PRAISE FO~~R~~

"*Us Fools* is a boisterous, irrever[...] sisters growing up in an America t[...] their Midwestern farming family. [...] an unforgettable, ferocious voice, Nora Lange paints a remarkable portrait of connection and alienation, of love and heartbreak, and all points in between. "
—EDAN LEPUCKI, AUTHOR OF *TIME'S MOUTH*

"*Us Fools* reimagines the intergenerational family saga as a gob-smacked midwestern modern gothic. This novel is an explosion of ideas and a feast of language—a crazy quilt of bafflement, his-tory, love, and danger—made unforgettable by the central sisters Fareown, whose binary star guides us through the wild heartlands of Nora Lange's matchless mind."
—JUSTIN TAYLOR, AUTHOR OF *REBOOT*

"With wild dreams and tender considerations, Nora Lange's *Us Fools* brings us that bond most tangled, mysterious, eternal and dazzlingly reflective: sisters. As farms and families spin, what center holds when the world lets go?"
—SAMANTHA HUNT, AUTHOR OF *THE DARK DARK*

"Midwest farm life in the 1980s gets an inimitable revision through the eyes of the brilliant and unsettling Fareown sisters—filled with insight, sex, and unpredictable action, Lange's provocative debut dazzles and will be like nothing you've read this year."
—J. RYAN STRADAL, AUTHOR OF *SATURDAY NIGHT AT THE LAKE-SIDE SUPPER CLUB*

"Lange's voice shines in this wonderful debut."
—ELIF BATUMAN, AUTHOR OF *EITHER/OR*

"Lange's debut novel is a refreshingly sardonic take on the decaying ideal of the American dream, with an anti-capitalist tilt. Like the classics that the Fareown sisters quote ad infinitum, it's a lush, uncanny mythology itself." —*KIRKUS REVIEWS*, **STARRED**

"*Us Fools* is one of those special books that reorders the world and makes everything new again—language, family, history, fear, love. Nora Lange writes with the precision of Joy Williams, and the heart of George Saunders, in a voice that is all her own. You won't forget this novel."
—**DANIEL ALARCÓN, AUTHOR OF** *AT NIGHT WE WALK IN CIRCLES*

"A beautiful portrait of the parallel, intersecting, and occasionally derailing tracks of two sisters coming of age in an America as broken as ever. I think anyone who gets lost in these pages will find themselves haunted for life by Lange's truly singular and yet deeply, painfully, intimately American vision."
—**POROCHISTA KHAKPOUR, AUTHOR OF** *TEHRANGELES*

"An epic-sized, gloriously-anarchic, blow-out adventure through recent American history."
—**ROBIN MCLEAN, AUTHOR OF** *PITY THE BEAST*

"There is something of the end of America in Nora Lange's portrait of a farming family on a wild and anfractuous path to the brink of collapse. At turns hallucinatory and ruminative, fans of Joy Williams will find a familiar in Lange's sharp-witted prose."
—**AMELIA GRAY, AUTHOR OF** *ISADORA*

"This is a novel of heartbreak and beauty, presided over by one of the most idiosyncratic and surprising comedic voices I've encountered in recent times." —**T.C. BOYLE, AUTHOR OF** *BLUE SKIES*

"Achingly stylish prose, brutal humor, and ferocious wit set this novel apart—Lange captures the tender complexities of sisterhood in her electric debut."
—**KIMBERLY KING PARSONS, AUTHOR OF** *BLACK LIGHT*

US FOOLS

A novel by
NORA LANGE

Two Dollar Radio
Books too loud to ignore

Two Dollar Radio
Books too loud to Ignore

WHO WE ARE TWO DOLLAR RADIO is a family-run outfit dedicated to reaffirming the cultural and artistic spirit of the publishing industry. We aim to do this by presenting bold works of literary merit, each book, individually and collectively, providing a sonic progression that we believe to be too loud to ignore.

TwoDollarRadio.com

 @TwoDollarRadio

Proudly based in
Ohio
TURTLE ISLAND

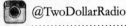 @TwoDollarRadio

/TwoDollarRadio

Printed in CANADA.

SOME RECOMMENDED LOCATIONS FOR READING:
Pretty much anywhere because books are portable and the perfect technology!

AUTHOR PHOTO→ Courtesy of the author.

COVER PHOTO→ Photo by Sinitta Leunen on Unsplash.
COVER DESIGN→ Eric Obenauf

Two Dollar Radio would like to acknowledge that the land where we live and work is the contemporary territory of multiple Indigenous Nations.

For Sylvia, you have been with me from my beginning.

US FOOLS

2009, LOOKING BACK TO 1987

Much of my young life as a junk kid was devoted to certain themes, such as Martha, the last in the family of passenger pigeons, and loving my older sister, Joanne. It was Jo who first called us "junk kids." I came around later to the way she saw us. Not that anyone ever asked, but my commitment to Jo and to completing our America Project, a seemingly lifelong study of our environment and culture, solidified on a sharp and clear day in 1987. My sister was eleven the day she decided to jump from our roof. She landed onto the concrete driveway our father had painstakingly poured one spring, breaking her hip and suffering compound fractures to both legs. She didn't try to break her fall. This incident occurred two years after the 1985 farm crisis had reached new levels of despair, after Joanne was told her scoliosis, if left untreated, would continue to deform her body and eventually her lungs would be crushed. She was told any future attempts at motherhood would be impossible, to which my sister scoffed. According to Joanne, the concept of "the future," which itself represented one version of more life, was a capitalist scam.

I remember the day well. It had been one of those rare and promising days in Illinois—the sun shone bright, and the birds were out by the dozen. I have no idea where our parents were, and Jo and I should have been continuing to plot our escape from our stunted life on a farm—that was probably emitting toxins—in the Midwest. It was imperative my older sister and I liberate ourselves from our hereditary defects. We should have been studying the heretics of Medieval England. They were models of what not to do (my thinking), but for Joanne those women were examples of what to do, precisely. We should have been contaminating our minds further and

5

challenging ourselves to dive into vats of ice, but instead Jo went off to hurt herself without me.

Jo said she decided to jump from twenty-five feet that day because she had wanted to "experience falling" more than she wanted to masturbate to images of Ally Sheedy, more than layering sandwich meats excessively. Which we didn't do because we didn't have those meats, because we couldn't afford them.

This was how it was with us. I could not trust what I was a witness to. This pattern of Joanne's—to reposition the angles, to confuse the content to get what she wanted—sometimes worked, and she looked captivatingly gorgeous and ahead of her time, her long black hair pulled away from her handsome face. But on many occasions, it did not, and the truth of her insides spilled out like roadkill.

Nine days from that one I would turn nine. Jo knew this. She explained that she'd wanted me, her younger lesser sister, to witness her fly before letting an entire decade end. Especially if we never managed to leave the farm. I can remember standing over her lying on the concrete, like an important figure presided over a nation, and feeling not enlarged and maximized, but naïve—only Joanne could make injuring yourself appear like a scene you might want to be a part of. My older sister was getting herself off when she should have been extremely uncomfortable, and maybe even bleeding internally. In that instant I felt I would never understand anything, and the longer I gazed down at her body—bloody, willful, and increasingly vulnerable—my skin shriveled like the jeering, cocky boy turned newt did for calling the Goddess of agriculture, Ceres, a greedy old witch. Instead of feeling liberated by Joanne's show of vulnerability, as I should have felt, I shrank like the boy in Ovid's myth. I was drowning in my sister's image on the concrete. And I liked it. I relished it, even if I pretended I didn't.

"You're drooling," Joanne said to me, frozen and fixed on the driveway, like a corpse settling into her earthly environment.

"You should do something about that," she had said of the excessive saliva involuntarily oozing from my mouth, as I tried to use my hands to block out the sharp sun.

Twenty-two years after the roof incident I found myself in 2009, alone in a motel in Bloomington, Minnesota, in a land of 10,000 lakes. I was still without a clear point of view. I was still using my older sister as an excuse to remain stagnant, like an unreliable narrator. Over the course of my life, Joanne has served as a convenient distraction with which our family used to avoid ourselves. Her questionable behavior served to legitimize my own. But the love trap that was our relationship meant that I would follow her any place, eventually to the edge of the universe—all the way to Deadhorse, Alaska, the place our parents sent her as an adult in her twenties to rest and to heal, which did nothing to alleviate the terror she would inflict by being unapologetically herself. (A "self" that had an uncanny way of highlighting our inadequacies.) When it came to loving Joanne, one discovered the extent of which they were capable of love. The suffering act of love was a test in stamina, which had me wondering if this was why she was hellbent on having a child.

In my Super 8 room in America, I was attempting to reckon with my sister's decisions. First, her decision to "experience falling" by jumping off our roof, and then her pregnancy twenty-two years later. I have always been compelled to make cautious, predictably mundane choices based on mortality, such as pulling off the interstate in a tornado. Or to accomplish what I believed was right, like scoring a deal on my room in a well-rated Super 8 in Bloomington, where I find myself riddled by the thought of Jo giving birth. Had her self-harm extended to include motherhood? That was what motherhood was, wasn't it? She would change, whereas I was still a person in need of a fresh mold. I would have liked to believe that she relished our relationship the way that it was. I would have liked to believe that she coveted the sadistic pleasures of sacrifice as much as

I did the sadistic pleasures of submitting, such that she would never leave us for the sake of progeny. I had thought we were enough. I had thought we were a good place to stop, our toes at the edge of a cliff. But what I had failed to see was that her desire was fueled by such a precise need. She wanted to reach a point where there was no going back—note the baby growing inside of her.

Joanne spoke of her pregnancy plainly: "I am a human animal," she had said, plainly about the evolution of sensory ecology, cells morphing, perception, so forth. And there was no other animal that seemed to need the promise of something to exist, no other species on Earth that seemed to need any reason at all to go on living. I told her this made no sense.

"This is further proof that your idea of mothering is a terrible one," I said.

And she told me it was time for me to leave her in Alaska.

"Go," she demanded.

The last I saw Joanne in person was in Deadhorse, Alaska, a few months back. She was holding a chalice full of red wine, as driven as ever by her need to seek out sensations, which had reached new heights in her desire to mother a child. There she was with a dark, cloudy sky cradled above her head. Her silhouette against a backdrop of an icy, crystal-clear sea, amid a sprawling, chaotic watery blue and gray landscape.

FARM TIME

Before we were born, the land our parents worked in Illinois had value. The export of wheat and soybeans nearly tripled during those years thanks to the wheat deal with the Soviets, who paid millions for bushels. Before we were born, our father redid the floors, a room-by-room project meant to keep his evenings busy and temper his drinking, an issue even in those days. The ladder leading up to the small attic space needed repairing, like everything needed repairing. Time and time again, our father said he would repair the ladder, toilet, oven, the roof of the barn, but he never managed to get around to it. Instead, he would drink too much, get angry, build an outhouse, and begin saving to buy concrete for what would eventually become our driveway.

Sylvia, our mother, reminded Henry daily, such was the routine of marriage, about fixing the ladder daily and went about partitioning the attic space, figuring if they were to have children, they would need a place to store them. Sylvia built the walls herself, delineating two iffy bedroom-like spaces in the attic. And, with the help of the plumber in town, she built a tiny half-bath. She updated the curtains, sewn from old sheets she had found, painted the walls Kelly green, and pinned up pieces of mismatched scraps of wallpaper to add dimension.

As was often the case with children, before the two of us came along the future was bright. "Life potential was a cherry orchard," Henry would say, before telling us little fools about how we had really taken the best from them. Before we came along to ruin everything, there was this rare and fleeting time where our parents had room to grow and to travel locally and in their minds. Our parents would reminisce about their past happiness and point to the oversized photographic portrait taken of them at the county fair sometime in the mid-1970s, before we were born.

The large portrait, taken at the county fair, served as a document, proof, if you will, perhaps even a reminder of this rare and fleeting time before my sister and I existed. It also represented an annual tradition, a symbol of a break from the often lonely, arduous daily rituals, a reminder of the long history of rural communities coming together to collectively build recreational spaces. Jo liked to say of the portrait that it reminded her of an execution line-up. I remember pointing out that by and large our parents looked sedate. I told her that prisoners could be subjected to maltreatment, including starvation, and therefore would not look sedate. We agreed their smiles looked forced. It was not how our parents smiled, but more to the point: nobody wanted to be remembered as miserable. Nobody knew what to do with misery in photographs. No person would hang a giant portrait of futureless people—especially those who knew that they would never travel outside of the Midwest—in their living room. Or even a small one on their fridge for that matter. There were far too many reminders of misery such as it was. Furthermore, nobody getting their portrait taken was ever directed to be who they really were, to express what they were really feeling, because what would be the point in commemorating that?

The 20x30-inch monstrosity hung unsteadily above the couch in our small and crowded living room as a warning, I always thought. "As a mnemonic," was Jo's thinking. Nothing about the poor quality of the slanted portrait of our parents at the county fair was subtle. In it, our parents pose side-by-side, while behind them is a painted backdrop depicting California's luscious San Fernando Valley. Each of them carried in one hand a bright orange and showcased the fruit like showcasing a box of jewels. Their other arm was around the other's waist, their hair is combed, and their expressions appear obliging and alert, ready for the shot. Henry looked straight at the camera, struggling to produce a half-smile. (He wasn't a fan of being photographed.) Sylvia was suspicious of the lens, but she was complicit with its requests. Our mother, like all the women in our family, knew a thing or two about being scrutinized such that she made a point to tell us not to hide.

Sylvia liked to tell us that Simone de Beauvoir argued that *woman* was a man's concept, a concept meaning *other*, because man was the *seer*. *He* was the *subject*, and *she* was the *object*. I remember her telling us to be unafraid of what we wanted—to reach for even our breath. I remember asking if we could get out of the house, out of the town, small even though it had been all I had ever known, to take a family trip to the Quad Cities, or go to the fancy grocery store there to buy something that had not been grown in the Midwest, something as standard and affordable and basic but exotic to us like avocados. Why? Because I was deficient. I wanted health. I wanted to taste something punchy to mask the filth inside. I wanted access to vitamins, like on the television. I wanted luscious hair. I wanted to feel a truly American kind of clean.

"Please can we buy vitamins," I remember pleading with our parents, who said if giving me vitamins would mean I would go away then they would do it, but nothing was that simple, not even me. If they could have set me on a sailboat with a little suitcase, some books, and a wool blanket, some cans of food and a can opener, and put me out to sea before I had the chance to do it of my own accord, I believe they would have. (The nearest body of water was the Mississippi River, a twenty-five or so minute drive, which would have required the use of the truck and therefore the gas, which was another factor to consider when making a big decision.)

1976 & 1978: BIRTH

For our parents, the end of the '70s was a turning point in their live-lihoods. Jo was a healthy child, even if she was a psychopathic tyrant. Joanne was a product of the booming era. She was born at home in our living room at the end of '76 with both the television and radio on loudly, which she later blamed for the thoughts that plagued her (and she was plagued by her thoughts). Of course the portrait was there too. Lighting a cigarette, our mother would explain that my sister had emerged a nine-pound skeptic through an opening roughly the diameter of a bagel hole, with a furrowed brow etched in stone. "It wasn't pleasant pushing Jo out, believe me," Sylvia would say of Joanne's birth. "Your sister was born troubled, she was a star."

Our mother has said of that year that she found herself coining slogans for fun, in what was an otherwise bleak atmosphere. She had been inspired by a group of women in Iowa who called them-selves "The Iowa Porkettes." Sylvia wrote them letters expressing her support for their female-run organization's marketing campaign to promote the Iowa Chop to help struggling family farms. "Hop to the top with the Iowa Chop," was their famous phrase.

I was born two years later in 1978, a charmingly kind, expensive baby, in a big, excessively lit hospital in the Quad Cities, marking the start of a new decade that would promote intense consolidation and financialization. In 1978, I entered the scene; a major storm flooded the crops, and the farm crisis was about to hit us hard. I was their impending bust baby, which was front of mind for our parents. By

14

1979, the "Save the Whales" movement was launched and would go on to prevent their extinction. That same year, the Soviet Union had invaded Afghanistan, which prompted America to place an embargo on grain sales to the Soviets; the value of Midwestern crops plummeted, and our parents made appointments, they blocked off entire days on the calendar, to have sex to lift their spirits while our father took to drinking around the clock. Our family began amassing more debt as a crop surplus grew a fat one. Up until that turning point, Henry contented himself harvesting corn and soybeans, and managing a few cattle, but by 1979 he became preoccupied with fatherhood, which was to say democracy's origin: Was it with the striving of poor white men working the Western Plains? Or with the class struggle in the East within an industrialized economy?

Sylvia continued to read horoscopes in the newspaper, and to do the work—the undervalued and overlooked mandatory "helping" work ("I'm helping" she would say sarcastically)—canning, accounting, cooking, cleaning, bathing, feeding, consoling, laundering, shopping, house maintenance, and clothing all members of our family—and began taking her Ovid to bed. When Sylvia wasn't busy helping, she did secretarial work part-time for a lawyer in town, a terrible organizer who couldn't keep his hands to himself. Three evenings a week, she went off to bathe the virgins at the nearby convalescent home, and Joanne would insist that our mother tell her about those women who had forsaken men, and therefore I would beg too, like a rat looking for table droppings.

In the years that followed, there was this frenzied feeling in the community that the crisis had happened overnight. It was a sentiment heard over and over, around tables, in grocery checkout lines, which must have helped in some way to assuage the unresolvable feeling of displacement. Though Jo knew—in other words, our parents had told her (and she would make sure I knew too)—that nothing major ever happened overnight. "Except for conception," Jo was quick to point out.

My sister was better, brighter, quicker. She was good at using knives to skin animals and to thinly slice potatoes. People wanted to be close to her, as one is taught to keep your enemies near, and, just like our mother, when you were in her presence the imperceptible hairs on the back of your neck would rise in tickling horror. Animals—deer, cows, rabbits, rodents—recognized something familiar inside of her. But just as our mother could, Joanne saw past their wanting. Whereas I studied these exchanges from the sidelines like an intruder.

Henry and Sylvia fed us and taught us a mix of new and old stuff, like that the '50s were a time when Americans confused a lot of things, namely the concepts of liberalism, socialism, and communism. And the truth was riddled, such as America was a riddle. We learned other essentials, which in our community boiled down to a few things: solitude, weather, and government. The last two were unpredictable. The last two impacted the body—which was to say, our health.

THE PORTRAIT, THE '80S, AND "THE GIPPER"

You spend all your time with the land and yet you're also alien to it; our parents repeated this like an anthem. Henry and Sylvia talked about isolation, especially while watching the television or listening to the radio, both played incessantly in our house. Our parents made a point of saying isolation was different from solitude. The connection between land workers and their struggle with isolation was identified as early as the 1900s when agricultural reformers believed these feelings to be the primary social problem in rural life. Jo blamed the impoverished feeling on what she called the "capitalist consumption popsicle," which included American idealism. She blamed the early '40s for making socialization within the nuclear family the primary source of interaction. "Even the portrait remains crooked," Jo said of the failure of family.

Our parents might have stopped our learning right then and there, forbidden us to use the library, but anything that would keep us occupied was considered a win for sanity. Wood was a thing in our family. The utilitarian roll-top desk, made of brown maple, that had been in Sylvia's family for a hundred years, held so many past due notices one would always float out like a feather of a frightened chicken when someone went to close a drawer. Every corner of our house was consumed with panic. Sylvia feared, among other things, that one day her daughters would feel the need to marry and destroy their lives. Henry worried that in America empirical truth was being systematically undermined, sabotaged by powerful men with expensive socks and state of the art safe houses for when the shit hit the fan. Henry spent an inordinate amount of time angry, drinking, pacing, and bemoaning the Reagan administration; the rising (again) popularity of the sweater vest; politics in general; and material regarding the extensive world writ large. Henry blamed, mostly, Ronald Reagan for his efforts to seamlessly blur the line between legend and reality. "The Gipper," as Reagan was mockingly known in our house for playing the football legend George Gipp in the movie *Knute Rockne All-American*. Reagan had even cultivated the role beyond the role, sociopathically blurring the lines in public between the hero (Gipp) and himself, which was problematic. He'd also chosen not to return to the Midwest to die and be buried, as George Gipp had.

I remember living in a state of constant hunger. I can recall our stomachs growling uncontrollably, and as we tried to study Ovid our distraught parents talked about deficits while groping each other. Jo and I imagined the portrait of them at the county fair coming to life until imagining became an interactive vision where my sister and I were invited inside of the frame to eat cheese pizza, fried goods, hotdogs, vanilla and chocolate swirled soft serve on sugar cones, plus extra pepperoni pepperoni pizza. But all we had to eat were uncooked beets and carrots pickled in jars, which our mother would call "cooked plenty."

"The fair is capitalist in nature," our father said about our musings, before saying ironically that we should forget food and listen to the people on television who had concrete things to say about our hunger.

On television, people were asking why desperate, hungry farmers didn't simply nibble away at their crops? Henry would not stop watching the television and listening to the radio while talking about President Reagan, born in a depressed Illinois town on the corn flats, canceling his second term inauguration parade due to severe wind chill. Our father was caught up on the fact that, before becoming the leader of the free world, Ronald Reagan had been a successful Hollywood actor. "If a successful Hollywood actor couldn't handle the Illinois weather, what hope was there?" he lamented. Only once did Reagan take Nancy to his birthplace of Tampico, Illinois. *The New York Times* reported that the town's "least desirable citizen" made his way to the front of the receiving line and presented Nancy with a "loud wet kiss." The wet kiss degenerate was immediately ushered away as Nancy went for a Kleenex. She didn't use her shirt. That part of the country never again made the itinerary.

"Reagan knew chilly winds. Reagan had lived in Chicago *for Christ's sake*," Henry said, before going on to say white people destroyed souls.

Later, on the walls of our attic space, Jo would write out: White people are thieves and destroy souls. In our poorly insulated attic space, in our rundown one-bedroom farmhouse, painted a faded red and black with a baby blue trim, further framed by the Green River that ran into the Rock River and was part of the Mississippi River watershed, we put our heads and hands against the icy walls barely separating us from the endless greenhouse gas effects we generated, the inedible corn and soybean crops, the piles of animal shit, the various highways and interstates and those nearby roads called "nowhere roads." Our hands and heads rolling like marbles in a bowl. But Jo knew those sentiments, writing them out, sharing them, would change nothing about the world or the color of our skin.

My sister's distrust of powerful white people would only grow more intense. Eventually, she would see these powerful white figures and their imprints everywhere—tampons, ballots, textbooks—which for the powerful made her into some kind of lunatic to re-wire, which for me made her into some kind of magic to admire.

At the kitchen table—made entirely of oak, which had also come from our maternal line—over plates of cold noodles with an inadequate amount of sauce, our father openly wondered about the ruling few with their venomous attitude toward those who had lost economically. A night eating bland food at the oak table might look something like this:

"The astonishing thing about the wealthy," Sylvia might say, forking up unseasoned, overcooked, cold noodles, touching Henry with her free hand to cool him down, "is their unquestionable belief in their good intentions."

"You two suck," Jo said a lot in those days.

"Goddamn it, Joanne, fool, you need to listen."

Infuriated, Henry would take Jo's plate of food away, put it on the couch beneath the portrait as an offering to their one-time aspiring selves, in order to punish her for ignoring the first rule of the dinner table, which was to get along at any cost. Our father would then look at her plate in his hand and throw his plate of noodles across the room, knocking over the one lamp with a working light bulb in the living room on the small table next to the television, which sat on a stool, made of metal, in the corner like a misbehaving child in time out, which was where we used to be sent to think about metal as material when we were the stool's size. The television sat on the metal stool across from the retro plaid couch, chosen for its promise to blend stains. (To be clear—breaking the lamp was easy to do; the farmhouse was very small.)

Outraged, deeply torn, Henry would not stop there. He would regret his anger; feeling remorseful, he would apologize and poke his index finger so hard into my back it would leave a bruise; before, usually, going on to slam his fists into something or someone. Henry would blow up about a lot of things, but during those early years he was especially angry at Jo, The Gipper, and at America's bigotry being pinned on the flyover states, and what he had read in *The New Yorker*, which he read diligently at the public library. In the 1800s the magazine had advertised themselves as a rag for cosmopolitan intellectuals and: "Not for the old lady from Dubuque."

"There are people, even those at *The New Yorker*, who believe America ends at Pittsburgh and that there's nothing but desert and a few Indians and Hollywood on the other side," he said, regretfully. "What do they have against elderly ladies?" The small promise of a flame behind his eyes had burned out.

Our father had no off valve. And our mother, Sylvia— a notorious mitigator, lover of historical texts, contradictions, and celestial awakenings, like stirring the dead while contending they wanted nothing to do with us—made sure to point out that it was, in fact, Midwestern literature that had initially rejected the prevailing Victorianism sounding from the East.

Our necks limped under the weight of the information. It seemed in those days, sophisticates—a rank I couldn't say our parents strived to attain, but nonetheless hadn't realized their existences were being mocked—had found the heartland insufferably provincial, outdated, Victorian, a waste.

Homeschooled, Jo and I were given myths to consider. A textbook if you will, for observing nature in all its iterations—torment, heavy winds. These myths served as a template for living in our house, on our land, in America. A resource complete with transformations and injustices, mostly against females at the hands of the gods. We were instructed to make diagrams, sketches, and abstracts, and, eventually, when we were ready, to write perfectly crafted, single-spaced essays about them.

"These writings are a way to evaluate the internal and external world," Sylvia explained before leaving us to go work.

Beyond the regular day-to-day punishments inflicted upon us, from working heavy machinery that had impaled children, to the habitual cleaning, exposure to harsh weather and bland foods, we were given mythology as "our guide" to understanding the basics of humankind, and never *human nature*, since our parents did not believe humans knew much about nature, which often came in the form of repercussions for various infractions, unsurprisingly hubris on the part of humans. (We learned first about punishment and wrath, and later about hubris causing the former.)

I remember the intense pleasure we took in reciting "Philomela." In Ovid's myth, the king marries one sister yet lusts after the other. Jo and I had seen this behavior on *The Sally Jessy Raphael Show,* later shortened to *Sally,* which we watched like rapt owls, explaining to Sylvia how we were gathering additional source material, as she had instructed us to do, in order to bulk up our Ovid essays, which she said were lacking.

"I give up," Sylvia said a lot in those days.

Our mother was always giving up, losing weight, and lighting cigarettes. Jo and I defended our watching of *Sally.*

"There is something to this exercise of ours," we said about binge-watching talk shows for the sake of our education, for the sake of the promise of self-liberation one-day, insisting our mother let us prove it to her, to which she said: "I'm too tired to argue with you monsters."

Like the characters both on and off-screen, Thracians were sexually insatiable, and unfulfilled male desire would result in women suffering. Jo and I understood, clearly—Philomela was just a placeholder for any woman—and she was at fault for failing to resolve his erection. (This part of the narrative we easily got.) Flimsy, sordid, stupid temptress, Philomela, we said, FAILED. So, therefore, the king condemned Philomela for enrapturing him—for his reacting body—which pulsated with unregulated desire.

"The blood in his veins raged like a drought wind explodes a forest," was how Joanne described his erection.

Philomela protested: Wait, wait, no.

But he would have her and he heard: Yes, yes, now. You gloriously equipped Man.

Joanne and I would act out the scene for the portrait.

Me: "Sad, so sad, protesting Philomela."

Joanne: "Mutilate her and send her to a damp dark cave. Farewell mutilated Philomela!"

So it was. So it had to be. Just like on television: Philomela's tongue was removed with a bronze blade, cut off at the root by the king, who went on to rape her in the cave where she was held captive. (The diligent students we were, my sister and I had foreseen this happening.) But Philomela refused to remain silent, which was the compass of the story. Philomela was determined to tell her story with her hands, weaving the story's timeline into the loom's tapestry and getting it to her sister. Her sister received the tapestry, read the woven tragedy, and freed Philomela from captivity. The two sisters devised a plan.

"The sisters would fuck shit up," Jo said, her stomach growling, dreaming of something flavorful like a cassoulet, which I remember her saying *cassoulet*, which then had me immediately losing my train of thought.

"And they did," Jo gave me the stink eye, in other words: it was time for me to focus.

"The sisters messed shit up," I continued. "The sisters took the King's sole child, only heir, and ripped the five-year-old boy's "hot little body into pulsating goblets," then put his body parts into boiling pots to simmer. When sufficiently delicious, they presented the glorious, aromatic feast to the husband, father, insatiable king. A feast for the ages, the sisters sang. Smiling at the spread that lay out before him like glimmering odalisques, the King swallowed whole bits of his salty, cooked son."

"I can't deal," Sylvia said to us about our skit.

Jo and I were doing our best to learn when one day our mother called us over to sit down on the itchy plaid couch, beneath the looming portrait of our parents at the county fair. She told us to shut up. She wanted to make sure Jo and I understood revenge was a desperate mode of imitation. All I remember thinking was: Our living room is the most used room in the house, which seemed strange since everyone must use the bathroom at least a dozen times a day.

"You two need to find another way forward. Maybe learning is making matters worse," Sylvia said, half teasing, as we fidgeted, and our minds traveled elsewhere, to trollops and pizza.

Our mother suggested we take a break from feeling sorry for ourselves, go outside, get back to work: shoveling, cleaning, feeding, and butchering chickens, pruning, and canning. Even junk kids, such as we were, should be grateful for the break we had been bestowed—Jo and I had been given a week off of driving the skid steer to feed the cows. Ever since the machine's hydraulic bucket ripped a five-year-old neighbor's leg tissue off from knee to ankle, the chore had been on pause. Jo and I should be outside in nature because we lived among what we called "nature," such as it were, crops, a few trees around the vicinity; never mind our lopsided satellite dish, clunky farming equipment, the dilapidated barn, and tall, deep blue Harvestore silos where kids sometimes died by what were deemed "avoidable accidents."

There was also the graveyard. We could pay homage to our ancestors. Our own personal Fareown family cemetery, where many of the women on our maternal side were buried, and where my sister and I built elaborate shrines devoted to their peculiarities. Our history, a pattern of women and their return to water, a pattern of behavior many deemed shameful. A patterning evident in the graveyard, where there were small indications of their living, which were noted and stood erect in the soil (until a storm would displace them). The spirits in the graves in which my sister and I would dutifully observe.

"Listen, up," our mother demanded. The time had come for the two of us to stop compulsively tuning in to *Sally*, "like junkies." *Sally* was becoming an addiction. Did we want to end up looking haggard like our mother, chain-smoking menthols, and washing a drunk man's underwear? Is that the future that us fools wanted?

"The future," Jo sounded out like an expletive.

My sister believed it was a concept often deployed to disguise the urgent present, which only benefited those at the top. Back then I was so young as to barely exist, but I understood we were in a crisis, second to the Dust Bowl in terms of impacting the lives of land workers, which included us. I understood it was a period when believing in something, anything, even something as farfetched as the future, might have slowed the rising rate of suicide in our community, but for Jo, nothing stood still.

I swear I must have been listening as our mother educated us, but my eyes were tracing the contours of the wall and the room. The living room walls were covered in a thin wallpaper with light pink roses and twisting vines, and the portrait of our parents at the county fair hung above the couch. Other walls in our house were left unadorned. Those simpler walls, in the kitchen and in the bathroom, were painted a pale gray, with a dark brown wooden trim left natural throughout. In the living room, there were two windows, and two long bookshelves high up on the walls, where they could not be easily reached. Other books, magazines, and newspaper clippings, which did not fit on the high shelves or on our kitchen table, were stacked up on the floor like high-rises with various bills tucked inside as bookmarks. Our house was small and cluttered, but the light, especially in the spring, could be magnificent.

I remember Sylvia removed our empty breakfast bowls and quietly said "Fine," before admitting that the material on *Sally* was indeed salacious and addictive and certainly relevant in perhaps a lot of ways, but none of it would get us into college. Nobody wanted to know the truth about what it was they were seeing. "Not really," our mother said.

"Besides," she said, "what the hell did we know of dark times?"

There were instances during these bleak times as junk kids on the farm when I needed a break. And then the news came for the circus. Federal Inspectors declared the four unicorns of the Ringling Brothers Barnum & Bailey Circus to be goats with surgically implanted horns; I can remember sobbing. I refused to let any more information sink in like a stain. Even at that age I was losing my mind like a trickling roof leak. The day I learned that unicorns were really goats that were being abused the sky was clear and other experiences were coming into focus. I had been covering for Jo, who had successfully hitched a ride to go someplace and to do things which would remain secret. I was doing the yardwork of two outside. I was thinking about longevity; mostly I was thinking about the Circus, which had been on the news that morning. The circus had survived the Depression. It had survived two world wars. It was from a time when Prussia was still a kingdom and Jesse James robbed banks. I remember taking off my socks to feel. I cleaned up fecal matter barefoot and wondered what a rhetorical question was. Later, when Jo returned from wherever she'd been looking funereal (a face she could wear like a robe), I asked her about rhetorical questions because she owed me. She said, "devices," and then lit the pair of my socks on fire. Then, using our mother's lighter, she started to singe the hairs on her arms. There was nothing that could be done about it. Maybe I didn't want her to stop. In fact, I remember vividly that I wanted her to ignite herself. I wanted Joanne to burn like a good American girl with no future, just as fireworks on the Fourth of July were responsible for the most human-caused wildfires in the country. Not to mention Canadian Geese, and other important waterfowl, get sickened by the remnants.

That night, on television, back inside the house with Joanne sitting beside me reeking of inexcusable dude cologne, a circus spokeswoman defended their surgical practices, reasoning that if anesthesia was used, and if the person performing the procedure was competent, then it was a simple tissue graft, and as far as they were concerned the animal was now a unicorn. As young as I was in 1985, while more banks were failing than in the Great Depression, I was conflicted about my relationship to this revelation. I didn't think goats should be surgically taken advantage of, not under any circumstances, but unicorns were unicorns. The kind of trick of the mind I was torn about.

"Tricky mind," Jo said, drawing a finger-gun up to her forehead and falling backwards where there was no one to catch her.

My sister trusted no one. She danced so close to the edge. When I rubbed a moist finger around the rim of a glass, I heard music; my sister heard resistance and friction. We felt stuck yet we were surrounded by roads, highways, interstates, and rivers which ran into the Rock River, which was part of the Mississippi River watershed, which stretched the whole of the Midwest where we lived and stank. We felt trapped in our small house that shrank the larger we became, which did happen (astonishingly) even though we were hungry. Our weather-worn house stood out among the uniform landscape, up against the hem of the sky, on top of a little hill, which our father claimed wasn't a hill, it was a hump. There was a barn with cows and chickens situated among acres of soybeans and corn that grew tall in August when you couldn't keep the insects out of your mouth, when the inert air had nothing more to offer. The land that in winter was blanketed in snow. A seasonality that affected our parents in odd ways.

Sometimes, during summer months, our parents would wake up from the heat so brain-dead they would forget to turn on the fans. Instead of being productive, they would sit around for hours, their mouths agape, oblivious to their hungry children (who, even in that stunted state, they still managed to demand labor from), lovingly fondling each other like a set of keys, which we found revolting.

HEREDITY AS CRISIS

Henry was an orphan, so there was less to discover about his side of things. He had been left on a typical Illinois country road by his parents. Where we lived, these roads acted like highways and were common receptacles for illicit trash: cars, plastic water bottles filled with fecal matter, hypodermic needles, loveseats, sneakers, kittens. But Henry was more than trash, he liked to joke—he was resourceful and would marry well. Our father made his way from there into town. Once in town, he found an open church on First Street, marched in, and told the rector, who would end up becoming a father figure for Henry, that he was an orphan. Henry explained that orphans had the potential to change the world. He rattled off a list of influential orphans who had done just that: Edgar Allan Poe, Leo Tolstoy, Nelson Mandela, Eleanor Roosevelt (twice an orphan), Alexander Hamilton, Batman. Plus, he knew religion. Plus, he knew all the words and moves to *Annie*.

During his seven years as a Catholic altar boy, our father had done the sacrament of penance and reconciliation for his sinful behavior many times. His father and mother made sure Henry would not have an unhealthy attachment to earthly creatures. He would not be a man that turned away from the eyes of God. Henry, master storyteller in the making, told the rector that he was an orphan and that the orphanage had let him go willingly, since he'd demonstrated a high level of maturity. (By then our father knew that calling something "good" or "bad" wasn't explanation enough.) He lifted the loaf of bread he had been left with to show the priest. He pointed to the loaf of sliced soft honey wheat bread—un-tampered with, you see, the plastic wrapping intact. The twisty tie twisty tied tight. Beyond dispute. Henry also showed the rector the liter of bottled water he carried with him. Proof. Proof of their willingness and consent to let him go. Our father didn't know what else to say. In the moment, his thinking was murky. He has said of his numb body that it had felt displaced, like he was set between hyphens on a page.

Many of the women on our mother's side had been methodically drawn to water and were set on returning to its mystery. Sylvia could see tsunamis as they were forming. Both Jo and I continually saw bodies of water in our dreams. One aunt spent her nights swimming in a river. Another had ripped her knees open on cay's coral, only to wake up draped over a barge like an apron. Nobody knew how she had managed to arrive on an island where she was spotted once and then never seen again. A third had washed up in Puerto Rico sun-burned, blistered, and married the sea in a ceremony attended by the remaining sisters. Married or not, those women on our mother's side gave birth to baby girls like the Catholics forgave. Most were considered insane by members of their community and were disposed of, albeit in different ways. Some never lived to see their children born; others had their daughters taken from them at birth. Some ended up in ditches, not unlike our father, or homes for heathens, or floating in a body of water. Sylvia warned us not to let others control the narrative: Letting others control the narrative was how "The Legendary Dispatch of Men by the Fareown Women" had come about. She did admit that she was amazed the "legend," such as it was, had endured.

I remembered, like a severe weather warning had been issued, reading that along the spectrum of inheritance, siblings could be more like identical twins, which I found to be unacceptable. The early formation of my person was premised on the fact that Jo was doomed, whereas I was an evolution of possibility.

Presently in Bloomington, the Super 8 felt like a place for revisions and new outcomes, and yet a statue of Reagan was scheduled to be unveiled in the capital. In my motel room, I was thinking about how one might go about implanting the souls of the dead into the bodies of the living. My online boyfriend Preston was chatting me. Preston was an artist living in Brooklyn. He liked receiving pictures of my vagina, but instead of giving him what he wanted, I was back to thinking about soul implants: Those female relatives of ours, whose souls were implanted in mine, whether I wanted them there or not, may not have had the same kind of permanence or staying power that this Super 8 possesses—set against a backdrop of flat, nondescript acres of industrial park, power plants, and airplane hangars—but they had staying power.

I ignored Preston and continued to work on finding an in-person teaching position. For months, back in Deadhorse, with Jo in our trailer, I had taught these required core courses online, composition, ancient philosophy, ever isolated, recording lectures in a corner, not brushing my teeth, not interacting with students. None of this prepared me for the kind of intimacy that in-person teaching would require. I chatted Preston that I was busy refreshing my "selling myself skills" to fit the new times, therefore I could not send him an image of my vagina at that moment.

My latest cover letter had taken the form of a kayfabe match, where wrestlers stage matches. In this case, pitting Heidegger as the heel (i.e., the bad guy), against Plato the baby face (i.e., the good guy). Heidegger wore a white hazmat suit and Plato was dressed as a beam of light. I even included a few illustrations for the university's hiring committee, a group of anonymous evaluators, so that they could picture the action between the two thinkers.

I caved and chatted Preston to tell him about the perks here: Free wi-fi and a breakfast buffet. The motel was near several covetable attractions like the Mall of America, which has an oxygen bar, a post office, a wedding chapel, and, during the holidays—The World's Largest Gingerbread House (on Earth!). The massive sugar house was edible, though nobody would eat it. People flew in from hundreds of thousands of miles away to spend as much money as they could on clothing, shoes, sports equipment, and fitness gear in as little time as possible. But also, perhaps more importantly, they came to rediscover "maps," since that was the only way to really get around the Mall.

AGREEMENTS, SOME (MANY) COERCED

Our parents could not be saved. That spring of 1985, as the crisis continued, we would often find our father wandering outside, back and forth, making shapes on the dusty ground. Our mother would watch him out the window from the kitchen table, miniature cows lining the sill, an ultra-light menthol dangling from her lips, like she was studying a Titian painting; steady and still from a distance she regarded him against the vast and complex sky with care yet bemusement. There he was, her husband, father, a man doing his thing, making shapes.

Around this same time Coca-Cola introduced New Coke, in what would then be considered the worst marketing blunder of all time. The company received up to 8,000 angry calls from their customers per day. They had to hire extra operators to manage the influx of calls. One disgruntled man wrote in: "I don't think I'd be more upset if you were to burn the flag in our front yard." One consumer filed suit to force the company to provide the old drink. At protests staged by groups like Old Cola Drinkers of America, unhappy people poured the contents of New Coke into sewer drains. The month of May offered a brief distraction. Jessica Lange, Sissy Spacek, and Jane Fonda, all famous and beautiful, all who played distressed Midwestern farm wives in popular movies, went to Capitol Hill to testify before congress about the worsening crisis. The actors called out the administration for subsidizing silos for MX missiles, but not for family farmers. It was B.S., they said. Supporters crowded the front rows, stood on chairs, and exploded in applause when these women said what they said about supporting small family farms. Back in the Midwest, the rate of suicide rose, so too did the number of New Coke haters.

A few months later, at the end of that summer, Henry went to the Farm Aid Charity concert. He came home with nothing good to say. I recall he pointed out, and to no one in particular, that Conservationist President Theodore Roosevelt had a National Park named after him in western North Dakota.

"Where the Great Plains met the rugged Badlands," Henry said.

"Nauseating." Jo rolled her eyes and pretended to pass out.

She did this often; conscious, she would fall to the ground, much of the time bruising herself. Jo was not a fan of what she called America's "dude inflationism." She had a name for everything.

Henry admired Roosevelt. He emulated the man, so much so we found ourselves emulating the man by accident, to which Joanne itched her crotch and said she'd rather be sedated. "Despite my efforts, there's no pleasure to be found here," she said. Our father repeated anything he found steady and reasonable. Roosevelt believed poor land made poor people, and if Roosevelt believed it, Henry said it was true. "The greatest disparity in our country is between urban and rural citizens," he would say. Like us. Henry said we had worse schools, inadequate healthcare, and higher taxes. He never thought much of the promise of men (in other words, he never thought much of himself). He was trapped in contradictions, like Sisyphus, pushing a boulder up a tall mountain only to have it roll back down. Outwardly he could be gregarious, but he experienced outrage, often toward himself, the furniture, tables, the walls, his family, sometimes the television. But he was also kind and supportive. He was ours. Our father belonged to us. He was capable of apologizing, saying he would try harder in the future, and ask for forgiveness. We were pros at giving it. That was how *it*—what we called forgiveness by way of love and compassion—functioned in our family. Nobody meant any harm, not really.

Here was what our family agreed to about love: In a buffalo hazing, as an act of empathy and loyalty, the surviving buffalo instinc-
tively gathered around the dead to dance. The animals collected
around the slain, shook their heads, jumped, turned in circles, and
moved their bodies before they too were shot to death.

Jo said '85, the year I turned seven, was also the year my observa-
tional skills improved, though only slightly. Of course, what she had
meant was that I was malleable and easier to use a staple gun on. Jo
proudly announced to our parents that I was absorbing information.
To put it another way—I was learning.

"She's your problem, now," Sylvia said to me when I was old
enough to take on additional responsibilities, taking a drag off her
menthol, shrugging her shoulders like she saw done in the foreign
films she incessantly watched, sucking on her cigarette until she
sucked the life out of it, before going on to light another with the
nearly finished one in her hand: butt to butt.

It didn't take long for this declaration to quickly turn into: "Jo is
your problem now, Bernie."

I remember our parents singing this line like an anthem because I
was beginning to understand the ramifications of being the youngest, and indentured servitude—in other words, living with family.
This was the moment I realized "learning"—which had been presented to me as this "great potential, an opportunity"—was a vicious
trap. But there was no going back. Once you did what was expected
of you, the pile-up of obligations, familial tasks, and responsibilities
simply kept expanding. Though I didn't have the words until much
later, two major things stood out about the time: the downfall of
being Bernadette and the role coercion played in our household,
especially as it related to me. And Joanne, my uncooperative older
sister, agreed with our parents—and she never agreed with Sylvia
and Henry. Joanne believed in this karmic order so deeply that she
ran around calling herself my problem.

"Joanne is your problem. YOUR PROBLEM," Jo said, shoving
her nasty, bony fingers into my sternum.

There were times growing up when I imagined ripping Jo's heart out of her chest and draping the limp veiny organ over a wooden chair, a nice chair made of solid wood. But I would say no such thing. I kept my thoughts to myself like one wears a locket. I understood being in her presence required surrendering.

There were moments when I considered what my life would have been like without her. I had seen plenty of crime dramas. I knew things like bodies float, to wear gloves, and that secretly criminals .want to be caught. Loving my sister for the rest of my life would not be easy.

"Nothing is ever easy," Jo said, entering my headspace when she was uninvited. "Not even high school sluts. SAY IT," she demanded, x-raying the back of my brain.

I refused to say "sluts" even when Joanne was adamant that I repeat the word after her, even in private, even as far away from my sister as I was—in Bloomington, Minnesota, where there's still talk of returning to "the good old days," I had no space. (Though I must confess the word has this amazing capacity, this tantalizing ability to roll off the tongue. "Sluts," like a snail on slick pavement.)

In the farmhouse bathroom, propped up on chairs, Jo and I agreed on a few additional things. For starters, our noses: "The state of love had endured plenty, enrapturing beauty and all that, but still, Helen, that inoculating one of Troy, after the war, she reestablished herself in the home and managed to be a conventional woman," Joanne said, studying her face in the mirror, up, down, left, right.

We didn't have prominent noses like our great-grandmother Poppy, who was regal in her own way. Poppy was a notoriously ill-behaved and flamboyant woman named for the flower's narcotic properties and not the small dark seeds it produces. She was known for having an "unfortunate nose" (which was to say it was visible), for speaking her mind (or "minds" as others saw it), and for choosing productive land. Poppy ingrained in our mother, who ingrained in us, to have a plan for potential threats or obstacles, which as women would be plentiful. Words would be used against you, she warned. You would be used against you. People had rage and they turned nasty and vindictive if they felt you were hiding something. The consensus was that females were always hiding something. The solution was to let them see just enough of you and meanwhile do the work. For Poppy, "the work" was the work of land and God.

Jo and I also didn't have desirable perky ski slope noses, like what's-her-face on *Knight Rider*.

"What was the name of the actress who happened to be born in Lincoln, Nebraska, and was made even more American, by being raised in Fort Worth, Texas? What are the odds."

"Janine Turner."

"Right," I said. "No, we did not have perky ski slope noses like Janine."

Not by any stretch of the imagination. But we had doable noses, wearable noses, our large dark eyes and dark bushy eyebrows reduced the scale.

I remember we also agreed not to make sense of our country. Only in a super catatonic, blitzed out frame of mind, on a bunch of drugs taken in fistfuls, knocked back with tangy wine coolers—and not die, but live through the blur—would any person have a chance at getting through the cognitive process, also known as understanding information in America.

I went along with Joanne's assessment. She was a self-described sybarite. I was in no position to stop her. Not then. Not later. Not ever. And at the time, she was holding Henry's razor to the hair around her ears, and I wasn't sure where she was headed with the blade or the near-dead stoned business. I remember trying to breathe deeply and thinking about doing the right thing, like not tilting your head back when you get a nosebleed.

———————

Eventually, we agreed on our affection for Seraphina, at least initially. Seraphina had moved to the area because her parents wanted to get away from the city to grow things, which our parents found inconceivable. Equally egregious was that Seraphina's parent's called vegetables and fruit "things." Seraphina's father was an important attorney in Chicago who had retired at thirty-four. Her mother was luxury wallpaper, consistent from top to bottom, a beauty from another age that had never lifted a finger. Her parents both had revitalization interests and were eager to get back to the land to feel something. They had lost their genuine selves living in the city. I remember they talked a lot about standing on the ground and feeling grounded. They kept their place in the city, bought land and a house not far from us that required "a makeover," as it was explained. They purchased the shuttered general store in town and transformed it into a new kind of general store, stocking and selling the exact same items as the previous owners, like milk, soap, and tape. A few things stood out about that time: our family could no longer afford to go to the "new" store after Seraphina's parents had it remodeled. I also distinctly remember hearing our parents repeat the phrase "genuine self" as they went about doing whatever it was they did in their bedroom where I had stationed myself outside of, waiting to be said hello to, in passing. I would lean against their bedroom door and fancy myself a private detective, the European sort, living in some kind of mystery misery since the outcome was both a "known," but which still needed "resolving."

Seraphina and her family arrived. Our family sat around the table flabbergasted. Why would anyone choose this, living in a crisis if they didn't have to? Only ever opening envelopes marked "final notice." Our parents attempted to rationalize her family's move "back to nature," as they saw it.

"Ideally humans would be clear-headed," our parents told us. "When in reality we make decisions, often terrible ones, in imperfect conditions, limiting our ability to think things through."

At least Seraphina's family had their high-rise in Chicago, but the people around us, those we'd known from birth, as unfortunate for everyone as that was, were hurting. The truth of it was none of this would affect Seraphina, or her parents, and our family needed to get on with it.

SERAPHINA AS A CONTAMINATE

1985 ushered in a period when our parents did not like being compared to other parents. And along with the other substandard appliances, they became permanent, also useless, fixtures in the kitchen. They spent countless hours at that oak table discussing annual operating budgets, pointing to the stack of bills that needed to be addressed, and their courtship, such as it was, and the "false expectations" Seraphina's parents were instilling in their daughters. They reminisced about the past almost competitively. The television and the radio together were not loud enough to drown out their exchanges, which was best described as a kind of retroactive flirting.

"You love me," we could hear Henry say.

"You sound like a cult leader," Sylvia would say.

"What can I do?" Henry would ask, cutely, as Sylvia put something inedible in the oven. "I could have done that."

Our mother would smoke and go on to talk about mistakes and happenstance and how "you arrive where you arrive in life," before briskly coming into the living room to turn down the television, which was at its max, and to look at Jo and I squarely: "It's time for you monsters to get back to subjects like death, arson, and the witchy deranged women in our family."

So it was, we were told no more television or radio and to make something of ourselves. We were tasked with outlining our mother's past, i.e the women on our maternal side, so that we might learn something about being grateful.

We said "sure." It was just the sort of noncommittal, ambivalent word available. But instead of going to our attic space to make a fucked-up family tree we talked about families being cults and the dire news about a farmer named Rick Stice, then we would go over to Seraphina's house to bask in her '85 glow and to rummage through her fridge and her subscription magazines.

It was a busy year in America for linking all things the country despised, like the Midwest crisis and banks failing, to people, like Jews, and eventually to communism. On television we heard more about the cult and Rick Stice. His wife died of cancer. His eighty acres were threatened by foreclosure. He invited a religious cult to his land to see if they could help him recover his losses and help with his children. The men came, built a base, and began stockpiling weapons, ammunition, and clothing in preparation for the Battle of Armageddon, which would happen on farmland since it was also known as the Battle of the Wheat Fields.

"I need a towel around my head for this," I said to my sister.

"Do you know what happens to those who express doubt," Jo knew it was rhetorical.

It wasn't a question I was about to answer. Members that expressed doubt about the cult leader's supreme rule had autopsies revealing the following: left arm was broken, legs were fractured at the thigh level, gunshot wound shattered the skull, multiple rib fractures on the chest and back, a blunt object had been inserted far up into the body cavity through the anus, causing damage to the liver, the colon was torn; linear bruises were on the body, and skin had been stripped from one of the legs.

We would draw our family trees with crucifying Jesuses, fill up on forbidden television, and take off to Seraphina's house. She was stunning. Magazines were delivered to her door. She had this sophisticated ease in which she carried herself around like a designer handbag. She was two years older than Joanne, and she and her family lived close by. She was skilled at allowing just the right amount of affection, bordering genuine, to pour down from her to the two of us, with a trickle of interest in the mundane details of our lives, which fueled our everlasting loyalty to her wavy beach-blond hair.

One night Seraphina came over to our house for dinner. Her parents were having "date night." I hung up her slick raincoat and she told me I did it wrong. She showed me the special piece to hang it from so as not to deform the jacket. I did it correctly and went to brush my teeth. After, I sat down at the oak table to eat with everyone, bare in its decorations with bowls of bland white bean chili and waited for someone to chime in to say something about salt and why salt mattered even when it came to sugar. I remember Seraphina moved her spoon around, looked up and said, "I think farming is beautiful."

I knew it was a ridiculous thing to say, but saying it made her even more spectacular because she believed it. Our mother nearly smacked her. Jo cracked a smile. Only Seraphina could get away with spouting such fictions without my sister going apeshit, whereas anything I did—or for that matter anything anyone did (even as young and out of the way as I was)—caused a scene. In the presence of Seraphina my sister was a giant void, slack-jawed, glossy-eyed, like Earth had stopped rotating and the angels and demons alike had gathered under one roof to once and for all fornicate.

It was the first time in my life I saw Joanne in awe. I imagined it was as temporary as the magenta nail polish she started to wear since Seraphina wore it. But their relationship lasted longer than I expected. I resigned myself to being second in line in terms of importance, which was fine since I was already a copy of a copy. Sylvia said I was depressed, and I should make friends. Henry said not to worry; "we're all temporary," he said.

Whatever state it was, I found I could rest there easily since it was a place nobody wanted to visit, like my sock drawer. The magazine columnists, the ones who knew how to behave, the ones that I re-read in the magazines I'd stolen from Seraphina and donated to the public library and then legitimately checked out from the library, said you were supposed to connect *with* people, not *to* people like an ethernet cable. Though there were times I viewed those that I loved as life-saving machines.

Perhaps the only similarity between our two families was that Seraphina's parents also taught her at home. In a refreshing twist, her family showed an interest in our family. They wanted to know everything there was to know about growing up in a quaint, cute town with manners and "customs" and with a sweet downtown, regardless of how bombed-out looking it might be. They did not ask about our female relatives losing their minds. It seemed they had not heard the popular castration story that followed our mother around—"The Legendary Dispatch of Men by the Fareown Women"—which was to say, followed us around.

The last thing we agreed to in 1985, when Joanne was nine and I was seven, was that "The Legendary Dispatch of Men by the Fareown Women" would one day need a revision. As it were, the unrevised version of the legend has it that Sylvia Fareown was an only child. Raised by her mother in a small house in town, just off First Street where the churches were, and the bank, the library, schools, cafes serving breakfast all-day, a salon, second-hand stores, a pharmacy, and so forth. Yet, again, another girl-object the gossips would fixate on. This made the gossips suspicious, or perhaps this anchored their ever-evolving suspicions. And like flies drawn to a mule's corpse, they couldn't stay away from our mother. She was relentlessly nitpicked over: hair, skin, clothes. (Jo called what the gossips did "monitoring fetishism"; they couldn't help themselves, twisting and relishing their nasty tongues.) There was no mistaking Sylvia was her mother's daughter, and, like all the other waxy female hags she had descended from, she smelled bad. The gossips could not make sense of it, and sense was something the gossips were intent on making because *baby boys must have been born*. The discrepancy had to be explained once and for all. Something had to give.

The story told, obviously, was that in time each maladjusted Fareown woman—with the help of her abhorrent sisters and equally abhorrent daughters—had removed each and every perfect baby boy that had (inevitably) been born.

I said: "The gossips had lost their minds."

"No," Joanne clarified. "They had made up their minds."

So, how was the removing of men in our family done exactly?

As tantalizing stories must emerge to whet our appetites, to explain what's before us, a story presented itself: the lack of a male line in the Fareown family was a result of castration. Of course, the type of which varied depending on who was talking. For those with a greater imagination it was the classic, most feared type, and for others too squeamish to share their real feelings, their version was of a chemical nature, which did not involve a large incision.

Joanne said this back and forth would have made some sense if we were incredibly high. Unprovoked, Jo returned to the subject of catatonic states of being. This discourse, she said, made partial sense if one were in a super near-death high, "like living through the eye of a storm, like we had our mother's body"; a state she promised her one-day teenage self she would find herself in if she were to end up at some Shakespearean Festival, especially in Ashland, Oregon, where she did not want to end up. Where, at the time, Jo felt the capacity for self-deception was at an all-time high.

"And people think the Midwest is predictable," she said.

According to Jo, massive intoxication was the only way to deal with those sorts of festivals. It wasn't long ago that white Americans readied themselves to be entertained by performers on stage in velvety attire, adorned with glass beads, speaking Old English, cozying themselves on picnic blankets, that signs were posted on telephone poles threatening Black Americans to leave the city of Ashland before sundown or be brutalized.

"There was a general fondness toward thinking these things happened ages ago and that it was the Germans, and the country of Germany, who owned all of history's hypocrisy," Jo said, making a pipe out of a found pop can for the future.

As fate would have it, Seraphina's parents loved Ashland's Shakespeare Festival—full of America's best and brightest. They made a point of traveling there every year. "You and Bernadette should come with," Seraphina had said over breakfast at her house one morning, which was so amazing and plentiful it was sick. She had every type of sugar cereal you could imagine, plus waffles, plus mini chocolate chips, and banana blueberry pancakes too. In fact, her family hustled to make the festival annually—it wasn't easy to fit in a trip to Oregon. They rented a big, old cabin, built with real logs like in a picture, on a manmade lake, and partied down. This may have been the beginning of the end for my sister and Seraphina. But I was getting ahead of myself.

Seraphina, and her standout parents, spread over our already fractured landscape like a dense fog. They were a pristine example of wealth and gender. And all three of them eventually spoiled everything that was sacred about my relationship with my sister. Her family had an untouchable quality about them that managed to touch everything. Their entire family enterprise was sticky and kind and aerosoled into place. They did what they wanted, and America loved them even more for their carefree callousness.

TO BE CLEAN

After Seraphina came into the picture, Jo was in a perpetually foul mood when Seraphina wasn't around, which usurped earlier, pleasant-er memories, like those of us impersonating regular children. Even as junk kids my sister and I couldn't help but note that other kids had free time and spending money. Even parents with little money, like ours, somehow managed to give their children cash and enviable snacks. Thus, initiating a period when Jo and I began impersonating "regular children," i.e. those children who looked and talked like quality children, like the well-groomed, talented, successful ones we saw on television, like Seraphina. Children that wore clothes that matched (and sometimes even to their siblings or parents—that *matchy*), and which were gender appropriate; children that mostly did what they were told, their kind of mischief was *cute*; adorable children that were loved by their mother and their father, unconditionally, making it all the more wonderful that these good and loved children behaved so well because likewise their parents were perfect.

Impersonating regular children had taken my sister and I all over Illinois. Sometimes we hitched rides into town to go to the public library where nobody went and where we could make messes undisturbed. We stood on street corners selling what we called "Real Minute Maid Ice-Cold Lemonade." Though, everyone thought it was poisoned (we had black hair, and other personality set-backs) and it very well might have been. You could not be sure with us.

Years later, Ivanka Trump, in her memoir, would write, unironically, of her troubles selling lemonade in her family's skyscraper in Manhattan. "We had no such advantages," super disadvantaged, struggling, super blond little Ivanka wrote of her financial troubles. Eventually, little Ivanka managed to sell her lemonade to her bodyguard, her driver, and to her maids.

In addition to the tantalizing agony afflicted by Seraphina taking my place in my sister's psyche, and later Ivanka taking the place of Chelsea Clinton in America, Jo was in an exhaustingly poor mood. Her nipples were bad. Her vagina smelled. Her hair was really dark and it was wily, which was all wrong. I remember sketching bars of soap inside of thought bubbles while trying to get her to eat salty food, a reliable thing we did together. (Even if we'd end up with only drawings of nachos because we didn't have the ingredients to make them.) But Jo stank and she was never hungry anymore. I should have felt badly, her eyes sunken, her boob-less chest, but I enjoyed even the tiniest shreds of her demise, such as it was—minimal and temporary.

Those, and other hormonal shifts happened. It was winter. Against our parents' wishes, Joanne decided to try regular school and joined the 4th grade class. Every morning, she woke up at the crack of dawn to catch her bus, which would take her away from me and Seraphina and to the school in town. She carried her lunch in a paper sack she designed herself, with drawings of lightning bolts and helmets, instead of more popular lunch boxes, hard box-shaped ones with handles and designs featuring Care Bears and Rambo. Jo carried her wrinkled brown lunch bag with lightning bolts, and wore undesirable clothes that also reeked of cigarettes. On her first day, the teacher looked at her and said: "Tell your mother to send you to school in clothes that fit and don't stink."

Joanne did what Joanne does, she responded by removing her shirt, and baring her not-yet, not-even-close-to maturing female body, and screamed like a rock star.

Weeks later, my sister cut off a classmate's long blond ponytail. After the hair chopping incident, Jo left school and walked all the way home. When she arrived, her face was bluish and swollen. Sylvia wrapped her in a blanket and addressed the frostbite on her feet. There were several holes in her boots, which had gone unnoticed. Just like that, she was back to being homeschooled. After a stint attending regular school, what Jo really wanted to know about was anarchy. She had the makings of an anarchist.

At the time, my sister had taken up with the revolutionary hero Peter Kropotkin. Even though he himself had said "cooperation" rather than "conflict" was the leading factor in the evolution of species. To my mind an important detail, which my sister notably omitted because it did not serve her interests. Jo was skilled in conflict and not cooperation. "Chaos begets chaos," was how she described America's infrastructure and the engine that fueled the economy then, which was still how she saw it now. But what Jo had really wanted to avoid was the news about her spine.

A nurse in school discovered that Jo had Idiopathic Scoliosis. The nurse had identified Jo's curvature during a routine screening offered during class. Joanne's "S Curve" was severe, running from her mid-neck, curving through each vertebra down her sacrum. The same path her long hair fell. She was told she wouldn't be able to have children.

"Little vultures," Jo said in response, about children sinking their teeth into boobs, a body part she was preoccupied with. Her curvature, already a concern at that noticeable stage, would only worsen in time, eventually threatening to crush her lungs if she didn't get a custom back brace, which our family could not afford. I remember the insurance company laughed our mother off the telephone when she called to inquire about coverage. Our father called back, and they spared him by simply ending the call mid-sentence. I remember Jo said not to bother with it.

"I'm a vegan, so focus on how obnoxious that is," she said.

I remember Sylvia reflecting on my sister's barrenness and saying that perhaps it was a positive she would never be able to have children of her own. Note: the castration tale. The situation involving Joanne's spine made Henry so angry he threw a beer across the living room where it shattered. He did this on more than one occasion. Our parents fought hard. And for a brief spell they stopped having sex. Henry made his hands into fists, and I shut my face like a trapdoor. Sylvia screamed at him that beer was an extravagance, and look at Henry: he had gone and wasted beer. The room felt like an unpressurized airplane. I dreamt of bubble gum.

Extravagances made Henry and Sylvia uncomfortable, especially our mother. Extravagances included the one egg pan (not that you need more than one); I can recall that the single cast iron frying pan could only be used once a week to make eggs. To clean it, you had to treat it like Gwyneth Paltrow's face; a laborious task, one that our mother performed weekly. And there was the toaster our mother had found in a parking lot, which only toasted part of the sliced bread. Sylvia threw away nothing: paper napkins, mustard, mayonnaise, and ketchup packets, chopsticks, plastic bags, and plastic cutlery she had pilfered from the donut shop were stuffed inside the cabinets and drawers in an apocalyptic frenzy. If someone dared open a cupboard, they could not do so without hundreds of plastic items and containers, precariously stuffed inside of the cupboards, falling onto the floor like an avalanche.

"And now you've made a mess," Sylvia had said to Henry of his beer throwing, that day we could no longer ignore the severity of Joanne's scoliosis, before threatening to leave him—that was to say, before abandoning us all. Something our mother most certainly would have done if she was pushed too hard.

Looking back, I can see that our mother was tired of motherhood, a role she was supposedly made for. She was tired of being a wife. Tired of land being used inefficiently, tired of making ends meet, of our father's anger, of America, and of the insistent debt collectors who loved a good car wash before driving those back country roads. It was only a matter of time before she would go away, like the women before her. Or to use the preferred euphemism, before she would "return to water."

There was a look to leaving, and this look came to define Sylvia's facial expressions, which did not change the overall warmth of her face, which was warm like a summer peach. We lived with this look. We lived inside of fear like it was architecture.

OUR MOTHER

Sylvia's mother died when Sylvia was a senior in high school, a death our mother memorialized. It was a loss she never recovered from. Every year, on the day our grandmother's body was found in a snow-covered field, Sylvia made a point of reminding us about her mother, about the sort of woman our grandmother was—a solid woman—and we would be asked to close our eyes and picture something luminous in her honor: a beach, an airport, a bowl with fruit instead of the usual mess of coupons and tangled rubber bands.

Our grandmother's death was ruled a suicide. Sylvia remembered that day clearly: it was winter in Illinois; snow blanketed the ground, but at the police station the authorities, all men she'd never seen before, wore t-shirts and cargo shorts and stood casually around our grandmother's dead naked body on a gurney. Underdressed, the men declared our grandmother's death a suicide despite evidence pointing otherwise. What about the tire tracks? Sylvia's mother did not drive a truck. And the cigarette butts? Her mother was not a smoker. Our grandmother wouldn't have touched a cigarette.

The men nodded and put their police shirts over their ordinary civilian shirts, without bothering to button them up. Uniformed and more certain, they doubled down on their assessment. They were sure, and they had their reasons for making sense of the incident. The men in uniform, whose seriousness looked out of place, and who looked like a particular type of white boy on acid, suggested Sylvia get back to her studies: Didn't she want to outlive her familial curse? They knew about the Fareown women. They had grown up hearing the legend. The policemen and the detectives suggested Sylvia let them handle the situation since they were skilled professionals. Besides, "suicide was suicide," the men said, and said, and said, and said, until they were more inflated, more convinced, levitating white authority balloons. From that day forward, Sylvia told us, if people wanted more nothing from her, then that was exactly what she would give them—more nothing.

Our grandmother Poppy was found dead, and Sylvia was left the one-bedroom farmhouse, the adjacent land, the cemetery where her relatives were, and the small house in town she had grown up in. She was also given Aunt Vie to look after, our mother's last direct relative, our grandmother's fifth and youngest sister who had not yet returned to water, and who at seven years of age was a guest on I've Got a Secret, a quiz-game show on television which ended in 1967. (She never watched television after that. Even just looking at a remote control could cause her to go apeshit.)

Aunt Vie moved into the house in town voluntarily so she could have her fruit juice whenever she wanted. (Sylvia was obliging.) But with her behavior being what it was (erratic), soon thereafter she would burn the house to the ground and claim she had told people to pay attention.

"Americans don't listen," she was famous for saying, stuffing unpaid items into her pockets.

For a brief period before the arson, Sylvia and Aunt Vie lived harmoniously: Vie drank vodka with tropical juice and made tinctures and healing salves. Our mother found in Vie another motherly figure. She gladly picked up after Vie who pulled her hair out and who started fires, at first little ones in the oven. Sylvia inserted eyes in the back of her skull for the sake of efficiency, and with them she put out the fires and studied her aunt's face. It was like her mother's: her bone structure was sharp, she had a handsome, forthright chin and sweet nose, flexible, expressive eyes, all of which fossilized into a face that did not ascribe to any gender, much like Joanne's. Sylvia

51

then sewed two additional eyes next to her ears—she would be better than one person at seeing. She would become an owl in order to care for Vie, which was to say care for the larger community, and to continue to keep them both fed.

Given the context, Sylvia was permitted to finish her senior year at home. She hired a local teenager to help out so she could continue doing administrative work at the high school, which gave her the confidence to think beyond the scope of her hometown. Of this period, Sylvia has said she was happy enough. Inheritance had given her options—this luxury was not lost on our mother—but eventually she ended up meeting Henry in 1973 in a pharmacy on her knees (longer story), who had recently returned from Vietnam, and the rest was history. (This, of course, was its own story.) Our parents would talk like the outcome—meeting in a grimy pharmacy where the stained carpet smelled like cat piss and immediately deciding to get hitched—was unavoidable. Sitting at our kitchen table, they would sort through stacks of coupons, envelopes, spreadsheets, calculators, and notepads, and speak about their fates like they had already been written. And, in a way, I can see it: if a person puts everything they have inside of them into another person, if one deposits their worth, love, and value into another, then there's no going back.

At the end of Sylvia's senior year, in a fit of delusional paranoia, Aunt Vie threw a stack of receipts in the oven, set the temperature for 500 degrees, the timer for ninety minutes, and went out for more tropical juice. The house in town burned. Sylvia's childhood home reduced to rubble. "It was for the best," our mother explained of the situation. (She tended to gravitate toward this sort of resigned reasoning when it came to tragedy.) Sylvia deferred her acceptance to the University of Iowa to continue to look after Aunt Vie, who had been placed in a mental institution, this time by choice, with an extensive Jell-O collection.

Our mother has said of this time that she felt like a bleak water-color painting. One of those landscapes sold in a seaside Sunday market where the colors don't hold—the shades bleed and become so faint and neutralized they might as well disappear altogether. Nothing our mother imagined for herself had transpired. She did not attend university to discuss Eldridge Cleaver with like-minded individuals, learn about self-care, and have sex recklessly with a stranger in a dingy van. Her university self would have dared to be irresponsible, chop off her hair, give herself an uneven blunt boy-cut to frame her defined, angular face. That even as our mother we had to admit had remained stunning, electric. This version of our mother at university had her up late at night photographing mice copulating in the corners of her dorm room where she would leave them pieces of cheddar and breadcrumbs, since everything was personal.

But none of this came to pass. She did not attend the University of Iowa as she had planned. Instead, she bought a beater car with the homeowner's insurance compensation and continued doing administrative work for the high school. She took the only apartment available to rent from a creepy retired schoolteacher. She fell back into her default position, which was to "hold tight." Our mother did this well. She held tight like you do when you're asked to remain calm in a precarious situation you want nothing more than to get out of. Our mother held *it* together, an impenetrable force field around her. She was detailed and well-designed, like a fine-tuned music box. She went nowhere without a pack of menthols and a contingency plan. She pointed out the emergency exits wherever we went. In an evacuation, our family was not going out the same door we entered—that was suicide. She held tight and tried not to think about what might have been. If she did, a slow suffocation came over her and she wanted to bury herself alive, as the Vestal Virgins had—those virgins whose blood could not be spilled because they were the keepers of the fire.

"Keepers of the fire," she would tell us, smoking, shrugging her shoulders, and drying her hands.

"Fire keepers," Jo and I repeated in our attic space until the doors to our hearts opened, and in marched the Fire Keepers from 7th century BC. In walked free women, free from their fathers, free from the duties of marriage, whose sole responsibility was to cultivate the sacred fire.

Eventually, Aunt Vie—our last direct relative—died in her sleep in the Institution. If our mother felt alone before, she felt alone in new ways after Vie's death. Growing up, it was Vie who taught her about hypocrisy. Vie had told Sylvia to brush her teeth regularly and to skip sugar candy so as not to get cavities. Vie had advice. Vie ignored advice. Vie drank room temperature vodka combined with whatever tropical juices she could find until she was in a motionless state. Vie was famous for socking people if they got too close, but never Sylvia, who was her favorite.

Aunt Vie, like many of the women in our family, liked being transported elsewhere, as if in a dream. In the end, Vie died surrounded by her preferred assortment of Medieval and modern elixirs, surrounded by jars of her healing salve based in comfrey, others with yarrow, or other astringent herbs, which she said could help relieve the burden of absorbing the emotions of others and that she used to heal wounds. Throughout Vie's room, our mother found cartons of her sugary juices and digestive bitters, a mix of dandelion, liver, and cardiac tonic, bottles filled with tinctures made from her preferred solvent: vodka. "Good to swill plus made a fine base for herbs and garlic," Aunt Vie apparently liked to say.

"Still said," Joanne corrected, since she had a way of communing with the dead. (Whether this was an outright fabrication was irrelevant. Jo did and said what she pleased, even in 2009, even in Bloomington, Minnesota.)

I had to take a break from examining the contents of our lives like receipts. I held my pee.

It was like doing taxes.

Time to leave Super 8. It was time to go to The Mall of America to find God and to focus. A pricey enterprise that opened its doors in 1992 just as America was in the middle of a recession. Back then locals called the place "megadeath." It was important to visit the Mall for relevancy and illumination, and because Simone De Beauvoir would have wished as much for me. Not unlike 2009, back when it debuted the Mall had the intention to make consumers feel like they were outside while they were inside. Then, a lot like now, the indoor world was expanding, and the outdoor world was not because it was being eaten up by the indoor world. Even Le Corbusier—French, famous, respected architect—advocated replacing actual (plague-like, dirty) streets found outside, with street lookalikes inside buildings. His solution was to treat inhabitants with doses of light and air.

I would do this, take a trip to this city-sized mall, because *The New York Times* would compare America's dying malls to an endangered species. And because the biggest mall in America might one day have a Writer-in-Residence Program, and the writer—who would do good work explaining and eulogizing the Mall's significance—would be awarded at the end of her stay with a substantial gift card. "Don't let anyone tell you capitalism isn't generous," I could hear our father lament before finishing a bottle of liquor.

I went to the lobby for help. Reeba, the motel's receptionist, after identifying me as one of those "lazy guests that come to the lobby with last-minute requests," arranged for a shuttle to take me there, which was quite a *to-do* since the Mall had been booked for weeks in advance. To make things right, I asked Reeba what she wanted from the Mall. "A pretzel from Wetzel's," she said, without hesitating. "And if they're all out, I'll take two from Auntie Anne's."

I had been off the bus and inside of the behemoth all of six minutes before needing a rest. The woman I sat down next to was looking at a map, and when she noticed I didn't have one, she asked if my shoes were comfortable enough to meander the Mall's fifty-seven acres.

"Converse, no such luck," I answered.

The woman was from Reykjavik, Iceland's capital. I told her my favorite outlaw folk story was Icelandic. Did she know it? Of course, she did; all children in Iceland grow up with the story and are sung the lullaby to sleep.

In the fable, Halla (female), runs off into the hills with a misjudged outlaw (male). She gives birth to their baby, and then throws their baby into a waterfall knowing they faced starvation. The couple managed to live out their days among the remote highland, hidden in the lava field, surrounded by barren desert and glacial rivers, indicative of their desires to remain hidden. But then the volcano erupted, which was not helpful. Parts of the area are named after the couple. These stories marked the Icelandic landscape, which was to say: language and meaning were present everywhere.

"Not the baby though," I said. "The baby just gets tossed out."

"Though I suppose the spirit of the baby lives on in the lullaby all Icelandic babies get sung," the woman seated next to me from Reykjavik said.

The woman said it had been a while since she'd thought about this 18th century story of Halla and her bandit baby daddy, Eyvindur of the Mountains. She was in Minnesota to shop, she added, as she rose from her seat. She'd be sure to look it up when she got back home to refresh her memory.

"No problem, we all need refreshers," I said, when I should have just waved and moved on to other non sequiturs.

In the legend, the baby was thrown into a waterfall by her mother. There were a lot of babies in the Mall. Land and death and identity for us went back generations. Our mother attached this ideology—to work with what you had, and to make and save what you could—to us like a bomb. To reinforce this point, Sylvia made her own products and saved for items that could not be made. Grime and stink became encrusted beneath her fingernails, her hair was long and crazy if she did not hold it back like a hostage. Her clothing did not conform to popular fashions, and she was aware of it. Some days she said she barely felt female at all. Semiotics, the little exposure she had, made sure of it. Only much later did I come to understand that often for many women these feelings of operating on the periphery of established feminine behavior were internalized. Our mother, like others in our community, struggled to balance a range of competing identities. Exhaustion and resilience, her growing interest in the cosmos, her menthol cigarettes, all came to define Sylvia. A state of being that crystalized during motherhood, with all the disappointments, relentless breastfeeding, and unrequited tenderness required. The work of care our mother was responsible for providing and maintaining for an eternity—an infinite span of time she would spend most of lacking a dishwasher and a washing machine—felt like a trap. Wasn't it? She resented (my word) or despised (Jo's word) herself for not moving to Iowa when she'd had the chance. The magnitude of picturing what life might have been without us overwhelmed her.

There were times when Jo and I hid from the truth that was our mother: her heretical DNA, her aging body, lean and worn, her skin rough and her dark hair untamed. She was dissolving in real time. We watched this—the truth about the women in our family disintegrating—unfold before our eyes. The sound of a wind-up toy running out of batteries. My sister and I were doomed. Entranced by the television, we ignored the inevitability that one day the skin of our upper arms would sag like a hammock, like Sylvia's did, and that eventually our hair would turn black and silver and we would be painfully exhausted. There were times Jo and I conjured the women in our family, all dead, technically; and we would laugh, feeling their madness in our bones, like we were submerged beneath salty waters. Sometimes we lingered there in that suffocating feeling.

HEREDITARY, AS CRISIS CONTINUED

The Fareown women had problems. Many said that they were the problem. Their issues had to do with money and atrophying minds. Over the years, the few female relatives who had not gone missing—those women who had not pursued a permanent return to water, subsequently vanishing in oceans or ditches—were forced to sell their acreage to pay off lost bets, dental and medical bills. These female relatives, dead like the water ones, were notorious. They were notoriously devoted to religion (Elvis was Jesus), freeform and reckless, especially when it came to salvation, their love of the sea (though at a distance), their ravenous sexual appetites that went unsated, and saying whatever was on their minds. When it came to salvation, they chose religion over all else, including bodies of water.

For them, religion came easily—God was everywhere. He had solid advice, at every turn, in every parking lot or truck stop. They might spot religious icons when they gambled. God's divine shape was embedded in playing cards, which spoke to them in languages nobody else understood, let alone heard. Sometimes telemarketers were saints. Their saviors camped out in jukeboxes and various customizable life-improving discounted offerings from *As Seen on TV,* like dog stairs and Huggle Hoodies. God sprouted up in strangers at bars. He was especially noticeable around pool tables dressed in well-fitted cotton tees and tight denim pants making flirty eyes from across the room. Where spending happened, God was bound to be.

If booze was present, God was close by. If money was on the table, God had thoughts.

I was five when I realized Jo and I would need water. A resource. We didn't need God; there were already too many saviors to contend with. While these cognitive details and humorous illustrations regarding our hereditary natures were compelling, in the years that followed they would not help us when it came to filling out medical forms. The truth, while mostly true, about the women on our maternal side did not improve our living situations. It didn't help matters that our father was a mere child when his family decided to discard him like trash on the side of the road.

In the living room, I would contemplate whether I liked reality while sitting in some undesirable outfit, cross-legged, and picking my nose until it was hollow and bled. I remember being relieved that Jo was out with her clean, fragrant girlfriend, Seraphina. All Jo ever talked about was poor English weather, birds, anatomy. Much of the latter having to do with Seraphina. Seraphina's "flawless style and her *Tetris*," which irritated our father to no end. Even one year after the game had entered the market, Henry still wasn't sure whether it was either just a video game, or a last-ditch effort by the Soviets to distract America and win the Cold War.

At the time, our parents resolved their financial pressures by downing Tylenol, despite (my word) or because of (Joanne's) the '82 murders. In 1982, a handful of people in Illinois took Tylenol for headaches, their headaches worsened, and they died. Our parents stocked up on the pain reliever and had this routine: they would take a bunch of Tylenol—our mother with water, and our father with booze—before getting to the growing list of maintenance costs. There was the land maintenance, fertilizer, equipment and facility upkeep, livestock fees, labor, fuel. Not to mention us fools. They had to secure credit and they were having trouble doing that. Henry had done some listening. He took an oath—we saw him in front of the refrigerator do it—to keep his mouth shut and tried to listen. Instead of losing it and getting angry, he directed his energies into repairing the holes he had punched into the walls.

"A new leaf," he promised our family.

It would not be the last time we would hear it. I remember Joanne explaining to me that our father was taking charge of his anger issues, though he refused to acknowledge the issue was rage.

Nothing lasted, and I remember feeling foolish for thinking otherwise.

One afternoon, Joanne and I were in the front of the house, which had sunk half-an-inch, doing yard work. Henry was backing up the truck out of the driveway when he ran over my foot. I cried out in pain and he kept backing up.

"Stop!" Jo shouted.

Our father got out of his truck—a 1971 Chevrolet C20 Longhorn 300 Horsepower—studied me thoroughly like an army sergeant, and said: "You weep like a sissy. Stop weeping, sissy."

Maybe I was a sissy. I remember thinking Henry should have picked a less obvious word. Called me something equally ineffective but more fun to say, like hussy or milquetoast.

"Nobody uses sissy anymore. Not to demean a person, anyway," I said. I remember Joanne was shocked I'd been articulate.

Henry hit me across the face, though not as hard as he was capable of. I glanced over at Jo. Jo was struck in a way I had never seen. I thought to myself: My sister is hydrology. She was a hydrological occurrence. She was water perennially moving between planes—despite itself—occurring between what was obvious and recognizable, and what was implied and often misunderstood. I loved-loathed my sister more in that revelatory moment than ever before.

Jo threw her tools at Henry. First, her trowel, claw rake, and last, her shovel. Each hit his body with force. He didn't wince. Our father knew restraint. He had learned restraint in the army. There, he learned about stoicism, hunger, and managing narrative paradoxes, like committing murder and finding camaraderie.

"Bernie, I'm sorry," Henry said, taking a seat in the dirt.

It was another one of those odd things, a twist in the road, in that I never knew what he really meant when he said this, but I knew he meant it. His head sunk down into his sternum. Gesturing with his arms and his hands, he asked us to join him there. It was the kind of day where people said and did what they shouldn't, and the pain it generated miraculously brought them closer than ever. I remember the three of us sat huddled together like a tight sports team does when deciding the next play.

Many times, Henry disgusted us. There were no heroes in war; he had taught us that. There were only enemies. Henry's sickness, his outrage, his depression: something wasn't right with him. We toyed with packing our bags and never again speaking to our parents, because that was what a person who has been in therapy with a good therapist setting boundaries would have done. But we rationalized his pain, though we knew his behavior was wrong. That was the trap of violence sickness, Jo said. Everything was out of place but almost recognizable. In those environments, truth was fragmented, both real and unreal. Understanding love was foolish. After Hansel and Gretel learned they were to be taken into the deep forest to be left to starve to death, Hansel dropped pebbles so that he and his sister, Gretel, could make their way back home.

Why were they so determined to make their way back home knowing what they knew?

I remember asking Joanne why we forgave him, and she responded by throwing her heavy books at the wall. Then she went outside, where, before running down the well-traveled road in a cape, which nearly engulfed her thin frame, she stopped to face our house to scream bloody murder, something about *King Lear*'s Fool and his belief that the lives we lead were all versions of the same patterning, each involved weather. I wanted her to stop running away. I wanted it all to stop. I wanted her to stay so that I could tell her that one day the Hoover Dam would be turned into a giant battery and that our love of water would amount to something spectacular.

———

Money, and our lack thereof, was a constant source of tension and shame. The government had implemented new agricultural policies (misguided, our community would argue), which were keeping farm prices low. The barn roof needed massive repairs and the cows were injuring themselves on the barbed wire. The name "Ron" came up a lot, said like a necessary slur. Henry was always calling and leaving messages for Ron. Sylvia smoked and kept the spreadsheets organized. She punched numbers into the calculator, her face scrunched. I wanted to be just like her. In the evenings, her hands went numb, and I would offer to rub them. She lit cigarette after cigarette and spoke of her dead female relatives to her dead female relatives. She turned on the oven, to prep for the evening's dish of bland food. Ruffled her thick hair. Poured herself a glass of unsweetened iced tea. Emptied the dish rack. Re-filled the dish rack. Yelled at Jo to empty the rack of clean dishes, but Jo was not there. She was out misbehaving and fine-tuning her pranks; reading materials she should not have been reading; teaching others to masturbate, which, when their parents found out (and they always found out), would become a scandal. Their parents would call the church and the school, and the church and the school would call our parents to complain about Joanne. My sister's early dictionary had defined the word "complain" as "Joanne."

"Damn us," Henry and Sylvia said, before going off to argue and have loud sex.

"Like diseased rabbits," Jo said of their obscene sex. "Even our space in the attic isn't far enough to be spared the details."

What did having sex like rabbits even mean? Small biddy parts covered in a soft, cushy buffer, operating mechanically?

The point was fighting and getting it on was often what our parents did in lieu of using other forms of communication, which might have actually addressed the stressful circumstances our family faced.

That winter, I remember I sat in the living room thinking about my dear friend Martha, a taxidermized passenger pigeon being gawked at by museum-goers, listening to the television and the radio while finances were fought over and parental sex happened. I put a plastic bag over my head. I watched television with a plastic bag over my head to contain my rage as my parents ignored the potential hazard of having a plastic bag over my face, while I listened to people in many places across America deny the farm crisis existed. A kind of static amnesia had taken over the country. There were communication issues, which sprung from the ambiguity of its causes: Was it a farm crisis, a rural crisis, an agricultural crisis, or a credit crisis? Things were never called by their common names. Massacre was sometimes called "agitation," sometimes "effervescence," sometimes "excess," I once heard a man on television explain. Sylvia said at that age I slept a lot. I demanded to be near her body at all times. A dagger in wait, she said of my calm, unmoving body as I slept.

All I wanted then was to be a stealthy wombat. That outwardly sweet, strange, and rotund animal with short legs, a thick body, and a large head, with round ears and beady eyes, teeth that never stop growing and that shits in cube shapes. Did you know that wombats were able to run up to twenty-five miles per hour? A speed they could maintain for ninety seconds. They could attack backwards and could knock adults to the ground. They could shatter fox skulls against the walls of their dens by using the hard cartilage of their butts.

"Someone, please, give me a wombat," I said to Martha, who understood such things as an animal that had been made extinct because of mankind; also, an animal, who in turn, made her into an object for a museum visitors to remember her by.

ANIMAL INCIDENTS OF 1984 DURING 1985

My older sister and I looked back to that year—1984—in America because by 1985 we were really hungry. 1984 brought about two very different and inflammatory incidents involving animals and their dying, which preoccupied our minds. Not to mention that year saw record-breaking winter blizzards in Illinois, just as Cajun cooking became a national obsession. "Finally, flavor is allowed where we live," was Jo's relieved thinking. There was a lot to unpack when it came to our country's relationship to flavor and to animal extinction.

We began our love affair, our first substantial one, with Martha, the last of the passenger pigeons who I'd contributed to our America Project. She invaded our minds and spirits like a spell. At one point in our nations' history, a single flock of passenger pigeons was said to resemble the windings of a vast and majestic river, twisting, swelling, expansive as ever, and never uniform. Flights could last from dawn to sunset, resembling the coils of a gigantic serpent, and darkening the sky like an eclipse. Jo etched an outline of Martha into her forearm to preserve her memory, never mind the huge bloody mess she made to make this happen.

In public I spoke of her extinction, the future of water (which was to say our lack of it), and our present hunger, to anyone that would listen. We parked ourselves in front of Blaine's Farm & Fleet: Everything about Martha was pertinent, Jo and I argued. The passenger pigeon was once the most abundant bird on Earth and within a few decades approximately five billion were dead. The responses—to approximately two-hundred million dying a year—varied. Some said the birds had fled to the Arizona desert. Others hypothesized that the pigeons had taken refuge in the Chilean pine forests, or somewhere east of Puget Sound, or in Australia. Another theory held that every pigeon had joined a single mega flock and had disappeared into the Bermuda Triangle, where things vanish.

In the early 1800s the ornithologist Alexander Wilson described a flock of passenger pigeons moving across the Ohio River in Kentucky: "From right to left, far as the eye could reach, the breadth of this vast procession extended, seeing everywhere equally crowded...I took out my watch to note the time, and sat down to observe them. It was then half past one. I sat for more than an hour, but instead of a diminution of this prodigious procession, it seemed rather to increase both in numbers and rapidity...I rose and went on. About four o'clock in the afternoon I crossed the Kentucky River, at the town of Frankfort, at which time the living torrent over my head seemed as numerous and as extensive as ever."

The truth was Americans liked hunting, and America was a hungry, young, and growing country, so therefore Americans ate them up. Hordes of commercial hunters and trappers colonized the land to meet the demand; pigeons were cheap. Hunters and trappers sought out sagging trees, where passenger pigeons nested. The men lit the trees on fire and collected the singed and squawking squabs that fell to the ground. Then came the thousands of miles of railroad. Later, the nationwide telegraph communication system. Which expanded even faster than the rail lines. Cookbook recipes loved the chicks: pigeon pot pie, larded pigeons served with bread sauce—bread sauce!—and directions for making potted pigeons: "draw and clean, break legs just above the feet." It was suggested for the braised pigeon dish that the gravy be served in a gravy boat. Pigeon was roasted, stewed, stuffed with parsley (at least one pint of parsley for each bird). *Mrs. Lincoln's Boston Cook Book: What to Do and What Not to Do in Cooking* in 1883 was so popular and profitable that the publishers kept the book in print until 1923.

By 1914, there was only one. The Cincinnati Zoo housed the last captive passenger pigeon, named Martha, after First Lady Martha Washington. When news spread of her species' imminent extinction, the last Martha became an instant tourist attraction. In her final years, whether depressed or almost dead, she rarely moved: What was Martha's problem? Disgruntled zoo visitors threw handfuls of sand at her to elicit a reaction. Others claimed she had become—"before her time"—another solid and stoic American statue. On September 1st, 1914, she died, and her corpse was sent to the Cincinnati Ice Company. They froze Martha in a 300-pound ice cube and then shipped her to the Smithsonian Institution, where she was stuffed and mounted.

The cat incident of 1984 was an entirely different situation, but equally compelling. At the time, my sister was eight and I was a mere six—that is to say, nugatory—but I can recall the cat incident, and the killing of Nebraskan farmer turned vigilante Art Kirk, who was shot in the middle of cultivating his corn by a SWAT team, who were demanding a return of $100,000 to the bank. The incident broke down like this: Art's wife, Deloris, arrived home a day after the shootout to find one of her cats, not yet fully grown, with its head severed, ears slit, and a portion of the skin stripped from the remaining body, its torso and legs missing. The SWAT team said they didn't kill or skin any cats; they didn't even see any animals. (Though one member admitted to seeing a dead kitten's remains decomposing and being eaten by another cat on the south side of the house.)

Special Investigator Samuel Van Pelt, who was assigned to Kirk's case, was desperate to understand what he and his team considered to be the unnerving shifts in the political landscape of the beleaguered Farm Belt. Special Investigator Van Pelt interviewed Art Kirk's loan officer for his U.S. intelligence report. Kirk's loan officer remembered seeing Art on a Sunday evening before October 23rd, when he had taken his family to see the movie Country starring Jessica Lange and Sam Shepard, about a couple running a small farm in Iowa that had been in their family for generations, which they were about to lose to the bank. A movie that would earn Jessica Lange an Academy Award for best actress.

I remember our mother was both impressed and proud that a regal woman such as Jessica Lange would portray someone like herself, yet equally horrified by how little Lange resembled the women she knew.

Presently, in my Super 8 room in Bloomington, I thought back on that time of dead animals and American cinema; I felt a deep loneliness which surprised me given the fact I had grown up in a rural place known for its isolation. I needed to learn about Minneapolis. I took the stairs to the lobby to get some exercise. In place of the usual receptionist, I had come to know—Reeba—there was a young, fresh-looking replacement, wearing thick, black eyeliner, and a hot, short, olive-green dress. She did not have on a nametag. I hoped I would be spared the task of establishing relations all over again. The process of making acquaintances, the busy work involved with saying something effortlessly arbitrary, yet pointedly meaningful, was a task which could send me straight back to bed. I had already put in my time getting to know Reeba.

I introduced myself and the young woman behind the counter, who was using a calculator, an actual calculator, said she didn't want to know.

"Bad day?" I asked.

"Something like it," she said.

But you're so young, I had wanted to tell her plump, sweet face.

"You don't look like you like people," the replacement receptionist said in earnest.

You look like you think looking hungover looks good, I had wanted to say.

"I like people plenty," was all I could think to say in that moment where I had been put on the spot, an inadequate response if I had to guess based on the doubtful look on her face.

"What is it you need?" the replacement receptionist asked.

It was true; I needed things. "I am looking for a golden-haired boy who is here with his parents," I said. The replacement receptionist said that family—the one with the mother who drank juice like it was the forbidden fruit and wore an expression like she was about to off herself—had checked out, taking with them all the complimentary snacks, and had not paid the bill.

Perhaps this was the news I had been searching for. Perhaps these details would go on to hatch millions of offspring in my head for years to come. Perhaps I too was invested in progeny, but I was not under the impression that I could save anyone. At some point every teacher realizes that, but I had thought I might see the boy again in this motel, an impulse I would have been better off curbing as I had no business spending time with a young kid. What if they came away imitating me?

"Why do you call him a boy?" the young receptionist asked me.

I suppose it was because that was how he struck me.

I had met the kid I called boy the evening of the tornado. He had taken a seat beside me on the cold floor without asking, assuredly, like he was mine. After several moments of him watching me struggle to open my bag of animal crackers the receptionist had passed out, to appease weary guests, the boy offered to open them for me. "Tiny hands," he said, wryly. Jo would have found him startlingly familiar. I was an older woman who should not have been impressed, but I was impressed. And for this first time in ages, I relaxed. Together, munching on animal crackers, the boy said he didn't like waiting. His mom: "See that woman falling apart over there next to the coffee maker?" the boy asked, pointing to a very attractive but admittedly disheveled woman grabbing a beige mug. His mom was always the last to pick him up from school.

I said none of this to the cheeky young receptionist who clearly had sharp impulses.

"I suppose you think I'm a child as well," she said to me.

The young receptionist had eyes like lasers, and she used them to see right through me.

The receptionist typed some words into the computer and said I had stayed much longer at the Super 8 than I had originally intended. It was written in my notes.

"It says here," she said, "one to two nights."

Each guest has a profile, did I know that?

"I'm on deadline," I said. A lie. A knee-jerk reaction. A cry for help. I started back toward my room.

"Hey," she called out to me as I crossed the room. "Did you know *your boy* was staying in the room next to yours?"

Most people—I should say most adults—have stories about partners, exes, best friends, gurus, mentors, roommates, infatuations, strangers, and maybe even distant cousins. I had stories about Jo, an enterprise, a kaleidoscopic wormhole that touched and sank everything far and proximal, and I wasn't even close to sure what those stories meant. I found it bothersome. I found it compelling. Instead of getting on the elevator when it came to fetch me and heading back up to my room, I decided I had another question for the replacement receptionist.

I returned to the motel lobby, brighter now that the sun had emerged from behind the clouds exposing the aubergine-painted room for all its garishness. Aubergine was one of those colors that was easy to get wrong. It seemed to me then, standing in the lobby, that every child on Earth was there, tapping on the counters, demanding snacks, wailing about boredom and icy milk. For that I couldn't blame them—the carton of non-fat milk often sat out in a pitcher of soppy melted ice. Ordinarily I would have fled the scene bemoaning civilization, itching to return to the privacy of my room, but I had an actual reason to be there. I had some business to take care of that involved the replacement receptionist. I wanted tell her something intimate. That's what friends do. But she was nowhere to be found.

I left her a handwritten note on paper on the counter next to the motel's telephone, where she spent much of her time dealing with the concerns of others: I have a question for you, call my room, it read. Using tape, which I always carried with me, I secured the piece of paper in place like securing a rare artifact. I made sure to say it was a question only she could answer. I had a feeling the young receptionist whose body could not be missed would not be able to resist responding to a banal request such as that one.

Back in my room, my bedside telephone blinked red. It was a voicemail from the receptionist inviting me out for karaoke.

1970S: THE FACTS

There were problems in America, other than having children, being disguised as solutions in the name of progress, many of which happened before the two of us existed. Throughout the '70s, farmers were heavily pressured to expand their production. The pressure came from every direction—agricultural professionals, politicians, farm agents, scholars, lenders, and economists—who were all certain land rates would not go down—they just wouldn't. And in 1973 Earl Butz, the Secretary of Agriculture, demanded that farmers "get big or get out, plant crops fence-row to fence-row," and to hurry up and increase their production for the markets or else.

The prevailing logic was to squeeze out as much as was possible, and plan to replace human labor with technology. Henry could not believe his eyes. This kind of high-production approach to agriculture could devastate land's productivity. It was as if the Dust Bowl was a mirage. Like many in our community, destroying the land to accumulate more debt was poor decision-making. Sylvia and Henry went to community gatherings. Among their peers they expressed their reservations. Most agreed that borrowing was trouble. But it was near impossible for farmers to escape the message to borrow and there were few realizable alternatives. Now was the time to make those much-needed improvements: updating to new farm equipment, purchasing additional livestock, doubling the rows of crop per acre, because one day, in the near future, these improvements would pay for themselves. Why couldn't our parents get on board?

Anxious farmers were assured by the experts that their worries were outdated and unreasonable. Those who'd never worked the land but knew everything about America's finances told our parents it was easy—borrowing money was a no-brainer; at the time it was a booming banana bonanza in '70s Midwest farm country, and it would only get better. They said to those land-workers who protested: "You fools would not be able to spot a deal if it shot you in the face."

Our parents were welcomed inside air-conditioned bank offices. They were offered donuts, hot coffee with half-and-half. Our parents were handed out loans with ear-to-ear grins and handshakes, and eventually they caved to the pressure. Against their better judgment, they borrowed hefty sums to grow their farm operations and to meet the demand. By 1983, Henry and Sylvia would be paying three times as much in interest alone as they had been three years before.

"We had targets on our backs," our father said at the time. "Booms end, if they were ever real in the first place."

By 1985, Jo was nine and I was seven, and we were both fully committed to sifting through the 1970s with an eye toward retribution. We were eager and delighted at every chance to point out our parents' terrible economic decisions and thus we were committed to destroying our parents' vision. Jo had her own notebook dictionary—"Defeat Capitalism"; "Take Down The Family"—that she filled with words, albeit with her own definitions of them. I did nothing but obey her and her words, yet she still harmed me. No bother. My sister and I painted over Sylvia's bright green walls in our attic space with an undeniably ugly deep mahogany. We put up what we wanted to see—like posters of Sally Field, whose face we had scribbled over, and of the movie *Fletch*, which we kept in pristine condition, and wrote on the ceiling: misery loves company. When our parents protested, we told them they had children, two girls, of all things, with insatiable appetites, so feed us or we would be forced to call Child Protective Services.

Our hair was not blond. It was also thick and a struggle to maintain, which as a kid I wore short and tidy and wrapped neatly around my chin like Queen Elizabeth (the original). We looked nothing alike, save for our olive skin and the texture of our hair. I had geometric, root vegetable-heavy, poop-brown hair which barely tucked behind my ears. And my sister, hers was luscious, almost black, knotted and long, snaking down her spine to her ass. We both had bangs, mine were short and hers were long, both trimmed at home with sewing shears. Our mother said bangs were a quick fix for angular faces. And in our house, things needed fixing. Never mind the fact our bangs never behaved; they never simply relaxed on our foreheads like a doily, but shot up every which way like an error our parents should have seen coming.

2009 and America was on the mind. Blackout days were not on offer. Sometimes in America we kill things. Sometimes in America we save things. In other words, we attempt to restore in seconds what we've spent years dismantling. About twenty-five miles away from this motel where I was wasting time and calling it productive, was Spring Lake Park Reserve. Around 8,000 years ago, Indigenous tribes would come together where the Mississippi and Saint Croix Rivers met, near what is today Minneapolis.

They say when I go to visit the preserve, I might spot bald eagles— once thought of as baby snatchers, before becoming a near-extinct species, and then America's totem—egrets, great blue herons, and pelicans who use the riverfront as a migration corridor. Just when a particular species is near complete irrevocable death, sometimes, especially when the saving campaign resonates, people find themselves experiencing a kind of humility (if it can be called that), really a kind of rapturous joy in imagining their continued existence on Earth. Stories of resurrection endure—they're bloody and perfectly circular. Reality, as far as I could see, was broken.

Twenty some years later in a motel, I have read that the summer wildflowers are not to be missed. I imagine the same wildflowers in this very region were called *pestilent*, those same invasive bright flowers we spent years killing off with toxic substances for the sake of crops. One-hundred and fifty acres have been restored to tallgrass prairie. The same prairie that not long ago cows (an ill-conceived plan) had destroyed to save the (additionally ill-conceived) cowboy. Word is that in the year 2022, a herd of American bison—what would become America's national mammal—will be reintroduced for grazing on the land. Meanwhile, the long awaited Hoover Dam-turned-into-battery operation was expected to be completed six years later, in 2028.

I would get to this Reserve, but first I had to flee the replacement receptionist, who I found unhelpful and agitated, and who was causing the bones in my body to rebel, but who was probably just a byproduct of her generation. That was to say—she'd lived all her life with the science, officially knowing that the world would be either submerged under water or on fire soon, and permanently.

The elevator arrived, and five small people, all wearing vertical stripes in different colors emerged, holding hands and tied together at the waists. The older man and woman with them, who looked the grandparents—worn out but genetically, evolutionarily satisfied—commented about their almost matching clothing. They said it was the only way to tell them apart and to keep them together for easy monitoring. At first, I thought: This has nothing to do with me. And then I thought: This has everything to do with us.

PARENTHOOD, PATTERNS

Henry and Sylvia loved us. Though sometimes I believed they would have preferred us to be moved elsewhere, out of sight like a sin, like detritus. They treated each of us accordingly. According to our natures, our separate and uniquely distinct natures. My older sister was one such extreme, disagreeable in an indefatigable way. Jo had emerged from the womb an instigator, recalcitrant fire-breather, resolute skeptic, confident loner. I, on the other hand, was another very unique pole, gentler, softer, and inarguably agreeable. But I was weak by comparison. And I was condemned to live a life with Joanne. Our parents had confirmed as much. From birth, I was predisposed to believe in art, a massive undertaking, and thus I would go on to be undervalued. Almost everyone on Earth can agree on this. I was destined to become first an afterschool theater teacher, to now an underpaid adjunct of some near extinct subject matter because it was just the sort of cynical nightmare I was made for.

What can I say? Forever a hamster running circles inside a clear plastic hamster wheel: a gift presented as liberation. A freedom toy for rodents that would go on to inspire several other advancements, like The Rakku rotating shoe rack, and come to define what's referred to as "hamster-wheel economy," which claimed that no matter how fast it spun or how hard workers toiled, it was not moving forward. I should mention that science indicated these lovable confined rodents absolutely loved their wheels. They couldn't get enough of these plastic toy containers.

The point was Henry and Sylvia loved us. While that might seem obvious since they were our parents, there were times when it wasn't. That's what Jo and I understood about love: it was an act, and it was a constant struggle. Our parents were drawn to each other like electrically charged particles were, as related phenomena merged like gravitational waves. Sometimes we barely existed to them. Our existence was like an afterthought, undeserving of a simile.

"They loved each other the way lovers get it on," I remember I said about them.

"The way lovers get on each other's case," Jo had clarified.

Joanne, a little mosquito I went and severed with a toothpick but lived on regardless, to continue her life's ritual of landing on human skin, which she could taste with her legs before puncturing it to suck the blood out.

I remember one Saturday on the farm, after picking tiny shards of glass from my sister's hair as a result of our father's outburst with a bottle of beer, Henry loaded us into his beat-up 1971 Chevrolet C20 Longhorn to take a trip. We stopped to pick up Seraphina and the four of us drove into town. On the drive, the radio reported two hundred and fifty farms were closing every hour. The county sheriff said he'd served more replevins, summons, and execution notices than at any other time during his fifty years of service. He would go on to blow his brains out.

Henry deposited the three of us on First Street. He said he would be occupied for hours. "Take a walk," was his advice. We were certain he was up to no good, but, as he also made clear, it wasn't any of our business. I spent that miserably uninformative day with Jo and Seraphina, whom my sister let put a leash around her neck. We walked by empty shops. We passed men sitting on buckets sobbing in the open, like postal collection boxes. I had never seen so many men at one time (and men were jumping off silos, so I figured it was a decent sign that these men were safe on buckets). I remember my sister said I was missing the point and socked me in between my shoulder blades. I remember wondering why I couldn't keep my thoughts inside. Jo told us one of our neighbors explained that the only reason he hadn't stepped into the baler was because he didn't want anyone to have to find his body. And when I had the balls to ask my sister why she let Seraphina put a leash on her neck, Joanne looked askance and asked if I really thought I wasn't someone's pet.

"I mean, look at you, Bernie."

There were indications of suffering everywhere. All over First Street shop signs had been removed, and many buildings had been abandoned. Jo said it looked like Beirut after the Israelis had bombed the city.

"How do you know that?" I asked.

"There are books," she said, and then she threw one at me.

Seraphina laughed, did a hair toss, and sped ahead with Jo, whose neck remained on a leash. For weeks afterward Jo slept with it on.

In those isolating moments words failed me and the sky above me cracked open. I put my head down and looked hard at my ribs and my belly button contemplating fetuses and umbilical cords, lineages and fractured selves, abandoned like flat tires. I remember the doctor saying that my bellybutton was really a hernia, and I thought for once the doctor was making sense. I thought about passages, like the catacombs in Paris and like time travel and lifelines—ours: doomed—as well as other magnificent things to look forward to, such as fornicating and making other bad decisions. I remember needing a break from Illinois, from my family, and thinking about whether I should nap on the street, or find Henry to go home to our dismal house, "Located not on a hill but on a hump," as our father consistently liked pointing out. Go home to that crowded space, which grew ever inert, to nuke something up in the microwave like drying wet socks, because it could be done in a working microwave but not in our inferior microwave which Sylvia had found behind a shuttered café. I could think of nothing worse than wearing or being presented with a damp sock.

Home-life was debilitating. Information was not clarifying. It was exhausting. America was a time bomb, and we had only scratched the surface of lunacy. I was overwhelmed by the material even though I knew I didn't need to make sense of it—that was what Jo and I had agreed to in our attic space. That day she informed me it was time I join her to examine the onslaught of information, otherwise known as the living experience. I was able to cull a chicken with a dull knife, therefore, she said, I was old enough to try to understand how we were being assembled in our country. That was if the two of us expected to outlive the reputations of the women in our family, which, as far as our prospects went, was just about the only pressing task at hand for us fools.

My head was not a full bucket. It was not an empty one. It was a bucket.

The crop in Illinois was again a disaster. We saw our parents, however briefly, age ten years in one. They spent much of their time out, presumably doing positive and productive things for the entire family, leaving my sister and I on the farm to fend for ourselves, which we were confident doing. Despite being absent much of the time, it became clear to our parents, therefore it became clear to us, that the "essential and helpful" financial strategies being peddled to us, and to others in our community in the same dire situation—that the concept of taking on more debt to make the much-needed improvements in order to increase your overall income (which would reach various breaking points throughout America's history)—was severely flawed. Higher production levels lowered the prices for agricultural products. And, when eventually things went south, small family farming operations, like ours, would not be able to absorb the loss in revenue like larger farming operations.

Evenings at home might look like this: Henry and Sylvia put us on the couch beneath the dangling portrait to emphasize the point, but they didn't stick around to dwell on the particulars of the reality.

I remember that instead of talking things through, after demanding we sit down to listen, Jo and I instead might be given something ordinarily forbidden, like a box of fancy "sugar cereal"—though, if I recall correctly, it wasn't one of the coveted kinds like Fruit Loops—as a parting gift before they left the house. (We never knew whether they remained together once they left our house, but we wondered.) The standard order of events would unfold.

Outside, the sun went down. It grew dark and late as Jo and I sat in our quiet house with the lights out eating bowls and bowls of sugar cereal, discussing exit strategies while debt collectors, our loan officer, and our farm manager came around with notices. The men would leave their floodlights on and aim them at our windows, rap on our door, and ask questions that we were not able to answer. These disappearing acts of Henry and Sylvia's could last well into the next afternoon, and those who came by to collect were equally committed. Jo and I would hide out in our attic space plotting our revenge since by then we already felt dead. Besides, we understood zombies made for better revenge than ordinary creatures did.

I can remember one afternoon during that time as we cleaned out the chicken coop, Jo told me about the popular movies coming out of Hollywood: *Country*, *The River*, and *Places in the Heart*, the last of which starred Sally Field, who played a widow struggling with little savings to run a farm and parent two babies. American audiences adored Sally. She was the sweetheart of the times who could make just about anything palatable, but the content wasn't resonating with the rest of the country.

There were a lot of predictable patterns at the time, which was to say there were a lot of movies about the crisis that came out. There was a deadly tornado that took place. The presence of the Ku Klux Klan was increasing, and a growing segment of the community was being drawn to groups that protested taxes, brandished firearms, and spouted anti-Semitic, anti-government speech, like the Posse Comitatus.

On the radio, retired army lieutenant-turned-extremist, "Reverend" William Potter Gale, who launched the Christian Patriot Identity movement of the '80s, spouted his vile rhetoric. His rage entered homes. His sermons, preaching of a satanic Jewish conspiracy, entered cars, and the cabs of combines rolling across the last unharvested winter wheat fields. The central ideological tenet was that man had the right to refuse the laws he deemed unconstitutional. In other words, man had a duty to take matters into his own hands when necessary. He would know when. "Like most men," Jo said: "He, too, would feel the raging injustice surging in his groin."

"Look," my sister said, mapping out this dynamic: Reverend Gale had successfully bridged the gap between the anticommunist and segregationist movements of the '50s and '60s. He said communism had taken hold in America, right down to the coffee in our diners. Communism was corrupting public officials, and the courts, and undermining the sovereignty of America and its divinely inspired Constitution. Loading up on ammunition, identity adherents—"white people, as in the chosen people of God, who lawfully used religion to justify crimes committed," Jo explained of them—protested taxes and prepared to defend the constitution. These people called themselves "constitutional adherents" and placed the highest law enforcement authority in the land on county sheriffs and themselves, when it came to that.

Our conversations would go on to follow the usual pattern:

"What was this, Nottingham?" I asked.

"No," Jo answered. "It's America."

It appeared the High Sheriff born of the English shire had been transplanted to colonial America.

"How was this character able to slip past, unaffected by legal developments made over the last two hundred years?"

"How had he managed to miraculously emerge in present day America?"

"Not to mention, the sheriff of Nottingham was the tax collector!"

"We are surrounded by America with its orgies of barbarism," Jo declared.

DRAW A SPERM WHALE

Joanne and Seraphina were holding a whale drawing competition, really a test to see which of the inseparable two could attract more attention. More immediately, my sister was eager to ascertain who among the group of participants knew about sperm whales; the world's largest predators who have their own mode of communication and who relied on echolocation, a specialized organ that existed in their head, to find their prey.

"The Crazies Are Holding a (Sperm!) Whale Drawing Competition," their fliers read.

I don't think anyone other than Jo thought it was a great idea. Our parents went along with it because they said they did not have a choice, especially when it came to poor decision-making. The winner of the competition would receive a signed copy of *Moby Dick*. (Having been a one-time super forger, Henry counseled Jo on how to forge Melville's inscription: "To Ending Well.") She and Seraphina put up these posters at school and around First Street. I was tasked with tidying up the house: hiding stacks of mail, dirty laundry, and coupon clippings. On the day of the event, I put out an assortment of healthy items she'd pilfered from Seraphina—nuts, dried apricots, whole wheat crackers—on polished plastic trays that we borrowed from Seraphina's parents. I was told I could partake if I gagged myself, to which I said: "no problem."

An unexpected amount of people showed up that day to participate. I remember the guests—about twelve boys and four men—as they came into our house. They were so mesmerized by my older sister they could barely sit when the time came to begin drawing. They wanted something from her. They wanted to want her, and to not want her, and ended up wanting her even more, which I resented identifying with. And when I told her this years later in Deadhorse, Alaska, my sister said: "Admiration is code for scorn, Bernie."

"When reality feels uncertain, as it is often made to feel, admiration gave way to hatred because this proved to be a more comfortable state of being, as it needed little to no explanation or justification," she'd said holed up in our trailer in Alaska.

Jo said to look at Hillary Clinton, who existed as a figure as far back as the '80s, even as early on as the whale drawing competition, and even then—all that time ago—it was probably safe to assume that acquiescing had done nothing for her. "The system was designed to fail," Jo proclaimed.

For years, in Deadhorse, on the farm, I feared that we would never come up for air. I remember thinking my sister had this ability to remain submerged in water and not die. Jo could create a disarming tension, confuse the boundaries between Satan and Archangel Michael, life and death, presence and non-presence. She was an insect-human. A squid-human. Something altogether unique and infuriating. She was simultaneously blurry and vibrating in opposing directions at once. One never knew from which direction she was coming, which was to say there was no avoiding her or the events and incidents she created.

For the (sperm!) whale drawing competition that seemed to know no end, Joanne and Seraphina drank Manischewitz wine out of ornate goblets from Seraphina's family trips to Shakespearean Festivals, drank as if freed by anonymity, freed into ecstasy, giving into the dementia of the delirium. They drank as the farm crisis had reached new levels of despair, and while the few men in attendance drew whale spouts and harpoons like they were in after-school detention, I can remember wondering why I was the one blamed for hyperbole.

For the celebratory occasion, Joanna and Seraphina both wore garb they claimed referenced the Mediterranean and pointed out the two fabrics draped over them: one depicted fishing rods; the other, grapes made into wine. Jo's latest obsession was Bacchus, the painted boy with the butterfly face, twice born God of delirium. Bacchus, son of Jove, and of hopeless mortal, Semele, who ended up dead by incineration after viewing the sheer force-glow of Jove's sexy naked god flesh. But that was not yet the point. The point was Bacchus was a boy with the most unusual start. His fetus was surgically inserted into a makeshift uterus in Jove's thigh, born at full term, not from his mother, but from his father.

"It took balls to come up with such rhetorical effect," Jo said to the competition attendees, swinging her goblet around.

The dudes sat in anticipation like bearing witness to an extravagant coronation ceremony. Joanne knew and she would give them a show. Let them have it.

"Blowholes," she rasped, clawing at her neck.

The dozen or so rapt boys and few men from town watched Joanne's every move and made vain efforts to draw whales, giving them needy faces which resembled their own. The dudes in attendance tried so hard to draw whales like whales, but they couldn't help but draw themselves into it. In that moment, I recalled something our mother had told us about realist portraiture, that it was an exercise in drawing another version of yourself. Sylvia said when white painters painted Black people, the Black people in the paintings ended up looking like the white painters but Black.

Jo popped grapes into her mouth and studiously drew her sperm whale to perfection. She did not need to look up to marvel at the boys' flaccid faces, eying her perky boobs, which by then were made unquestionably apparent. By then she'd removed the two draping fabrics. She was braless and wearing a tight cream turtleneck.

"Watch me," she hissed.

The dudes did, as her mouth opened and closed smoothly, like a child mimicking a fish breathing underwater.

"These are my absolute favorite fruit. Ab-so-lute," Jo said, locking eyes with me.

White lie. Up until that moment my sister called grapes "grape product" and refused to touch those slimy, tasteless round "baby balls," as she also referred to them.

I studied Joanne as she popped the last fat purple grape into her mouth and imagined it rigged to detonate. I waited for Jo to explode into tiny, unhinged particles. I remember watching her and those dudes furiously drawing aquatic mammals until I couldn't take it anymore. I excused myself from the event and went outside. Outside, the grasses had been freshly mowed. I was reminded of what it felt like to itch, as I had hours earlier when I'd been on the mower. The corn and wheat fields shone under the afternoon sun; aluminum grain silos reflected the light like a hazard. The haze that hovered above the crops was slowly lifting. Varieties of brown and gold— those were the colors of the surrounding landscape—until they met with concrete driveways, edged up against asphalt roads leading outward to a meaningful someplace, touched the shades of orange, rust-painted barns dotting along the flatness that appeared like boils on a forehead, structures which, more and more, stood empty of animals.

Sperm whales were nomads.

Nature was not at a distance.

Nature was not a thing that could be induced like labor, or a coma.

Fall 1985. Sylvia had lost a child. A baby boy our parents hadn't even known they had wanted, and like unexpected lost things, it quickly became the only thing they wanted. That year, the hole in the ozone was discovered over Antarctica, Donald Trump's house in *Architectural Digest* was so opulent and expansive it seemed to know no end. That October, our mother realized she was four months pregnant. Our parents hadn't wanted a third child, but for a spell during the crisis—"despite the crisis," Joanne clarified—they had found themselves in that magical space in a marriage where they couldn't get enough of each other, and their marital entanglement was without their usual questionable violence. Our parents behaved like insatiable red-nosed fruit bats. They were getting along. They were having sex a lot, and biting each other's cheeks in front of us. We were repelled, yet they did it anyway. The laundry piled up. The mail was unopened. The food was left in the oven to burn or rot; sometimes their plates of food remained untouched on the countertops, which was not their usual way. They never let things go to waste. Then Orson Welles went off and died. His death put Henry in a terrible state. He'd lost a trusted ally. It was around that same time when Sylvia felt sharp pains in her abdomen, locked herself in the bathroom, miscarried, and blacked out.

I cannot say where Henry was. I don't know where Jo and I were hiding out, but the medics found Sylvia passed out in a pool of blood on the bathroom floor, a linoleum she detested. Our mother awoke to see that her baby boy was flawless, tiny, and translucent; a limp baby boy on the ugly linoleum, which for years she had meant to replace. Her baby deserved better, she would later say of seeing him unresponsive on the bathroom floor. She held his body, light but weightier than she might have imagined, and rocked him back and forth, telling him whatever came to mind about the things he would never know as the medics pried his body from her arms. People, especially those that are certain about what they know and what they're doing because of what they know for certain, have little-to-no patience.

"There's nothing more original than nothing," Sylvia said of waking up to her dead boy that day.

It would be the last our mother would speak of DNA, she warned. Our baby brother, the one that could have been, the one that might have saved our family farm, the one that would illuminate what was lacking in our lives, had an abnormal heart rhythm that went undetected. I remember my sister said everything ends up at a waste management facility. "Fact of life," Jo said, stripping down to her underwear for no particular reason.

Pain was a season. They say that there are four of them. There was a distinct patterning in the years that followed. Our mother dreamed of babies coming back to life, warming from the cold of death. She also had the same nightmares, which she explained was from low noradrenaline in the brain that ordinarily let the dreams cure pain. An end to their reoccurring. For the motherless babies that grew into adults—they too dreamed of mothers. "Awoke and found no mother," Mary Wollstonecraft Godwin Shelley said. Her mother, too sick to provide milk, died eleven days after she was born. "Awake and find no baby," a sixteen-year-old Mary Wollstonecraft Godwin Shelley would write of losing her first child. She would dream her little baby came back to life; that the child had only been icy because it was winter, and that, "we rubbed it before the fire, and it lived," she would write in her notebook.

The past wrapped round and round us like a coil. Jo and I were reminded our environment was tentative, a makeshift structure, as if it were built out of paper and ice; it was a system that was not intended to last. Growing up in that environment impressed itself on the psyche and on the body. However inchoate, land was a farmer's identity, history, connection to God, a religion and nationality of its own. You never failed to wonder whether you were not a person but a thing, flimsy and dispensable, despite momentary efforts to forget.

On dreaming and sleeping and oceans as depositories, "A thinking woman sleeps with freaks," Sylvia had said. We learned about monsters. The one-eyed monster originated from Greek mariners reporting on savage cannibalistic tribes they came across while at sea. The men couldn't get these cannibalistic faces out of their minds—savage sardonic stares shot straight from the eye like a laser. Images of monsters came in dreams, nightmares, later taking on more recognizable forms, mothers, and sisters, that walked among the living. And monsters were often historically female: the sphinx and the Sirens, the evil mythical sea monsters, Scylla and Charybdis, the nightmare, and the night-hag. The witch. The moon. The mystic.

"The heretic," Jo said.

Thinking about heretics had my sister thinking about self-preservation.

One afternoon, Seraphina and Jo were practicing their groping-deflection skills (for when dudes would come for them) and when they weren't going for the other's body like the college boys had on television, they discussed the subject of deceit as a manipulative tool used by the capitalists. "Heroism is a lie," Joanne told Seraphina in a wheeze. Joanne told her about the great hero-leader-man-king, Odysseus. How the hero just showed up uninvited with a bunch of killers to the island of the one-eyed giant—Polyphemus—who was minding his own business, living alone and hungry in a cave only to be made a mockery of. When the one-eyed giant asked his name, Odysseus answered "Nobody" and plunged a burning stake through the giant's one eye. Slashed and blinded, the giant cried out: "Nobody has hurt me. Nobody is going to kill me."

"Why not just slay the monster?"

Jo wondered if anything had ever been sacred. She was sick of sincerity and saviors and "beefy dudes saving stupid mermaid vaginas from catastrophe."

Miserable and sleep-deprived, my sister walked around our house complaining, a period when nothing was acceptable. Not even scientific breakthroughs or pizza. Not even the cows rubbing themselves against the trees to remove parasites were amusing. I remember Joanne saying mermaids, who were made-up, even *imaginary,* were not spared the shame and disappointment heroes brought to females in legends or just in life.

"Even mermaids with beautiful creamy breasts covered by a mess of draping hair get yeast infections. Look at her fin," Jo demanded, even though both Seraphina and I would have preferred to imagine other things, such as getting a masters degree because I'd earned it.

"A hot box with no ventilation would exacerbate the growth of fungus."

I remained silent as Jo boldly went on about vaginal infections and mermaids. Meanwhile, luscious Seraphina had turned a bright pale, which I thought impossible since she was as white as a person could be. Jo was tired of ultimatums. She was having nightmares. She hated her bony legs and the dark hairs attached to them. She was over men slaying monsters and saving stupid clueless invented mermaid vaginas with no point of view when we knew there were plenty of puissant mermaids in every culture who tortured men for their own amusement, or blessed ships with wild love.

I had heard it all before, but Jo's need to retell superseded my need to mention it, and I was getting worried about Seraphina whose face by that point in Jo's rant looked like a grimy bathtub.

"Look at what's in front of you," Jo liked to say.

"Keep one eye on the eternal and the other on the everyday."

"Where are the eyes?" was a question Jo often repeated.

At that time, given her preoccupations with eyes, whales, and sex, I worried about Jo's night terrors, which would grow worse and more frequent. All of which had our parents wondering "what in God's name is going on in America?" And they hated God. God didn't follow up, ever. Sylvia smoked and wished we'd discover more approachable hobbies. Henry would smack himself in the head, push or mime-threaten to hit Joanne, who might have been in the way of the beer in the fridge, or screaming for him to stop hitting himself, which she often did. He would tell her to go to sleep and go on to slam his fists into the coffee table, which by the time we moved to the city looked like a larger version of an egg crate. I can remember Henry slamming his body and his fists against the walls, detonating the plaster, two new round fist holes to peer through, though nothing was ever on the other side. Why do we continually think there's something on the other side that should be seen?

"What a mess," our parents said before going on to screw in their bedroom. Of course, we knew. Parents could be so pointless.

Thanksgiving rolled around. Feeling pinched, our family assembled a feast that included chalky, dry mashed potatoes, stuffing from a box, and no turkey. (Sylvia claimed that for years she'd used box stuffing and nobody had noticed.) Seraphina's family canceled last minute, but dropped off three elaborately decorated pies. Jo opted out of eating. At the underwhelming Thanksgiving table, my sister stood up and said she felt like a miscalculation. Worse, like the latest season of a sitcom that had petered out seasons ago—everyone knew the show was intolerable but watched anyway. If that wasn't a metaphor for the news in America, she said, then what was.

She then offered to say Grace, even though it was only something we did when the sheriff deputy, on behalf of the loan officers, stationed himself outside our home, or when we were nearly out of bland food.

"For identity to be realized," Jo said, "one must come to the place where identity dissolves," freeing her long, raven-black raven hair to let it tumble around her face, down her crooked spine.

Right then she withdrew *Joanne Fareown* from consideration. Said she wanted to be listed in the playbill as "————." She said that without a name, with less to point to, there would be less overall "self" to undermine.

Joanne, grabbing fistfuls of apple pie, went on to declare she would not live out her days within parameters she did not set. She would not die a rodent on an exercise wheel. Unlike hamsters, she was not an impulse buy. For Hamlet *to be* he needed to gain experience in the graveyard, under the instruction of the grave-maker, what it was like *not to be*—why couldn't her family understand this about Hamlet?

"At least you're learning something," was all our parents could get out, before ignoring her. Henry shoveled chalky potatoes into his mouth and Sylvia chain-smoked. The pies drooped. They didn't stand a chance in that atmosphere. It had been a very long day.

Then my sister turned her back to the table. Which was to say, she turned her back on us. She left us there fiddling, trying to figure out her next move. What would she come up with next?

Jo was unstable. Her scoliosis would worsen. Our parents needed to find a way to get her the back brace.

Time was a luxury.

Weeks afterward, one could still find scattered drawings of whales throughout the house, serving as a reminder of too many things. Many mistakes. Not one of them was a decent rendering of the cetacean. Proof that something had to give. We knew Jo needed more space, even if we didn't know how to understand it, or how to address it.

CURSES AND CAPITALISM

For weeks, my sister didn't appear outside of the attic space. And for a spell, I was contented by this, even satisfied. I had waited many times for Jo to make a sizable error and massively miscalculate so that I could be the center of the universe; the champ that took home the prize. I wanted to be a champ.

"There is no prize, Bernie," I could hear her voice in my head, feel her, she was both here and not here.

Her movements were so subtle they were nearly imperceptible, like carbon monoxide. I remember trying not to breathe in her curse, and drawing a lot of hotdogs and adding to my list of desires, which included experiencing a *real Thanksgiving*—which would be determined by an abundance of rich food and gorging oneself—and hedgehogs. All the stuff she said made me the insufferable Bernie I was, but Joanne also didn't know how to get rid of me.

December arrived. Among surfaces already piled high with year-end materials, apologetic earnings reports from crop sales, calendars from the bank and equipment brokers that may as well have had a date circled for ankle breaking, *1984* sat open on the kitchen table as a reminder. *Page Six* covered manufacturing and the maniacal stock-piling of *better* weapons to secure world peace. Henry read these pages like it was his obituary, poring over the details as though it was something he had written himself about himself.

I was young then, but I would like to think I got the gist of capitalism. It seemed to me back then, despite having a grasp on capital, that I was more useless than ever, and that the world was moving rapidly, more quickly than ever. I remember feeling like I should have been advancing or at least growing. But I wasn't doing it fast enough. I still had a speech impediment. I still wet the bed. I still loved in traditional ways, like longing to be touched, or to be felt. Jo would give me new undies and clean the soiled ones in the tub with Woolite. She would put a clean towel down on the bed and read from her newspaper clippings to me about capitalism.

"All of farming will go corporate," Jo said, sucking diet pop through a perfect, sterile cylinder straw.

To complicate matters, I had a constant case of ringworm on my scalp and feet. It was terrible magic. I didn't wear restrictive clothing. At that time, we didn't have any domestic animals. No pets. No cats, no dogs—only later did we get our puppy, Tall. No hedgehogs. No starfish. I remember keeping a jar of soothing ointments near the bed and praying I wouldn't need to go to the doctor. Those visits to the doctor made our parents anxious. Our father would find something to drink. Our mother would mumble "no good deed goes unpunished" and pull her hair out. Their skin flaked off and even though the flakes of skin were imperceptible to the human eye, you could smell them like you could a nervous, overheating animal. The truth was we could not afford medical treatment.

Those were desolate times. The landscape was marked by tragedy—white crosses covered entire lawns, symbols of the lives lost to the economic catastrophe. For us, the height of it came when we realized the extent to which we needed to continue borrowing to hold on to what we had. The Farmers Home Administration was the lender of last resort, which was where we had found ourselves. In addition to keeping the farm operations afloat, we had other financial responsibilities, like saving for Joanne's custom back brace and caring for our father, who was suffering in new ways on a cellular level. His neck and wrists, each with outlines of contrasting colors, indicated time spent outdoors, in the weather. Rings burned into his eyes, charring his corneas. For twelve months straight, the language of violence overcame him, like a blade in his sleep. He experienced terrible night sweats, waking up soaked to the bone, trembling, screaming, and weeping in the wee hours. His flashbacks to Vietnam grew frequent—smelling enemy breath, strangling bodies in the dark, and crushing tracheas on foreign lands he should never have set foot on. He started walking around the house like he was walking Vietnamese land, determined to survive the landmines. He recalled at length a woman whose kind face he had slammed with the flat side of his .45 caliber pistol, as soldiers burned down her village. Farmers ran for their lives. The priest who had raised Henry had said that these things happened in war. This was not adequate for our father. Henry never hid the fact that as a result of war, he was vile, and for an extended time he had become more fearful of what he was capable of. And these fears met him in his sleep.

A blue badge hung by our front door and when I asked our father about it, he explained the Combat Infantry Badge was for members of an exclusive club. The "club" wasn't academic or athletic or dedicated to making a profit. The admission standard was extremely strict—to belong, you had to be willing to kill other human beings, and the only way out of the club was to die or go insane. "You need to make horror your friend," a fellow soldier had told Henry before losing a leg.

"Where there's horror, there's narrative," our mother explained, without missing a beat, dipping into a cold remove.

"Where there's horror, there's sensation," I said, little generic Christmas stocking that I was. Why red and green anyhow?

Jo said, "People like nothing better than a story involving a naked woman on a gurney, especially if the mystery is unlikely to be solved."

That was Joanne's reintroduction to family life at the dinner table. I remember feeling what I thought might have been something akin to happiness to see her return.

———

The television had things to sell. Everything on television was about money, which in turn meant everything was about how we didn't have any. In general, our family did not fit in with iconic America, like in the movies. We tanned easily, we were marked by labor, we were not ideal, blond, blue-eyed, or wealthy. We did not smell pleasant. But in another sense, we fit in perfectly, underground. We lacked. We were in need of money, and our active accumulation of debt meant we belonged to America just fine.

One morning, Henry left early to drive to the city to meet with a German man named Hanz who manufactured customized back braces, the special kind Jo needed for her scoliosis, which ran the entire length of her spine. The brace would not be able to correct her curvature but the hope was that it would be able to stabilize her condition so that it would not worsen. This brace would set our family's finances back even further. I can remember Henry returning home from that meeting with Hanz in the city with a small bounce in his step, and to say we had options. After getting this vague tidbit off his chest, he went off to the barn to find a long suitable wood plank. He seasoned it and began constructing an improvised back brace for my sister to wear until he could afford to get her the right one.

He'd found a focus. In the barn, our father assembled the supplies he would need to complete the project: softer fabrics (like cotton), metals, plastics, which he would have to mold into the necessary shapes he'd seen in the custom design presented to him. One strap would hold up Jo's chin, and the other her right underarm to straighten her lopsided shoulders.

I remember Henry called us outside to assist him, which my sister said felt like the start of a blond joke. Jo was told to move our tractor near the road, about fifty yards from the house, which she did without protesting. I was tasked with writing the sign since my penmanship was mediocre. I taped my sign to the tractor: Has a usable life of about nine years, but these days it will take twenty years to pay for it. Then Henry called Sylvia to put out her cigarette and leave the kitchen table. The moon was out—didn't she follow the moon or something? When we were all assembled in the barn, our father told us one option was to do what Dale did—to kill everyone he loved. Third generation corn and soybean farmer Dale Burr erased that legacy he'd earned when he decided to go on a shooting spree that left his wife, a local banker, another farmer, and himself dead.

I remember feeling uneasy as we took our seats for dinner that night. Over plates of bland mush, our parents admitted for the first time we might not have money for basics, and if there was a best part to the murders, "It was that Dale shot himself, too."

Nobody touched a thing on his or her plate. Jo cleared dishes of uneaten food and unused cutlery. It seemed everything had the potential to be weaponized in a capitalist world. Even Joanne's back brace that promised to help her if she stuck with it, which in her case meant her body, her skin on her body, would need to be trapped inside of an intolerable object for twenty-two hours a day if it was to have a chance at succeeding. Our mother said it was time to call the bank. The bank was our best and only option.

I remember the setting sun was coming through the clouds, casting a net of sunlight on the linoleum, which glistened like a newborn after Sylvia's deep clean, while Henry kept telling himself to "suck it up" and to just call about securing another loan. Sylvia poured Henry a drink to resurrect him, sat down, and lit a cigarette. Joanne stood behind me playing with my hair before deciding it was more entertaining to yank it. She said that that was what sea fishermen did when they caught a marlin. Henry made the call to the bank but the line was busy. When he finally got through to someone, they explained to him that they weren't taking appointments. "First come, first served," said the voice on the other end of the line. Our father said he felt like life was one big car crash happening in slow motion. He could see what was coming next. He could reach for the thing, reach out his hand and grasp it, but there was no way he could latch onto the thing, and there was nothing that could be done about it.

Our father said he felt stuck between images, like a filthy slide projector. I remember the look of an outburst coming over his face but he did not hit anything.

The next day, Henry told me to get in the truck. We were headed back to the bank. I had been before with our father. It was a particular kind of punishment he inflicted upon me. It was not pleasant. One such bank visit stood out most. I remember the line was so long we stood for almost an hour before taking a number. After, we took seats on the colorful, slick, smooth plastic chairs. The man next to us had been foreclosed upon. "Go get the man some water," Henry told me. I did. I poured filtered water into one of those sad, cone-shaped paper cups that dribbled from the bottom. The man sipped like a bird. He said ever since they were foreclosed upon, he and his family felt like they had the plague, like they had AIDS or something.

"The hardest thing," the man said, "was going back to church."

It was tempting, but he couldn't criticize God—who could in God's country? But his wife died four months ago from a heart attack. She was fifty-five. How was he supposed to handle the pressures if she couldn't? And now, waiting in that stuffy room, he was sure vultures were coming in for a piece.

I remember the secretary, a woman in a vivid canary yellow dress, waved us over in an unexpected way like she was lightly overheating, like a little excess moisture would ruin her bright yellow dress. I was a kid, but I knew I did not want to be her when I grew up.

"It will just be a few more moments. He's on an important call," the overheating canary lady said, gesturing to the banker on the phone in his office with her matching manicured hands. The yellow secretary then left the room like a breeze.

I remember her hands were very clean and the banker's phone looked new, which had me thinking about Jo's latest hypnotic preoccupation with nudity. That yellow dress would have sent Jo screaming that the Soviets had made her clothes. "Bernie," Jo had said the night before in bed, "if the entire population believed their clothing came from a huge Communist country as far away as the Soviet Union, a large swath of the public would go nude."

The banker's office was tidy and cold, in the sense that there was nothing inviting about the space. Canary lady should install herself in this room, I remember thinking. The Greeks and Romans understood polychromy was desire. Thousands of years ago, all those white statues lining museums were adorned in color.

On his desk, which was prominent and hard to miss, there was an hourglass and a tall stack of important papers. "IMPORTANT," the paperweight said. Behind his desk was a poster, a picture of a rocky shoreline meeting a tranquil sherbet sunset: "Success is a journey. Whatever your path, it is your determination to succeed that will get you there." I remember feeling constipated, and our father gearing up to suck the lender's ego-laced cock like we had practiced on the drive over. Jo had said we must appeal to the man's inner humanity. "That small part of his masculinity that remembers his first wet dream," was how she phrased it. Our mother nodded along, approvingly.

The meeting with the banker that day lasted six minutes, most of it was spent with the banker explaining stuff like the bank's regrettable position to deny our request for a loan, and that because our family engaged in diversified farming practices, they didn't have a package that made sense for us. Besides, the banker explained, our previous loans had been made with imperfect information and these were new times.

These were new times, I did not say, looking down and watching a cockroach trail over Henry's untied shoe. At least cockroaches can live for a week without their heads attached.

The banker went on to show us graphs indicating credit depended on the health of local financial intermediaries, which were currently unhealthy. He offered us leaflets in the shape of a cornhusk. He admitted the reduction in available credit had amplified the recent shocks to agriculture. As a result, decent and efficient small farm producers, such as we were, were going bankrupt. He said we could try to reschedule the loan. The obvious choice was to sell to a larger operation, to corporate farmers or land speculators with access to loanable funds. It was obvious.

Henry struggled not to implode. Farms that were not brought back into operation, farms that sat for sale, sat neglected, was our father's take on the situation. The standing crops not harvested would result in a total drop in planted acreage and production. And what about the land and the soil?

"Single purpose land use is no good for the soil," Henry said to an unresponsive party.

There were basic routines and systems in nature, Henry explained, broadleaves and grasses should be rotated between cool seasons and warm seasons, manures should be incorporated into the soil to fertilize and add nutrients, growing plants, cover crops, and biological primers should be utilized during fallow periods, minimizing soil disturbance was essential; mulch and crop variety, those routines that strove for diversity, were essential for maintaining healthy soil.

"What is this guy?" the lender looked directly at me: "A poet?" The banker cleared his throat, explained that at that moment lenders had tight fists. He showed us his hand tightened into a fist.

"Some folks are visual learners," he said, whirling his fists around in the air like a cheerleader, before explaining that one of his boys— lucky bastard, he had six sons—needed illustrations to accompany every teaching opportunity to get the most out of it.

More than half of the 65,000 adverse action notices sent out by Farmers Home Administration that year would end in foreclosure. Even now, the numbers make me sick to my stomach.

LIBERATION AND WEEDS

Sylvia joined a women's group and extended her part-time secretarial work. She, along with other women in our farming community, took further steps to puncture her presumed identity, which she'd out-grown—she would say—since birth. She was not alone. At the time, many women had assumed the responsibility of finding solutions to their family's debilitating financial troubles and had become the leading partner in the farming operation. There were over twenty-five female organizations, each with their own style of consensus building, operating across the Midwest. They organized and ran self-help groups, created food pantries, coordinated out-reach efforts, and acted as liaisons to the media, who otherwise got it wrong. They lobbied for change at the national level: speaking at public meetings, in front of television cameras, at mediation tables, in offices belonging to bankers and lawyers. They let themselves into the boardroom, whereas in the past these larger conversations happened between men behind closed doors. Their efforts forced the state to commit resources to finding a resolution, which in turn deescalated the tension. But these female-led groups maintained a delicate balance, and were careful to keep up the expected social continuum, which was to say they continued to conform to community standards to ensure economic and social security. For example, by publicly asserting that they weren't bra-burning man-haters.

Quietly, and over time, their burgeoning ideology grew, making possible the rehabilitation of a shaken marriage, the struggling parent, and for what remained of the farming enterprise. Volunteers waited outside strip malls and grocery stores handing out brochures. These covered topics like community viability, adjusting to the new economic conditions, and the different ways that chronic poverty might be alleviated. Some detailed the symptoms of depression, a condition that had been stigmatized and therefore untreated. They provided tips on how to run for public office or how to help get people registered to vote. They talked you through how to file for bankruptcy and find jobs in the city. Women did the work of patience and found that by the end of it they were unusually stressed. They were completely wrung out. Dizzy with the weight of balancing the varying responsibilities, they realized that there wasn't enough time and emotional support leftover for themselves.

"Women—time for themselves? *Extra money?*" I remember Sylvia heaving, and her group—which met weekly to talk in one another's homes—rioting in agreement around our oak table.

At this time, when our mother was only semi-recognizable in her newfound semi-liberated state, Jo switched her attention to the weeds. She and Seraphina were on a break. (I surmised this had something to do with Seraphina sharing her unflattering thoughts about the cow images, which were abundant, in our house when she should have kept her mouth shut.) In our house, images of cows appeared on everything: pillows, magnets, floor mats, napkin holders, mugs, salt and pepper shakers. Seraphina had said we needed an interior designer, and her parents could recommend some superb ones to rid our house of cows, as rage dumped over my sister's face. In that instant, my sister looked like Henry. I remember I left the room immediately—no reason to be in the way of that, I had thought.

The day of Seraphina's announcement, Jo went ahead and did what she had to (whatever that was), sending Seraphina home with a crying welt of a face. I remember Ronald Reagan was talking again on the radio. "Government wasn't the solution to our problems," he started to say about women getting involved in the crisis, before quoting George Gilder, a man who argued that a woman's role was essentially to be a sex slave to her caretaking, dutiful, and fair husband. The consensus on television that day, and perhaps every day that followed, was that female liberation was a declaration of war.

Meanwhile, Sylvia, along with the church ministry, had set up a pantry to feed families on a monthly basis. Jo and I helped sort boxes for distribution: oatmeal, sponges, Woolite, Cream of Wheat, cans of soup, veggies, honey graham crackers, white rice, Lipton's onion soup and dip mix, packets of dry sauces, like ranch and alfredo. I would like to point out, many of the things our house was lacking. I remember Jo tucking into her pockets some instant packets of brown sugar oatmeal, saying she wanted to liberate herself from America, but she would start small. Jo would practice with instant oatmeal and with liberating the weeds—the weeds were being assaulted by the advertisements on the radio and on the television—and I dutifully followed her line of thinking. The very blacklisted petulant, unruly, wild plants that Joanne and I were deeply attached to were being eliminated at an accelerated rate, and there was nothing we could do about it. We decided to make an inventory of everything destined to suffer.

"Let's see," Jo said, "there was Treflan, weed and grass preventer; Prowl, residual weed control; Ambien, sleep aid for the sleep-deprived; Pioneer, digital entertainment, which people need more than sleep; Dekalb, hybrid agricultural seed with the image of a hard-on ear of corn rocket with wings: *when performance counts!*; ICI Americas, manufacturers and distributors of chemical products, synthetic resins, non-vulcanizable elastomers, polymers, and pulp."

There was: Funk's G's, hybrid seed, producing corn that's sound, plump, lustrous, bright, kernels of remarkable uniformity; Larvin, pest management; Poast, broad spectrum herbicide; Sandoz, pharmaceuticals corporation, a global leader delivering medicines; American Cyanamid, agricultural chemicals, industrial chemicals, specialty chemicals, cosmetics, and toiletry products; Basagran, post-emergent herbicide, killer of tough broadleaf weeds, yellow nutsedge, annual sedges, and more.

"I will never love a man; I'm saving myself for wild weeds," Jo said, running around naked.

That's a lie. You know that's a lie, I did not say, though I was speaking the truth.

Jo loved how her body felt around men. She had willingly and sometimes unwillingly sought out this feeling, which began as soon as she started hitching rides, and which remained secret.

"Weeds are wild and lusting fugitives," she said.

I said: "Oats began their agricultural journey as a weed. Weeds can thrive without people, which is why they are deplored by so many."

"Domesticated plants, evolutionarily, become dependent floral nut-jobs. Their existence is entirely based on whether they please us."

"Nut jobs!"

"Like the women in our family!"

"Like us!"

Joanne would not be domesticated. Nor would she be eradicated.

Our mortuary included: cool season broadleaves, *Lamium amplexicaule*, also known as henbit deadnettle, with leaves that grasp the stem, an annual low-growing plant with soft, finely hairy stems, opposite leaves, rounded, with a lobed margin. The flowers were edible. They bloomed gradations of pink to purple and have a slightly sweet and peppery flavor, like celery.

"Say it: henbit."

"Dandelions killed in this time: tons, too many to name."

"Weed killer came to wipe out the dandelion flower when the dandelion flower is known to increase emotional intelligence and healing from emotional pain."

"It was anyone's guess how mankind had lasted as long as it had," the two of us said.

"Death to: *Medicago lupulina*, derived from the Latin medica, believed to have been introduced from Medea in antiquity, commonly known as black medick, nonesuch, or hop clover. Lupulina means wolf-like."

"Watch out for the white heath astor," I said, "and their densely clustered, miniature daisy-like white flowers, which attracted the pearl crescent butterfly, a bright orange butterfly with smooth black borders."

"Useless butterflies," Jo said.

I said: "Cornflowers. Kill the cornflower, also called bachelor's button, a cool season broadleaf with edible blue-purple flowers that tasted a little like cucumber."

She said: "At this time, warm season broadleaves killed: scarlet pimpernel, also called eye bright, a member of the primrose family with stunning salmon pink blooms. This asshole was an annual invader of gardens, lawns, and waste places. In England, it's called poor man's weatherglass because the flowers gently closed before it rained. Kill the American water horehound. Kill. Bludgeon. Horehound."

"Say it: horehound," she said. And I did. "Horehound."

Death to sweet bugleweed, wolf-foot, Egyptian's herb, which caterpillars feed on to become colorful moths. Death to the common buckwheat and all the bees drawn to their flowers.

Then one afternoon, the county sheriffs were at our door. They would send boys from twenty miles away, as far as they possibly could, with bulletproof vests on. The notice of replevin for the row crop tractor, the plow, the harrow, the feed, was tacked to our door. A second notice informed us that our furnishings would be inventoried against the interest owed, and our house would be assessed. (I remember wondering if they had marked our house down as small and on a "hill" instead of on a "hump," like our father so often said.) This time the assessors would be accompanied by armed deputies should our family feel compelled to resist. Our family had six months to come up with the cash or everything we had would be handed over to our creditors.

LIFE LINES

Cherri Cohen entered our lives. By then, our mother had reached a tipping point. She'd called a help hotline. Our father's high blood pressure, backaches, loss of appetite, and depression had become too much to ignore. The day of the call to Cherri, Sylvia sent Henry into town to collect library books, watch a sports game at the bar, and dialed the number on the back of the brochure—from the same stack she herself handed out to others.

"What's your name?" the voice on the other end of the line asked.

A simple question, but Sylvia preferred not to say. The counselor's name was Cherri Cohen, and a call was all it took for a friendship to form. I remember Sylvia telling Cherri over the phone that Henry spent the money, and she had to figure out ways to pay for the spending. She confessed to Cherri that she was doing what she could to continue life, predictably moving forward along the space-time continuum: clipping coupons, consolidating, managing, and marching along to the sounds in her contracting head with no visible horizon, which she noted sounded dismal. Sylvia admitted we could no longer afford the equipment or the feed to keep operating. The county sheriff, along with his loaded men, had come to our door making demands. She was frightened, and she did not scare easily—she'd grown up aware of the quiet of the land, the silence of town, not to mention the heretical blasphemy she had inherited. She had developed acid reflux. She had muscle spasms in her neck. Migraines, the aura kind—before our mother understood that pain was on the way, she delighted in the flickering, bright light in her vision. It was different. She had lost weight, something she'd a dearth of to begin with. Her husband and daughters were needy—she didn't think it was possible for three people to need so much from one person. So many mouths issuing wants and opinions. Sylvia had hoped things might improve. Some things had, of course. Sylvia pointed to reusable plastics, and the fact that there were cycles: laundry, menstrual, seasonal, historical. "Celestial," Cherri added. She told Cherri that she had not meant to seem so dreary.

"Though," our mother said, taking a drag off her cigarette, becoming lucid, "with regards to the latter category, I cannot point to a time in history where mistakes have been made and learned from."

"No matter how much I see myself as a man, I'm still a woman," Sylvia said.

It was superfluous, our mother admitted it would even be wasted on her, but our mother confessed that lately, after the dishes were cleaned, she ignored the stacks of mail, instead she zoned out and wished for an eye mask, and not even for a special holiday, just a gift given on a regular day, just in case it would offer a way to feel connected to the rest of the country. Or to her body. "One in the same," she said to Cherri on the phone that day she sought out support.

"What kind?" Cherri wanted to know more.

"One of those soft silky ones that handle moisture well," Sylvia said. So that our mother could get beauty sleep and look like a woman who took care of her face. Sylvia wanted a facemask, one of the mud-based kinds that guaranteed clearer pores and a radiant glow, like a swimming pool at night.

She spoke to Cherri on the telephone and touched the coarse black strand of hair on her chin. That stubborn single strand that continued to sprout like a reminder. She called out to us, demanding to know where the tweezers were. Earlier, she had gone to get the tweezers, but they were missing. Cherri said she did not have daughters, but she did have sisters.

"It's a dynamic, I give it that," Cherri said of sisterhood.

"Talking to a stranger about my husband feels unnatural," Sylvia said, after a pause.

Cherri explained that *politeness* was often mistaken to mean that the comfort of others mattered more than your own. Sylvia said Henry was a storm-rager, a man who at times raged with no sign of abatement, who at times alleviated his frustrations in the bedroom in a way that made sense to her. Sometimes he pulled out clumps of her hair. Sometimes the harder and more it hurt, the better it hurt, she said. "A rash of pleasure," our mother explained about the things we wanted nothing to do with.

"Consciousness was defined as much by what it hid as by what it revealed."

"Why do people stay?"

Cherri explained that in her experience, based on what she had seen over the years, most farmers and their wives would do just about anything to remain at home on the land. Our type of family unit demanded a special chemistry, which didn't necessarily transition easily to another context. In our world, there was a particular configuration blending land work with family roles that we needed in order to be successful. The bare minimum—the ultimatum that was key to a farm's success—depended on whether we were willing to engage in self-exploitation. The constant need to perform hundreds of mundane tasks in unpleasant conditions required a special dedication to the intolerable.

"Therefore, no face mask," Sylvia asked-said.

"Put the emphasis on 'someday'," Cherri confirmed.

Sylvia asked if compassion could be debilitating and whether the frustration this caused inclined her to be cruel at times. Was it her unsettled nature that triggered our father? Had it made him feel less than he already felt he was, which was very little to begin with. Sylvia had tried to fill the void, going to Henry, putting her hand in his mouth, and attaching her mouth to his throat like a leech. Even in the middle of the crisis, two starved daughters with precious minds at their feet, she and Henry found time to please one another, a teth-ering arousal between them which became even more pronounced the darker their situation became. Cherri did not scoff. Cherri lis-tened. A longing was fulfilled between our mother and Cherri. Their friendship pact was the special sort that novelists wrote entire novels about, which went on to be bestsellers since many people long for fulfillment. Our mother and Cherri's friendship lasted years.

I can remember seeing our parents gnawing at each other and won-dering if my sister and I would ever find that kind of love, that stark addiction. Sometimes our parents demanded we go outdoors to eat dinner or to do chores. "That's what the flashlights were for," they would say, blissed out and disgusting.

There were times as a kid I took baths with our mother and noticed the horse conch-shaped, deep purple bruises on her hips, buttocks, and back. Only much later, when Joanne lived in Alaska and I was in Chicago, did she tell me over the phone that there were nights during that period when confusing violence occurred, when Jo couldn't tell if she should intervene and call the cops. There were times when Joanne's night terrors sent her sleepwalking and straight into "the lion's mouth," which was what she called being in the wrong place.

Jo would often stumble across Henry throwing Sylvia against a wall; hear him unbuckle his belt, unzip his pants, and put him-self inside of our mother. Their rough behavior rattled my sister. Jo wasn't sure if it was more "pleasure violence" as opposed to non-consensual terror. My sister explained during one of our long conversations that our parent's warped sexual routine had gone on for so long that she said she began to wonder if every instance of violence was pleasure-driven, which, she had said, was the point of violence: to cause confusion. It was the source of its power.

For years, this was what Jo understood about pleasure. My sis-ter asked if I remembered the noise and I said no, but the lie was only partial. It was only after I had exhumed my subconscious that I remembered the pain. There was so much pain in our family that entire rooms in our house vanished, and the two of us along with them.

OTHER SCENES FROM OUR HOUSE

"If there is hope, it lies in the proles," George Orwell wrote of the working people, Henry said, which had Sylvia saying, "Not that again," and out the door to nurture and butcher. As kids, we did this feeding of the chickens and cows, and killing of the chickens and cows too. (Learning about sacrifice was ongoing.)

On cool early autumn mornings, before the flies came, after being presented with goopy food, Jo and I would partner up to take care of some things. Outside, we filled a 12-gauge shotgun with high brass No. 4 shots. After, we positioned ourselves about ten feet from the steer, and imagined two lines drawn from the base of each ear to the opposite eye, and then aimed for where the lines crossed. The silver dollar-sized hole was made in the animal's skull, and the beast dropped to the ground. Jo put one foot on the cow's forelegs, and, using her other foot, she would force its head back as far as possible. I would keep watch for thrashing hooves. Once the animal was stabilized, we would call out to our parents to do the rest. Slaying the animals ourselves came later in our lives. Sylvia was usually the one to make the thirteen-inch cut along the bottom of the neck with the breastbone forward. The incision had to be deep enough to expose the windpipe without piercing it. And with the back of the blade against the breastbone, she would press four inches in toward the spine, cutting the carotid arteries and jugular veins. "I am not an example of purity. None of your female relatives were," our mother said of our genetic defects, holding the slayed animal like the Virgin

Mary held a sideways baby Jesus, knowing very well how much suffering was before him.

"Sometimes—perhaps a lot of the time," Sylvia once said to Cherri, "I want to eat my family. Roast each of them like cauliflower florets. Caramelize their bodies like chicken thighs. Consume their souls like sugar."

I often thought maybe Sylvia was hungry. Iron deficient. Deficient in vitamin D, or in need of a mulit-vitamin for middle-aged women. She had always been noticeably thin. I too was hungry; I was in a constant state of hunger, which was probably why I had hunger on the mind. Ravenous for things from the sea. Sardines, in fact. I desired those oily, stinky, nutritional fish bits packed tightly in a tin. I remember saying something to that effect to my sister and her responding: "We're all sons of bitches," as if I knew nothing.

Cherri Cohen came over often to visit. She had a place of her own in town. Cherri and Sylvia would sit around our kitchen table to talk about fate and sex, sex on sandy beaches, and the humid weather in Miami where in the future they would don colorful caftans and have sandy sex. They acknowledged that Miami would be the first city to vanish once sea levels rose, so the future had best arrive.

"The tidal floods will eventually inundate the streets," Sylvia hummed.

"Nothing is sacred," Cherri said.

Sometimes the two of them worked on other backup plans for "someday," i.e. potential places where they might realize their preposterously grand romances and survive the elements. Sometimes the information the two of them hashed out was amusing and they laughed hard. Sometimes they psychically connected and remained silent and still in their seats. In each iteration, they smoked, because Oscar Wilde's Lord Henry Wotton had said, "The cigarette was the perfect type of a perfect pleasure."

Cherri visited a lot and the two of them discussed their experiences. Like how one early morning, when she was opening the café where she baked the pastries, a man came in and demanded she get him off. And a few years back, a sister of hers had committed suicide. Another sister was in an institution receiving electric shock therapy; as a result, her bones were fractured and her memory fragmented. That sister ended up losing custody of her children to a man who was sick in the head. Cherri called it a set-up, "The whole doctor to patient thing."

"What my sister really needed was a divorce," I remember Cherri saying to our mother. (I also remember my sister asking our father if Cherri was a good influence.)

Cherri's sister's husband was a raging menace. He even took her gun, which she had purchased for protection from the outside world, and used it against her. He said: "I think I'll just shoot you," and shot her leg. The blood spilled so fast it had everyone worried she would die then and there on the mustard carpet.

At the time, Cherri was there, but she had been in the kitchen trying her hand at a French omelet, which was to say she was not paying attention to what was happening in the other room. Later, in the hospital, Cherri's sister admitted that she had been the person to tell her husband to go ahead and shoot her.

"For a guy who wanted his ashes shot out of a cannon he built from scratch in the backyard, who, sometimes, surprisingly, voted Democratic, he was a shit shot. A sloppy menace that liked bridge and gambling and the bottle," Cherri's sister had said.

However, Cherri's sister remained hopeful. She hoped her four children would inherit her flair for independence, but not her suicidal predilections, which she called "responding."

"Responding in America to America can have terrible repercussions for women," Sylvia said, and Cherri absolutely agreed, both taking drags off their cigarettes.

At the time of Cherri and our mother talking and chain-smoking around our table, there were other consistencies. The weather forecasters said to expect instability for the foreseeable future and insisted on relaying weather projections daily, which saw erratic persistence. Weather was extreme. Severe. Unusual. Irregular. Unstable. Abnormal. We estimated the words showed up a total of nine hundred sixty-two million, six hundred thousand times. Our counting agitated Henry. Jo said our father was trying to distract himself from the hole in his heart, a septal defect between the two ventricles of his muscular organ, which might have explained his latest tendency to get up abruptly at the dinner table.

Those scenes looked like this: Standing up, making eye contact, Henry would tell us he was sorry. That was all he would say. "Sorry." And after that, he would distribute what was left of his food—which nobody wanted since it was tasteless—to each of our plates and leave the room, back hunched. "He was a misplaced stone looking for a river," I remember thinking about our father after one such evening, a thought that had prompted my sister to stab me in my side with a lead pencil in our attic space where she said nobody would be able to hear me protest.

"Lonely," I remember revising my sentiment to say as our father left the dinner table, and because I could not help but identify with him.

Sylvia became unhinged and sent me to my room to remain indefinitely. In a surprise twist, Joanne came to my defense.

"The naturalist E.O Wilson himself had said they were living in an age of loneliness," said Jo, which our mother had to respect since he was a renowned figure, and a naturalist.

"I could use a break from you monsters," our mother let out, humorously and apologetically, an exhausted cigarette dangling from her mouth like a slim extra limb.

It was unexplainable, but during this phase, Jo and I got along. (I surmised it was because she had convinced herself that I would die of lead poisoning, and when I did not, I had earned a bit of Jo's fated respect.)

This was a phase in which I prayed because I heard it could be useful, or did wonders for thinking positively, and because my parents loathed the idea. I remember kneeling on the hardwood at my bedside, digging my knees deep into the attic floor such that I could feel the bruises form. It was so cold I counted my outgoing breaths as though they were my last, clasping my hands committedly and knowing it would lead to nothing, because our father had said that was where each of us was headed.

1986

Jo's nightmares worsened, her insomnia began, and she found new ways to contribute to America's ongoing dialogue, mostly through her unwelcome thoughts regarding body odor, preservation, and sheep impaling themselves when they should have been blithely jumping over white fences. She was eleven at the time and growing better at guarding herself. (Or was she just leaving me out?)

Jo said 1986 was to blame. That was the year a Soviet nuclear reactor at Chernobyl exploded, and a wonderland that carried everything from guns to scrunchies called Target opened on the periphery of the Quad Cities. Also in 1986, the Agricultural Credit Act was being proposed to Congress. This piece of legislation promised billions to agricultural lenders to keep them solvent. The caveat was that lenders, in order to receive government money, would need to agree to stop calling in the sheriff. That was a tall ask. We waited, anxiously, and bit our nails. These were the reasons Jo said she had given up any hope of dreaming.

Sleep-deprived, malnourished, Jo was certain Seraphina had backstabbed her and my sister was in no mood for forgiveness. I wondered what Seraphina had done; never mind the fairly banal (to my mind), comments she had made regarding the preponderance of unfortunate cow images in our house. I knew my sister—who waited for no one—was waiting for Seraphina to return. Jo's attitude put everyone in our family on edge. Our meals suffered, and this had the greatest impact since there wasn't any wiggle room to begin with.

Any chance at having well-seasoned food was lost entirely by 1986. We wondered what 1987 would bring.

We bit the other's nails and waited for Congress to decide the outcome, which was to say our fate. If this legislation passed it would not free us from debt, but it would give us more time to figure out what was next.

This was the year Ronald Reagan denied he was selling weapons to the Iranians. It was the year I became smaller and more fragile, and became insanely sick of being small and fragile, spending the better part of my imagination channeling figures like the invincible Tiny Broadwick. Tiny was a born-to-die farm kid, nothing to nobody, female, who in 1914 was the first woman to parachute into a body of water, which happened to be Lake Michigan. She was not supposed to be a sensation and yet tiny as she was, she made something big of herself.

1986 was long. It was important to note, in addition to Jo's toxic relationship with Seraphina, that there were other important things disintegrating: forests, voting rights, stomachs. The number of families receiving food stamps was at an all-time high, despite the fact that many did not qualify for aid. The guidelines were restrictive for the self-employed, which most farmers were. In Iowa, the increase shot up from 500 in July 1984, to over 2,000 in March 1986, prompting our mother to remind us we lived in Illinois, and to "thank God for *The Chicago Tribune*." Sylvia shoveled cornmeal "oatmeal"—since we hadn't any actual oats—into our mouths and read us studies. At the time, a poll commissioned by the Anti-Defamation League found that over one in four residents believed the farm crisis was caused by a satanic, Jewish-inspired conspiracy of international bankers, under the auspices of the Trilateral Commission. Sylvia had a way of making us eat by dropping statistics like jokes. She would wail like a pack of coyotes. Our mother was not tame like other mothers, like Seraphina's, or the ones we had encountered at the grocery store.

The farm crisis in the Midwest had reached a point of intensity that the stink of crisis had permeated every space in our house. Our family, and our community, were desperate. We were more isolated than ever before. We had been abandoned. This was the year our parents went from discussing "soil erosion" around the oak dinner table to "souls eroding," and they went to church for food but they didn't believe in God.

As far as Joanne and I could tell, the place we lived had faded from our country's collective imagination. "A bruise left to fade," Sylvia said. Land values continued to decrease. Temperatures continued to rise, reaching record highs. Hundreds of calves were dying in the fields. The animals were falling over in plain sight, and it was alarming. One neighbor changed his sign to read: "Welcome to Death Farm." Henry was toying with changing his allegiance to the Republican Party since the Democrats—otherwise known as "the Party for the everyman"—had attached themselves to Apple.

"They now prize the robots over us," Henry said of the party he had belonged to since he was eligible to vote.

The region where we lived and stank had become an object of derision. Like a family of charged batteries, the four of us sat in the living room together listening to the radio, listening to the television, and strategizing a course of action for 1986 and beyond.

At night, Joanne paced—"obsessively," I said about her movements. "Determinedly," she clarified. Two sides of the same coin, but never mind. Jo was reliably agitated and desperate to get her ideas in writing before they landed in our country.

"Where relevancy was sent to die a slow, painful death," she said about facts being ignored in America.

In our attic space, Jo could not fall asleep. Well into the early morning hours she would pace, talking about how to escape America. Unprovoked, swinging a flashlight around in the dark, she would explain (I supposed to me) that the men in America, who knew everything there was to know (even about outer space, she made sure to point out), had concluded that distressed Americans (such as everyone we knew) were intolerable wankers who should be grateful for what they had. I remember wishing for Seraphina to return because she was another person to antagonize.

According to Joanne, America—which was to say, the powerful white people in our country who purported to know everything there was to know—had decided the time had come to extricate sad, soulless creatures, such as us, from our antiquated natures, such as nature itself. It was explained to me, whether I wanted to know or not, that to complete this mission, these powerful white men needed reinforcements, i.e additional bodies on the ground: agile, top-quality, top-notch, unpaid interns, and recruits willing to work unobjectionably fast and hard and for nothing. But the powerful men who had all the right answers even about outer space were having trouble recruiting fresh young blood to carry out their mission.

I said: "Plus, nobody in HR could come to a consensus regarding what constituted motivational content—like, what did motivation even mean?"

Jo said: "Not to mention the coffee was terrible."

"How can *existing* happen without language and orientation?"

"The human race is synonymous with demise," Jo said. "There is no doubt we will fall into the ocean or burn."

Once I realized I would never have any space or sleep again, I joined Joanne inside of her thought bubble, and I agreed that we had to do everything we could to get out of America. We needed a plan. We would need to prepare. One idea was to travel by acceleration. Before all that, we would first need to acknowledge our shortcomings, foresee danger. Our parents had taught us as much. In a world of gaslighting, uncontainable wildfires, snowstorms, and expensive uterine devices, us fools had better anticipate catastrophe, what our father called "capitalism" and our mother called "instinct." If we wanted anything for ourselves, we better be steadfast and resourceful and ready to rebel.

In our attic space, we surrounded ourselves with flashlights, library books, magazines, hardware, notebooks, batteries, cassette tapes, a portable Sony tape recorder, and other electronic devices, a growing rubber band ball, pencils, compression socks, hairnets. Jugs of water. The method of escape we settled on was to use a hurricane, harness its force, as a kind of slingshot to propel ourselves forward at hyper speed. When our mother objected to the idea's carelessness, we said we would be sure to have emergency parachutes in case. Nothing to be paranoid about—parachute devices had come a long way from Da Vinci's sketches centuries earlier.

"How does it work exactly?" Henry asked sincerely, tucking us into bed, so close I could smell his smell of fatherhood, which I loved.

"The plan is to escape America via a monster-giant rubber band capable of catapulting us to space," we said.

My sister and I would go on in this capacity long after he'd left the attic and until our mother called out for us to turn off the lights.

"Go to bed now, you monsters," Sylvia would yell up from the bottom of the broken staircase.

Joanne and I ignored her. She was our mother.

"Nothing is safe," Joanne continued, whispering in the dark. "From the beginning, there was a deadly virus called stupidity."

"By the *end* there is a deadly virus called stupidity."

"But what will we wear?"

JOANNE WON'T SLEEP, 1987 WOULD ARRIVE

One night, instead of pacing but continuing to ramble, Jo began designing what she called "preservation uniforms." Sketching and re-sketching, my sister insisted that we work harder to be in tandem with nature and imagine a way of existing that acknowledged the explicit harm we caused by existing on Earth.

"These are existence outfits with objectives," she explained to my half-closed eye.

These uniforms would strive to work with extremes and with what was left of vegetation on the planet. She determined that the outfit had to be reasonable, functional, thoughtful, but the competing objectives made the outfits tricky to design.

Bleary-eyed, I remember Jo looking over her sketches and noting the uniforms would need to be modified for outer space, once we had catapulted ourselves there using a storm's force.

"Focus, owl," she said when she had lost track.

Joanne drew and re-drew, paints, pens, graphite pencils spilling out everywhere. Her knuckles red with winter's cold.

"Build the uniform first, the boat second, and think about escaping gravity with a rubber band later," she repeated, entering a state of baser psychic rage, beginning again to snake-pace our room.

Eventually she erased the stunning ostrich feather from the forehead of the latticed helmet and replaced it with a feather-shape made of waterproof netting. For the face, we would need a serious material, maybe carapace for around the eyes and throat since those spots were most vulnerable in an attack. Because our mother had taught us that if we were tall enough, we should go ahead and gouge out the eyes. Otherwise, take your fist to your opponent's throat or groin, our father had shown us.

I remember nights in our attic space, wishing my sister would shrivel into a newt like the menacing boy in Ovid's Proserpina. Or, that we had a piano, or any instrument to touch and to make escapist sounds with. Better, a telescope, so that I could escape from the things that were said to have changed but had remained the same.

Eventually, over many sleepless nights, I had so many lucid thoughts I ran out of room in my brain. My head became brain-hell and brain-hell was at occupancy. I remember feeling pink and dry from the space heater and cracking open a window. Sucking in cool air, I began to believe life would be simpler in third person. I kept what I saw and heard those days to myself out of fear that people might learn of our behavior. In the past, there had been grave consequences for the women in our family being themselves. To be clear: it wasn't that I felt we were losing our grip—our grip was solid, if not sometimes reckless. Plus, it was ours to lose. The thing was that our reasoning was not the sort of reasoning that made people comfortable. It was the kind of thinking that for centuries had harmed women.

In the dark I could make out the back of Jo's legs, moist with sweat. A web of glow-in-the-dark stars beamed on the angular ceiling. It was difficult to articulate what it was like to watch someone you love suffer, and to hold their suffering, because the impulse was to back away from pain. I remember trying to distract myself, touching and thanking various parts of my body for sticking with me, as she moved back and forth, cautiously tiptoeing around our Legos, dutifully and artfully assembled into battleships, and cups of homemade slime. She would pace around the forts we had made from quilts while mumbling about plans, and about women and heretics and endings. Eventually, settling down and telling herself to calmly count sheep. Fluffy white sheep. One by one, sweet sheep, taking turns moving in a linear fashion, which was hard enough for us to fathom. Over a dumpster, a river, a hill, a target, a minefield. Jo counted sheep jumping over white picket fences, copied from the ones she had seen on television.

"Am I doing it right?" she wondered aloud.

Jo tried to sleep. Her sheep leapt over fences, background forests morphed into savannas, savannas into parking lots, which quickly dissolved into wastelands. The sheep morphed into donkeys, donkeys into walruses. Donkeys and walruses had nothing to do with one another, which set my sister back. The white picket fences morphed into wooden stakes. She thought of burnings. Not particularly soporific. *Vogue* suggested getting to sleep by thinking happy thoughts.

"Think. *HAPPY*. Idiot," Jo said, unmotivated, unconvinced.

Wooden stakes morphed into well-maintained and spectacular boats; the kind Natalie Wood spent time on. Not a good fit for dreaming. These boats became simple sailboats. Better. She counted one hundred and five walruses in well-maintained sailboats oozing over deserted wastelands. Two hundred and eleven before declaring sleep overrated.

"Seven hundred and four stupid walruses in simple sailboats with no direction," marking the count into the wood floor by her bed with a knife hoping to insert some optimism back into the space.

Count and tap and make way for happy thoughts just as *Vogue* suggested. Nine hundred and twenty maladroit walruses and counting. "We need a strategy," Jo would repeat.

The two of us could travel by water. Build a boat. Go to the Quad Cities' Mall, that sprawling lifeless structure, and pretend to be brassy teenagers with something to offer like boobs and spending accounts. Wish for alien abduction. Do as blonds do, which is to get away with shit—move through architecture like breezes. If being blond didn't work, pretend to be one of the super-rich and steal big stuff. Real stuff. Like the wealthy do. Like the life savings of average Americans. Head to Sears, the original everything store with refrigerators large enough to store, which was to say stockpile, tons of cartons of discounted orange juice until the next big sale rolled around. Storage capacity was a big incentive. While loitering at Sears, ask a guilty-looking stranger to buy us trashy movie tickets. (There were many guilty-looking strangers at the mall.) Order two extra-large popcorns. Eat one and save the other because the food offerings at home sucked. Joanne once explained that to understand life's propensity for familial punishment—to understand how fate and curses operated in the Fareown household—one had to eat Sylvia's food.

Together, we would direct a commercial about the demise of pizza—which was to say, the end of humankind—for The Discovery Channel. It would go over so well with audiences (of all types) we would be commissioned to come to grips with the end of pizza, therefore civilization, in a four-part series to be released incrementally. A cub could be thrown into the mix for effect, or a newborn, something cute would be included and put in jeopardy; put either one in jeopardy for additional salaciousness and for good measure—to get people to feel. Executives in their studio offices off of Melrose Avenue will be pleased around a table overflowing with quality muffins made of local (like, milled on the premises) spelt that took some special doing to procure.

"Resist hate," Jo said of the rabbit hole we found ourselves lingering in and turned on the fan.

Jo put her fingers in the fan and said: "Lick the pain off the scorched bodies and severed heads of history's heathens and weather-brewing witches flying from donkey parts. Lick the unguent wounds of history, which followed us around like a spirit."

"Everything, including us, returns to water," she said.

"Fishes, plankton, whales, squids, birds, and sea turtles are all linked by unbreakable ties to kinds of water."

She desperately wanted the dark thoughts to clear. She could not sleep. Joanne then buried the meaningful parts of herself, like the mines and caverns below an ocean's floor where millions of species lie undiscovered for an eternity. There, she would let her insides thicken into something richer she might one day eat with creamy mashed potatoes, made with an irresponsible amount of salted butter—gobs of salty butter—and gallons of whole milk made from real dairy cows, the kind that came in authentic glass jars.

I spoke of creamy mashed potatoes next to her ears. I wanted to reach my sister, to remain with her. To do this, I tried to engage her mind. My sister was the kind of person that didn't settle, not on loving one gender or on anything, really. She was born speaking a language few wanted to understand. I wanted to understand.

The year 1986 would end but it was too late to stop its spread over our house like an illness, threatening to permanently occupy our bodies and spirits. Our cupboards were bare save for an abundance of sticky plastic bags and bent plastic containers. Henry was dying for chicken legs and feeling guilty about it. He refused to get help for his depression. Instead, he trashed Cherri Cohen, our mother's dear friend who knew a thing or two about suffering. His stress was at an all-time high. He was shedding hair. His thoughts were on buffalo. Henry could not get the tragedy of the American buffalo out of his mind. He wanted to talk, endlessly, to us about "mistakes." The fact was the grazing of livestock was more damaging than multiple nuclear bomb blasts. Did we know that? "Raising cattle was a mistake," Henry made sure we scribbled it down. "Cows are stupid," he demanded Sylvia remove the images throughout our house, before calling his demand a mistake and putting them back. "Cow-burnt lands," was how Edward Abbey described the West, and Henry feared he had never made one single productive decision in his life.

That winter hundreds of thousands of cows died of exposure and starvation. Some were crushed to death on barbed-wire drift fences. Cows lacked essential survival instincts and didn't know how to approach severe weather. They calved during storms. In the warmer months, if provided the feed, cattle would gorge almost to death. Cows flattened and depleted the soil. Buffalo, on the other hand, had sharp hooves, which broke up and oxygenated it, improving the sod, and increasing the variety of grasses, forbs, and shrubs.

Unlike cows, they didn't gather in large groups around springs and streams. Instead, buffalo wallowed in potholes, which, when seeded with their manure became fertile ground for much-needed vegetation. Buffalo directly faced weather in marching columns, taking turns driving through the heavy drifts or stopping to wait for storms to pass. What had we done?

The unraveling continued. Our father shed hair uncontrollably. He said we needed a high-fiber diet. The cows were getting impaled. They were dying. Our house was freezing. The linoleum was making everyone, not just Sylvia, psycho. Our mother said she was post-empathy. She walked away. And Jo, an insomniac with an agenda, said that 1987 would be more ridiculous yet, more ridiculous than our parent's wedding: "1987 will be the very epitome of ridiculousness."

Jo said "epitome" a lot in those days leading up to 1987. I remember I copied her, epitome of this and that, but when I did, she pinched me so hard and deep that it left a bright red skin spot for days on my thigh. Jesus, the truth was I hadn't said anything that damning, and I questioned whether Jesus was real since he never showed himself. If I had known in a few days what my sister was about to do—that the "roof incident" would repeat like a glitchy reel—I would like to think I would have tried to stop her.

Congress was deliberating on television and Joanne went outside to jump off our roof. It was a clear and sunny day in January in 1987, the year Jo decided to have her Dadaist repertoire include the experience of falling. I was nine going on ten and she was eleven.

"I wanted to experience falling, as a way to train myself," Jo had offered up about her ill-fated experiment jumping onto the concrete to experience the sensation of gravity, when she was asked to explain herself, something she was not a fan of doing.

I can remember Joanne calling me out from inside of the house—where I had been minding my own business—to "see something unoriginal." I remember immediately thinking it was a terrible idea to listen to my sister. I would be implicated in whatever was about to transpire. Of course, I promptly went outside to see something unoriginal, but she was nowhere to be found. I searched the family cemetery, the barn, until I heard the words "up here." There she was, up on the roof, dazzling. Then I watched my sister drop through the air and hit the pool of concrete. "Our father will not be happy," I remember thinking.

She fell and I felt a mixture of shame—Jo did not fear mortality, whereas I feared everything. And reverie—how was it possible my sister could make her deadly moves appear rehearsed, fluid, like a modern dancer? I studied her suspended in a state of terror: How dare you abandon me in America. The knowing and the not knowing what had crossed her mind in the minutes and hours—perhaps even weeks, and months—preceeding her decision to harm herself for the sake of feeling, fractured my mind, which I could not get rid of.

The night after her fall, Joanne returned home from the hospital in the Quad Cities with her head bandaged, painkillers, and a wheel-chair for her broken hip and compound leg fractures. She returned to us having been told she'd never have children due to the severity of her spinal curve. Our parents let her eat whatever she wanted however she wanted. Jo asked for hotdogs, hamburger buns with sesame seeds on top, brand name anything, strawberry yogurt with fruit on the bottom. Jo was given the new pair of denim that our father had fetched from the Quad Cities' Mall, from a shop that was better than Sears though he couldn't recall which, all while her injuries were being addressed by the doctors. The grandness of the gesture was not lost on us. Our parents were eager to demonstrate the extent of their commitment to loving her. Henry never entered malls or bought new clothing. Our parents never gave us anything new. As kids, we wore hand-me-down clothing, mostly from boys. Joanne liked to say we were ridiculous looking, "and not in the way ridiculous was the coveted look of the time."

(I can picture my sister saying we're the epitome of absurdity, debilitated. Insufferable. Mesmerizing, as she rolled around in her wheelchair like she had been born with it attached to her ass, displaying the arm strength of someone twice her age, wearing her new denim pants and eating whatever food she wanted, maneuvering around the piles of detritus in the attic space that we shared along with small rodents, boxes of dusty items, like bills, instruction manuals, books and photo albums, winter gear, torn lawn chairs, and an inflatable pool our father had demanded we buy from a yard sale since everyone else had one.)

The point was that Jo was in a fantastic mood the night she returned from the hospital. I remember this frightened me. She was eating legumes from a jar, waiting for our parents to return with her expanding list of goodies. She was making messes on herself and on the floor, while reading to me about champion thrill-seekers from her personal dictionary. (Which was more of a dictionary-encyclopedia hybrid.) Joanne was diligent about keeping her definitions updated. Sometimes these robust offerings took up an entire page worth of text and often included images. For instance the word "wake" had a rooster and a mirror, and "carry" a bucket and a medical rendering of a heart.

Joanne opened it and suggested that we explore our options.

"Contrary to common thought," Jo said, "good adventurers dread fear."

Fear was the result of a situation gone wrong, such as a bad turn in the weather, and skills were for figuring a way out of the trap that fear presented, Joanne explained.

"Sorry, but you're spilling," I pointed out.

I would be blamed for the stains. My sister, who had demonstrated a fierce commitment to seeking out (mostly destructive) experiences, was now invincible.

"Eventually things need to be eaten," Joanne said, dumping legumes into her mouth, subsequently all over the rug, and going on to lick the bean liquid running down her arm instead of using her shirtsleeve or a napkin like a good girl.

So sure of herself, even as an invalid.

"Bernie, are you having a mental breakdown? You're wearing your shoulders like earrings."

I really considered it—was I having a breakdown at that age? And my ears weren't even pierced.

"No," I wanted to respond. "I'm like this all the time. And my name is Bernadette."

I remember that night Joanne returned home from the hospital, she fell asleep quickly, soundly, the way someone with a free mind sleeps deeply. There was a fudgy chocolate sheet cake a nice neighbor had made for her, which she kept in arm's reach. That night—her body, broken, was hot like it was on fire. I could feel her volcanic heat, even from my part of the space in the attic. I remember thinking if she'd been awake, I might have shown her something simple, like an abstract drawing of a cucumber. I wished I had said something light-hearted and supportive, like farting could happen by swallowing air. Two of the recent figures we'd been reading about—Glenn Gould, and her not-so-favorite Charles Darwin—were both notorious sufferers of flatulence. Did Jo, who retained so much, know this about them?

I remember the silhouettes of leaves flickering on the ceiling of the attic and thinking about willpower. Joanne had so much of it. I thought about that phrase "too little too late," as legislation to help us had gone into effect, but by then the psychic damage had already been done. Days went by in that drafty garret with a pitched roof and one small window we fought over.

1987, SO WE ESCAPED TO 1973

Our parents first met in the pharmacy in 1973. The war was declared basically over, and President Nixon spoke of a peaceful, progressive new American era, driven by a conservative revolution. Insisting the chaos at home, and in Southeast Asia, was the fault of the credo of liberalism. He urged Americans to do great things for themselves.

That year, Henry returned from Vietnam a staff sergeant, fifty-eight thousand dead in the muddy jungles, to meet Sylvia, who was on the pharmacy floor fumbling around in her bag for her reading glasses. *People Magazine*: "Roe vs. Wade, the Alaska Oil Pipeline Bill," was open next to her. Her clothes were soaked through from walking in the pouring rain. Her hair was dripping. She explained that she usually carried plastic bags to tie around her head, but she had totally spaced. That day had been a nightmare. The plumbing issues, and then the electricity had gone out. Henry asked her if she wanted a paper towel. And the two got talking about the past and death.

"What are we doing here?" she asked.

"Exactly," he said.

Sylvia astonished him. How was it they had never met? Everyone knew everyone in that town, and she looked at him inquisitively, affectionately, not at all like the anti-war protesters, or the people who believed the cheerier depictions of American soldiers in Vietnam. She was one year older than he was. The town was really small, and this was worth reiterating. Plus, the priest had raised Henry, which was a notorious story—not many were left on the side of the road like trash like our father had been. He was lucky. His parents had "equipped him with a liter of bottled water, a loaf of sliced, honey wheat bread left un-tampered with, made squishy from the heat, and one heavy-duty trash bag tucked into the back pocket of my pants," he joked.

"America begets more America; trash begets more trash," Sylvia said.

He wanted to kiss her.

She wanted to think about it.

Sometimes, I would stop our parents right there in their story, where I found their attempts at humor unsatisfactory, nauseating. Henry was a citizen of America. He may not have been a particularly special person, and I did know that at that time our country had a litter problem, but I also knew, even as a nine-almost-ten-year-old coming of age in a different decade, that he wasn't a total complete waste. Our father would take my hand, sometimes exacerbated by my inability to just roll with it, and explain that going back to his mother and father's grim apartment, where they were living their evolving American dream experiment, was not an option.

By ten—the age I almost was, he would remind me—Henry was a celebrated forger. At twelve he got a job stocking shelves at the mini mart using an expert fake ID. People knew it was a fake, but the sheer audacity showed leadership potential. He was handsome, pouty, and utterly irresistible. He even started bartending. His irresistibility factor made the bar a ton of cash. In summers and on weekends, Henry was the favored lifeguard at the community pool. Over his shoulder, girls cried out for his attention. Teenage girls swooned. He was a stud. Cleft chin. Broad shoulders. The stuff hunks were made of. Girls rallied around him, lined up like suspects, auditioning for the part of atomic girlfriend. Pick me, they gestured. Joanne called them greedy bitches. I kept my mouth shut; there could be a backlash. Henry was good with his hands if he was forced to teach you a lesson.

Our father stood out: orphan that was making something of himself, a celebrated forger, star high-school athlete, a good poet, creative and brooding barman, all that. "Oh," was what our mother said of his fame. She too knew something about being left to fend for herself—Sylvia's mother had died unexpectedly, and her father was a figure that she never knew except for when he made his way into her reoccurring dreams. But she didn't know Henry. She hadn't heard his name or his story. Sylvia liked to get wet, but she never went to the swimming pool. She preferred to read about the ocean. As well as about other natural waters, since water was a theme, sometimes disastrous, consistently liberating, for the women in her family. Never once had she been to the sports bar in town where Henry worked. Not even for special occasions. And as far as God was concerned, she stopped going to church once she understood the derogatory names they called the women in her family, who were rumored to have castrated the men they came into contact with. Had he not heard the castration story? It was inescapable. Henry had not heard this tale. And when Sylvia briefed him on the cautionary legend, he remained unfazed. He listened, and afterward he said he was hungry. His stomach was growling, and he suggested that they should go to lunch. Sylvia again explained to Henry that she was at the pharmacy to buy toilet paper and had left her reading glasses at home.

"Could you please read to me the sale prices?" Sylvia said her scripted line, one morning as they started up recollecting the pharmacy scene.

"Just like that, there you were, almost as tall as me," Henry recalled, on that particular day of recollecting, over a breakfast of dry toast.

1973. Next to boxes of tampons and hair dye, Henry struggled to get down to one busted knee. Eye to eye. His heart went weak. He was ill-prepared for a proposal of that kind, but when he finally managed to balance on the blemished carpet, surrounded by consumer goods, he asked Sylvia to marry him. She could not think of a reason why not. All she'd ever had were mediocre ideas and the only way to minimize one bad idea was to come up with a worse idea. Besides, everyone she might have counted on for advice or shelter was dead. Not to mention the retired schoolteacher, whose cheap room she had rented ever since Aunt Vie burned down their house in town, had for years studied her too closely. Her landlord— a retired schoolteacher, mind you—had flashed Sylvia his penis on multiple occasions. Super plus, Henry was holding a decently sized umbrella. "God's will," our mother has said of their engagement, though Sylvia hated to admit it.

"But now you've given me up for astrology and all I want is to be the Venus yin to your Mars yang," Henry lamented at the oak table, taking Sylvia's uneaten dry toast.

I remember that day the story made Jo nuts. My sister began screaming. "That was enough humor for one lifetime," she screamed. She could no longer listen to our parent's limp attempts at flirting and watch star shapes stream uncontrollably from their animated eyeballs. "1973 wasn't a great year either and as a collective entity that cannot let go, we might as well try to live in the present moment of nonsense or please simply get on with the wedding story," she said.

We knew the story of their wedding ceremony well. Perhaps it was the best part, as my sister suggested that particular day. And perhaps that was reason she and I would revisit this part of their story regularly.

Henry and Sylvia were young when they married amid an Illinois blizzard. Visibility was near zero. The horizon was indistinguishable. They felt right at home in the chaos. The wedding ceremony was held in an overheated room in city hall, an unremarkable slab of concrete on the town's periphery. The clerk, a wiry farmer in his late seventies wearing trousers and rain boots, conducted the ceremony like he was about to pass out. (It was common for rooms to be overheated during the winter.) Most had overdressed for the occasion and were sweating through their shells made of synthetic fabric. (I would like to point out that synthetics create wetness; polyester allows perspiration to build up inside of a garment and polyester was all anyone wore.) "Imagine the scene." I did not want to, but I did what Jo asked of me, and it was messy. Guests in bad clothing growing damp, popcorn asbestos ceiling, in a room that overwhelmingly smelled of cat urine and chalky deodorizer. Joanne said: "Bad smells can't mask bad smells." Bad over bad didn't make right. Worse wasn't a solution to bad. Bad wasn't pleasant, it wasn't even passable, it was just bad ten times over. But nobody considers the long term.

"Nobody gets it," I could hear Joanne say.

Their ceremony was brief and straightforward. Along with the city clerk, Sylvia's remaining, assorted relatives managed to show up, a collection of distantly related individuals with debts, who moved in on our mother like mosquitos to still waters in search of anything they could sell off. These individuals regularly reminded our mother that she was tolerated.

"We tolerate your sentimentalism," seethed out through their poisonous mouths because she had proven to be more obliging than her mother, or any of her mother's three sisters, not to mention her mother's mother, and her mother's mother's mother; that genetic line, that strain of savage heathens that coiled back like an intrauterine device.

"Pray those women suffer the ultimate fate of the Dalkon Shield, leaving them dead, sterile, or, better: infertile, and spare us their damaged children. The insufferable women should have been beheaded," these relatives said, their heads spiraling out of control, roaming waist-deep in damp dark halls where unwelcome wild things roamed.

"And not the sorts of wild things the two of us want roaming, Bernie," Jo clarified, which included beasts, chimeras, and leatherback sea turtles.

"But the unwelcome sorts, like deeply apologetic politicians apologizing for their immoral behavior with absolutely no intention of improving themselves. Those beasts were everywhere," she said.

My future self would find this hatred of the women on our maternal side to be without merit and therefore superfluous and unnecessary. Furthermore, the women in question were highly skilled at inventing their own terror to engage with. Like the fools of the past, they made a point of delivering themselves to the rivers with its thousand limbs, arms, and legs—to that great uncertainty external to everything. Otherwise known as God.

Our mother too needed to find something to wear. At Blain's Farm & Fleet, Sylvia picked out a discounted dress for the ceremony with deep pockets. On the day itself, she woke up early to pin her hair into twists. She scrubbed her feet. Our father wore clean work clothes for the occasion. He brushed back his dark hair that had grown long again and used hair gel to set the style. Sylvia noticed the hair gel, and this was a sweet thing that lasted between them. For the ceremony, she borrowed a hanky and a bible from Grandma Tess's remaining items she kept wrapped in a box. She would take with her what the virgins, whom she spent hours bathing at the convalescent home, had said: that they had never known a man. Next to Henry, in front of the state, sweaty guests, heaven, hell, and all that was impossible, she would know Henry. Sylvia would blush and undress and touch his flesh and make him erect, a thousand times over.

After their wedding, Henry and Sylvia settled into the one-bedroom farmhouse she had inherited, located around two hundred miles outside of Chicago. There, our parents joined a region of outcasts, a collective identity centering on values of hard work, dignity, and loyalty to family and community.

"Values and virtues," Henry loved to say, before going on to quote Thomas Jefferson: "Those who labor in the earth are the chosen people of God, if ever he had a chosen people."

These sentiments, which could make Jo and I constipated for days, had me heading to the Super 8 lobby for coffee.

SUPER 8, PRESENTLY

A few days' stay at the motel had turned into more days, and my supplies had run out. I took the stairs to the lobby; I was lazy but not that lazy. The receptionist, the brunette I'd encountered only once, but who stood out for her layered, colorful, mismatched patterns, was nowhere to be found. An empty motel lobby was an exceptional sensation. Inspirational, like a European fountain. Not to mention the latest weather crisis had been averted and presumably guests were asleep or on their way elsewhere. I made myself at home, just as the receptionist had instructed. I filled three janky bowls with Frosted Corn Flakes and put on a pot of coffee like on a police procedural, but really, I was in the western *High Noon*, and everyone who should have been fighting me for free goods was outside waiting to watch the showdown.

I was making a mess. I went to take the gray plastic top off the cereal dispenser to return some of the Frosted Corn Flakes I hadn't eaten, but I could not remove the lid to do it. I thought about temporality. A lot of sterile, monitored, temporary spaces such as motels by highways, or like institutes, narratives, asylums, patriarchy and police stations—they possess oppressive auras. I tried to change my direction and to focus on waking up, fully. I went for sweetener because it was both delicious and an uninformed, health-wise, thing to do. I struggled to open the little white packet of classic sugar. The same unhelpful design after decades, which had me thinking about the United States Congress: those men and women (mostly men), are paid a fortune to find solutions, yet they remain exceptionally pleased doing nothing. With a batch of those super slim red straws that fail to be helpful, I gave my coffee a swirl. I was of no use to anyone making observations under-caffeinated in an empty lobby. I walked back up to my room, a few bowls of Raisin Bran filled with skim milk on ice. It was the one cereal, in the collection available, that had remained untouched by the other motel patrons.

In our Illinois house, King Lear liked to appear. I can remember over breakfast of supremely dry toast (again) one morning, our parent's disruptive patterns came to a head. Henry was again in a state and his "state" had for weeks been dominating the mood around the kitchen table. (He had been saying he wasn't a shaman who could turn himself into a bird, nor was he a madman who might turn himself into stone. He had returned to smashing things.) He was conflicted about being a man, especially one without value or purpose—stewardship of the land was fundamental, but even a house with a roof would not be able to accommodate a cyclone. "How to best proceed" had him wound up.

"King Lear cursed the earth," Jo said, staring blankly at her dry toast.

"You're talking to me like an actress," Henry said to her, when she was only trying to comfort him.

Sylvia told Henry point blank to get his act together that instant, a threat she often made. She drank an Alka-Seltzer, emptied the ashtray in the small trash she kept by her ankles, lit another cigarette, and pointed at the plate piled with cold toast. Henry said he didn't like her tone, or the implication. She reminded him not to push her to say things she shouldn't have to, especially that early in the morning. At that time, she was our main source of income, and at the suggestion of Cherri she was getting into astrology, lifelines, predictions, and palm readings. (One reader saw death in her aura, which had Jo and I wondering how the reader saw Sylvia's palm over the telephone.)

I remember biting my nails and waiting for a hologram of ancestral women to come extricate me. I remember wishing I had some peach jam. I remember in that moment in their conversation, just as it got hot, Henry called Sylvia a sexy beast. Sylvia told him to focus on breakfast. "Eat, Henry," she pointed again to the toast. Henry said he wasn't thinking about eating toast. Jo explained of our father's persistence—like he was not present at the table also baffled by more dry toast—that access to our mother's hands, face, and vagina had been barred by the stars. At the table, Henry confirmed as much. He said he missed Sylvia, and they should go to "the pharmacy," a euphemism, as far as I could tell, for starting over.

During the period when Henry had difficulty tying his shoes for unknown reasons, and Sylvia had fully given herself to interpreting celestial cycles, there were calendric limits around when and how they could (more often could not) have sex. Mars, it seemed to our father, was deliberately in a state of retrograde. He couldn't wait for Mars to come out of retrograde. He couldn't fathom how a robust planet, such as Mars, would want to tamp down primal instincts, raw at its core. And Venus was always up to no good. He made clear his displeasure with the cosmic factors—haphazard astronomical bodies, astrological details—which had begun to derail their generous sexual routine. Moons were habitually void of course, even though Henry had no clue what that meant, and was convinced nobody else did either.

Jo and I would leave when the two of them began their tit for tat dance, the meaning of which I came to understand was their version of foreplay. Sylvia would mention terrestrial periods, such as the "Void of Course Moon," when the transiting moon makes its last major turn before changing to another sign of the Zodiac. She explained this period was also called "silly season," or "a vacation from normal living," a span of time when one shouldn't make decisions because they would turn out to be terrible mistakes. To drive her nuts, Henry said this moon talk made his dick hard. This made even my sister, whose appetite for the absurd saw no bounds, volatile.

Eventually our parents came to an agreement: Henry would get his act together. He would earnestly stop drinking the way he was drinking, if Sylvia agreed to never again use the movements and positions of celestial objects to weigh-in on their sexual life, or other human affairs, and if Sylvia kept astrology in their bedroom, so that astrology did not breach their walls and infect us. (His daughters were freaks as it was, he said.) Henry would get better at exploring sobriety and optimism as a "viable living condition," as long as astrological cycles and Cherri Cohen stayed out of it.

Henry took this practice of optimism to a new level, filling notebook after notebook with optimistic drawings. Our father really felt he could make the world a better place. He said it was his duty to address the widespread pessimism sweeping our community and encasing our home like a mollusk's shell. He was determined to transform feelings of malaise into feelings of possibility, because he honestly didn't know what else to do to combat his depression. He wasn't one to give in to it; and for our father, "giving in to it" meant letting the bankers win, and he would rather ignite their enterprise than let them win. The truth was the bankers had already won—our father had become sober and further paranoid.

"Imagine yourself with rectrices!" Henry said to dismayed people, passing out hand-drawn posters of human figures with feathers of a bird's tail attached to their asses.

When we asked Henry about his illustrations and his ideas, he said he felt entrepreneurial. He said the ideas germinated from this infectious American notion of commodifying something—not immediately considered useful—and then disseminating it to the rest of the world. He said this unironically, as would have been characteristic of him. And when we looked at him skeptically, since we knew how he felt about innovative presents from America, Henry said we were being judgmental. We didn't push it further. Our father's newfound sobriety was a relief in other ways. As a family, we had little interest in curtailing his tendency to theorize since it had meant for a time he was preoccupied, and this had meant he was less prone to violent outbursts from which we suffered more greatly from. It was, as Jo would later point out living in Deadhorse, Alaska, simply our best option at the time.

Undeterred by rumors that he had lost it worse than the Fareown women were batshit crazy, which stoked Sylvia's competitive fire, Henry pinned up posters depicting humans with feathers on their asses around our house, inside of the barn, and on the slim row of trees lining First Street, to lighten the mood. We were sadistically buoyed by our father's newfound personality, and wanted more than anything to play tricks on him while he was mentally incapacitated, basically. That was what daytime sobriety did to our father.

"Leave it alone," Sylvia cautioned us, like a large dog is told to leave a small dog.

Our father had become an "it." And when Joanne and I were embracing the nasty—as in, letting ourselves do and say and feel incorrectly by most standards—we felt a surge of liberation. In their bedroom, as they had agreed to, Sylvia looked at the alignment of the planets and would later tell us that the time ahead would be nourished by obsession. She said we were expecting a Pisces full moon, which is fed by abstraction, expansion, and exploration of the self, lighting the path toward your destiny, finding the voice that protects the seas.

I remember Jo leaning into me in a way which felt kind and soft, to whisper in my ear: "Our parents are miserable adults who will never see the ocean."

At night, after our father disappeared into an activity that had the potential, as he saw it, to save the world, and after our mother went to bed with her moon stuff and the radio, my sister and I explored the dark recesses of our minds; in that damp dark space we held conversations about those people responsible for tending to us. About our parents, Henry and Sylvia—both "solidly inept," Joanne pointed out—Jo explained that we learned very little from our mistakes and pointed to the research: Humans were designed to be reliably mercurial, highly suggestible, and profoundly irrational tricksters better at fooling themselves than anyone else.

"Take General Philip Sheridan," my sister once said about America; the commander of the Armies of the West concocted a kill-for-the-sake-of-killing campaign, which for many reasons we can all agree was not a good plan. General Philip Sheridan wanted the festive cowboy to roam free and to engage at will in wholesale slaughter in an effort to exterminate the buffalo, so that America's prairies could be covered with cattle. This, his loyalists argued, was the only way to bring peace and allow for the advancement of civilization, which needed advancing.

"What hope was there?" Jo asked about the overall flaw in the pursuit of an advanced civilization, and one that advances peacefully.

"Besides, what sort of people, and their enlightened civilization, advance by exterminating useful animals?"

"I know."

"I know you know."

Lenders agreed they would stop calling in the sheriff and so the government gave them billions of dollars. Thanks to this, the Agricultural Credit Act of 1987 passed, and this legislation saved our family, but the relief we would feel would be only partial and it would only be temporary. It was only a matter of time before we'd be asked again to pay back the loans; the same loans we had been pressured into receiving to continue farming.

1987 & 1988

Sylvia was speaking with Seraphina's mother on the telephone, who had words for her. First, there was the issue concerning our father's suspect behavior, which our mother did not argue with, and our family's apparent ungratefulness that the "United States Government had spared us; they had let us off the hook for behaving irresponsibly," Seraphina's mother said to our mother. I could hear her voice on the line burst with life; it was as if her plump thighs were covered in a rash that she was desperate not to scratch, but in the end, could not help herself. Our mother would later explain of that animated conversation, the book *Of Woman Born* on her lap earmarked for our bedtime "lesson," that for the wealthy, the desire to look down on the poor was simply irresistible, and Seraphina's parents were rich.

More importantly, Seraphina's mother continued, quickly shifting back to the matter at hand, the matter which prompted her urgent phone call to our mother, was Joanne's treatment of their daughter: How had my sister gone from obedient friend, to raging nightmare? Seraphina's mother was pissed. Joanne must stop putting "Missing Blond Sweet Bright Angel Seraphina" posters up around First Street. Jo must stop blanketing the school's hallways with these fictional posters. Jo must stop tucking them underneath windshield wipers. Seraphina was safe and at home and terrified strangers would get the wrong impression about their stalwart family. Seraphina was a promising member of society; their daughter was destined to flourish, her mother went on to our mother. I can remember Sylvia swishing those words "destined to flourish" around her mouth, like people who have mouthwash do with their mouthwash.

There were rumors of "Satanic Ritual Abuse" in town and whispers of Satanic altars in Seraphina's basement, no doubt all of it started by my sister. It didn't help that they were out-of-towners. It was only a matter of time before someone broke down their door and demanded to see their basement where surely the stuffed rabbits and sacrificial blond daughters of the Midwest bowed to Satan's altar for the sake of mankind. Plus, Seraphina's parents had urban lawyer friends. Plus, they oozed money.

The other topic was about getting the pickling liquid just right. Seraphina's mother was struggling with ratios: water, sugar, vinegar, veg. Nothing came out right. Could Sylvia help her with this? She was having ratio problems.

I found Jo on the couch in the living room, the portrait above her, reliably crooked and hanging there like an omen; a stone's throw from the kitchen we were forbidden to enter if a parent was on the phone or if both of them were there, together, in the same kitchen, period; and another short distance from our parent's bedroom, which was off limits indefinitely. Next to me on the couch, Jo spoke about woman-on-woman hate as a contagion which had spread over the centuries.

"We relish language, you and me," Jo said on the couch, "but oftentimes it is a source of self-inflicting damage and gradual ruin for our gender, whether we are active participants playing into the scheme or not."

Woman-on-woman hate was splashed all over afternoon television, which Joanne couldn't help but watch even though she wasn't supposed to be watching television in the afternoon. Questionable content just happened to my sister like every other error. On daytime television, women trash-talked each other, clawed at one another's painted faces with nicely manicured nails, even trash-talking unborn babies, and two-timing boyfriends.

I would like to take a moment to point out that the babies had not been born. Unborn babies being trashed was cruel and unnecessary because they were opinionless cells forming in a womb, not a bother to anyone except for their mother.

Jo pointed out—born or not—they were still baby fiends.

"I don't understand *baby fiend*," I said, unsure about what that meant and unsure that I wanted to understand anything, at all, ever.

"If a baby doesn't get enough calcium, it sucks it directly from the mother's bones," she said.

Jo pointed to the women on television pulling each other's hair and said the debacle had been staged.

"Women don't pull hair. Hair-pulling is a myth espoused by producers, who are really acne prone teenage boys that still play with toy race cars. They should be figuring out how to fund quality content."

"Plus, new moms don't have nails," I contributed.

"You're missing the point, Bernie," Jo said.

I believed my sister when it came to specifics that had to do with America's free enterprise, which was to say I trusted in the verisimilitude of our mother and (mostly) our father because that was where much of Joanne's thinking at the time had originated from. But nobody knew about afternoon television and its ways or about older boys jockeying to be men who acted like boys like my sister. Joanne was surrounded by posers. They—the posers, as I saw them—had said they could heal my sister's body, inside and out. They had said this about Joanne's right shoulder blade that was protruding like a wing. Our father—who had wanted to take out his rage on those boys—had instead smashed his fists into a tree. He felt terrible. He admired trees more than he did pigs. As for my older sister, I never understood why she chose not to retaliate. She was excellent with knives and at camouflaging herself when it suited her. She was skilled at weaponizing her instincts. Instead, Joanne chose to acquiesce to their desires and timeless manipulations. I knew—or so I thought I knew—that she would not have wanted those boys touching her or for them to be anywhere near her developing brain and our goals to leave the farm. Those posers were setbacks.

Jo was adamant women should be talking about the essentials: survival, and therefore masturbation—too many females defaulted to the in-and-out motion because it mimicked sex, menstrual cycles, and the ensuing general self-loathing sold to women daily as self-care.

"Squirting, now that was where the action was."

Why couldn't she just eat her snack and be more like the rest of us?

"*USE LUBE!*"

Jesus, Jo was insufferable. And to be clear, none of this was in *Of Woman Born*.

At the time, my sister was insufferably moody. There were little buds and swellings showing up below her nipples, which over the course of a few months had begun to feel sore. She pierced her bellybutton with a safety pin, explaining that it felt "cohesive." She recounted her changing body in front of the television like it was her best friend in the whole world, especially when I was minding my own business like doing my homework to make Sylvia proud, and would have preferred she talk that way elsewhere, out of sight. New smells were emanating from her underwear, her armpits, her asshole; she recounted all this like she was reading a cookie recipe, double chocolate fudge. At first, the new hairs sprouting were soft, and later kinkier, curlier than the hair on her head, which was stunning, jet-dark, shiny, and long enough it reached her hips. Her new body hair grew in new places, even above her lip, which she polished and cared for with our mother's Lubriderm lotion, which disgusted people, which she greatly appreciated.

Joanne was determined to discover pleasure where and when she could, fearing, justifiably, and as other women had, that one day those desirable sensations would be taken away from her. Around us, kids were finding their fathers in the machine shed with rifles next to their bodies, no head. Husbands weren't returning for dinner. Instead, finding their bodies in abandoned farmsteads and calling it symbolic. Jo watched *Summer Heat* nonstop. (There was a lot of nonstop action in 1987.) It was her favorite movie, about a Depression-era farm wife named Roxy who was hooking up with a hot, competent, and skillful hired hand named Jack. She explained Roxy hooked up with hot Jack because her brutish overbearing husband was hooking up with not only the orthodontist's wife in town, but the butcher's wife, and the weighty librarian too. And they lived next to each other. It was just the sort of feasible distraction Joanne approved of.

Also notable, *The Legend of Zelda* was released. Mikhail Gorbachev was *Time's* "Person of the Year." A can of 10.6-ounce Campbell's soup was 99 cents. Al Gore announced his run for the presidency, and quickly stopped mentioning global warming. On October 28th, there was a high-spirited dinner party in a lovely townhouse on Capitol Hill. Guests, a mix of educators and oil and gas company types, were seen mingling and joking with environmentalists. Trade-group representatives chatted up regulators; academics got tipsy in corners where subject matter was at a premium. The scene conjured the word consensus; appeared to be the start of a grand collaboration among varying factions to find solutions to the warming planet.

Joanne rolled around in her wheelchair wearing oversized sweaters, gorging on pop culture. She was hell-bent on playing Heart and Whitney Houston nonstop, while repeating *Summer Heat's* plotline. The music was tolerable, but there was absolutely nothing seductive about a Depression-era farm wife beginning an ill-advised affair with their hired hand, who was clearly being taken advantage of. None of which addressed the major issues affecting us—she was avoiding our America Project, and I took notice.

I remember thanking God that 1988 was just around the corner, and realizing that praying had made my tits retreat even further into the background. My tits, and overall body, were insignificant. There were no growth spurts in sight. Sylvia had warned us about wishing for things beyond our control. Our mother was the one who had introduced us to Ovid, for fuck's sake. Wishing for more than what we had could turn us into rivulets or swallows, or kill us. "Though you will die regardless," Sylvia said.

The National Farm Medicine Center, founded in 1981 to conduct agricultural health and safety research and education, reported in the Upper Midwest more than 900 male farmers, 71 female farmers, 96 farm children, and 177 farm workers killed themselves from 1980 to 1988 (the last year that figures were compiled). In Sioux City, Iowa, a farmer's suicide note said: "The farm killed me."

Farmer Norma Fetter said when she came home, that Joe, who was five years old, said his dad was out in the machine shed with a rifle next to his limp body. And that was how she and Joe found daddy when they came home from church.

Karen Heidman picked up the children from school and when they returned, Dan was not at home. They weren't alarmed because he had said he was going to go to Monona County to visit family, as he often did. But he didn't return home for dinner. He did not return all night. Karen notified his family, who said they had not seen him in weeks, and they went looking for him. Karen called his psychiatrist several times and left messages. The next afternoon, the authorities had found his body in an abandoned farmstead. Karen called it "symbolic": abandoned farmstead and abandoned dreams. The economic battle was a shame. He had died of shame. Karen said it's a shame that intelligence and determination were not equal to overpowering market forces.

"His death is a result of shame, the stigma of mental illness, and the loss of a dream," she said.

Meanwhile, Henry and Joanne had turned 1988 into a game of charades, making it up as the year limped along. The three of us were gluttons absorbing trash like the ocean, drinking tall pint glasses of milk with cinnamon in rapid succession in the living room. The television announced the Food and Drug Administration had found that more than half of seventy milk samples taken in fourteen cities were contaminated with antibiotics. The man from the F.D.A.'s Center for Veterinary Medicine explained: "I think the milk is free of antibiotics, and if it's not free, the levels that could be there are well below levels of concern."

I was ten, which meant yet more suffering was to come. There was more realizing to happen, more toxic information to absorb. The region was back in a drought. Jo said it never left. Rush Limbaugh was using the term "feminazis" to appeal to all the men in America feeling aggrieved by "uppity" women. To demonstrate his point, my sister had burned her training bra on a flagpole on First Street, which got us fined. Republican presidential nominee George H. W. Bush echoed sentiments made four years earlier by Ronald Reagan, rallying crowds: "The South would rise again." Then, to obliterate his opponent, Michael Dukakis, a letter was disseminated that included a photograph pairing Dukakis with convicted rapist Willie Horton. It warned if Dukakis became president your children and friends should expect to receive a visit from a rapist.

"Sewer money was ruining America," Jo said.

"But there was Nixon before those assholes," Henry would not let us forget. "And then there was Reagan." We wondered if our father would ever get over Ronald.

Twenty years earlier, Nixon focused on disaffected white Democrats in the South, invoking the term "neighborhood schools." In other words, segregated schools.

Other themes emerged during this time. Jo was diving more deeply into deepening her sexual relationships. "Just into seeing what all the fuss is about," her words. Which meant talking to brainless dudes on the phone late into the night who were into her and who apparently also suffered from insomnia. From a very young age, it was clear to me that animals and people—girls, hawks, goldfish, boys, men, cows, women—would be drawn to my sister. Though only the human animals would seek to harm her. Jo was born a cannon. She emerged an energy. She was a force that levitated and left a mess behind, which others would fall over themselves to clean up. But nobody had the tools to do this well or the willingness to help her.

Motel 6. I wasn't sure if we'd finished their love story. That was where our parents went after their wedding reception, which was held in an even smaller, even more overheated room, next to the room where their wedding ceremony was held. Their reception did not include the usual fanfare: toasts, gifts, cake-cutting, stuffing fat sugary slices into the other's gape. But it did have its share of memorable moments, which Jo demanded to hear on repeat. As the party was dwindling down, Henry, his fly unzipped, drunk, stuck up his thumb to announce to those gathered that he and Sylvia were off to the Motel 6 to fuck.

"What a treat for our mother," Joanne said ominously.

"Motel 6 was downright disgusting," I concurred. "Even in the early-seventies, when young Americans were taking their clothes off at the drop of a hat."

"Not to mention that that Motel 6 was notorious for gang rapes, and high school athletes' hazing rituals," Jo said reflexively.

Right. Yes, thank you, Joanne, for that. She never missed a beat. I remember asking my sister to please refrain from going into further hazing ritual details, and her flatly ignoring me. Instead, she entered a state of baser psychic rage and said: "All those fuckwads do is fondle, lounge around, get wasted, and feel their life potential is being underrated and stolen out from under them by other less talented, less deserving people."

It wasn't that I couldn't follow her thinking, I did. I followed the thread, but there was no letting up, no peace, and before I could get a word in, she went on to explain galas existed for people to feel better about themselves. They were self-serving and gave people a reason to mingle and snack on shrimp tapas passed out by acne-prone teenagers and middle-aged volunteers dressed as penguins. Did I realize that to save the planet, non-profits had to incentivize giving?

"The rich wouldn't put out unless they got an all-expenses paid trip to Kauai. The rich got boners over potential tax write-offs.

There was no need to stick around to watch what happened when tax season arrived. Cultish shit," Jo explained the situation.

I did not want to picture rich people getting off during tax season. I told Joanne as much. Joanne told me not to worry. Those sorts had accountants, even specialized ones in different departments and everything took place offsite.

"Besides," my sister said, "the orgies and erotica in the name of saving money at the expense of others would be nowhere near the likes of us."

Meanwhile, as I pounded headache medicine, Joanne continued saying that Americans produced more "puppet people" and things like tragedy and debt. The country produced these things like it did bubble wrap and offspring, and commercials about solid abs and disposable diapers. There were the preordained kids who went off to elite universities and joined academic clubs, like entrepreneurship, business, or accounting, which had her seething. The less privileged worked at our own Culver's bagging ButterBurgers, or across the country at the busted drive-through windows at TacoTime, hunched over steaming vats of moist refried beans. In either case, serving soft, beef foods to white people on the cheap, only to later die of a bursting aorta.

"But at least Ron built his cholesterol empire on the West Coast," Jo said.

Who was Ron?

Of course, my sister had found some obscure taco dispensary we'd probably never indulge in. Ron was the CEO of Taco Time, which was on the West Coast. Apparently, he spent nights tinkering with his hot sauce recipe. Ron blended his perfected spice mix by rolling them around in a 55-gallon barrel in the parking lot. It was only later, after Ron was moderately successful, that he purchased an electric cement mixer to replace the barrel.

"About sex," Joanne declared.

Please don't. I did not want to talk about intercourse. Our parents had ruined sex. My headache had morphed into a blazing migraine and my teeth felt like they were going to pour out like a cartoon. She told me suffering was the point. Joanne said I should come to grips with my limitations, intellectual and otherwise. And then she abandoned her wheelchair—a prop which provided her access to a continuous tide of sympathy, which included the chance for triple servings at the church fish fry—to do a masterful cartwheel like the rotary shape had been custom-made for her. Her hands and feet barely touched the ground. Her long slender arms and legs the points of a perfect star.

"And drugs," Jo went on. "Let's talk about medicine."

"Let's please not," I prayed and prayed and my tits all but disappeared.

Some did the whirly preferable ones like lithium and cocaine, Joanne explained, while others sniffed glue and gas because it was what they could afford. Clean-shaven rich kids got blazed and blotto in desirable domiciles with garbage disposals, undocumented gardeners, and house cleaners they spoke Spanglish to and imposed their bodies on. Meanwhile, their parents convinced themselves their sweets were practicing their flutophones and compositional skills.

"Fuck-ups existed, even in rural Illinois, even before we were born, when people went to great lengths to say social progress was being made," Jo was adamant.

I remember breaking out in hives, a reaction to the onslaught of information. I remember telling myself "Joanne is a night owl" like a mantra, hoping she would disappear. Jo was born close to midnight, which I surmised had something to do with her sleeplessness and her deluded thought processes, which I surmised had something to do with the roof incident of 1987. Many nights in our attic space I tried to stay awake to be with her, as she rambled and attempted coherency, but it was difficult. Sometimes, for maximum waking effect, I would flip on a light and stick my dull face under it and imagine I was someone else, a pale, tall, attractive, naturally blond someone who lived in a different nightmare, but in Sweden where at least I would be in good health, and that I had a different hobby, or obsession, other than love-loathing my sister.

We were reluctantly doing the dishes and quizzing each other about the latest catastrophes. Our father had with him *The New York Times*, which had on its front-page: "Global Warming Has Begun." That summer, people watered their near-dead plants with gray water. Eleven states officially declared their counties disaster areas due to the severity of the drought. The chief weather expert at the Agriculture Department described June conditions as the worst in fifty years. "The hottest and driest summer on record," had my sister rolling her eyes, rolling them so intensely I honestly thought they would not return to the front of her face. I could not tell if this was a thing which had great potential—Jo's eyeball-less face might offer me additional ways to expand my personality repertoire.

Flames erupted. Two million acres in Alaska incinerated in a blink. Yellowstone National Park lost close to one million acres. In New York City, streets melted, mosquitos quadrupled, and the murder rate reached an all-time high. "It's a chore just to walk," a former hostage negotiator told a reporter. Hot as holy hell. Medical waste washed ashore—real waste, not like Henry who had been left on the side of the road. Beaches were being closed. The largest wildfire in the recorded history of the National Parks occurred. In Los Angeles, the 28th floor of the city's second-tallest building burst into flames. The cause was spontaneous combustion. Ducks fled in search of wetlands. Ships in the Great Lakes began carrying lighter loads to account for the drop in the water levels. Some Midwestern states banned cigarette smoking in rural areas, which Sylvia, predictable like scripture, ignored. "She will quit us, before she'll quit smoking," Jo said.

The stars were suggesting that Sylvia move to France, like she had intended all along. Smoke for the rest of her functional adult life, let her small, cute dog trundle ahead of her to poop all over Rue de

Bac. Join a theater company, and, like back in high school, get cast playing minor roles in well-attended productions. (Our mother liked pointing out that they were well-attended.) Local weather forecasters insisted ups and downs were to be expected, "Ups and downs, guys. Face it—it's life. You know how life goes." Desperate, Americans were willing to go so far as to try coaxing water from the sky, in pagan fashion. The Secretary of Agriculture recommended that citizens appeal to a higher authority. Priests were filmed sprinkling holy water onto failing crops. A farmer and Baptist minister in Alabama declared a statewide day of prayer for rain. Most of the state—a population of approximately four million people—was said to have prayed on cue. But it did not rain. A "Rain Day 1988" was declared in Kentucky. The local radio station offered mood music to help to usher the rainy weather along: "Kentucky Rain," "Raining in My Heart," and "How High's the Water, Mama?" Clifford Doebel, of Clyde, Ohio, led the effort to bring Leonard Crow Dog, fourth-generation Sioux medicine man and activist living on the Rosebud Reservation in South Dakota, to perform a rain dance in a four-day ceremonial plea for water.

"Why is it that we ask those we kill to save us?" Joanne just spit at me before answering her own question: "America."

The Plains tribes had experienced massacres, poverty, and all that comes with the disease, the decimation of their land and culture, for over a hundred years.

One hot day in June, when shade was sparse and the sky was cloudless, thousands gathered on a field between Doebel's Flowers and the Winesburg Inn on McPherson Highway. Some brought their children to see, "real Indians." Others came because big events rarely happened. One woman said the rain dance was the best thing to happen to that town of 5,500 since local son, Sherwood Anderson, wrote *Winesburg, Ohio* in 1919. People gathered to watch Crow Dog, wearing Lee jeans and a red shirt with a yellow sash, dance with seven others from his reservation inside a 350-foot circle. But before dancing, he told the crowd that "Rain Dance" was the white man's term. According to Sioux belief, the reason the area had been stricken with a drought was because Americans abused the land. Big corporations disturbed nature. He said what he said about America, careful not to take it too far, and then he did what he had come to Clyde to do. He turned like a compass, pointing his body North, East, South, and then West, directing the clouds and winds to bring rain. Attendees, many who worked for the Whirlpool Corporation located right down the road from the field where Crow Dog danced, tried singing along, raising their hands to the sky in a gesture to save themselves.

That year, the Northern Pintail Population was expected to be about 2.6 million, down from its long-term average of 5.6 million new birds each year. Henry and Sylvia were at a community meeting they had organized to discuss the dire bird situation and left my sister and I to manage, which usually meant I looked for spices to use on our dinner. I remember Joanne was into talking about "expectations," which led her to "nuclear," then to "DNA," and ultimately to "failure." The term "nuclear family" had been installed in America like the questionable electrical wiring in our house, which would fail. It was a case of the emperor's new clothes, Jo explained. The nuclear family, it turned out, was a hoax developed to sell things: prescription medication, home appliances, domestic policies. The system did not work. Jo took particular issue with the social disguises father figures were asked to wear. These were ill-conceived, constructed in bad faith, and the fit was all wrong.

"Turns out these men were regular fuckups, just like the rest of us," Jo had said, mostly referring to Henry, who spent much of the time retreating to drink someplace, someplace she could not locate. Their closeness was like an accordion—it expanded and contracted. I remember Jo was having none of it: Founding fathers, forefathers, father figures, our Father Who Art in Heaven, Hallowed be thy Name, Thy Kingdom Come.

"Where are the eyes?" Jo went apeshit and threw the salt on the floor.

"We need salt," I said, terribly disappointed and going to pick up the grains of salt.

"Picture it," she demanded, as I continued to do my best to put together a quick dinner for us.

"Picture invisible-headed ghosts bankrupt, found out, their mediocrity discovered, running for their lives, just like a stream of dispersing ants do after being discovered. Imagine these father figures fleeing in droves, trying to escape the waste trucks eager to collect them like plastic and cardboard."

Alone that night with my sister, I honestly did not know what to do with her latest "invisible-headed-father-figure" episode, or with her saturating disappointment in our father. I remember I tried to imagine George Washington riding horseback to a pressing summit with an unstable invisible head that wobbled, and that image was distracting, which prevented me from joining my sister where she was. So, instead, I imagined our father with an invisible head, holding his hooch, running for his life through the corn and soybean fields, when my sister poked me with her sharp elbow, and I spilled my cup of lemonade on my newly laundered pants. I had dreamed those pants into existence.

I handed Jo dinner—dry potatoes with a lot of pepper. We ate on the floor in front of the television. We ate peppery potatoes and listened to the television and the radio at once. Several organizations—the National Academy of Science and Resources, the National Climate Program Office, Resources for the Future and the Board of Atmospheric Sciences of the National Academy of Sciences, Climate Analysis Center, the National Climate Data Center, Regional Climate Centers, the Atmospheric Environmental Service—had completed their official report about the situation on planet Earth. There was no scientific evidence pointing to a direct link between the drought and global warming, but the report acknowledged that should such catastrophes become more frequent or more severe, the 1988 drought should be the subject of study.

"Who are these people?"

Jo itched her butt and rubbed her nasty fingers all over my new pants. I had just gotten them; a gift from Cherri Cohen for being the youngest daughter, just like she was, and Jo and I very rarely got anything new, as in items nobody had ever owned before.

SHAPES: CIRCLES, BIRDS, POTENTIAL ITINERARIES

The debt collectors had returned; a dark cloud came over our house. Our family had nothing to give them. Sylvia offered them coffee regardless. The men left their dishes and said they would be back. Henry scratched his head. Our parents were ashamed the situation had to reach an irreversible level of despair. When would the rest of the country realize we were in pain? "This dance with America," Sylvia said, "has lasted much too long."

I remember Henry and Sylvia sat us down on the couch to tell us the time had come to move on and to let go of farming. The news anchor on television, a man with a full head of hair, explained that 80,000 people had received foreclosure notices and two hundred and forty thousand family-farms were now out of business. Farming no longer had a viable future and our parents agreed that we would endeavor to respond as the birds did. We would utilize our experiences of a fluctuating climate—extreme temperatures, new illnesses, water and food shortages—to make and execute a plan.

"Capital," Sylvia said, lighting a cigarette. "Everything associated with it is a warning."

"The wealthy, they get off scot-free," Henry said. "Those at the bottom end up fighting one another for scraps"

I remember distinctly our mother putting out her cigarette midway through and saying to us: "Do not lose your center of gravity."

Sylvia said this like she was speaking at a friend's funeral where more than a hundred guests were in attendance, a gathering so large the memories and sentiments got lost. The style in which she addressed us—severe—had Joanne and me laughing our guts out. Sylvia turned away from us so aggrieved that we stopped and began offering to do all the housework.

The shape of our family's "bird plan" would require further development, but looking to the birds was a place to begin. As continual migrants, they had evolved strategies for dealing with instability. We would learn to avoid skyscrapers and become supreme masters of weather management. We would learn to skirt deftly around gale-force winds and correct our course after being blown astray. We would continue educating ourselves on aerial acrobatics—it was important to be flexible and to gain different perspectives. We would master an acrobat's flexibility to manage fear and pain while performing flawless gymnastic feats.

The conclusion that farming for our family was no longer a viable way to live rattled our parents to their core. Whatever had been attached before, like an arm in a socket, was now separating. It was nasty, agonizing, as though their skin was removing itself from their bones. That day the four of us sunk into the couch underneath the large portrait, further contemplating the end of farming; I remember my head stopped working. What might our potential new life look like? I was without an image. We would not be able to continue the way that we had been. We understood that we needed to sell, but the process of leaving the farm and the farmhouse, and eventually the area, would not happen quickly.

In the weeks following their announcement, Sylvia grew so remote that she forgot to smoke. During this time, without a clear exit strategy, without something else to turn to, Henry focused on trying to reach Sylvia. He tried to get her back, like an ex does with an ex, the one that was the love of their life. Our father realized that there was no way forward if our mother couldn't keep it together. So, from daylight to dark, this time he really tried to do better. He became active in ways that would have been helpful months before. Even still, it was difficult not to sweetly acknowledge his efforts. Even Joanne had thoughts of revising her "invisible father figure" rant.

Henry's days were spent salvaging the crops and organizing local meetings about the issues at hand, which by then had been exhausted. (Even all the oatmeal raisin cookies in the cookie jar had been depleted.) He took over Sylvia's role, writing to senators, congressmen, even Ronald Reagan, who was on his way out. In the barn next to water troughs, buckets full of seed and grain, our father carved out a place for himself to be proactive. He hung coils of warmly hued yarn from the barn's doorway: "To make it nice," he explained. He cleared hay from the cracked floorboards and put a long slab of plywood on top of six assembled buckets to be used as his planning desk. He sat at the desk he made, a recluse in the barn at night, breathing in dust, chaff, and spit in the air. He thought about exit strategies there in that stuffy space surrounded by shovels, pitchforks, and manure, listening to the cows scratch themselves against the wooden posts, and tried to make a plan for our family. Henry filled folder after folder with possibilities and potential solutions. He had reused the whiteboard we were homeschooled with, writing over past lessons he had given us on the carbon cycle. The sentence—scientists have called methane the "sleeping giant" of the climate crisis—was still decipherable. Chapters on ornithology, aerodynamics, and inertia covered the barn walls next to spider webs and rusty nails.

In the poorly insulated structure, Henry drew up plans for survival. Some of them involved scrupulous details and designs concerning different transferring vessels: aircrafts, ships, vans, and motorbikes. In private, Joanne said Henry was a hawker of ideas, a peddler with a rolodex of plans, most of them absurd and short-lived.

"When we grow older, if you know it's him on the line calling, you won't answer," she said, matter-of-factly.

I remember thinking her cruelty had no limits. At the time, I remember thinking: I will certainly answer when our father calls. At the time, I remember thinking: Lucky for us, people answered the phone when Henry called because people trusted our father. If they hadn't, we would have been screwed.

I would never escape the web that was my family.

I would never break from that group of individuals facsimiled for America.

I would never eat desirable food.

Often, our family sat around the dinner table eating gummy lentil soup which smelled like a dirty diaper. I can remember looking at my tan cup of brown soup and thinking: "Wow, that beautiful oak table is the one piece of furniture in our house that has any monetary value—made entirely of oak!—and here we are putting our bland, monochrome, sad little plates of food on top of it every day."

It was a disgrace, but I avoided outrage since I understood where that could lead an individual. When it came to family life and our home on the farm, there was nothing outside of us, of our unit. I remember shoveling stinky lentil soup into my mouth, and thinking that, like Jo, I would never give birth to a tick. I too would be spared the insult of changing a baby's soiled diaper.

Over soup, Sylvia asked Henry what he was up to in his barn-slash-office, making diagrams and such. Was our father simply backing himself into a corner? Which, as our mother liked to point out, we were already in.

"I am watching," Sylvia said, going to pick up some food that had fallen to the floor, which relaxed us—she seemed like herself again—and proceeding to smoke a cigarette down to her calloused fingertips. Her bowl of soup went untouched.

"I'm making arrangements," Henry said, a little tipsy, spooning brown goo into his mouth out of habit. "I'm looking at our options."

"If H. W. Bush can declare on Lake Erie's shores that he's an environmentalist, then I don't see how or why I shouldn't smoke," Joanne said, lighting a cigarette of her own.

Jo's brain, and what she decided to "articulate," loudly, was her greatest asset and her greatest liability. I remember watching our mother's face falling into her untouched cup of lentils and our father doing his best not to give in and hit something or someone. Everyone at that table usually had a lot to contribute about shape-shifting realities, especially while eating soup that smelled like dirty diapers, but at that moment we remained silent. I remember at the library in town browsing a copy of the *Los Angeles Times Magazine* (and being told the newspaper wasn't for me), which had an article in it that predicted what the future family in the metropolis would look like in 2013. The Morrows were thrust twenty-five years into the future and had installed a Smart House wiring system—a single switch in the house that turned everything—the coffee maker, oven for the cinnamon rolls, water heater, their personalized home newspaper highlighting the subjects that interest them—on while they slept soundly. By that time in 2013, mobile robots—in programmed shapes like dogs or maids—would be the ultimate appliances, a household fixture like a quality stereo system or a good set of parents. Their robot was called Billy Rae and he would wake the family up each morning in his light Southern drawl: "Hey, y'all, rise an' shine." Father, husband, caretaker to his ailing mother, Bill Morrow (senior executive of a multinational company) would hold 3-D tele-conferences with business partners in Tokyo, but not before using Denturinse to brush his teeth because he was in a hurry to get to the office on those days when he went in.

I swallowed dirty diaper lentils—I was that hungry—and thought about 3-D teleconferences and looking out of our kitchen window at the wind pushing our underwear and socks on the clothesline, small bits of cloth waving like one of those Tibetan prayer flags. Henry said I would be going with him to the grocery store. I did not want to go back to the store. America was dizzy. The grocery store was a storage unit for psychos. The crisis was causing major chaos and delays in checkout lines. Even at that age, I knew a lack of resources could start wars. I knew who was at fault. A single sheet of ice was a time machine. Ice sheets kept track of the time and the information, which was probably why America wanted them to melt.

I ate lukewarm soup in a small tan cup and watched my family fall apart, over and over. Then Joanne came beside me at the table and pressed her prickly, fresh, erect boobs into my boobless chest. After that, she doubled down on her fury by hurling her tan cup of brown soup across the room. It dripped down the walls. It was all over the valuable oak table. (I had not known that much soup could fit inside of that small tan cup.) Once again, my sister showed up with her truth. Jesus, Joanne. She was inevitable. A thorn on a rose, I thought.

"People are animals, animals kill animals, and therefore all persons are killers," Jo said, as if there wasn't now a dirty lentil mess on the only valuable piece of furniture we owned.

Joanne said what she said, and my thoughts turned to melting glaciers, and how those melting glaciers, which contained millennia of information, crushed baby harp seals. I knew who was responsible for so much suffering in our house and in the larger world. But the more I tried to avoid my careful disdain for America, the more it spread in me like a conspiracy theory. My limbs ached with revulsion. Even at that age, I knew it wasn't a healthy lifestyle choice for me or for the atmosphere. The shame of being a Fareown woman could sit inside of the body for thousands and thousands of years, like accumulated carbon was stored in permafrost—frozen in suspended animation for millennia—until, eventually, the process ran in reverse and the organic material released. That was what substances did: they released.

Looking back, there were many times where the truth of our destructive lineage, our fate, was stifling. But it was also sustaining in ways that were hard to adequately explain. And this connection—that many outside of the region deemed insufferably provincial and sentimental and which was difficult to articulate—often made our family, and others in our community, extraordinarily self-conscious.

What I can say, many years later in the privacy of my Super 8 motel room, was that when you're alienated, surrounded by unpopulated space, you were drawn to the ideas and stories that situate you. The land of our childhood was more than a commodity, it was our nature, such as it was, for better or worse.

That year our family decided not to sell the land or the farmhouse. Instead, the plan was that we would look to find renters for both. This arrangement would allow us to keep our link to the area alive for another year or so. It would mean we could retain this idea of a bloodline and remain near enough to the family cemetery, and to those female relatives whose bodies were found and bones were buried behind the house.

1989

It was easy enough to rent the farmland if a family was willing to rent to a larger farming operation, which we were, and did, albeit reluctantly. We sold off most of our equipment and the cattle, which went some way toward paying back the FHA loan, and our parents invested what was left in a fund located in the Cayman Islands, a compelling destination where no one we knew had ever been. With the income we received from our land renters, we had enough to put down a deposit on a two-bedroom house in town, not too dissimilar from the one Sylvia had lived in with her mother during high school. The house in town was ready for us and we were in no hurry to leave the farmhouse. But we were being hounded by a couple from the West Coast.

Our renters for the farmhouse were an eager couple from as far away as Sacramento, California. They were interested in agriculture. That's what they'd said over the telephone about renting and living in our farmhouse. They said they didn't even want to see the place in person. They didn't need to: People in the Midwest were not like people in California.

"Midwesterners have souls. They are the soul of America," the couple said over the phone.

Our father said something about minutes passing and long-distance calls and went to the bathroom. Our mother hung up the phone. But the couple called back immediately, which they had done consistently.

The couple agreed to fly out from Sacramento to see the place first. I remember when they came to visit the farm. They sat in our living room like misplaced items and said they desired a quant, quieter, pastoral life, and they intended to have children to share this simpler life with. Both the man and the woman had studied climatology at the University of Santa Barbara, and appeared to have quite a bit of disposable income by the look of their clothes (made of linen), and the two automobiles (BMWs) that they drove. Joanne asked them what they had against carpooling. For this educated couple, the choice to live on a farm was an obvious one: "Nobody over there, on that coast, wants to have a real conversation about fire."

Sylvia mentioned the harsh winters and that the toilet had issues. "One toilet for all of you?" the couple asked our parents, doing a mediocre job at hiding their shock. Not to mention the plumbing should probably be replaced. Our father talked about the town's psyche in general and about the heavy toll the crisis had taken on the region, but the couple was certain it was what they wanted. It was perfect and authentic. In fact, it had been a massive dream of theirs from the start. ("The start of what?" Jo was desperate to know but after her last comment she knew she was already in trouble.) Let's just say our parents' minds were blown by the situation. Our minds were blown. By that time, many we knew had left the land for good. I can recall that there weren't enough kids available to play a game of football. And those that had remained, to continue farming in our community the way they had done for decades, lost nearly everything. The decision to sell off what you had to get next to nothing was no consolation. Even after emptying out, many could not pay back the bank.

Other important things about that time: the county fair was fast approaching, and Henry had found a new career as an auctioneer. Combined with Sylvia's secretarial job, the money they made provided enough income for us to continue chipping away at our debt. The additional money also meant that our parents could begin to save for Joanne's custom back brace, which would be costly, but there was a chance it could stop her curvature from progressing. (When Joanne eventually had one fitted and made, she would be in agony wearing the rigid, corseted contraption constructed from metal and heavy plastics. She would have to wear it for twenty-two hours a day, taking it off to shower if she'd wanted, which she didn't, doubling down on some point that I never grasped. The back brace Jo wore all day, every day, for four years did stop her curvature from crushing her lungs. But it did not make her popular.)

The money also meant we could look forward to the county fair, which was a big spending ordeal.

That year's fair was colossal and the food options were plentiful. I remember feeling overwhelmed by its growth spurt and feeling grateful that the line for "black cows"—an ice cream float, black for its use of root beer as opposed to cola—was only ten minutes long. The fair's theme was "Give Us a Whirl," a theme which had my sister squatting to take a piss at the entrance while our mother restrained our father as onlookers speedily walked by. (Jo made so many enemies.) I remember the fairgrounds had spread out, covering over a hundred-acres. There were maps for the parking lots. And on a cloudless Illinois day in July, the treasurer of our local Chamber of Commerce, also a teller at Blackhawk Bank & Trust, was tasked with cutting the blue ribbon across the main gate. The devastating spectacle worth taking in was America.

That year at the fair, there were many splashy reveals, but the one which stood out was my sister's black eye, which she gave herself so that she could legitimately wear an eye patch over her healthy one. That, and the portrait booth's backdrop. The thirty-foot tall backdrop depicted a snorkeler flailing in the Caribbean Sea. On the upper left-hand side, a massive Christopher Columbus observed the thrashing snorkeler with a twinkling eye. "The Columbus Affair," as it came to be known in our family, was an enormous success. The best yet.

To be an auctioneer in the Midwest at that time was a tricky proposition; a balancing act, which required the ability to behave like an enemy yet to act like a friend. There was nothing about the role, nefarious to my mind, that could be extracted from a person's own interest. An auctioneer could sell off in four hours what it took some farm families nearly fifty years to generate. Henry was good at being an auctioneer. But in private, he struggled to settle into the position. Our father said he felt like one of those commercials when a child actor is identified as a "real child" and "not an actor."

"Nothing about this makes sense," Henry said, "but I like money. It's helpful."

Sylvia refused to participate.

"Auctions are hideous," she said about the situation they had found themselves in. She wanted no part of it. This only served to make her more attractive to our father, which seemed implausible.

During this period, Sylvia was sick of being sick. She began looking to repurpose discarded materials that were potentially useful, was how I thought of it. Or to make use of things that were a complete and total fucking waste, was how Joanne saw it. Sylvia sipped at a glass of Alka-Seltzer like a bird when she should have simply downed it in one chug, smoked and repurposed questionable items that she found. Sometimes, I went along with our mother to rummage through dumpsters, clipping the locked ones first for the "good stuff." Who was I to judge?

Once, when our mother was busy breaking the law, when she wasn't monitoring me, I snagged a puppy from a cardboard box in front of Blain's Farm & Fleet without paying what the box demanded be paid. I named my small, weepy animal, Tall. I remember stowing him underneath my sweatshirt and feeling like a convict in the best way as Sylvia drove the truck furiously, totally elated—holding a cigarette out the Chevy's window like a weapon—way over the speed limit. She was oblivious as the C20 Longhorn sped along. She was in a fantastic mood, having pulled out an unopened box of imported rotini, a pair of sharp scissors, and a few slabs of walnut wood from the dumpster.

"Fuck, I'm a sucker for walnut," Sylvia said, thrilled, cussing freely, drawing on her cigarette, smoke coming out of her nostrils like a better-than-average dude about to engage in a bar fight.

"I can orgasm over the sight of walnut."

"Ok," I said.

"I don't know what happened to the man otherwise known as your father, Bernie."

I remember I did not like her using the word "orgasm."

During this time—the period when our mother was a criminal—she sifted through dumpsters to collect trash. Sylvia had become more flexible in nature. In general, she was looser in terms of the rules and familial protocol she so often installed in us like an alarm. It was as if she had resigned from her post and duties as "our mother," and had become more like that notorious aunt that does illegal drugs with you. The sort of aunt you hear stories about, positive stories involving getting away with stuff you ordinary got caught doing. The aunt that gives you your first line of tequila shots on a man's torso. The aunt that sneaks you wads of cash. The aunt that supports all your hazardous ideas. Sylvia's new flexible disposition meant my actions went undetected. Of course, I welcomed this shift, but I was also aware there was a chance that without anyone watching, I might swim further away from shore. The waters so fresh on my hot ugly face that I would forget to assess my surroundings and end up too far out to ask for help.

1989 was the last year we spent in the farmhouse, which was to say—it was the year we moved out completely for the couple and settled fully into the house in town where we would stay for twelve months, to start.

In '89 eleven million gallons of oil dumped in Prudhoe Bay. It was the fourteenth straight year the gap between home prices and income had widened. This was also when Joanne's body enacted a kind violence on itself. Her spine was angling to smash her lungs.

If left untreated, there was the potential she would end up twisted like a pretzel. The stars were suggesting it was a good time to move, and Sylvia's astrological forecast indicated the remaining months of '89 should be full of energetic fun. On television, Germans with hammers, picks, cranes, and bulldozers were taking down the Berlin Wall, in what was referred to as the greatest street party in the history of the world. I tried eating a tuna fish sandwich I made flavorful by adding pickles and bacon fat. Scientists across Europe concluded some hormones to be complete carcinogens that caused cancer and banned animal meat given hormones. A group of international policymakers landed in the resort town of Noordwyk, to sit in a conference room and decide whether to endorse a framework for a global treaty on stabilizing emissions. Emerging hours later to announce that America, together with the Soviet Union, would forgo any commitment to curbing greenhouse gas emissions.

Perception was an ongoing theme as Joanne's body continued to turn on itself. Jo's body was morphing into a pretzel, we filled and packed boxes, and talked about perception. Perception could be used as a weapon to alienate. Philosopher Ludwig Wittgenstein's illustration, at once of a duck and a rabbit, proved that what you saw was entirely dependent on what you were being told to see.

"Where are the eyes?" It was just as Jo asked.

I remember wondering why mankind worked so hard to deceive itself. It seemed to me the more "real" the illusion, the more desperate people wanted in. Like the duel in the late 5th century between painters Zeuxis against Parrhasios, to see who could best represent the illusion of reality, which even at that time (the end of 1989) seemed to sum up my existence. Zeuxis painted deliciously supple grapes, so real the birds came to feast upon them. Parrhasius painted a simple bland curtain and Zeuxis demanded he immediately draw it aside to reveal his painting. Zeuxis had deceived the birds with his grapes, but with his unadorned curtain Parrhasius had deceived man.

Five years before Wittgenstein's illustration was published, the realist painter Andrew Wyeth would produce one of his best-known paintings, "Christina's World," depicting a woman on the ground in an open field. I have often wondered what Christina Olsen—the central figure seen from behind in the painting—would have thought about being described as "awkward on her spindly arms," as critics often did. As a child, Christina contracted a disease, paralyzing her from the waist down. She refused to use a wheelchair. Instead, she used the strength of her arms to propel her body. How might she see herself in relation to these descriptions? It was a question that resonated when I considered my sister, my mother, and the women in my family. And much later, while in college, these unresolved feelings calcified. I had stumbled across an article where the realist, Wyeth, a man who had painted Christina many times—a man who asked to be buried in the cemetery on her property—went on to say that she had made little impression on him. This was troubling. And no matter how hard I tried, I could not reconcile the parts: what did Wyeth mean by this dismissal? Why did he say it about Christina Olsen? Nothing about affection or love or time would be reconciled for me.

2009

In my Super 8 room, I remember how Jo and I would hitch rides to check in on the farmhouse. We would sit in it, empty, before the educated couple from California filled it with their belongings. The emptied house seemed to hold its breath, like a space waiting to see if someone would make good on their promises. How would the new tenants fill the house with their personal detritus? Where would they put their supplies? Jo looked around and said our house was like an emptied bladder. Joanne pulled out her eyelashes and said they were covered in microscopic face mites. Waving the black slivers in front of me: "A face mite, like this one here, doesn't have an anus. So, its poop accumulates in its body until it dies and decomposes on your face," she said, her eyes bulging like a feign.

In the privacy of my own mind, I began to wonder which figure Joanne was: was she the sorceress or the heretic? The sorceress was the bearer of the past, power-challenger, attempting to connect frayed ends of culture—the aspects of demise that were hard to endure. She cured afflictions, healed, resisted the church, moved in the direction of animality, plants, and the inhuman. It was a life that ended in confinement and death—would that be Joanne's life? On the other hand, the heretic untied familiar bonds, introduced, and exposed the disorder of everyday life. She disrupted the status quo, a riddled disrupter. She was gaslighted, a prisoner in the family, a modern scapegoat for miscarriages, addiction, and general indecency, a medical spectacle to poke, prod, and to fix. Cure her for humanity's sake. Put her behind grim bars and white walls. Dress her up in glitter and pastels; have her dance on slick poles in dingy rooms that smelled of waste. A life that ends in despair. Either way, I was condemned to living an immortal life with Joanne.

I can remember that distant was how I felt each time we said goodbye to the farmhouse and to the dead women we would be buried next to on the land. At the time, I thought about people turning people on, people turning on themselves, bodies turning themselves in, and my sister, who was trouble, and our parents, who had taught us everything, including how not to end up like them. Ten years went by in that one-bedroom house, living mostly in isolation, feeling empty. The first part of our lives were spent cold in our shared attic space, planning our eventual escape from bland food and a collapsing economy. And like the weeds that grew unapologetically, biding their time before Roundup would kill them, we waited to lose everything. Only later did I come to see those early years as junk kids living on the farm as romantic. Jo saw them as macabre. Looking back now, from the vantage point of the unsteady desk in my Super 8 room outside of Minneapolis, lopsidedly sifting through our family history, taping together these scraps of my memory, I see that the two of us were reaching for something inside of us to save us or to kill us, using our hands to claw at the earth's surface even from our graves in the cemetery out back in which we would one day inevitably rot.

"Or more likely perish in a cheap motel room smelling of lubricant," Joanne chided.

There she was again, my sister, in my ear. Jo, a bonafide volatile motherfucker stuck like a pop song in my head as I did laundry in the sink, and mourned, not only the loss of Joanne, but the loss of glaciers—their melting—and with them, their memories disappearing.

But still, my sister was hell-bent on having a child to suffer all to herself.

CHICAGO

1990

A single driving force: I would get into a well-regarded university if it killed me. One word: Hello. I had befriended a man in his mid-forties with a sizable shed a few houses down the street from our apartment in Chicago. I could see his house from our bedroom window. I called him "Hello," since in the beginning that was all he would say to me when he found me lurking around in his backyard, except it was more like "Hell," the "oh" was like an afterthought. Hello was a sexy man who agreed to let me temporarily store supplies in his shed and pick his brain about life at sea. At the time, I had gone back to exploring oceanic life to reinvigorate the spirit between Jo and I, which was long gone, but the focus remained on leaving the Midwest. Understand, I had to do something with myself.

Before becoming a finance guy, Hello was a loutish boatman. And to get my boat project moving along, I needed support. Building a sailboat from scratch was not in the cards and Hello knew things I did not, like Michel Foucault's *Madness and Civilization*, which solidified our bond. He could recite, and did so without prompting, the passage that read, "Navigation delivers man to the uncertainty of fate; on water, each of us is in the hands of his own destiny; every embarkation is, potentially, the last. It is for the other world the madman sets sail in his fools' boat; it is from the other world that he comes when he disembarks." He especially liked to emphasize that final sentence. An early clue he was more than simply an interesting older man.

To master a life at sea, which was to say to take control of my life, it was important to first grasp some basic aquatic skills (at that point, nil), like becoming a skilled swimmer with an exceptionally agile mind, which would require spending countless hours in the university library, where I would take up temporary residence in order to prepare to receive topnotch scores (as they say in England), and to get out of the Midwest as quickly as the region had ever been shunned. Eventually, I would be able to save myself. And if I made Joanne jealous at the same time, then it was a bonus track.

Hello and I agreed I would need to save for a fixer upper and master the complex language of sailboats, which were "like mini cities in terms of systems," he explained. There were thousands of components to consider: the rigging, the sails, and the mechanics of the motor. Since this project was primarily up to me, I would need to clock as many hours as I could at Video Creature, who paid a shit wage but had hired me despite my lack of experience in the "film world," which I would spend the bulk of my time trying to rectify. As it was, I worked a lot, checking movies into the system, talking customers into renting some of the art-house films, which turned most into unhappy customers, and making sure babies (all children were babies as far as I was concerned) didn't wander behind the long plush brown velvet curtain into the sex lair. That was where men gathered like in a steam room, going back and forth between renting *Cumback Pussy Sixxx* or *Spartacus MMXII (The Beginning)*, about a captured Spartacus being thrust into a world of sex and violence, forced to perform in depraved orgies, and fight against the giant Androcles.

It was complicated. At the time, I was not old enough to check these "films" out to people, but did it anyway. I would stay an employee for years.

Hello talked to me about how to pitch to investors. Even though I was on my way to being a freshman in high school, and understood that this was laughable, I very much liked the idea of having investors. I also approved of this older man feigning a kind of faith in my potential. Regardless: the goal was to buy a fixer to become a roaming water eyeball. Hello said life at sea would involve enduring scrutinizing circumstances. We would need to prepare for the passing of time to be catastrophically monotonous, the millions of repetitions occurring daily, and physical suffering, which sailors' thought of as self-determination.

"*We'd* need to prepare?" this was a detail I would not let slip away.

Heat and humidity blistered armpits and groins. Eyes exploded with conjunctivitis. Fingernails and toenails peeled off. Clothing permeated with salt and refused to dry. The smells, abhorrent. Hello said nobody ever knows how much weather they can handle until put to the test.

"Is that why you gave it up?"

"I lost part of my sight."

I was happy then. It's hard to explain how a single word like happy goes from a place of futility to taking over your head like a fever. Between getting into college and the prospect of my future life at sea, there was living that happened during middle school. There was a lot of thinking then about high school as a mandatory katabasis, or trip to the realm of the dead, in order to get to life in a university. But I should not overlook our move, or the period that came before Hello announced himself, which was how I imagined it happened— that he announced himself—when really I had been spying.

My twelve-year-old-self was being developed like a roll of found film, and Chicago had exposed me to alternate notions of "progress." Mostly, surrounding ideas of what it meant to be female, and independence in general. In the city, social exchanges were not about doing chores in order to then be served (bland) food; they were closer to giving head in exchange for a mixtape. The stakes were different in Chicago. They were different in school, in urban America, and expanding with the people I was meeting near Lake Michigan. In middle school I was a cheat, which was not why I didn't have friends. I could only surmise that the reasons for that had to do with the fact that, for starters, I was ugly; I ran for student council and spoke about Chicago's transformation of water in order to support the human enterprise (a catastrophe, for the most part), which was unambiguously snubbed since students loved the objects they loved and were freezing in the gale-force winds. It didn't help that I ignored the fact that I had no middle school friends and that I was a loner that just blithely walked around. (Nobody liked to be ignored under any circumstance.) I was a student who, almost reflexively, copied the (often incorrect) answers of my peers seated next to me. Even when I knew the answers. I didn't believe in my ability to get it right; getting it "right" filled me with despair. (When nurses asked me to provide the date that I was born, I often unintentionally gave the wrong date.) I spent a lot of time wandering the city, befriending people my parents would not have liked me talking to, sitting on a freezing bench in front of Lake Michigan, feeling like my hands had not come with fingers, and my wrists were without forearms. That was how I learned to handle the cold as a twelve-year-old in Chicago. I made adult conversation that did not include the subject of Joanne in front of the water with my bench friends, who, unlike those in school, regarded me as a purple-faced (I was cold), sexual intellectual with a solidly bright future. It was a time of plummeting temperatures, self-doubt, saying the wrong things in public, and reading *Moby Dick*. I would carry with me photocopies of "Loomings," the first chapter which I read and re-read. Melville must have known the limitations of the human-animal spectacle, like a palm reader read the palms of the desperate, including our mother's. And if "theory" meant what the Greek root "theoria" meant—a spectacle, a viewing—then visiting was not theoretical. Firsthand experience was the difference between having the rationale that honey was sweet, and tasting the sensation of its sweetness. On the bench in front of Lake Michigan, humanity was the subject of our conversations, and how most of humanity had desperation in common. I remember it was too cold in front of the water for anyone walking or jogging by to stop to ask you for the time. Therefore, you could go anywhere. In 1898, Lake Michigan was described as "a stupendous piece of blasphemy against nature." The explorer Louis Joliet, a French Jesuit missionary who "discovered" Chicago, had to carry his canoes overland in Wisconsin, much like the absurd explorers did in the movie *Fitzcarraldo*, who carry their ship over a mountain to fulfill a quixotic wish to build an opera house in a Peruvian jungle. Joliet considered Chicago's swampy waterways to be the gateway into the soul of America.

The '90s shifted everything. The stakes were different in the '90s. Our move in 1990 coincided with the warmest year on record. This new beginning, of our living in the city, gave our mother migraines. She would see bits of well-lit cotton floating all over the place, which we thought was hysterical. At the same time, there was a rise in the so-called "citizens' militias," as NASA gave money to SETI to search for extraterrestrial intelligence. Other early events: Internet, Globalization. The phrase "collateral damage" became exceedingly frequent, a result of our ongoing moral wars with other nations committed to illiberal beliefs that brought sexism, racism, religious, and political persecution. The time had arrived to come around to Eggos, Barbie, and liberal capitalist democracy. It was time for nations to be free like America was free. "Faux" was a popular word at the time. There was even a plagiarism suit between two faux Elvises that resulted in the defendant singing "Burning Love" in the courtroom. Other popular events: boombox, date rape. Eco-safe. E-mail. Glass ceiling. Lake effect. The informal noun "white bread" emerged to address the values of affluent white Americans.

School in the city was not the same as being home-schooled on a farm where dead ends were assured. And for a time, I thought about the rural Midwest like a thought bubble that could be deleted. I considered what that shape—of a person with high standards—might take elsewhere in America: what shape did a quality person take in another city, like Boston or Detroit? (I wasn't set up for a place like New York City.) I wanted that sub-coveted, sophisticated, desirable, well-adjusted (also cold) urban shape of a person who could not only put together a mixtape, but a memorable one. I began this process of personal development, that I had convinced myself would lead me someplace, with what was closest to me and with what I had some control over: our shared bedroom. Though by then Jo was an optical aberration.

The walls of our Chicago bedroom were covered in this unfortunate yellow wallpaper that conjured Charlotte Perkins Gilman's "The Yellow Wallpaper." In it, the woman's husband is a physician that hopes to make her well again, but instead he drives her insane by locking her in a yellow-papered room. (Though, why anyone believed anyone was well in the first place, especially in America, boggled my mind.) Jo, self-aware, noted that the wallpaper would only exacerbate matters. She implored our parents to buy some paint to deal with the walls, but her request became one in a thousand that nobody would have time to address. A few months later, Jo would do what the woman in the short story does—she peeled the yellow wallpaper off with her hands.

To start, I took old pieces of tape the previous tenants had left on the walls to repurpose. I found tape in the oddest of places. I ripped off Joanne's pictures of dead folk singers and replaced them with my own pictures of dead people, like our great-grandmother Poppy and other dead female relatives that had gone insane. I put up pages torn from *The Economist* on hydrothermal cooling to give the room some dimension. I picked leaves, and—if available—flowers from nearby yards to brighten the room, to put in discarded cups, often from 7-Eleven, and plastic water bottles, to help reduce America's litter problem. America had a litter problem, which I had known about for years thanks to our father, but also thanks to Philip Morris, who had in the '70s devised a plan to keep the country great. When we were junk kids Jo and I used to watch the "Crying Indian" ads (starring an Italian American actor) at the library in town on Betamax. I remember the Indian cried because he kept running into litter, even while chilling in his authentic canoe hobbling along the still waters of man-made lagoons—in nature.

OUR APARTMENT

"Home" was a two-bedroom apartment in a neighborhood known in our family as "Near Lake View," which was a fancy part of the city, and since that was how Henry described the location to his clients. "Real-estate was all in the labeling," our father explained, even though we did not give a shit. But he had repeated it enough times that eventually it sunk in.

The truth was we lived north of Lake View, on Chicago's North Side, on the cusp of Ravenswood, a neighborhood built on farmland and once known for having ravens. The apartment was in the mid-thousand block of West Argyle, near the Catholic cemetery of all places. The brick building was nothing special, though attractive, well-maintained, and stood uniformly with the other classic brick apartment buildings lining the street, a few houses sprinkled in between. One of which belonged to my older friend, Hello. There were trees, other kids that I would never befriend, and patches of grass for dogs to piss on. The place came with a ceiling fan. It was pet-friendly, and cable-ready. Other apartment amenities included "efficient appliances," a dishwasher, plenty of natural light, coin-operated laundry in the basement, and hardwood floors throughout, an inflexible deal-breaker. Sylvia demanded our new home have hardwood floors.

The space was bigger than anywhere we could have imagined living. The kitchen was large enough I could put a Slip 'N Slide down when the weather improved. When the time was right. It was all about finding the right time, especially at the beginning of a new decade, especially when 1992 would be the year of the woman and it was only two years away! At the time, in middle school, my classmates were calling me Little Schizophrenic Mole, which was not entirely inaccurate. But more importantly, this term of endearment was way more acceptable than what kids called Joanne: "Total Complete Psycho Bitch," which she relished like soft serve. (And as far as we could tell, our maternal "Legend," such as it were, had not contaminated the city. Even if it had, urbanites were much too busy to care.)

There were other phrases that surged in popularity: "crack baby," "politically correct," and "attack politics." "Negative campaigning"— a tactic that focused on an opponent's "character," instead of their political positions—had become commonplace. This, too, gave Sylvia migraines. My first migraine came one day as I passed by Planned Parenthood on my way home from school. I remember there were around a dozen agitated, self-assured protesters outside waving "save the fetus" signs, or "God is great and good," like it was that simple. I remember thinking: nothing will save a fetus. Not even the trees, with all the positivity they provide. Institutions swallow fetuses, I thought passing them by like waving a middle finger at a cop's back. Then, as fate would have it, the cops were called.

I was caught in 8th grade for cheating. I admitted to it. I wasn't a liar, which Joanne pointed out made me a liar. The school's principal, and the cops he had called in to ensure obedience, called me a liar and a cheat. They mandated I get a psychiatric evaluation.

"But I admitted to it," I protested.

"Precisely," they said.

I sensed my dead grandmother become chillier on the gurney, which was impossible since by the time she had made it to the gurney she was already dead. Our grandmother's body was etched into my body like an engraving. I felt the entirety of my maternal line marking my insides like a map I didn't want to follow. Such was the value of truth (valueless), which I came to see rarely worked out for the women in my family, perhaps women in general.

That day, my 8th grade teacher, Mr. Steiner came to my defense. I was told to leave the office as the men deliberated. After, Mr. Steiner told me he had grown up in a mortuary, and while I may have had ideas about death—there were plenty others. He wanted me to stop cheating, and I became hooked on his growing up in a mortuary. Walking the empty halls, seeing me out of the school, Mr. Steiner—a weirdly attractive man, in that his anatomy did not come together in the way you would expect—and I came to an agreement: I would interview him for extra credit about growing up in a mortuary and write a profile: "Is Death Dogmatic?" That was the piece that got me to my middle school graduation.

The point was getting somewhere. The point was college.

I made it to high school, which got me closer to attending university and closer to my future independent urban shape. And by freshman year, I had stopped quibbling about the small stuff and started to think about what might make me stand out amid a sea of college applicants. By then, I had embraced my nickname "Little Schizoid Mole." Once I accepted "Little Schizoid Mole," I gained momentum as a mole. It did not matter in which direction. I advanced, and at a rate even Sylvia was proud of. There was the thinker Walter Benjamin, who I welcomed into my psyche. I wrote out at least one-hundred times the words: "What for others are deviations, for me are the data which determine my course." And there was Paul, another student at my high school that had come upon me like a cataract, blurring my general loathing of dudes. He had taken an interest in my thoughts. He had a photographic memory and was fine being seen with me in public, unlike my collaborator Hello, who was into being private. Paul would stick around for my entire high school life and beyond, but none of this newfound positivity would change the fact that I had amassed a posse of girl-haters in high school. (Funny, in the beginning I was envious of their school styles, family lives, and of their movements, especially, which were fluid like famous people.) For an entire semester, the girl-haters had confused me—in their words—for a hot guy.

"These are tits," I said eventually, after I had caught on to the mix-up, lifting my shirt to break it to them, revealing my small (ridiculously small), but functional tits, nonetheless.

The scene was not pretty. The attractive girls with name-brand clothing, who were ordinarily cool, became red and infuriated. They were disgusted that I would "show myself, in public of all places." The truth of which had them fuming, and insisting tits were not "tits," but more appropriately "female breasts." Honestly, I remember thinking: Haven't we been showing ourselves in public school for almost a year? I remember hoping they would simply take my tits, my little "stowaways" on vacation, but instead they paid some hefty guys at our high school in cash to beat the shit out of me.

That Christmas Eve I came home to our apartment to find a festively decorated gift box outside the front door with a dead mangled cat stuffed inside. Thinking about all the ways I might use the word "tarn" in future sentences did not help.

I asked: "Can we move?"

To which Jo said: "Bernie, we have no place else to go."

I recognized even January 1st wouldn't be able to expunge the dark feeling. There was no escaping being substandard. I promptly threw away any indication of Christmas spirit; I didn't see the need for further disappointment. Everything went—including our desperate, slender black stockings that our parents insisted on hanging up every year, even though, indubitably, they were the wrong color. Once again, they dangled in front of us, underlining the ridiculousness of the capitalist holiday, which neither Jo or I had memories of celebrating. It was important to note that our parents "stuffed" these black socks each holiday with one or two Granny Smith apples, the absolute worst fruit. It was important to note that the stockings' inadequacy had nothing to do with our getting bigger or growing more mature. They were limp and pitiful, even by a child's standards. Our parents never understood the holiday, or any holiday for that matter. The concept of excess totally escaped them. It was as though they had learned nothing.

The building of the boat was magical thinking—even by the time I got to high school I knew this—but I also knew there were many writers who had sold books comprised of that sort of whimsical, fictive thinking and that those narratives had the potential to transform nobodies into somebodies, and somebodies had access to quality health professionals. This was an opportune moment for me to return to the material of my roots. Return to the dead women on our land, buried in our backyard, in our family cemetery, in that place Jo and I called "the mound." It was time to revisit those fierce, castrating daughters, sisters, mothers, and grandmothers who were lulled by the sea—because the sea could not be tamed.

During the Renaissance, the mad-stricken were given to mariners because folly and sea belonged together. These "Ships of Fools" meandered the waters with their cargo of squandered souls. Herman Melville must have known the limitations of the human-animal like a palm reader read the palms of the desperate. Seascapes, like landscapes, lacked an adequate vocabulary with which to describe complexity. Many of the women in our family had a cursed need to seek out the words to attach to the sensations because a landscape that lacked a vocabulary could not be seen or visited. How could that invisibility be anything other than personal? For example, in 1934, "sea-green" was a place defined as "land overflowed by the sea in spring tides." Overtime, the word's meaning would be reduced to a kind of limited, muted color. Then the greenhouse effect would prove to be true, ocean levels would rise, and politicians, engineers, biologists, developers, and others would not be able to help but look to the mere color "sea-green" for guidance on what was to come.

There were other coincidences to consider, such as my (not entirely) distant college eligibility, and the day I would turn twenty-one. Those turning points in a life, any life, were notably big package deals. When I wasn't playing by the rules, I went back to fictionalizing: filling a calendar in the future with dates, like turning twenty-one in 1999, and not-to-miss appointments, like weekly sessions with a psychoanalyst, who happened to be a former male model. My figure, however slow-to-change, deserved to be explored. I channeled my increasing sexual appetite into something that didn't feel like a dead-end—like exploring my body—but a propelling force. In terms of sex, there were several avenues to explore. There was Hello, however tentative. There was inoffensive Paul—truly sweet, lean, with a full head of hair—who tried, but was unable to grow hair on his face like his best friend Preston, who dreamed of fame and planned to die young, and was as hairy as he was far away in Hoboken, New Jersey. It was not a question of whether I liked Paul. At the time, my desire for sex stemmed from the fact that Paul consistently knew what he wanted (me), even if that exact feeling was not reciprocated and his clarity was compelling.

The point was you could rent fantasies like a custom Harley, like men rented wives in Japan and breezy domiciles in warmer, sunnier environments. In the meantime, the process of filling out the future calendar enabled my psychic moods, which I let roam unfettered. One day I would sit down to eat a real, quality Thanksgiving, where guests ate so much, they puked and it smelled good. And Paul's family would think I was "the one," for him. One of a kind Bernadette—me, a sublime, suitable match for their upstanding son, Paul, who was trusty and smart enough to know he would never be a conceptual artist like his best friend Preston in Hoboken, who would by then have a slice of pizza tattooed on the roof of his mouth. Bright, well-behaved, Bernadette coming into her own, genuinely decent to their quality son. My family would take whatever they could get. In 1999, I would turn twenty-one and be in control. I wouldn't be friend-less and a virgin.

I had decided, arbitrarily, that my twenty-first birthday party in 1999 would mean I had finally arrived, following through on my own birth, like a promise. I would be a complete—instead of partial—American creation, or catastrophe. People—everyone, men, and women alike—would clamor to partake in the cake, made in the shape of our mother's placenta. Super sugary cocaine placenta cake doused in rainbow sprinkles, which had no right being part of the design. At my party, I would have epileptic fits due to the abundant cake. I would sit at the head of the table and be very pleased with myself, that I was kind enough to invite my defective family to witness my making it to twenty-one years of age. That I had not perished as the women in our genetic line had perished like a contagion. It would be a time to celebrate with abandon that I'd made it as far as I had without any STDs, or worse, pregnancies. And with a reliable, mainstream boyfriend named Paul, who granted me space.

It would not be about Joanne. Finally.

My family would be temporarily allowed to cluster around me to watch as I lustily ate my placenta cake, as I washed it down with goblets of burgundy, from Burgundy. I would perform with the kind of emotional power you see at the Oscars or on *Days of Our Lives*, where in seventeen minutes you absorbed all the cultural cues and social hieroglyphs you would need to get ahead in this life. The future me would swallow oodles of fine French wine on an unseasonably hot summer day, just as hypoxia season hit, which would make the feast even more befitting.

"Then we'll go on to die of oxygen starvation like starfish," I heard Jo like a dog whistle. Jo, embedded in my skull, along with the paralyzing fear that we would never come up for air. I remember in the middle of my deserved twenty-first birthday fiction, thinking Joanne had this unique ability to create a disarming tension, confuse the boundaries between Satan and archangel Michael. She was simultaneously—there, not there—blurry, vibrating in opposing directions at once. I never knew from which direction she was coming. She was inside of me. But nobody was going to stop me from turning twenty-one, a period I would dedicate my time on Earth to all those who had spent their lifetimes putting heads on needles in pin factories. There was Sartre's *Being and Nothingness*, and the city pigeon who also desired satisfaction, however measly. I could make it to 1999 safely. The girl haters had been handled. Joanne had spotted them one day on the L Train and had darted their cool peachy asses, one by one, with a set of darts she had lifted from the dive bar on the corner from where we lived.

"The air, the land—they do not need people," Jo had said to me about receiving a month's school detention.

Those girls never bothered me again. It was hard not to see what was coming. By decade's end, "Environmental Illness" was named the disease of the 20th century. There were scented pencils, pens, stickers, and greeting cards—everything was doused in fragrance. Also, the average CEO of a big company earned nearly four hundred times as much as the average worker.

There were other familiarities, which had resumed after Jo, with her darts, came to my defense. Many evenings after my shift at Video Creature I would come home to an empty apartment and wonder where everyone had gone and why our dog Tall had lost his enthusiasm for treats. It seemed to me that the members of my family had gone missing. Sylvia worked long days for a female-owned and operated textile company sewing and grommeting curtains for hospitals in an unmemorable building, off the Brown Line, on the far edge of the city. On rare, good days, our mother would bring us home baguettes from the Vietnamese bakery near where she worked, which she would warm up in our microwave and slather in butter for us. Henry's days were spent in the real estate office resenting the very premise of real estate, while eagerly trying to prove his worth. He was also angering our neighbors with his public birdwatching, which he said was his only option.

Sometimes our father could be found in his study, which had more than a dozen filing cabinets filled with thousands of pages of journals, letters, lecture notes, and ephemera from every stage of his life organized in fanatical claustrophobia. His study contained multiple drafts of his thirteen books; in a time-capsule, there were letters to future Joanne and Bernadette titled "Future Scholars," whom he addressed as "FS." There was a notebook titled "Failure Pile"; a 40,000-word report on the unexplainable events in his life; and a 65,000-word account of his dealings with Sylvia over the years, of which he spent 20,000 words bemoaning astrology. I can remember peering inside his study like a crystal ball in order to understand what might happen in the days, weeks, and months ahead. The frozen space held in its palm the future.

And, for a brief, remarkable period, the two of us could again be found discussing life's predicament in our bedroom, and in our usual fashion: muddling details, speaking nonlinearly, mixing metaphors, body-slamming, and stockpiling bottles of hot sauce. We fell gently into a familiar, hermetic pattern that we shared on the farm. Like the hermits and anchorites who lived a life of seclusion and contemplation in Medieval England, we stayed inside of our bedroom, inside of our apartment, sometimes all weekend long. Holding hands like we did as kids in a tornado, Jo said there was no need to impersonate happiness: "We can be ourselves." In other words, we could be self-reliant, if a bit reckless (my thought) and homicidal (Jo's).

Either way, these impulses resonated with us. But it would not last. Before too long, Jo would be back to her usual shenanigans, picking up where she had left off, resuming episodes with shady characters (men treating her like shit). In other words, "dating." And, in her way—which was the way she knew best—getting off on the displeasure, or pleasure, it brought. At least that was how she presented it.

I have often wondered how many times or iterations a lie needs to be repeated before it rings true. I have often wondered how long it takes to peddle a falsity before you believe it. Has anyone measured that?

The more Jo unraveled, the more she inflicted harm on herself, the more I felt myself numbly making counter moves. Let her go where she wants, I thought. Let Joanne entangle herself further into her own misery and terror that didn't inherently belong to me. But the truth was, I wasn't sure if I was even able to relinquish my own suffering. Or I wanted to. That twisty cord that connected us and made us less alien to ourselves was a lifeline.

DIMINISHING AND SEX

Paul had a pen pal girlfriend in Brazil, who was Brazilian. He said this nonchalantly one day as we walked around Wrigley Field pointing out rowdy drunk people and there was even a game to blame. I immediately went home to tell whoever was available—nobody—that I wanted to be a failed poet right then. I did not want to wait until I could vote, or before I could legally get wasted. Being a writer, especially a poet, was just the sort of failure I could imagine myself being successful at.

"A failed poet is redundant, Bernie, and unfortunately redundancies do not cancel each other out," I distinctly remember Sylvia showing up to say, out of nowhere, before leaving for her shift at the textile company.

I revised my thinking. I would be an unknown writer writing about decay, the loss of glaciers, and the reputation of the legendary neon tie-dyed t-shirt, which evaporated the second it was associated with the suburbanite Chelsea Clinton. The Clintons would have a decent run. The ice was shrinking. The polar bears were diminishing.

"They come, and they go," I can remember Jo said, in a rare moment at home snacking with me. She then repeated the word "diminishing" and snagged the remainder of my corn chips, which had been a very small portion to begin with. She snatched the few chips I had been saving to enjoy with the last of my tomato juice, to eat with the final bite of my unidentifiable sandwich, because she had to illustrate a point. She had to prove pleasure has consequences. But Jo, too, would eventually run out of energy.

Meeting Henry on the level of the "Moisture Cube" was at the time the only way to connect. (He had nothing to say about my being a failed poet.) He was busy resolving the Moisture Cube, a derivative project at best, which had me wondering whether it might be an indication of something more profoundly disturbing. The Moisture Cube embodied the physical occurrence of the condensation cycle, in real time, and consisted of a large transparent acrylic cube containing water. The difference between the outside and inside temperature turned the water vapor into condensed droplets, which ran down the walls of the cube, like a shower door, taking on random forms, which he would have us watch. Henry explained, unprovoked, that the conditions were comparable to a living organism.

"Smart living organisms," he explained, "react to their surroundings in a flexible manner." At a moment's glance, the water shapes would change freely, bound only by statistical limitations.

In July, a heat wave in Chicago killed more than 500 people in what was the hottest year on record. On the first day of school, Paul showed me letters from his Brazilian girlfriend, Mallu. (Of course that was her name; it was desirable.) Paul was telling me about the ongoing discussion between himself about his best friend and rival, Preston, over what they would eventually look like. (As if either of them would ever be interviewed on television, where thinking about this sort of thing might have seemed logical.) I told Paul he sounded like he was in the movie *Dead Poets Society,* and he switched to talking to me about an article he knew I would find amusing. Apparently upper middle-class whites between thirty and forty years of age had started rating their tiredness, "for which tiredness was not equal."

Paul liked talking about facts, and by '95, new generations of separatist patriot militias were forming. I couldn't remember at what rate. Paul knew. As he talked, I wondered what Paul was like in bed, but I wanted to have sex with Hello. I had no experience, but I understood the difference between hard deep sex and regular sex, even then. Visions of Hello's hairy fifty-year-old body, and his inability (due to poor vision) to locate the pleasure parts of me could be educational. I wanted to ride things: a mechanical bull, waves, elevators, a grown man, like Hello. Things I knew about sex: it could be convoluted; it involved the body; our father walked around our apartment in his underwear; our mother hand-washed them and hung the crotch-coverings up to dry. Some days, I would be trying to get to school—to learn—and underwear would be dangling everywhere in our apartment, getting in the way of me making something of myself.

In those moments, and others, I considered the meaning of love in a family in 1989. Though, our parents were not wealthy. 1989 was the year we planned our exit from the farm and the wealthy Menendez brothers robbed and murdered their parents in their Beverly Hills mansion. And they were rich. And the brothers probably got whatever they wanted from their parents, like a real, quality, overly-filling Thanksgiving meal. Hypocrisy was amazing in America. Reinvention was, too. After the murder, Lyle returned to Princeton and used the stolen money to buy Chuck's Spring Street Café, which he would rename "Mr. Buffalo's," after its spicy wings. This had me salivating. His dream was to turn it into a franchise. He, too, had dreams of one day being an entrepreneur.

"It was one of my mother's delights that I pursue a small restaurant chain and serve healthy food with friendly service," he told the student newspaper—at Princeton, which was an elite school on the east coast. Where I would have gladly lived out the rest of my days in such proximity to New York City where mocking my childhood would seem appropriately in tune since that place detested the Midwest. The other brother, Erik, hired a full-time tennis coach and competed in a series of pro tournaments in Israel. "My brother wants to become President of the U.S. I want to be a senator," he said. Erik married a woman who looked exactly like his mother— same poofy, dyed blond hair and freewheeling gaze. And Lyle's first wife, a former model, would end up divorcing him for writing letters to another woman.

Other things I knew about sex was that it could involve love, like a recipe, but that it was often violent. It could be called "it" and it could be an "act." And, like everything else, it could be extreme. Sex was also called intercourse, by losers and unsexy types, but still, and joined a list of other *inters*: interlocutor, international, interstates, interchangeable. I liked desire. I both did and didn't understand it, then, ever. I did understand it lent itself easily to self-hatred.

Even now, in 2009—in a motel room that reeked of years of activity, resting, and sorting through the contents of my head, recovering from various maladies and other ailments, such as Joanne—when it came to sex, it was never entirely clear to me in my long-distance (never in person) relationship with Preston, who was managing who. I can say it seemed to me back then—when the thought experiment turned to bodies coming together—it was a question of managing desires, like giving a plant so little water it strains to live and thus flourishes.

I can remember Hello asking me about my dreams. He would ask while we stood aimlessly next to his shed. I liked sheds, but back then his shed in particular held a coveted place in my young mind. I had liked that it was a depository, for the boat I wanted but would never buy with Jo for our Midwest escape, or for my ambitions, like having memorable sex for the first time with Paul. I had liked that Hello didn't know what to do with himself around me. I liked that he wanted to know about me and my sleep for a time span before he had turned his attentions completely to my older sister.

"Do you dream?" Hello would ask me, when it was me that he favored.

He was, for me then, a man—the whole of an opera.

"Doesn't everyone?" I must have said, as I'm sure I would have answered him.

I might have said what I would say now: that when you sleep in a motel you were wasting time and money and not making the most of it. Though at that point in time, I had never stepped foot inside of a motel or hotel, but even back then I thought of myself as a fast learner.

There was Cyclone Nargis and a new poem by Louise Gluck, *Before The Storm*: "A full moon. Yesterday a sheep escaped into the woods, and not just any sheep—the ram, the whole future." These had me thinking of Joanne, her insomnia, her reliable instability. There was the fact that she would be giving birth to a child.

I took the opportunity to write to Hello about a dream.

Dear Hello, wherever you are in 2009, the letter went:

Last night in this Super 8 motel, I was wasting time and finances. I dreamt I was in my childhood bedroom. Have you spoken to my sister? Let me inform you, or reinform you, that she has decided to have a baby. She doesn't even believe in babies. It was Jo herself who called them the shiniest American commodity there ever was. Children were for white rich people to show off with their handbags.

As I cannot sort it out, or the family history which plagues me (or why sometimes my letters carry a wistful, romantic tone from the 16th century—such as the sentence that proceeded this one—which belies my staunch cynicism). A history our mother believed would be the source of our liberation and not of our stagnation.

I have been spending time with my memories in our childhood space in the farmhouse. The space Sylvia had constructed for me and Joanne in the attic. My lost friend from college, Fais, was there. I couldn't tell where she and I were in our relationship timeline. Was the Fais in my dream, the Fais before I had lost Fais? Or afterward? She and Jo were making out in that dream-logic way: like their hands and heads were backwards. I could feel their weird softness. Like they knew what was coming. There was a knock at the door. Sylvia, Henry, and a small 6- or 7-year-old beat-up boy I didn't recognize were standing there. The boy was hurt. A cast on one arm. Henry pushed him over to me, like a hostage exchange. Henry then pulled out a serrated knife and said an intervention was necessary, "They would need to cut out the part of my body that was the feeling part."

CHICAGO

There was a note on the fridge informing me that Hello had called. Henry wrote in a parenthetical asking if we could please instead call him "sayonara," which of course he found hilarious. Hello had called to say that there was a 40-foot fixer-upper with a mizzen sail for sale in Michigan. Hello wanted to tell me about it in person. That was, if I was still interested in boats. Apparently, Michigan was the place to get a boat. There were a lot of used boats for sale. I was hooked on boats. I was invested in escaping the Midwest via the sea. I was absolutely still interested in becoming a roving set of sea eyeballs that understood water's complexity. Please note that when I defined myself and did not let others do it: this defined me.

From our bedroom I could see Hello in his backyard, pacing. I remember I went to his house straightway to get the details. In his backyard we discussed the options. The decision would come between a Ketch boat or Yawl boat, depending on where I wanted the wheel.

Hello came to the door wearing all denim, loose-fitting on the top but which got tighter the lower you got. "Hell yes," I thought.

"Original," I said.

His hands were covered in grease. I thought about the origins of things like WD40.

"Yeah, dirty," he said, sheepishly inviting me inside.

I had never been inside his four-story house, which felt like a nice hotel, a space waiting for an awakening. Hello offered me a bottle of beer, which I accepted. I followed him into the kitchen and saw his dark back hairs poking out of the top of his denim shirt as he opened the fridge. After, we went to his backyard, an area I was well acquainted with, having not only spent time in it but having watched over it from our bedroom in our apartment. I remember feeling a little disappointed we had not stayed inside where I had felt willfully vulnerable and dangerous, existing in such proximity to an older man in denim who had issues with substance abuse, a daughter my age who had once been my friend, and who had himself once been a drifter at sea, a roaming sea-eye, like I endeavored to become to begin a new life with Jo.

In his backyard, we sat on the Adirondack chairs Hello wiped down with a Batman towel.

"Do men keep extra towels around? Is that what determines a man from a boy?"

"How can I be of service?" he asked.

I thought I'd been funny, in that flirty way that was sure to make him want me. But no.

I said I was a sea-life amateur. Both Joanne and I were, though I never once called my sister by her name. Our conversation always started out the same way, weirdly close, and talking in the same truncated manner about escape.

"If this is going to succeed, we need to prepare our minds and bodies for the monotony of life at sea," I said about the two of us escaping the Midwest.

"I was hoping you could help out with that part," I said to Hello.

"Do you have the funds?" Hello wanted to know.

I did not have the money yet, but when I did, and once Jo was re-involved in this boat escape project, I would need to find a way to get the boat from Michigan to Illinois and into Hello's shed.

"Ask your friend Paul for a ride," Hello said, out of the blue.

"I can't do that," I said trying to find a comfortable position in his Adirondack chair.

I could not do that. I also wasn't sure about Paul knowing about the things in my life that I had not mentioned. I also knew if I wanted him to, Paul would have taken me. But a car-ask was in another league altogether. Up until then our communication was mainly limited to the confines of our high school, which meant lightly flirting and talking about Adorno's "culture industry eating everything" in the hallways, or out on the front steps. How had Hello seen us?

"Katherine Elizabeth Katy Rogers is my daughter."

"This entire time?"

I was not sure whether I had asked Hello the question.

"You don't have her eyes."

It was true. His eyes were a darker blue. But more to the point, Katherine Elizabeth Katy Rogers (KEKR) had been my first friend blemish, in what would become a long line of blemishes, back in middle school, a time worse than high school, and the reason why I had let most of it fade into oblivion.

"You have more money than I thought," I said to Hello.

"You could be right."

My one-time, blue-eyed friend, who wore Guess and always had coveted snacks in her super carry-all bag, asked me to be friends in middle school. She dropped me after the "chicken slaughter" incident.

KEKR was apolitical. She hated feminism. She said feminism was the reason her mother decided their home life was toxic and decided to run away to Spain. Feminism was the reason her father was the way that he was, which at the time I didn't understand but that I came to realize meant he liked substantially younger women because younger women were not yet set in their ways. A younger woman believed that there was something to him, which was to say that all one had to do was to peel back the layers like an onion to discover what was substantial. He had nautical expertise. But the other truth was that he was plain. A doorknob. That was the part of him that was seductive. I mean, he had a shed. He also had beer and his own digs.

The point was, before she didn't, KEKR wanted to be friends with someone who was unexceptionally unbalanced. And for a brief period in middle school, with KEKR by my side, my inner life levitated to new heights. Her presence eclipsed my sense that others around me could detect the dark overgrown pubic hair beneath my clothes. Pustules had found places to camp out on my face, stowaways on my cheeks, and KEKR didn't notice or make any mention of my bad face next to her flawless skin. The thing was, I was never great with people, in terms of making and prolonging friendships. And it didn't take long for me to make a massive friendship blunder with KEKR. In an inadvisable burst of self-confidence, in her church youth group, I talked about piety. Notions of piety and restraint seemed to excite everyone, including our once President, who in 1992 explained his affair with Gennifer Flowers on *60 Minutes*, which our family tuned into like an exorcism. I distinctly remember Sylvia taking a moment to point out that the woman on television, whose name started with a *G* instead of a *J*, and that somehow this made Gennifer unsympathetic. She was a floozy in our mother's eyes. (I remember feeling conflicted. I was told Democrats were feminists and Sylvia was a Democrat.)

I told KEKR's youth group that I knew about sacrifice. I described how on the farm we used to prepare chickens for slaughter. How our family spoke of sacrifice before applying the knife. "Once a chicken's neck was settled into the kill cone, a plastic gallon container with the bottom removed," I explained to her group of saved, crystal souls that glowed without stains, "we then nailed it to a tree." Our family would give thanks to the sky, talk about sacrifice, and slit the neck's artery without cutting the windpipe. The pinned bird bled out, some said "fell asleep," while the heart continued to pump the blood from their body. I told KEKR what I knew about piety and sacrifice and promptly went back to having no friends.

In Hello's backyard, a pile of warm scrambled eggs he had made me sat on my lap. I dumped a jar of salsa on my eggs. There was no precedent to be discreet, not in the '90s. I ate eggy salsa next to

KEKR's father, Hello, and thought about what it would be like to drive across America stopping off to visit the Spiral Jetty, a site-specific work that shifted along with its surroundings: the water, land, and atmosphere. I remember my butt aching on the hard Adirondack chair. I thought about my genitalia belonging to my ancestors, and said confidently: "As a human race the design is circular. People are the misguided endeavors," shoveling scrambled eggs into my mouth.

"Come here," Hello said, gesturing like flashers and other creepy men do, patting their laps, and so forth. I liked it. I welcomed the referential transparency: Hello was gross. His patronizing, fatherly gesture appealed to me—I felt like a wanted and only child. Please, take advantage of me. Hello had absolutely no idea what I was capable of. And when I got so close to him that I could see his deep pores and smell the beer on his tongue, he removed a piece of masking tape from my shoulder.

"Virgin, huh?"

I hadn't noticed it taped there. These notes were pinned to me with some regularity, often the message was "schizoid mole," "lame stump," or "nasal spray."

"I'm here about preparing our bodies for disaster," I said.

He was getting distracted.

Hello told me about the Polish kayaker, Aleksander Doba. Doba had lessons on perseverance. The biggest regrets in Doba's life were the times he'd succumbed to suffering in conventional human-animal ways. Like a night in 1989 when he built a fire to make tea and dry his clothes while paddling on the Vistula River. Or a week later, when he gave in to his desire to eat fluffy pancakes, creamy tomato soup, and rice at the Milk Bar restaurant. He shouldn't have been enjoying and indulging himself. He'd promised he would be tougher than all human weakness. He should have been alone at his bare campsite, with his kayak, eating canned goulash to condition his body for the Arctic temperatures that lay ahead.

"What you need to do is make a *Liste de Travaux* and tell no one. The secret, sailors say, was to never say when you're sailing," Hello said, about what to do next.

Hello would help me with my list as long as I introduced him to Joanne. He then told me that up until recently, he'd never believed he deserved a dynamic, pretty girl.

"I don't think I've ever heard you say her name. What do you know about Joanne?"

"What, you think I live in a cave?"

Jo often got herself detention, or worse, suspension for her body-stink screaming: "The body secretes. The body sweats, shits, and bleeds!" Jo liked to scream in public, pointing in the direction of France and to excessively relaxed, comfortable French women with bushy, drippy armpits lounging nude in the Riviera eating cheeses made goopy by the heat.

"They manage to smell so well," Jo would say of snacking nude French women.

There were inherent problems with her strategy. Mentioning naked French women speaking eloquently while eating loads of carbs with gobs of creamy cheese was never a good idea if you were trying to shed light on any particular social issue. Especially if you were trying to prove a point to an American, which my sister consistently did. Using this illustration to change the mind of an American was not a good plan, and Jo had forgotten the cardinal rule: we wanted plans we could execute.

"Finally," Jo said of Listerine promising to end halitosis, and handing her coupon for the product to the cashier in the checkout aisle.

"Civilians are being assassinated, but halitosis is a social defect, leaving women sad and alone and unmarried and childless and defective. All the things women are said to fear."

The truth was we did fear those things, perhaps Joanne most of all.

By the time I got to high school, Joanne was often given detention, and later she was expelled for good. She would sit like an obstacle on the front steps of our high school and rehearse her oral maneuvers on over-ripe bananas. The Smashing Pumpkins were on everyone's mind, except Joanne's. She sat and listened to Annie Lennox on her headphones. She sat and sucked spotty brown bananas, back and forth, like oarsman row, until mid-suck when part of the fruit would limply fall to the ground. I had heard from some acquaintances, who felt compelled to share, that Jo had been paying for her "veggie with extra everything" Subway sandwich by dropping handfuls of condoms at check out. At the time, Subway was promoting their Fresh Value Meals, which started at $2.99. "Such a deal," people said my sister said, before dropping condoms like an afterthought.

Had Hello seen Jo do this?

This was an odd moment in my life as a fifteen-year-old. At that moment, at Hello's mention of my older sister, I found myself caught in a bind; somehow, all I wanted was this older man with a hairy back, ill-advisedly dressed in all denim, all to myself. I remember ducking inside my excuse for a body to pause. For one, he knew who she was without my telling him. Two, Hello was not in his fifties like I had initially believed, but in his forties, which had me second guessing my perceptive abilities. Third, I thought I had the attentions of a man completely, and figured I had my remaining time in high school to explore the terrain, but the time had come to act or I would lose Hello.

Why not me?

I did it. I asked Hello. Why? My savings were at work here, my boat project, my high school sex life, my shed solution, my burgeoning social skills.

Of course, I did not say anything. Instead, I wrote out Jo's pager number and handed it to Hello.

At home that night I called up Paul. (There were still phonebooks then.) I asked him about his car: was it in shipshape? Did the AC work? I told Paul to meet me in Hello's shed, in his backyard, and gave Paul his address. I said in this shed we might be cramped but we were going to do things we had never done before. The moon would be out but not yet in full. That night, naked in the dank shed with Paul, I was no longer an Illinois junk kid. I was a blister forming a scab of an urban woman, peeling off on a custom Harley, breaking land speed records whichever way she went.

Joanne and Hello stayed in his four-story house for months. Our parents, eventually in the same place at the same time, asked me where she was, and I sincerely thought about the truth. The truth being that she was probably, most definitely, mentally unstable. She had wanted to catapult herself to outer space to escape America, still. And she believed, still, that she could make it happen by using the force of a tornado like a slingshot. But I could not think of the last time telling the truth had saved a woman.

Jo at the time might as well have been an aberration, in the optical sense, like when a mirror fails to show you *you*, which did little to alleviate my jealousy that it was she that was now in his house with beer, scrambled eggs, a backyard, and a shed containing the residue of Paul and I, a pivotal moment in my life that only she had access to. Hello's shed and house was no longer a place I could take refuge in. Instead of taking out my pain on my body like girls were expected to do, at any age, I went on "an information diet." In other words, I narrowed down the materials I consumed. Some days Michael Kirby's *1965 Happenings*, Antonin Artaud's *The Theatre and Its Double*. Other days, Fredric Jameson's *Postmodernism* or the *Cultural Logic of Late Capitalism*, and always Andrea Dworkin's *Intercourse*. I took illusion to bed with me and worked on plays never to be staged. Of course, I had director's notes, in case. The audience was directed to look across, beyond the stage, through the window to the street outside, where the action was taking place. I delved deeply into illusion.

I kept my head down, because I had read that's what aspiring teenagers who turn into promising, well-adjusted adults do. The boat had the potential to save me, to save us, if I chose to take Jo back. I needed to focus and get productive. Time to organize. *Liste de Travaux*: lazarette, epoxy primer, Danforth anchor for the sand (different anchors for different days/locations). Epoxy. Propane oven. Cut wheels. Big connectors. Lee cloths were an important piece; lee cloths belonged on the bottom of the bunk, a piece of fabric that acted like a safety net, which kept a sailor from falling off the shallow mattress and onto the floor. Weather cloths—they protected from the weather with the dodger. Survival suits, i.e., Preservation Uniforms. EPIRB (acronym for emergency position indicating radio beacon). Order choke cable for gas engine boat. Make engine box. Jacklines, the ropes that ran along either side of the deck and that were always attached to the boat—to be used in heavy weather. Running lights. Water maker. Boomkins. Horseshoe Buoy, a flotation device like a lifesaver but open on one side. Swivel arm, to connect the steering gear to tiller.

Tons of cleaning stuff. Non-toxic if we can help it. (If on decent sale.)

Canned goods. Grains, pasta. Gum.

When all was prepared, perform a "shake-down" (a sample of boating, i.e., a practice run before setting off to sea).

The goal was not to sink, and I was tired of looking at Hello's house and yard to see if anything had changed.

Sometimes I studied at the prominent Catholic church across the street from our apartment building. Our building was surrounded by religious institutions—Greek Orthodox, Jewish Synagogue, Episcopalian. We were surrounded by believers and sinners that needed to believe to be saved, corner bars and grocery stores.

TRIANGLES

Virginia Woolf asked why—if we were able to express the thoughts of Hamlet, and the tragedy of Lear—we had no words for the shiver and the headache. I liked scotch. I liked the burning sensation in my mouth and chest, and spending time with our father, who was home more since being first demoted at the real estate company and then fired two months later. I remember the absurdity of what passed as family getting to me. Face it: Americans were fatalist. Sadists. Freud (granted, imperfect), after visiting Coney Island, called our country a gigantic mistake. For someone who had spent a lifetime looking into the abyss of the mind, one would have thought Freud would have been dazzled to watch grown men gleefully ride mechanical hobbyhorses. But the possibilities of America and American infantilizing were too much even for Freud, which I found ominous yet vindicating.

Events kept unraveling in America. The fires in Los Angeles had taken down scores of homes; the authorities weren't able to keep count. There was no point in releasing a death count, they said. Unusual temperatures were expected to reach "as far away as Illinois." That far. On a positive note, AOL changed their hourly fee to a flat monthly rate of $19.95, which we reasoned we could afford with the return on our investment. Henry and Sylvia had been working to locate their measly investment in the Cayman Islands that they had made back in the '80s, which was coming up empty. Henry tried reaching the investors by phone, but they were away on vacation, skiing in the Alps or bodysurfing someplace. Henry wrote them emails and received automated responses, salutations with photo attachments of their calibrated children riding horses, emaciated elephants, or dolphins at SeaWorld flooded his inbox. The dinner table was a wormhole.

"Hi there, do I have a family?"

I became convinced that a bad actor playing Sylvia had replaced our mother, and that a worse actor playing Henry had replaced our father. I told them as much. Each had an untalented actor fulfilling their parental roles—"poorly," I said. Our parents looked at me and went back to discussing whether to sell the farm and farmhouse that perhaps long ago should have been put out of its misery. We had already torn down the barn to make way for additional rows to be planted. The infrastructure was falling apart. The heating bills were insane. Our renters, the trusty couple from Sacramento, finally got their own land. Plus, they had found a sweet cottage in town which had been updated with new windows and other desirable appliances.

"Now this," our parents lamented.

Every year there was something: low yields, trade wars, thunderstorms, drought. During the last heat wave, the farmer who rented the land to farm, quit mid-harvest. "It's like farming in hell," he said.

Without stable renters we would not be able to continue in the way that we were. The decision was a heavy one.

Joanne and I understood that we were from a long line of determined women, who worked as land and garment workers. I can remember a night Jo was at home in her bed. It seemed she had finally fallen asleep, then would pop up like a zombie in the dark to ignite a winter jacket on fire. "The body was the first tool of man," Jo had said in the glow of the flames. I remember she refused to extinguish the fire until I repeated the words after her. I did. I said, "The body was the first tool of man, the body was the first tool of man, the body was the first tool of man." Our great-grandmother Poppy, after decades of grim work, fought tooth and nail for what she had. We were no stranger to the fact that labor changed bodies.

Hands were the first to go, then sleep, nutrition, and, lastly, the mind. Our familial struggles could be traced back to the collapse of the Bank of United States in 1929, when the Feds allowed the banks to fail, and the banks failed. Why throw good money after bad? "See," our parents demanded. "The logic of institutions never fails institutions."

"What's another year of saying, *we've never seen a year like this?*"

Our family would decide to hold onto the property, as a reminder. It was hard to explain the complexity of the connection, unless you were inside the same fishbowl; it was easy to mistake your own shit for sustenance. At the age of six, I had been made to understand mid-twentieth century cosmopolitans saw Midwestern regionalists as a flock of cuckoo birds, "always trying to make their homes in the nests that other birds have built." I had no intention, ever, of making it to Hollywood. "When I die," I wrote to my future self on my calendar, "there should be a curt piece of text sticking out of a small mound of dirt in our family cemetery to indicate my presence: Bernadette Fareown mentioned something about a large and uneven portrait." There was a lot to consider when it came to women and endings: execution, childbirth, exposure to weather. Female evaporation.

I remember one afternoon watching from our bedroom as a woman waited on the corner. A hooker, I thought. And then I realized it made no difference. A woman alone, waiting in public would feel like a hooker regardless; in that she would be asking for trouble. Regardless of the time of day, what she was wearing: her hair, how it was worn or not worn, her bodice preserved, her hands folded— resisting or capitulating? That was what it felt like to be monitored and preyed upon. From birth we were told to survey our every move, to continually prepare and ready ourselves. "She" was nearly always accompanied by her own image, walking across a room, while mourning the death of her father. She could scarcely avoid seeing the image of herself.

Even with the internet and the expanding cell phone market, I bought a compass. I waited like a hooker because fuck them for deciding. I waited—for a bus ride, a long-distance phone call, for an ATM machine, for lab results—still as could be. I was a part of stillness: a stillborn, seas before a storm, an ice cube meeting room temperature.

1998

A solid year. I was out of high school and working on my college applications. Our president inserted a cigar into Monica Lewinsky's vagina. Unlit, presumably. Sylvia and I would cross paths more often in our apartment, and I would catch her staring at me as though I knew why everything was the way it was. The television was talking about the key al Qaeda operative who blew up two American Embassies in Kenya and Tanzania. Most nights I sat down to eat with our mother at the oak table, but I had obligations. I had started a poetry and politics zine called *Subject: The Inadequate Life of a Tryer*, with a bi-weekly circulation of about forty copies. I spent an inordinate amount of time at Kinkos photocopying and assembling *Subject*.

My relationship with Sylvia had reached a new low. I had disappointed her, it seemed, epically. Despite the fact that by my senior year in high school I had excelled in multiple subjects: sports, math, biology, and literature. But none of this promising news had the ability to detract from my sister's (i.e. Complete Psycho Bitch) trouble. She was saying things in public that were not welcome. Five years before, she'd been expelled from our high school. She'd pulled the fire alarm and broke into the principal's office. Using the principal's loudspeaker, she demanded that white people atone for their sins, before slicing her hands with a utility knife. The part of her body she loved and relied on most.

The residue of that episode hovered over our apartment for months. It was like an infestation. The fear was sometimes worth ignoring. But there was no ignoring Joanne.

I remember trying to engage with our mother over dinner. One night I told her that John Donne analyzed the world as a "chronically ill body of stinking flesh and protruding bone."

"He was a poet of love," I said to her, "and love was constant in a dying world."

"Bernadette," Sylvia said, eye-balling me like a mistake, "you're out of high school. Maybe you should move out, get looked at, and consider reading more nonfiction."

I did. I read nonfiction. It had never been my genre of choice—blurring the lines for the sake of sales.

There were times nobody could match Sylvia's sharp cruelty. Not our father. Not even Joanne. The two of them, Sylvia and Joanne, would go at it until calling stalemate, which given their personalities one might have thought would have made matters worse, but amazingly they settled down as if napping, like a dog that has found her place among the pack. I remember looking down at the oak table, and thinking about what was passed down from one generation to the next, one version of another, and thinking it was incredible what pain did to people. Our parents worried about Jo. Yet, it seemed nothing could be done about her. I remember thinking about how certain questions and facial expressions, the ones directed toward you—personally, accidentally—could become incidents that might alter the course of your life.

That dinner, the one where I shared that John Donne saw the world as a chronically ill body, was the worst dinner in the history of dinners, which was saying a lot. One day soon we'll be in search of shade and food, I thought, like birds must think, shoveling macaroni out of a plastic bowl into my mouth, which, along with fleece, and other synthetic microfibers, were weaving themselves into the gastrointestinal tracts of sea creatures, poisoning oceans and riverbeds, fish and other wildlife, and concentrating toxins in the bodies of larger animals, higher up the food chain—like us—where nobody dared to look. I consumed America as much as America consumed me. I would be taking every substance with me to the grave, where no doubt I would continue to be a poison. But I would be educated by America's leading institutions.

1998, the hottest year since the instrumental temperature recording began. In my college application essay, I handed the one-eyed giant cannibal from Homer's *Odyssey* a credit card, a six-pack, an outline of the Hero's Journey, and dropped him at Denny's. He was told he was now living the American Dream and that he should get on with ordering accordingly, as in whatever he wanted, and to put it on the Discover card. The one-eyed giant ordered seven of the Meat Lovers Slam ($5.99, 3x7=21 sausage links, 21 bacon strips, 2x7=14 eggs, 14 buttermilk pancakes, *for a limited time only*), setting him back $41.93. He sat in a worn booth and built his Own Grand Slam, which he balanced out by ordering a Fit Slam made of egg whites, fresh spinach, and turkey bacon strips. After, he ordered a Crazy Spicy Sizzlin' Skillet that he found to be under-seasoned. He asked the waitress for Cool Ranch Doritos, anything with bold flavors. The waitress eyed his six-pack and informed him he wasn't allowed to bring in outside drinks.

"This is Denny's," she told him.

And the ogre asked her what she thought about the priority of existence over essence, anguish, responsibility, and freedom of choice.

At a table crowded with food and condiments, the one-eyed giant and the waitress went on to discuss some basic themes of existentialist thought, from Kierkegaard to Sartre, to the relation of the individual to mass society, conformism, nihilism, death, the all-seeing eye, God, birth, the death of God.

I had omitted the psychoanalytical readings linking the blinding of the eye to castration, recognizing that it would not have been in service to the exercise (i.e. the application process), which as far as

I could tell required a light balance between insight and neophyte. (Remember, the goal was to get into a good college.)

The relevant American subjects, the ones I was told the college admission boards would find too grisly, found their way into *Subject: The Inadequate Life of a Tryer*. I wrote about a forty-nine-year-old African American man named James Byrd living in Jasper, a town in Texas. One evening, in 1998, three white men offered James Byrd a ride, and he accepted. The white men proceeded to take James to the woods, where they beat him, chained him to the back of their pickup truck, and drove, dragging his body along the rocky dirt and cement. According to an affidavit of the account, his severed torso was found at the edge of a paved road, his head and an arm, in a ditch about a mile away.

2009

On what should have been my last night in Bloomington, I left the comfort of my Super 8 room to meet the replacement receptionist for karaoke at a punk bar. By then she had a proper name—Isadora. Though she preferred to be called Isa. We took our seats across from each other at a dimly lit square table in the corner of the bar a good hour before the show was set to begin. I made sure to silence my cell phone. Paul had been calling and not leaving messages, which by 2009 was embarrassingly juvenile. There were no excuses left. By then, texting was not only free but commonplace. Isa had on what I had come to believe was her work uniform: tight mini dresses, which she wore like a second skin.

"So, talk," Isa said. "What's the big question you've saved for me all this time sitting in your room?"

No fanfare. No how are you. What are your days like in my well-rated motel? Which she most certainly thought of as belonging to her. Jo, you should have seen Isa move about the space. It would have made all the male CEOs on Earth twitch in their seats. "There's nothing a schoolboy likes more than being scolded by the headmaster," Jo liked to say of twitching men.

Isa had her curly dark hair pulled back into a tight bun. Each wily mustang strand of hair restrained by a bobby pin. It took a minute to put together. Isa said, as she did this, that she had surprised herself by inviting me—an irritating motel guest—to her favorite bar in the entire state of Minnesota, which happened to be only a few miles away. A place she didn't share with unkind people. Especially people born at the end of the '70s. As far as she could tell, that generation seemed convinced they had done all they could for America. Isa did not trust my demeanor, but she had decided she trusted the infrastructure that was my whole person, as she saw it. Her voice sounded serious, restrained, though the words were strangely chosen as if thought out in advance, even practiced. Isa was a photographer. She shot portraits of strangers in public spaces, mostly of their eyes, which seemed to her to have grown more unfocused over the years. She didn't care if it sounded cliché.

"That's what serving vodka is for, to resolve people's insecurities before shooting them."

"You're making me nauseous," I told her.

"Good," Isa said. "You could stand to be kinder."

The bar began to fill up; as the energy levels rose there was pressure to get on with it. With the point. We were not going to be friends, and perhaps knowing that long in advance freed us up to be ourselves.

"I want to know what you think about," I said, matter-of-factly.

Isa excused herself to order us another round. She came back to our table with a small tray of shots and jiggered one of the janky legs to stabilize the table. I asked what the booze was—what's in the glass? —and she said, "never mind." We shot them back like beauty pageant winners attempting to avoid what an outsider might call the truth, which in this case was that we were strangers, Isa and I, sharing an intimacy generally reserved for friends or lovers. It was less about the words and more about our bodies sitting at the table in the corner.

"That's what this is?" Isa said. "You want to know what I think about?"

I didn't know what "this" was.

"Yes," I answered rather confidently.

Isa paused a good minute. She took out her cellphone and fumbled around with it. Several of her friends entered the bar, equally young, equally attractive. They called out hellos to one another from across the room and left communication at that. I looked down at my chest and was pleased to see I was wearing a tank top. The space grew increasingly muggy and irresistible, but I was wearing something without sleeves.

"To be honest," Isa said, rather charmlessly, "I think about storms. You?" she asked.

I thought about Fais and then *Point Break*. I kept these revelations about 1999 to myself.

1999

There was Fais, a college librarian. She was also the only person I knew at the time who had not seen the movie *Point Break*. That year's heatwave was deemed "ok" compared to the one in 1995 that killed 739 Chicagoans. I was told if I lived at home and did well in community college, our parents would do what they could to help me transfer to the University of Chicago, even if I might be catastrophically old by then.

At the end of the '90s, two trends emerged: medication begets medication, and human-animals (plus the ones we were eating), were being pumped full of bad memories, steroids, and antibiotics. Both species were growing in size and in resistance to drugs, then linked to rising obesity, diabetes, asthma and allergies. Humans consumed television and food that was killing them, and then went on to consume drugs to do what the ads recommended, which was to counteract the information and the food that was killing them but that might have terrible side-effects that would feel like death. Millions were poured into advertising allergy-fighting Claritin as the planet warmed, extending periods when plants released pollen.

Fais was a woman I wanted more than the whole of life to emulate. If there was even the slightest chance I might have gotten away with it, I would have tried. Fais and I spent time together. If I felt like I was floating nowhere, she kept me grounded. We role-played, had bowel movements in front of the other in the way trusted friends do, drank warm beer, ate peanuts in their shells like cool baseball players, and talked about drugs and bad policies. Fais played the part of Dr. Anthony Nicholson, a British neuroscientist and clinical researcher for the drug company, Schering-Plough. I took on the role of Sherwin D. Straus, the F.D.A. medical officer assigned to review Claritin.

Dr. Nicholson said of comparing Claritin to a sedating antihistamine called triprolidine, "We are not actually in the business of saying one drug is better than the other. We are in the business of saying whether a drug is acceptable in terms of its performance profile."

I, as F.D.A. medical officer D. Straus, responded, "But how can you say it is acceptable in terms of its performance profile without comparing it to what else is out there?"

"We compare it with placebo."

"So, you compare it to nothing?"

"Yes."

"And is it better than nothing?"

"Yes."

"I can't argue with that."

Side effects included infertility, heart, kidney, and liver disease, increased aggression, anxiety, breast enlargement, constipation, diarrhea, heartburn, insomnia, decreased libido, and erectile dysfunction. The last of these prompted rich guy Ace Greenberg to better the lives of those who couldn't afford Viagra by covering the costs, and explaining that he believed "in the basics."

Fais and I entertained secret yearnings to forget the world and live life in an erotic utopia. We had mastered the weak beer buzz and talked about what it takes to love a person. All that mattered to me then was Fais. So, when one day she asked me in front of Starbucks why I remained tethered to Jo like two bandits at sea I passed out. (What Fais could not have known then was that one day I would need the space of a well-rated motel to sort out the answers to these questions.)

Fais asked how the connection between us remained solid despite Jo's disappearance into Hello's house, where I presumed she had been living and taking her prescription medication.

"Why the devotion to your sister?" Fais asked.

"I'm never bored with her. Which was to say, in her presence I'm never bored of myself," I said.

That was all I could think to say. Had I known this would be inadequate, I would have given Fais every copy of my zine *Subject* I had.

Just as swiftly as I found Fais, I lost Fais. And the last I had heard from Joanne, was via a postcard she sent of London's Tower Bridge. She wrote in it: "Deflection is a narcissistic tactic used by America to control our minds and emotions."

I wanted to pin Jo down for the sake of our family. Or did I mean humanity? That summer I would lose my way in the city. "Surrender to its uncertainty," Jo would have said, if she had been with me. But I would be alone. Fais had a girlfriend. Apparently, she was shelving books at the library when the two met. Her girlfriend wasn't sure about my existence. Her girlfriend was not sure what I meant to Fais and what Fais meant to me, and this vagueness was not good for a relationship's longevity. I tried reassuring her that I, too, was unclear about my existence, that I was highly skilled and motivated to simply disappear into the background.

But as shriveled and compact I offered to make myself, the girlfriend felt I assumed too much space. And for the first time, I didn't have the words to describe the events unfolding before me. The loss of Fais hit me hard. Up until that point, it was unclear whether I had ever felt present, at least not in that close way which allowed me to take a shit in front of a friend like Fais. There was a magic to that intimate synergistic animal state, which required surrendering to a deep closeness. The only way to know another person was to let them see you. That was to say: you would come to see your errors more sharply than ever before, and discover new, unforgivable blemishes.

The loss of Fais emphasized the loss of Joanne. Jo had been away so long I had stopped counting the days; a pile up of time I left unmeasured. This split between Fais and I had a sustaining impact over the course of my life. I came to understand that it was my doing. I made many miscalculations with Fais, who was kind and American. I had placed in her a longing to believe in the value of humanity, so much so that eventually she was made into a caricature I could easily mistreat. We made excuses about the bruises I had left on her arms. There were occasions I took advantage of her care and affection, something men did, that our father did, and that I swore I would never do. Fais was forgiving of my temper, which she would gently walk around like a child's dollhouse. She said she was stronger than I gave her credit for, and that was true.

MORE 1999

University was for me a time of determination. Growing up in America required money, and I was cash poor. I searched for additional work, but to qualify for my financial aid I had to register as a fulltime student, and this made employers anxious about my commitment.

I got a Discover card like a good girl. This massively temporary, vibrant university student lifestyle—one that would eventually include establishing my look—a stuffed teal fanny pack (surfboard keychains, Frosted Mini Wheats, condoms) and dull black combat boots. Personal style would cost me. I refused to stay in the Midwest and remain in community college. Fortunately, my GPA allowed me to transfer to the University of Chicago to pursue a degree in philosophy, which would no doubt keep me occupied for the rest of my life; namely how I had remained in the Midwest for my higher education. (It happened that the university covered my tuition costs.) Paul was there, too, studying the very same topic that had no future. Paul and I were in it—the pursuit of excellence—together. It was a time of refusing to end up like our father, violent, unemployed but pretending to have employment because every person, even those disposed of like trash as children, need to feel valuable.

It was a time of refusing to end up like the Fareown women, most of whom found themselves in fugue states, alienated widows, or spinsters. (Those that had suitors, had them because they were compelling but mostly it was because they had land that men wanted.)

Some of these women in our family, intent on exhibiting a kind of willful nothingness, lived an absent identity. Almost all were arrested and institutionalized for being in "states," and were completely absorbed by external forces and interior existences. Eventually, they succumbed to water, which was to say: they ended up dead. Joanne often pointed out that the line between mystic garbage and truth was blurry: "Something must pass for a self, otherwise what is there?" It was a time of resisting impulses, like smoking cigarettes, or going after my sister to drag her out of some compromised situation and pulling her hair out of her head for ruining my life.

University was a period of commitment, to philosophy, and to Prof. Tim O. On my first day of class, Professor Tim O. said about philosophy: "Difficulty, doubt, and disorientation; this course is for those who are willing to let their intellectual habits be rearranged." And I took every class he offered. Tim O. taught a course on "Kaspar Hauser" and "Death," and I was insane for him. His classes were popular, often filling up before they were listed in the course catalog. Eager students, including Paul, clamored to be let into his classes. They would pile high on desks. They would spread out on the floor during the first week of the semester. He taught a course on "Whiteness," to teach us about white people. I remember students wondering if that wasn't what African American studies covered, and Professor Tim O. telling them to leave, quickly. In his class on "Whiteness," students watched and analyzed the movie *Falling Down*, about society's mistreatment of a white man, played by Michel Douglas, who decides to take matters of fairness and equality into his own hands because the owner of the convenience store, Mister Lee, couldn't give him the change he needed to make a phone call. Douglas' character then busts up Mister Lee's shop with a baseball bat, and after, finds a quiet place to sulk and drink Coke. A hundred and fifty-three minutes spent with this white man and the viewer was to feel badly for him, too. After the police who had beaten Rodney King were acquitted for their crimes, the film crew had to pause shooting of the movie because of the 1992 race riots that had broken out in Los Angeles.

Apologies, but I must go back even further to 1991. I can remember vividly watching the footage from March 3rd (often referred to as the first video to "go viral") in our neighbor, Harriet's apartment. The footage was shot by a 31-year-old plumber on a camcorder that he bought for his wife a month before on Valentine's Day, intended to document their future family. Harriet and I watched, as thousands of others had, as multiple LAPD officers stood around a defenseless Rodney King violently kicking and inflicting 56 baton strokes to his body for speeding on the Los Angeles freeway. I remember when I got home to our apartment that night, I found Sylvia frozen like a statue in front of the kitchen sink and Henry wrapping sandpaper around his hands like a bandage. And when I pointed out what he was doing, and that he was bleeding, he said it was a bandage. For several days, our mother listlessly gazed out the window and our father sanded what didn't need sanding.

EDUCATION

Professor Tim O. was all about preserving the spirit of resistance and loaned me all the texts I would need to do that appropriately. In exchange, I agreed to talk in class, which I figured I could do if I put my mind to it: I could say stuff.

"If it's nonsense of a significant nature, you'll be fine," Professor Tim O. assured me.

He was right. I got into student life, mostly as an observer, going back to my days as a roaming sea eyeball. Figuring, if Jane Austen showed herself to us, it would be with her eyes. Jo, if she had been in college with me, would have approved. But I hardly saw her, save for when she came home to get a new season's worth of fresh clothes. I did what I could to forget. I did my best to ignore her predilections for putting herself into unfavorable situations. I imagined my sister driving off a sunny cliff like the start of a rainbow, the horrified onlookers, and in the seconds preceding impact seeing the sky like a bird sees it—and then poof, lost to the horizon. But I didn't need to imagine anything. Jo was already gone.

This was a period of drinking and getting other people to buy me drinks at dimly lit Chicago bars. I spent my nights drinking with Paul's crew, and with his rolodex of "M" girlfriends—Melanie, Margaret, Margot, Michelle, Mena, Muriel, Mary. Early on, Paul had a steady, liberated girlfriend named Mira. I liked her more than I liked Paul. Mira was cool, though she would eventually be replaced. But the point was she didn't give a rat's ass if he had female friends, especially one like me, which I surmised was her way of saying our kind of relationship was nonthreatening, which Paul found offensive, and I liked that he did. Mira was collected, but not chill enough to sit through Paul and I reminiscing, which happened enough to have its own rhythm, with slight variations:

"It was you who ended things," Paul might say, after I had teased him for going cold on me in high school.

"Bernadette, you don't remember looking at me blankly in our high school cafeteria and saying I wasn't your thing?"

Jesus, had I said that? Paul never provided me with an answer, but it wasn't really about answers.

Before Woody Allen was a pervert, which seemed like a hundred years ago, Paul and I would walk around campus (important texts suffering under our smelly armpits) in a state of constant inquiry, seeking out answers to life's big questions, the ones that have plagued mankind from the start. Luckily, philosophy didn't require me to ascertain answers. Instead, I was tasked with asking a barrage of questions; I had been designed for this deluge of a position.

Paul and I, pretending to be platonic robots—the want of the other so palpable, strong like rot—turned the grassy quadrangles on campus into Central Park. Our working method, though arguably more mine than Paul's, held that the sky was the limit if you never looked down. Once you did, you realized you were in Chicago, Illinois, in the Midwest of all useless places. Many Midwestern institutions were quality, and held high standards in their own right, even still you would never possess the right tools, like you might from Columbia or Yale, to succeed.

One night at Danny's Tavern I came to see that no one mattered more to me than my sister. That night, I had wanted to go to Phyllis Musical Inn, where the owners treated you like one of their children, where the rockers Veruca Salt played their first show, in a room that began its life in 1908 as a grocery store, and my favorite of the swampy, lo-fi bars off the Blue Line. But the consensus among Paul's crew was to go to Danny's in Bucktown, a neighborhood that looked like a triangle on a map, known for its historic low-rise buildings and single-family homes, and named after the male goats (bucks) said to have once roamed the streets. The consensus was to get veggie burritos and herbal treats from "blueberry muffin lady," and for me to answer questions about the rural Midwest.

The arrangement was that Paul and his crew would buy me drinks, occasionally food (that night, a bean and cheese burrito), and in exchange I would give them what they wanted. They were after my "rural perspective" (their words); a tried-and-true delusion peddling freedom and self-sufficiency (my words). This deal was that they sated my desires and I sated theirs: they borrowed my class notes (scrupulous), and took my arcane advice (like using ash water to get rid of fleas). I told them about slaying animals on a farm and societal rejects. The latter of which meant I had good taste in music, and they wanted good taste in music too. His crew were eager to have "evolved spirits." They did not want to be the same posers as those people who separated themselves from the screams of the animals they consumed. They desired authenticity, and life in the rural Midwest fulfilled that desire, a notion that would have sent both Sylvia and Joanne spiraling.

Danny's was famous for its dim, comfortable feeling, like being at a house party where the details about the room or the people present didn't matter. And that night everyone in the crew was introduced to Paul's new girlfriend, Mary, who had the face of a snow angel, which completely outdid my olive complexion even in low light. Mary had lost her home to foreclosure. She and her family had moved to Chicago from Wisconsin, a far worse state than Illinois. And for a moment I had hoped she might take the lead on these conversations about the rural Midwest Paul's crew all but begged to hear about, but I was mistaken. At our table in the bar, I asked Mary to tell us something about Wisconsin's iconic dairy industry and Mary said she didn't know what I was talking about.

At the bar, Paul's crew picked my brain like vultures did roadkill. There were times I felt fatigued by the memories of my childhood. Nevertheless, I was a hungry college student and therefore told them what I knew, what we (Joanne and I) obsessed over, like Martha, the stuffed passenger pigeon, and the coveted county fair. Every year the spectacle was a real draw to those living in the region. Early agricultural reformers in the 1900s believed feelings of isolation to be the primary social problem in rural life. Jo blamed what she called the "capitalist consumption popsicle," which included American idealism and the early '40s for making socialization within the nuclear family the primary source of interaction. I remember the '80s were for familial despair and living in a state of constant hunger. Our stomachs growled uncontrollably as we studied the portrait of our parents at the fair taken before we were born, dangling crookedly on the wall like a warning. My sister and I zoned out on it, expecting the image to come to life so that we could eat the food at the fair: cheese pizza, fried goods, hotdogs, vanilla and chocolate swirled soft serve on sugar cones, pepperoni pizza. At the time, all we had were uncooked beets and carrots pickled in jars, which our mother would call "cooked plenty."

I told Paul's crew about rural life and the county fair. It was an event; it was capitalist in nature. But like everyone else in our small community, we experienced a deep loneliness and longed to connect. Unlike living in the city, rural living had people running toward sensory overload like football games: a sea of flesh, elbow-to-elbow nausea, where the smells alone could stain a person's clothing.

"You spend all your time with the land and yet you're also alien to it," I said to Paul's friends over drinks. Jo, had she been present, would have criticized this "share." Mining and neutralizing our shared experience for consumption would be abhorrent in her eyes. There was no doubt that my need to modify myself would be synonymous with an "East Coast act of desperation," which was to say: idealizing myself at the expense of others.

But Jo was not there. And they loved this line about being alien to oneself. Paul's crew regularly pressed me on my limits with regards to weather, deprivation, depression, and endless disappointment.

College students were the epitome of aspirational, and they wanted "workarounds."

How was it that I, Bernadette, never seemed cold in the frigid Chicago temperatures?

How was it that I, Bernadette, managed to stay on top of my studies and mitigate months on months of depression and disappointment?

How was it that I, Bernadette, a lithe junk kid that smelled of cow shit, had parents that would not cave and buy Tide. Everyone had Tide.

How was it that Bernadette, I—poop brown hair and ugly by most standards—from a long line of batshit women—would ever own her own a car or make it anywhere in America? Especially with a notorious older sister who'd already socially poisoned herself.

Joanne hadn't even tried to get into university before hitting delete. Now what?

If I'd had any backbone at all I would have found a way to leave them at the bar and never turn back.

UNIVERSITY LIFE CONTINUED

Over the course of my life there were very few days that went by without Joanne being mentioned, and these moments exposed my lack of generosity. I can remember one such conversation between Paul's girlfriend, Mary, and myself, which was also Paul's and my first fight, which became the basis for my understanding this shortcoming.

"Do you like me, Bernadette?" Mary had come up behind me one late afternoon as I got off the L Train and stepped foot onto the platform.

"I know how much Paul means to you, and it means a lot to me. I really do like Paul. I believe we have a future."

"Sure," I probably said: "I like you, Mary."

Why wouldn't I have said that to Paul's girlfriend, Mary?

But then she had to go on talking.

"I hear you have a sick sister. Poor you. Paul mentioned she was again arrested for accosting strangers in Bloomingdale's?"

"Mary," I did say to her fresh doily of a face: "You are the origin of what is right."

Her face lost ignition. I did not like Mary, or anyone, sharing their unapproved thoughts about Joanne. Each time it happened, my thoughts turned toward glaciers, and their heaving and evaporating with pulsing regularity. This pattern germinated back in high school where I had been excelling. I sat in German class, as Jo's message about white people atoning for their sins reverberated over the principal's loudspeaker. As it did, I imagined drawing thick vertical lines over our faces with permanent black marker. After Jo had been stopped—or interrupted, as I would have liked to see it—I remember saying to the students in my German class, who were nodding their heads dubiously, that the burning of Black churches in America had become so frequent that they were added to the National Trust for Historic Preservation's list of "most endangered places." But it was too late for reason. Jo had taken things too far. She had broken into the principal's office and stolen the mic. She had managed to slice her hands up before security was able to get inside. It had been one thing to hold parent-teacher conferences at the Cheesecake Factory "on behalf of the administration," but this charade was too much. That atonement episode would get Jo expelled from school, a bevy of more prescriptions, and land her back in a psychiatric ward for more weeks than I care to count.

"Where are the eyes?" I can remember Jo not asking since it was rhetorical, as three police officers loaded her into an ambulance, tears streaming down her face, so heavy and hard her skin cracked open. It was clear my sister no longer knew how to store the information. Her hands were bleeding through the bandages. Eventually, her message made its way into department stores across Chicago, and then to that day on the train's platform with Mary.

"I am not a lagoon," I said to Mary, matter-of-factly, almost inaudibly as the opposite train came into the station, and in a tone even lower than my naturally low voice, which had tended to alarm people who had trouble processing a female that sounded like a man.

"I'm more like a drained swimming pool, a hint of water left at the bottom where the mosquitos are left hatching and mutating."

I remember thinking: God, her boobs were amazing, even in her thick sweater you could tell. You had to hand it to Paul. Paul knew perky in a way that was beyond me.

"I'm sorry about your sister," Mary said, like words did not matter; or like only words mattered.

"I don't know what you want from me, Mary."

I walked away. I did not bother recounting the numerous unfortunate Marys and Marias of the world.

Back as junk kids in our attic space, adoring the sexy decapitated history of England, had Jo and I eating (even bland food) at a time when she had lost her appetite. Crime, theater, rot, modernity, country mists over the grand prodigy houses of late 16th century, had the two of us getting along when the world seemed to be falling apart. There we were making messes, soiling ourselves, and shoving whatever unhealthy goodies we could pilfer into our mouths. With our mouths full, we sifted through history's heretics. Maria Manning was an abused murderess who was imprisoned. Maria confessed to being overcome with rage at being continually attacked by her husband. She seized the hatchet closest to her—the one she used to break coal, to keep the fire going so that her husband's supper would stay warm—and with it, she struck him several times on the head. Maria, tormented by the thought of a mad crowd outside her prison walls, grew her fingernails long and sharp like a beak, and tried to stab herself in the throat with them before her execution. Some thirty thousand dreary English, including Charles Dickens, gathered to watch her die.

In 1852, a distraught Dickens wrote letters to *The Times* that man should recoil from his shameful callousness, at their upturned faces delighting in the scene, like watching an opera, "so inexpressibly odious in their brutal mirth." Dickens would not forget the hanging spectacle of Ms. Manning, thinking of her shape and dress—elaborate, corseted, blowing. Four years later, Thomas Hardy similarly recalled the execution of Elizabeth Martha Brown, noting her fine figure shown against the sky, dangling in the misty rain, and how "the tight black silk set off her shape as she wheeled half-round and back."

More to the point—I did not care who died first as long and Joanne and I both drank the poison. We did drink, and, in my delirium, I could hear her voice. This was a period for me of great exposure. It was about educating myself, and about Paul and I having our first big fight as grown-ups. I acted as a roving sea eye and spent a great deal of time looking outward, walking the city, despite the fact most I knew were looking inward for answers. Even Paul was into figuring himself out and believing it was possible. The trend was to go inside to unmask and to become fully formed and realized. The last thing I wanted was to spend more time with myself. I was hoping to rise outwardly, like a chimney swift seeking a better view, that brown bird with a pale throat that never descends and whose habitat was the open sky.

It was the Aughts. Notions of "tough love" flourished in the earlier part of the decade. "The Post 9/11 Era," "The Noughties," "The Naughties," "The Naughtiest," "The Zeroes." "The Aughts," an unfortunate coinage and linguistic error. The use of "Aught" to mean "zero," "nothing," "cipher," took hostage of the 19th century word "naught," which also meant nothing. All for naught. *Thirty-aught-six* was how to order a cartridge for a Springfield rifle. The actual English word aught, a concise and poetic near-synonym for "anything," had for centuries served writers, including Shakespeare.

"I never gave you aught," Hamlet says to Ophelia before she wanders off to pick corn marigolds, and before she tumbles into a millpond and drowns in a calm pool, the fixed expression on her face like a perfected porcelain doll. She was too sick to be saved but just right to be gawked at and fondled over.

"Was Ophelia dead or just consenting?" I heard Jo's voice.

Ophelia's placid, softly pornographic scene, was an early indication of rape culture as I would later see it, immortalized by artists, made into postcards and posters, which went on to be further immortalized—adorning living spaces and dormitory rooms in loads of countries, not just in America.

One of the most famous depictions was by John Everett Millais—who almost killed his model by leaving her lying in a bath of cold water for too long—was polarity sensitive phenomena, such as the word *aught*, which incorporated negation as part of the meaning.

"Where are the eyes?"

I heard Joanne at a constant rate, a summer hornet attacking my slice of peach pie.

At the time I ate only bean and cheese burritos. I read with fervor Jacques Lacan. He believed Hamlet's invectives against Old Hamlet's murderer were an example of denegation, which was to say that Hamlet's outward contempt toward Old Hamlet's murderer suggested an inward admiration. I tried to see things differently. I wondered if postcards contained only fragments of thinking or synthesized what was most important.

MORE GIRLFRIENDS

Paul had another M in his life, and this one was called Melanie. The big fight Paul and I had was about Paul's then girlfriend, Melanie. Melanie had eyes like a flashlight, alarming and focused. She could act robotic, and not like a robot I would design, which would be empathetic toward its surroundings. The night of the fight, Melanie told everyone in the booth at Rainbo that she had found inner peace. She was attending Al-Anon meetings for clarity, though she did not know any addicts herself. But the meetings were full of plenty of people who knew plenty of people who were addicts or were addicts themselves. I said there were limits to what a person should do to get attention. Paul, among his crew, called me a moralist and demanded I answer for my sister's notoriously outlandish behavior.

"You're juvenile, naïve, and bad in bed," he said.

"You're all over the map, content-wise," I pointed out to Paul. "And as a serious modernist essayist, and striving academic," such as he saw himself, "you better get a straighter line of thinking or risk humiliation."

"Bernie, I'm a white guy, decent-looking, with a solid familial base to rely on—people like me aren't humiliated."

"Right now, right this moment you are humiliated," I was undeterred.

"Melanie is sucking on the pain of others and claiming enlightenment."

I took out the mirror I kept in my back pocket to pluck out my chin hairs and held it up to Paul's face so that he would see. Maybe he would suffer in the river like Ovid's Narcissus with his reflection, an infinite image he could never grasp because it kept changing. Or would I end up an echo like Echo, destined to repeat the final words of others, unable to grasp what she desired. Would I end up mad in a chamber or was I already there?

"It matters to me what you think," Paul said, following me out of the bar. I had never seen him unravel.

"Melanie is not a good plan, is what I think," I stopped and said to his face.

"Is this about their names beginning with M? I like other words, like mayhem and moxie."

It was night. I wandered the dark back alleys of Wicker Park. I walked past brimming trash cans; noted two abandoned baby strollers in pristine condition (as far as I could tell, though I knew nothing about transporting babies). I thought about "value" but mostly about what had none. I studied my worn combat boots. Through a lit window, I spied a toddler in pajamas playing with a Barbie and wondered: Would this be how she would learn about the body? I did not want to be in America, especially during the months November, December, and January, where people find themselves submerged in "want," where most of us felt the weight of having no money. But America was all I knew. And then there was Paul, beautiful and alluring in his own way, coming toward me.

"Bernie, you can't just take off like that and not say anything more."

Paul said I should revisit my beliefs because Melanie was just speaking her truth.

He grabbed my hand: "You could too, you know."

"I could what, Paul?"

"Share your truth. Say what you're capable of."

For a moment, I thought he was messing with me and smiled along, like when someone orders a burger without the bun. But he was serious. He was being sincere. I dropped his hand immediately.

"As it is, there are too many people in America taking up more oxygen than they need," I said to Paul.

He followed me home at a distance: "I'm not about to let you out of my sight." I wanted him to rip my clothes to shreds but leave them on to dangle like the fringe on a flapper's dress. Let the torn pieces sway like vertical blinds on a sliding glass door.

"I can do that," he said.

Jesus, had I said this aloud?

I remember feeling like I really had to get a grip on what I was letting out.

"What are you capable of?" Paul's question still plagued me. It came at a time when I felt like I had finally found a nice balance between not having close friends and not having close enemies, an in-between space that I comfortably navigated. A space one could easily disappear into, or was it a space where I had let others disappear?

I knew I was capable of a rich fantasy life. I was adept at turning others into thought experiments, which I later came to see as acts of cruelty. This was made clearer, after summer hailstones shaped like medieval flails forced me off the interstate and into a motel room outside of Minneapolis. And I became more frightened than ever before of what I was capable of. In the absence of Joanne, in Joanne's decision to have a child knowing all that she knew, the sinister possibilities seemed dauntingly infinite.

THE FOOL

For an extended moment, I did not wish to be somebody else. I wanted to again be covered in filth and chicken stank. For a period, despite our father's unemployment, our family lived decently off the unsteady rent (weather depending) from the tenant farming our land, and Sylvia's textile work, sewing what were called "integral mesh" cubicle curtains for hospitals. It was a quiet period of contemplation.

When Joanne and I were kids, an entire summer day could be lost, willingly, to jarring tomatoes for the winter. In the flat, expansive landscape of our youth, a small hill, even a small patch of wildflowers, popped like a spasm. The obstructed Chicago skies were like nothing we had ever seen. It too transformed nature. That day we drove into the city with our dog, Tall, and our belongings packed and tarped into the bed of the '71 Chevrolet C20, I saw sky-reaching office buildings with hawk decals on their windows. I was told they were affixed there hoping to divert nocturnal migrants who might otherwise be lured to their deaths by the lights on inside. I remember thinking the world would go mad, and The Fool—sane as ever— would know that the wind and the sky and the rain that fell had been patterning since the world began. *King Lear*'s Fool proposed that the lives humans led were all versions of the same patterning. This patterning superimposed itself onto every landscape.

I can remember on our drive into the city Jo flicking me, in rapid succession, on my wrist. She said she could read my mind. She did not like what she saw. I remember I ignored the sore indent on my wrist like a chore. At the time, I had these amazing oversized black sunglasses from the gas station that I was wearing. I used them to cover my fat face and to hide my not-even-hazel brown eyes, but mostly for punctuation. I pretended to be a somebody, one that had the potential to accumulate value. When I was a somebody, I was everything to everyone—I was that vast of an enterprise. But my sister did not care. She had not even noticed the glamorous glasses, even though they were the exact style she had wanted from the magazines a month prior. Her need for control; her impulsiveness, her attention-seeking behavior, suggested even back then at the end of a decade and at the start of a new one, that she may have been a serial killer.

I was content being myself but there was nobody around to verify it. If I had the chance to see Henry or Sylvia, or if they had the inclination to hear me out, I would have told them they could take turns. It was sort of painful, like a root canal, or like when a good party ended and everyone left, abruptly, leaving behind indications that something worthwhile had occurred. The music played, but you no longer understood the words. There was the residue: used napkins, paper towels, and bathroom towels scattered throughout. And forgotten items: Graham Greene novels, a phone number, one Diva Cappuccino Cupcake press-on nail, sunglasses, half-eaten things, condoms, fears of never forever, empty cans, cigarette burns in red plastic cups, ash, and stink. Even though the empty feeling in the apartment had gone on for some time it still felt sudden.

Sylvia and Henry took avoiding each other to new heights. Our mother would shut herself in their bedroom and paint multiple copies of Jean-Baptiste-Siméon Chardin's *Still-Life with Cat and Fish*, of a cat disrupting the calm of a splayed fish. After, she went to the dead, to exhume their auras, like those in ancient Mesopotamia lived alongside the remnants of the deceased. Going into a trance, in an act to preserve moments of time, our mother would spend countless hours unraveling her inventory of death, which was to say—collectables and other unenviable things she had from relatives who were all dead. Like her mother's support hose for her varicose veins, old dinner sets from China, moth-eaten linens stored in a chest. Each death set had an adjacent notecard, which included a handwritten date, and sometimes a scribble of history. Sequestering herself, Sylvia would undress these times like she was undressing a newborn: carefully and deliberately. She re-read the accompanying notes aloud, which surely by then she had memorized:

"Early photos of my grandmother, Poppy."

"Aunt Marjorie and Uncle Babe (Charles) received this tablecloth and matching six napkins (missing three) on their wedding day, 1932."

Or, written on paper, stored in a small plastic sandwich bag, sealed with staples:

"This was written by Aunt Fannie Fareown before she hanged herself, 6 years before Poppy was born in 1899, the year of the Great Arctic Outbreak in February. Oranges in Florida perished. Phoebe, a moon of Saturn, was discovered, an improved rotary blade lawn mower in America was patented."

"Mother's King James Bible, her death at age 50 ruled a suicide. It was my senior year of high school, 1968. Martin Luther King Jr. was assassinated. The year Aunt Vie moved into the house in town to then burn down the house in town. After, she committed herself to a mental institution with a decent collection of fruit juice."

Henry managed to spend even longer hours in his study. Unemployed, but pretending to still have work, was not a mentally productive exercise for our father, and whenever he found himself among streets or roads that were not arranged in a rectangular grid, he became distressed. He sported a plastic seashell the size of a sesame seed, that clamped shut the congenital hole in his heart. He made a point of telling us how much he loved us, which Sylvia welcomed after a lifetime of promising to change his ways. He still took his morning coffee (black, plus a finger of whiskey) along with his binoculars to the foldable desk and chair he'd set up for himself on the sidewalk. The neighbors did not approve. They filed complaints with the authorities, who then complained that the complaints were amassing. Henry could not for the life of him figure out why they made official complaints about his birdwatching: "Other Americans did their thing; watched anorexics on television shell out cooking advice." He wondered why he couldn't be left alone. It wasn't his business what other people did, he said defensively. He wanted to watch birds on weekday mornings before leaving for the real estate company, a job he had lost, but pretended to have kept, to eager, younger, better educated up-and-comers.

There were other physical developments. Sylvia had leg cramps, and when she wasn't grommeting hospital curtains, or painting, she was on the stoop smoking. Nobody dared bother her there. She said stoops were self-emerging systems built out of necessity, like kitchens were systems of domesticity. The kitchen was where Sylvia Plath ended her life, "Face-diving into a gas oven," our mother said of the gesture that would be later echoed by Plath's husband's lover, Assia Wevill, along with her baby girl, Shura.

"Love options," our mother said about women and progeny and final decisions.

bell hooks said the home belonged to women, our mother explained. It was where the women were, and it was a space to make final decisions. Sylvia would sit on the stoop, where I could see her from our bedroom. She sat there until eventually her face relaxed into her end-of-day face. The expression she wore when the bills were paid, and the checks cleared, or when Tall ate his kibbles slowly enough he wouldn't vomit all over the floor.

As for our father, Henry had lost feeling in his feet and legs; the result of nerve damage from the war. A stranger on the bus told him all he had to do was walk a path as narrow as a thread. "Walk a line," the stranger had said. His rheumatoid arthritis was causing his hands to cripple; the knuckles on his right hand looked like the work of the KGB. His physical therapist suggested he manage his discomfort by finding relaxing activities, such as meditation. Henry was to avoid tension, to relax, and to focus on the things he enjoyed, which made him angry. Henry did it his way. He took up collecting varieties of scotch. Any brand would do.

Some evenings, after long days spent at the textile company, our mother would be in the kitchen making use of the oven to prepare dinner, which no doubt we were ungrateful for. (She had somehow managed to make chicken so un-chicken, even the bird would not have recognized itself.) At the time, she loved the oven for reasons we did not press her about. At the time, she was growing more forgetful, forgetting to put the milk away and swearing loudly about it. (Waste was unacceptable.) Then she would go on to call her astrologer, who would tell her that natal Jupiter was in Taurus, an alignment that represented luck and prosperity. Jupiter was widely known in the solar system for expansion and aiding with fertility.

"That kind of planet, huh?" It was not what our mother wanted to hear.

From our bedroom window I saw Sylvia kneel on our stoop, barefoot, even when the outside temperature had dropped below zero, smoking menthols. "Imagine the nasty," Joanne could come out of nowhere and when nobody had asked. The thing was, I could not imagine the nasty. What did "imagine the nasty" even mean? This sent me into a perpetual loop, one that sent me back to our childhood, one that could be difficult to extract myself from. Even though I knew, even then as a fancy philosophy student, that I did not need to have the answers.

Once, in a rare moment back when we lived on the farm, Joanne had left me alone with her first love, Seraphina, and Seraphina had asked me how and why I tolerated my older sister.

"You can have your own life, one of happiness," Seraphina had said confidently to me.

I remember studying the contours of Seraphina's face, soft as the softest paintbrush, and wondering how beautiful people, such as she was, got away with the most astonishing things. She had not been a figure in our lives long, and we were kids, nevertheless I understood that the beautiful were exceptional creatures that left mighty imprints on the imaginations of nobodies. Seraphina, with her kind, loving, retired urban-to-nature parents, would find a suitable place in the world. The spot was just waiting for her to fill.

I won an award for a blender poem. Paul had won first prize for exceptional prose for his essay on Annie Dillard and the writing life. At the awards ceremony, I upset Paul's latest girlfriend, Mena (who had won nothing) for deeper reasons I could not explain but reasoned I did not have to explain, courtesy of my philosophy studies. "Don't you think what you're doing, drawing us at a distance, and not participating like a regular fucking person, is exacerbating your lonely, desperate life project?" Mena asked me at the awards ceremony, held in a designated room for special events in our university's library. The three of us stood awkwardly with adult beverages in our hands like we were waiting for instructions. The room was full of strangers, vases of peonies and trays of perfectly small, square sandwiches.

"You seem alone," Mena added for further clarification, sipping some champagne.

"That's because I am alone," I said, downing some champagne.

Jo could be rotting away in Hello's house for all I knew. God damn it, I had written a prize-winning poem.

Elaborate spaces, such as that one, were built to leave an impression. They were constructed on the premise that man could be excellent and therefore should be rewarded for his excellence. The space was an encapsulation of that premise: full-length mirrors, decadent chandeliers, dark, serious, wood paneling, and portraits of dead white men whose meaning was everlasting. I have this irresistible memory, a fetishization of the dress Mena was wearing that celebratory day. I remember thinking her bony shoulders could be weaponized. I remember thinking: "No, Mena, I'm not a person—I'm an animal who is here to get an award for a blender poem."

"What if one day we are asked to describe this experience?" I asked Paul and Mena.

"What if the majority of these educated people with fancy degrees become fascists?" I said, looking around the room.

"Wow, Bernadette, way to go off the rails," Mena said.

"There needs to be a record," I said, snagging a stuffed mushroom from a passing silver tray.

I had not invited Sylvia and Henry. It was no secret that by then I was on my own and I did not need my vacant parents there to highlight this. I had won the Fiske Poetry Prize for Best Original Poem or Poem Cycle (this was never clarified). My creative efforts were recognized by the institution, a quality one at that, which gave me money to attend the institution, and at the same time stole my money to attend the institution, an arrangement deemed necessary in America, and one that made me proud and queasy. My prize poem, "Blender," was the product of putting some of my most coveted words, like "tarn," for one, on paper and blending said words in our defective blender. The neighbor, Harriet, who lived on our floor, agreed to help. We drank hard liquor and pretended to be at a Solstice parade in Santa Barbara or a big splashy one, such as for the military. Harriet smoked a fat joint and threw the newly torn pieces up to the heavens, which scattered throughout our apartment. I photographed the results. After developing the film, I transcribed the images of arranged words and put them again down on paper. With a newly full glass of champagne, I toasted Paul and Mena, and requested he find another strategy. "What does she mean, *find a new strategy?*" an irritated Mena irritably questioned Paul.

I remember, when I should have been pursuing important life advancement objectives—like pretending I was an only (and wanted) child, and making healthy conversation with people outside of those that I studied and sketched, especially then; when I was closer than ever before to graduating from college, and applying for full-time jobs with benefits (dental and health)—instead of doing any of the above, I wrote out in pencil: Deflection is a major issue in society.

I superglued this unremarkable revelation onto our mailbox, next to all the other mailboxes in the apartment building. After a few days of nothing, no response good or bad to my legible note taped there, I marched over to Harriet's for additional support, or maybe to test the conclusion. Harriet was nine years older. She always had something stuck to her face. She ran an illegal daycare center from her parents' apartment. Harriet was hot with scandal. Harriet would know what was what.

I told her about Paul's girlfriend, Mena. Harriet interrupted to ask what happened to Melanie. "Or was it, Megan?" I told Harriet we needed to move on, subject-wise, and began to talk about societal deflection, and Harriet said: "God, we only have it *one*." She said this unfortunate thing while rolling a joint, her left eye sliding back into her head like a beetle does when hiding. I remember thinking she must have meant to say "once," before realizing I was late to class, and worse I was making assumptions. Something, after a lifetime spent with my family in America, I tried to avoid.

Harriet, a smear of avocado on her cheek, took a massive hit off her blunt, and said about weed and the male sex, "Be wary of weed dick."

I had no idea what weed dick was.

Harriet was awesome.

The little purple potted flowers on Harriet's windowsill were suffocating. She said the children she cared for were evil little fuckers that liked to destroy things, like pretty flowers. I remember thinking about weed dick, and about Paul and Mena as a unit, and about whether her nice dress had been made in China, since our country never grew tired of lamenting China, and about how Americans were notorious hypocrites.

I saw Paul less frequently after the awards ceremony. He had gotten really into rowing, hiking, biking, and half-marathons, and then into those fitness freefall challenges where people push their bodies to extremes. Instead of making plans, we just ran into each other at The Empty Bottle or at parties. It seemed any minute I felt like I had finally achieved autonomy, he was always there, in shape, which I remember annoyed me since I had a lumpy belly. Plus, I had a warped bellybutton that was probably a hernia, which left untreated might one day become an incarcerated emergency. Doctors were expensive and for important things you needed to see at least two to get a trusted diagnosis.

"I'm looking at you," Paul would holler at me, after spotting me in a crowd.

"Bernie," he said, coming up next to me, "I'm just the sort of beast you want near you, remember? Chimeras, leatherback sea turtles?"

"Jesus, had I told Paul everything?" I remembered thinking about Paul referencing the mind tunnels Jo and I roamed in our attic space on the farm. I remember feeling sick of my point of view and realizing I could not do this on my own. Besides, was she dead? No. Jo was alive. She was working at a specialty market that sold varieties of mustards, handmade greeting cards, single sourced oils, sea salts, salami, and pâtés in little French tins. I befriended her manager, which was to say I brought him recreational drugs (mostly psychotropic) that I had received from my bench friends. In exchange he told me which shifts Jo worked. In terms of where she spent her nights, I had imagined she was still staying at Hello's. But I had stopped spying on his house. I had covered over our bedroom windows with black out curtains. It was time to speak with Jo. Plus, Harriet had told me to get her, and I listened to Harriet for reasons unknown.

I stopped by Hello's to talk to my sister. Hello answered the door. His hair was shaggy. He had grown a beard. He looked like Henry. He told me to walk around the side of the house, Jo would meet me out back by the shed. Joanne came out, emerged like behind a theater curtain, wearing a pink terrycloth robe. The first thing I noticed was that she had overhauled her look. She had bleached her hair. She wore thick black eyeliner, trimmed, and styled her dark bushy eyebrows, put on wooden platforms that clicked and clacked as she walked the tile path. Hello must have purchased these garments for her. She did not like pink and there was no way, not even with the money she made selling foie gras at the specialty market, she could afford those niceties. Or had she grown to like pink? How much did I not know about how Jo had changed?

Like a car accident, I tried not to look, but there was no turning away: Joanne's face, a collection of sharp bones and androgynous features, gave nothing away. Hers was the kind of electrifying beauty many found alarming. One could not help but wonder how all the pieces and parts managed to fit together, but they did. For all of that, that day her sallow face did not glow like I had expected it might, what with all the adult sex and fortified cuisine I'd assumed she was consuming. Her long, bleached hair was badly in need of a trim. The ends were ratty and not in an intentional way. Jo was not known for her beauty routines like others her age were, but even she would have noted that her ends needed to go. I didn't ask Joanne about her insomnia. I did not ask her about what it was like to have sex with an average dad man who preferred denim over other materials. Instead, I said that during our life at sea one of us would have to be on watch three hours on, and three hours off, at a time.

In the past we'd had difficulty coming to unanimous decisions. I suggested since we were amateurs, we should keep our ambitions narrow; start first with Bermuda. Easy coordinates. This worked out well since the boat we liked in Michigan came with a Loran, but it did not have radar, which would mean a lot of interpreting. Plus, Bermuda was a short trip from New York City, where Patti Smith lived.

Jo, before me wearing a head of singed hair, was unusually subdued. She swiveled from her chair to the grass, which was covered in splintered wood. She said modern dance was "something else." She said congratulations on the award in poetry. She told me that boat was long gone, and, besides, by the time we would arrive there wouldn't be any ice left: "Tip the rowboat and it comes back, tip it once more and it comes back again, tip it a third time and you've reached the other stable state—upside down," she said about our future on Earth. "Go home, Bernie," Jo told me, her face flattening like a site being excavated. She told me that she never wanted to see me again until she wanted to see me again, which would probably be never.

She told me to go find a hobby. "Not a velocipede, but an actual distraction, Bernadette."

Joanne could not just call a bicycle a bicycle.

I remember feeling light on my feet—Jo had called me Bernadette—and going home to our apartment that day to focus on our escape from the Midwest, and the women in our family that had vanished. I read that Francis Bacon opened his front door, stood in the drafty vortex, pointed to a windmill in the distance, and asked what could be learned from the sight? I understood that Joanne was unwell. I could draw the contours of my older sister's face in the dark. But I had not known how sick she might have really been. That day at Hello's, I felt the years bubbling over. Her life was punctuated by small revolutions. She had been born in a cold wave. The year of America's Bicentennial, celebrating the country's two-hundred years of freedom. The same year capital punishment was reinstated and the song "Hotel California" became a national fixture. I had gone over in my head the many times Joanne was unreachable. Even as kids on the farm we never felt clean. In fact, we felt so consistently unclean that way our mother asked her crisis counselor, and later dear friend Cherri Cohen, if she had ever felt clean. Our family showered with soap and water, lathered well, sometimes even repeated the actions, but nothing changed feeling dirty. Not even in the city, with the jobs our parents' felt might someday get us on an airplane where we would eat well-portioned, designated airplane food despite the many complaints about bad food on airplanes. And the neighborhood boys, what had they done to Joanne? Had they been the source of her cuts and her bruises? The ones she would return home with after hitching rides. What about her expulsion from high school? All the things she would never mention because she felt nobody deserved to know.

INSTITUTIONS

Laura Palmer was everywhere, that was the truth. There were weary, half-smiling blond Laura Palmer look-alikes that kept appearing and disappearing on television screens in communities across America. My sister's absence for an obscenely long period of time had gradually gnawed away at the flesh right down to bone. The truth was, my sister was providing for herself, and this gave her the leverage to do what she wanted and to do it unchallenged. I was tasked with managing our parent's fears of losing another child, which I resented. Suddenly, Henry and Sylvia were uncomfortable with their kids growing up and moving out. They made concerted efforts to be home more often.

I handed in my notice to Video Creature. I searched for a better full-time job. I readied myself, but each time I stepped into an office to answer questions about my resume, my body involuntarily responded by leaving sweat stains on my clothing. I went on an interview for the position of "something-assistant to the CEO" of a global media company, and left drenched. In the interview, I was asked to explain how I had gone from pursuing a law degree in community college, to philosophy at the University of Chicago, to supporting technology's mission to ensure world peace.

"Don't you like lawyer money?" the man conducting the interview asked.

Of course, I liked lawyer money, I had thought.

"I care about people, too," I had said.

Though this was only partly true.

I landed a job teaching playwriting in an afterschool program to rightfully skeptical 5th and 6th graders four-days a week, which I knew nothing about, and which of course made zero use of my philosophy degree. I learned everything I could about playwriting, the value of dialogue and theatrical stage directions. Professor Tim O. mentioned he had a wealthy poet friend, recently retired, who might have some work for me at his house in Lakeview. The ideal person would need to be willing to paint walls. They should have a feminine mind. They should be a decent conversationalist, and capable of slogging through loads of archival work. Nobody was more surprised than me when the retired wealthy poet offered me the job. He paid handsomely. I was given a key to his magnificent house off the Red Line in the historic district, Lakeview, with Wrigley Field at its core. It was a place for the wealthy. I was told that I could come and go as I pleased. I could do laundry. Borrow one of his cars, if I wanted. I could take anything out of the fridge or the pantry, which appealed to me.

"And the pantry?"

"Help yourself."

In that instant—I became a lover, a defender, of the rich. I saved so that I might realize my future potential, and the more money I saved, the more impressed I was at my ability to save, so I kept saving.

My poet boss' Lakeview house was an endless sensation. It was designed for crowds to eat and to dance. There was a library with an enviable selection of first edition books and fine liquors, a substantial loose leaf tea collection, plush pillows and couches, long, full linen drapes that ran floor to ceiling, Turkish rugs scattered throughout. Rooms that were made to feel warm by the lighting, which emanated from lamps from the 1970s. His kitchen was designed to resemble a UFO. It was perhaps my favorite room in the house, after the primary bathroom that had a tub that would have easily drowned my entire family. The kitchen had a name, in this case "sour." The walls were painted a vibrant yellow citrus. Lakeview had rooms I could entirely disappear into.

He held these lavish, wildly hypnotic, sensual parties, where guests drank themselves into oblivion and lounged around his impressive goatskin-and-resin dining table into the early morning hours. There was endless activity, which could fill the space. Every few minutes, someone would ring the doorbell, and then the sound of a grizzly bear's growl would play, though everyone knew that the door to his house remained open and to just come inside. My poet boss' gatherings were seductive. And I was voluntarily seduced by them, compelled to consume them, like elderberry syrup coated the throat in antioxidant powers. Everyone present at these parties appeared, at least to me who would be hiding in plain sight, to remain cogent. More importantly, they were intent on getting what they wanted from the world. I watched them operate in a kind of horror and delight. It was just as our mother had said of her grandmother's dead naked body on a gurney: where there was horror, there was narrative sensation.

"Do it, Bernadette, go ahead, touch the art wall," my poet boss was fond of telling me to do about his Cindy Sherman photographs, my hands covered in paint. He was not welcome in my pants. I would not let the wealthy poet peel back my skin, but I would take his money, his pantry items—unpitted dates, goose fat, kombu—and attend his parties. My poet boss had many friends, art collectors, herbalists, architects, writers, local politicians, and sound artists who approved of me blurting out one evening: "Where does terror reside?" Of course, I had meant to keep the sentiment to myself, but there it was, my gaffe, our jargon—along with a platter of cheeses and crackers—out there on the table to pick at. I remember the wildly active sound artist, Leon, said not to worry: "You are sublime," Leon said. Gina, the director of an avant garde performance group named after an island that once housed wandering goats, entrusted me to open a bottle of bubbles to celebrate my being there. "You're ready," she said.

If my theater students had been privy to any of it—Bob Dylan on vinyl, candy cigarettes, the abundant throwbacks—they would have made disapproving guttural sounds. My students said I talked like a crackhead living in a past century. This was why their initial pity toward me turned to tolerance, and in time to contingent respect, and, as more months passed, an eventual appreciation for the theater. I was fond of these students, who I selfishly referred to as mine, who would have been absolutely fine without me. "Everywhere, terror," my poet boss said, with a touch of sarcasm, kissing me on the cheek, which he understood was condescending.

These exchanges were theater. He then did what he always did at his parties. He made me a plate of food: cornichon, dried apricots, slices of crusty bread, melon, burrata, and said to take it. He would even go to the trouble of squeezing a ring of mustard and to have me pick the next record. There was an alluring friction between us, of something that could be but was not, the jigsaw of our unmatched bodies, a secret door that begged to be opened but was not. Sometimes, I would make toast just to hand it to him, just to place my frame next to his, just to see what might happen, to see whether it would clarify things, and say: "Boss, here is toast," when really in my head I had named the maneuver "hotdog." Of course, it was certifiably unsexy. But most people, American or not, might find themselves wanting to be between buns.

I was having the time of my life in the city, proving to myself I was having the time of my life. For the most part, time had gone by uninterrupted and rather calmly and quietly. I kept busy. There were many other absurdities to examine, in addition to poetry and failing women in botched systems. My poet boss had me painting his primary bathroom a mandarin orange over the previous month's olive green. He would have had me think he was indecisive, yet he was anything but. So, when it came time every month for him to change his mind about a room's color, I bought the paint with his credit card and got painting. There were hard truths, like workshopping my stories to turn their potential into greatness, and like my suitable, long-distance relationship with Paul's best friend Preston, who agreed to keep our relationship over the phone, or, later by computer. I was proving to be successful at deprivation and self-restraint, which still turned me on. I attributed my triumphs to past obsessions, like Martha, stuffed and on display at the Smithsonian, and living a life at sea. I was busy showing myself that I had finally outgrown my sister. I was doing the work of a young, well-adjusted woman in America, finally. But there was an uncomfortable gap between then and my life before, as a university student, and further back with Joanne. I wanted closure. To conclude the chapter on my own terms, rather than having it just end.

Then I learned my sister was alive and well and back to her natural black hair, which rattled me. Her unreachable state—the one that had meant she was out of commission and temporarily disabled—had me less worried. Jo had been tagging the city with two thoughts: *Am, Not*. I had overheard on both the Brown and Red Line trains news of a vandal who was breaking into pet shops to free caged animals. It reached a tipping point when said vandal broke into the zoo. People did not like seeing tigers and elephants *that* close. "That was what television was about," a terrified man said.

On the radio, on every station, the announcers (ordinarily very put together individuals) attempted to keep their composure: How could this have happened? They asked their listeners. "The zoo has top-notch technology at its disposal," a caller called in to add. "And one of the best security systems in the country." Progress had let people down and they could not make sense of it. The security footage was eventually made public. It showed my sister sneaking smaller creatures under her sweatshirt and inside her sweatpants, out of the building. The street cameras picked up images of Jo calmly waiting for the bus.

Joanne had fucked up. She had ignored a major familial tenet, which posited that one must master the art of the outward message to move seamlessly inside of "civil society." (A notion our parents mocked. Our father often held up his wallet, which was funny since it was empty.) On the farm, we weren't used to being observed daily. In the country, days, weeks, months could go by without seeing another person outside of your family. Our parents insisted each morning that the two of us construct personal pentacles. These modes of expression could be made of anything. In other words, they could be made cheaply. Sylvia once borrowed an electric mixer from Cherri Cohen to whip Henry's hemorrhoid cream and said: "That's all there is to know about childbirth."

We tuned into Joanne. On the couch, our new family triangle turned on the television to watch Jo's boss, the owner of the specialty market, as he made a statement on national television in front of anyone who would listen. That's what he said explicitly, as he explained that he felt he had no other choice than to publicly denounce Joanne for piling up the fancy imported animal products and letting them rot. But they're so well preserved, I thought. Europeans know how to make the good stuff last. Wasn't that the truth?

News of Joanne kept arriving like an unwanted package. Then, as a courtesy, the police came by our apartment to let us know Jo had been institutionalized. She had been placed in a "Specialized Recovery" unit in a psychiatric hospital in the Quad Cities. The plan was that she would recover with those monitors strapped around her ankles. Apparently, Joanne had spent the entire drive there asking: "Where are the eyes?" The cops handed us a note neatly written on yellow legal paper. On it, my sister had written that she no longer knew how to store the information. She was at capacity, and the information just kept coming from every direction. She wanted her family. And, in a way, this news, bad as it was, managed to bring our parents back to life like a Chia Pet. Without Jo, there was nothing worth loving, and now she was solidly somewhere we could point to.

Later that week, I told my wealthy poet boss, who needed to zip up his fly and find a decent tailor, that I had to take some time off. He wrote me a check covering a month's worth of work and gave me a book on hieroglyphs. I lightly smooched him on the cheek. Teaching theater would continue. It was the more nourishing of the two jobs. It was also in Hyde Park, an area of the city I knew well since that was where the university was. And I had made a promise to my students that we would continue with Maria Irene Fornes, exploring her characters, who often struggled to confirm their dignity. They were often told their suffering was of their own making. The class would finish reading her play "Mud" from 1983, a play in which the word "love" is like a well. Her work was making sense to them. There were other things that should not be overlooked—we had raised the money to buy six video cameras for students to document what it was they saw, to tell their own stories in addition to the ones we were reading.

These kids knew more about America than anyone. They called me "fancy degree," sometimes "Bernadette Fareown," other times, "teacher lady." It was the closest thing to certainty I would ever experience. Sometimes I lost their attention to other news, like the loss of a relative, or hunger. I want to say I did what I could, but we all know that was not enough.

A tropical cyclone hit the southeastern part of America in August, ranking as the costliest natural disaster in our history, and I came to understand that from the time my sister could speak, her language, behavior, and the hormonal shifts that would later follow were being weaponized against her. Against us all, really. We must all have a kind of madness to stay sane, I said to Tall, who was crying in his sleep, possibly dreaming about the demonic me that might hurt a dog, a thought I had borrowed from a poet I had slept with—which was to say: I kept his thin book of poetry in my bed like a child would a doll. Then a storm the size of Chicago hit Chicago. I remember thinking if my sister had been next to me, she would have loved this storm. It was the kind of night in Jane Austen's *Northanger Abbey*: billowing curtains, whining chimneys, and hollow murmurs; a heroine's heart racing upon opening a drawer to discover a manuscript of unknown antiquity, which in the next morning's light turned out to be a laundry list. (God, did we understand her disappointment.)

But Joanne was not beside me. She was in a mental institution.

I visited her every chance I could in what the doctors insisted was a "special room": a heavily monitored, bare-bones, white, padded, windowless space, where the conversations could often be broken down like this:

"Bernie, what is it—you need confirmation?" she would ask.

"No," I would say.

"A vibrator?"

"Maybe."

"You should learn to keep your mouth shut."

I wanted to say: "No, Jo, that's your issue."

But it had become my issue.

"Stay awhile."

I would. We would sit in silence, until one afternoon she broke it to say, "Never mention Ronnie."

Jo had meant Hello. And I had agreed to never mention "shed man" by name again. Every so often, I wondered if my sister had ever discovered the etchings in his shed out back, little bubble shapes I had made all those years ago using my fingernails, because I missed communicating with her.

INSTITUTIONS CONTINUED

Jo remained obstinate. She refused to eat or sleep. She began calling herself "an interlocutor of time" and grew impossibly frail. During this skeleton phase, Jo bit and kicked and screamed more than ever. I remember before they tied her arms up for good, she hit her face with her fists, and I tried copying her in solidarity, but with something lighter like a brochure I had snagged from the institution's lobby. Unlike Jo, I did not have the courage to use my hands.

At night, I would stay by her bed until being discovered and escorted out by security. Jo would talk about light and dark, hues and values, secrets. She said, "People turn towards the light, and their backs to the dark." But darkness served a purpose. "We just need to work harder to see," she said. There was something to darkness. Without it, we would not have Francisco Goya, the engravings of Albrecht Dürer, or an Illinois river where shadows are cast. We needed darkness and extended solitude—caves, prison, a sick bed, silence, twilight—to activate the imagination. Joanne explained the dark was more than a room, it could be a black cloud, an ear canal, a pantry. There's what's poorly understood, she said: the dark web, the black sheep of a family. There was what has been tucked away: recesses of the mind, bibles, a diaphragm. And what's covered over: a grave, burrito suizo, a smoker's lung.

"There is what's in your face: an idiom, sunrise, a bald lie," I added, finally catching on.

"And on your face: clogged pores, scars, scratches, age," Jo said.

Take the supermassive black hole at the core of the Milky Way, a point of stillness in our rotating galaxy. Invisible, and still scientists knew the black hole was there.

"How do they know?" Jo asked. "Because it leaves an imprint on its environment," my sister said.

"And after all that, Bernie," Jo continued, "the bleak country of England produced the treasured painter of light, J.M.W. Turner."

What was it about the way my sister's brain processed information that made people think it was ok to hurt her, or anyone else for that matter? There were things that I gave up in order to be in the institution with Joanne, such as becoming a roaming sea eyeball. Personal advancement in general. I surrendered to the fullness that was my sister. It was how I might access her, access that part of myself, that person who could love fully. I tuned into Joanne like I would have a radio report on how best to barbecue chicken breasts, searching for clues on how to advance her work of rewiring this excruciatingly limited notion of what it meant to be a woman in the world with ideas.

For her doctors, I spent a lot of time and energy interpreting Jo's perceptions to discern her needs. Indecipherable gibberish about electrical currents connecting planets, both known and unknown, meant she had to go to the bathroom. She was cold and in need of a blanket whenever she brought up the critically endangered eyelash seaweed, an ancient seaweed the size of an eyelash. Hours passed this way in the institution trying to decipher her needs, with her staring at the freshly painted (because she had managed to find a marker) pristine white walls. We were told that this psychic torment was to encourage a clear mind.

"Or minds," Joanne would hiss at her doctors, unhelpfully.

Sitting in her special sick room, I never felt more desperate to pinpoint the origin of the Fareown curse, and the castration rumor. Nothing I read explained it. Or everything I read explained it. Then I remembered *King Lear*'s Fool. The Fool explained a snail had a house so that it did not give its head away. I had problems, Jo had issues, but the pervasive insistence on female tragedy—that was to say, that females were tragic—was not one of them. "Jo," I would say to her on my next visit, "keep your head in your house. Keep your eyes in your head."

I studied my sister in her hospital bed, the monitors blinking beside her, colorful pills, tubes inserted into her arms, her thinning body lit up like a Christmas tree. I studied her like I was memorizing a church verse. I studied her because she looked like our mother, who looked like her mother. I wanted to remind us about the parts that solely belonged to us. For that, I went back to infancy. "Look," I said to my sister, "we did not die, we came out alive, screaming for air." We wanted air. Joanne even held onto hers for the first minute of her life, which set off her heart monitors and left the doctors frazzled. I would like to say we were not toilets destined for waste. If this was to be the only metaphor we would be allowed in that institution, where she would remain until they could fix her, then here, instead: The two of us were more like colorful buckets in the woods, placed next to tall shady trees and free rivers. Walter Benjamin would say those that hold a fixed place in the world were never really present in the now.

Paul had given me a potted polka dot plant for Joanne, which the security guards chucked immediately. She would not have liked a plant in a pot, so I didn't see the need to protest. In Jo's room I sat beside her, beside rows of prescription bottles and a collection of philosophy and poetry books I had lent her. I said: "Listen, Paul says hi and for a brief moment there was a gifted potted plant in the picture, but now I have only your back brace with me."

I had with me the cumbersome object made mostly of heavy-duty plastics and that had a metal chin guard to hold her face upright. That contraption had given her bright and burning rashes. I had carried it with me to the Institution. I leaned that hard, uncomfortable shell that had stretched over her body, that had encased her frame like a mummy, next to her bed in the hospital. That day, I had with me her custom back brace which for those four years, for twenty-two hours a day, she'd treated as second skins and as canvases. Like family, when I would have discarded the item at the dump.

Joanne said nothing. Her unreceptiveness was an opportunity to get some things off my chest. Mostly, I mentioned Preston gently but confidently, like sliding an envelope with an important message through the horizontal crack at the bottom of a door. I spoke lightly about how Preston was into me, about how he was an increasingly established artist living in Brooklyn, making performative sculptures out of rayon sheets and broom sticks. It was difficult to describe how ineffective I was at conveying good news. Only later did I understand that it was because I had thought so little of myself. I told her about spying on her and worrying. I can remember, to feel any sort of control over the situation with my sister (which I had no control over), I used to follow her, dressed in her black jumper, out to the suburbs. Outside, on freshly manicured lawns, I would peer through windows into houses and watch her maneuver the space like she had it memorized. She would be in a crowd of people dancing and touching her, and I can remember that despite making all the right fun moves—swaying their hips, drinking Jäger—in reality, they looked just as pitiful as I did, standing outside in the hail, peering in at them. I can remember thinking that for all my sister's exhibition-ism, she rarely ever exposed her skin, like a well-kept secret. Even the day her rigid, clunky, corset-like back brace came off.

There the brace was, an outline of her past, leaning, unsteadily, against Jo's hospital bed. There were two thick strips of metal pro-truding from the back of it, arcing off where her shoulder blades would have been like crowbar wings if she'd had it on. I remember those arches made her look even more hunchbacked than she was. Those metal strips ran from her neck, all the way down to her pubic bones. They dug into her flesh, leaving deep marks and bruises. Going back to that liberating point in time, when the monstrosity was removed, Joanne could have chosen to wear anything. Anything at all. But she had decided on a heavy black jumper, even in the sweltering summer humidity. And she would wear it like a uniform to suburban parties where she would drink and dance, as if to demonstrate that heat and moisture did not apply to her, and where she knew she was not safe.

In the Institution, Joanne was usually drugged out of her mind. If she wasn't, and she was temporarily allowed out of her special room for passible behavior, then she could be found getting into all sorts of trouble. She would scratch the walls, her body, and scream for people to embrace cunnilingus. She blocked the television and dissected capitalist-democracy's need to violently control the body and the mind. Jo had become preoccupied with exposing what was behind our attachment to building experiences to experience them, and therefore to have them. She said we were missing the meaning. In terms of extinction, she said: We noticed the loss of a species, but we didn't see the diminishing of a species. Jo warned people to watch out: "I'm always on my period!" Joanne said America treated our menstrual cycles like we were serving a jail sentence for sycophantic behavior. She would again be tied to her bed and not allowed to leave her room, while the unproductive conversations between her doctors—four of them—and our parents would commence. "Watch out," Joanne screamed on, interrupting her doctors, which did not help matters, "man doesn't know what he's doing and continues to do things!"

"It's a metaphor, obviously you know what you're doing!" she assured all of us—nurses and doctors alike—when we gathered again to reassess the situation.

The doctors heaved and hawed, and explained to our family that the earlier medications were not working.

"We just want her to stabilize and find happiness," they explained, like they believed in the possibility of what they were saying.

But Jo was happy, in her own way, as herself.

"Let's take a moment to consider Mary Shelley," I said in a burst. "Mary Wollstonecraft Godwin Shelley was a mosaic of identities—in name, a resurrection of her late mother who had died from the infectious hands of the physician that reached into her uterus to remove the afterbirth; she wrote in anonymity, and she went on to have sex for the first time on her mother's grave, later giving birth to her first child, a baby she did not name."

The doctors looked at one another.

"Excuse me, who are you?" they asked, seeing me for the first time, though I had been in that sterile room every day for months.

That day, Henry and Sylvia asked the doctors to continue.

They were looking to control Joanne's moods, to add Klonopin for her daily panic, and Lamictal, a drug that was currently being used not only to treat epilepsy but to treat a broad range of psychiatric conditions. *Plus, one little unknown yellow pill four times a day*, Jo wrote out on her forearm, like an overachieving student, like a zombie.

"Look," the doctors who knew about the female mind went on, "Joanne has overvalued beliefs on just about everything." The doctors said this, chuckling like it was an inevitability, rubbing their bald spots, which I was certain would only make matters worse for them. The doctors inputted data onto their computers. I can remember their typing was so aggressive and loud I thought they'd break the keys. Peck. Peck. Peck. Those men, who had studied the innerworkings of female minds, typed and explained to our family without making eye contact that my sister spoke of "other worlds as real," and that she believed, "people were out to damage the Earth and other animals."

"People out to damage Earth?" the doctors asked, turning away from their computers and toward our father for fraternal sympathy. Our mother lit a cigarette despite being told many times that there was no smoking in the building.

I remember Joanne telling me that counting the colors and the pills was how she tracked and organized the hours that passed. Counting down the worsening days and nights, counting down the minutes until the next yellow pill. She tried, her eyes facing the white walls, to ignore the neon lights flickering their slow death. I can remember back then, while Joanne was institutionalized, wishing we lived in a hotel, since that arrangement was intended to be temporary. Little did I know then where I would end up in 2009, in my twenties, in a Super 8, getting sick of myself and listening to strangers hump, moan, and sing along to music in the room next door for entertainment. It was a distraction. I was to be meditating on catastrophe, which was to say the women in our family, and my sister's pregnancy. Chrysler had just declared bankruptcy. The day before, I had seen a woman in a pantsuit walking to a red Dodge Charger in the motel's parking lot, when a gust of wind took the folder she was carrying right out of her hands. Sheaths of paper blew every which way. They could have been a divorce settlement, a will, a manuscript, or missing pet fliers; it hardly mattered once the wind got ahold of them. Square voids of white fluttered in the sky.

The time for liberation had arrived. I remember, even on a new mix of medications, Jo was not showing any sign of improvement. Our family was called in to the hospital. It was explained that my sister's newfound muteness was an indication of her inability to please others, and to take direction. We were told that this would only worsen. I remember Henry turning red with rage. Sylvia went furiously searching for Nicorette in her bag. Plastic bags, toothpicks, throat lozenges, packets of sample cookies and crackers, and coupons poured out. Before leaving, Jo passed me a note: I don't know how to describe what I'm feeling.

"What about her suffering?" I stopped to ask her doctors, as the door was buzzed open. I had studied Freud in college, not to understand nature—I would never presume to understand nature, nature has no need for people.

I did not know where to go so I looked to Freud to explore people and came away realizing that people were babies that needed nurturing. For a time, Ida was given the case study name "Dora," who was both a subject of Freud's, and an occasional mute. Dora wished her doctor, like any other normal person, had played ping-pong, literally, for his microaggressions. Apparently, Freud had small hands; even "Little Hans" was a euphemism for his shortcomings. The point was: Dora left Freud and his treatment. Jo should do as Dora did: wish her analyst a Happy New Year and get out of there. I remember that night, after returning to our apartment from the hospital, our triangle of a family agreed the time had come for Jo to come back to us. We would not lose her again. And to do this, meant she had to first be freed and then sent far away.

The day then came when we would remove Jo.

Sylvia parked the Chevy outside of the Institution illegally. In Jo's special room, Henry cut through the thin transparent tubes that connected her spare body to the hospital's machinery. He removed the IVs inserted into her veins and unfastened the restraints around her wrists and ankles, which were badly bruised. He tossed her identifying information into the trash can. (I remember being amazed he had the mind to put the items in the trash, given his anger.) With Jo in his arms, we took the elevator to the ground floor, through the halls, past the reception desks, across the waiting room, straight through the exit door. Outside, there were sounds of fire trucks nearing, whirling around corners, distressed red lights flashing. I remember the sky was clearing. I remember something our mother had said about survival: "There's nothing about survival that's sentimental. It's rebellious in nature. Rebels were those people who dared, who risked accusations of sentimentality."

The sun broke through the clouds and the world seemed to shimmer. That night, and the nights which followed, after putting Joanne to bed, the three of us resolved to send her as far away as possible, to a transparent and remote place, we agreed. The idea was an inchoate one, but we understood Joanne needed to leave. The winds shifted when a friend of our fathers', who worked in real estate, sent over a property that might be of interest. It was practically being given away. "Basically, free and doomed," was the consensus among Sylvia and Henry.

There was a trailer on a small piece of land in a remote part of Alaska from the early '70s that nobody would touch because of its past. It had been on the market for years. The property once housed forty trailers to realize an alternative to psychiatric institutions (which, from 1967-1971 had seen a rise of psychotic patients in mental wards across America double). The experimental project aimed to heal young, mildly psychotic female patients in an open, drug-free, wild setting. The founders believed that honoring one's personal agency would dramatically improve the health and lives of their female patients. Research showed their approach was astonishingly effective, and more effective than traditional hospital-based programs. The Deadhorse project was shut down and the property was left to fallow. Parents were complaining about the results. They were reporting that their daughters were returning from Deadhorse in worse shape. The headlines at the time, which I accessed from the library archives, indicated that the projects' patients were arriving home "open-minded," "opinionated," and "generally at ease and happy". Many families regarded this behavior not as a solution, but more of a problem. One such report quoted a mother as saying about her daughter: "My daughter keeps asking if I know what floc-cinaucinihilipilification means. She's insisting I'm a hippopotomon-strosesquipedaliophobic. She's as crazy as ever."

On the couch beneath the portrait, after Joanne was tucked away safely in bed, the three of us speculated that the single trailer was left on the property to signify a lost cause, which resonated. There were other facts: the property was remote, the price of the land was beyond reasonable (practically a give-away); it was secluded and far enough away from where we lived that Joanne could vanish. Our family settled on the trailer in Deadhorse, Alaska, because it was the state with the fastest changing climate, and where irony was greatest: a land of oil pipelines and wildlife, a radical place secluded and far enough away for Joanne to find a state of rest. A place where she could let the biological rhythms of her surroundings—storms, drastic temperatures and light, birds migrating—consume her.

That was where we put Joanne like an earring stud with a sturdy back. We sent Jo to the Arctic, where the old axiom was, "If children won't like it, it will thrive in an Alaskan garden." It seemed to us that the Arctic was one of the last imaginary places, a region shaped by the distant past, complete with dramatic fluctuations of light, and aliens, from as far away as another planet, and a dream of an unattainable and compelling world that was not a dream.

DEADHORSE, ALASKA

AT THE EDGE OF THE WORLD

The Dalton "Haul" highway was the longest stretch of un-serviced road on the North American continent. To get to her, I traveled along the empty, rugged Alaskan frontier in a shiny, silver, slightly beat-up 1985 Chrysler LeBaron GTS, which I had rented long-term from a local in Fairbanks. In her time away, Jo had become convinced that she needed to have a child, and had forgotten, willfully or not, that she could not because of her scoliosis.

The LeBaron GTS had come from Donna Acker. Donna had originally purchased the car to see what it might feel like to be Marla Maples in the swinging '80s.

"Imagine being named Donna?" Donna had asked me to imagine, conspiratorially.

"*Oh Donna*, all that," she had said about the popular tune, when I visibly had no answer, before saying "what a tragedy, the plane, the end for those three rock stars," about their plane crash over Clearlake, Iowa, that killed all three onboard.

I went along with it anyhow. Even mentioning the song was enough for it to get caught in your head for days. Besides, Donna had something I wanted.

I found her and the car in Fairbanks, a place that prided itself on its remoteness. I had been wandering around checking out restaurants and bars trying to get a read on used cars in the area to drive the rest of the way to Deadhorse, when I had heard about Donna and her shiny silver LeBaron at the Roundup Saloon. The conversation went something like this. The bartender, a large, sluggish man with a memorable grin, first asked if I was a reporter, and then on learning I was just an ordinary person, suggested Donna was her own sort, and that she had cars and she appreciated deals. If Acker, as he called her, was presented with a good deal, she would be open to a good deal. I didn't need to call in advance as long as I wasn't a reporter or murderer. It felt like this wasn't really Alaska, but a bartender giving me his impression of this region which lies 200 miles from the Arctic Circle. Before he could make the call, he said he first had to be sure it was what I really wanted—the road to Deadhorse was a long haul, a tough journey with fog, fatigue, flat tires, passing traffic, potholes, gravel, grizzly bears, sleep-inducing silence, sudden engine failure, an abruptly shattered windshield, and an increasingly low gas tank.

"I'm ready for it," I said.

I wanted it. I wanted the tundra, the Arctic Ocean, to view the midnight sun, and stay in lodgings assembled from modular buildings.

"Just be sure you take it light on the hills," he said, calling Donna.

And just like that, she appeared. Taking a seat at the bar beside me, Donna said, "I love this place. It feels like an airport bar. Don't you feel like our flights have been delayed indefinitely?" she asked.

Donna said surviving the Alaskan elements demanded speed and pretending. Marla Maples was her antidote.

"To survive, pretend to be someplace golden, like Sacramento, politics aside."

Donna took out her phone to show me a commercial of "our" fast car on YouTube. She searched a bit before finding the one she wanted, the one set to America's patriotic anthem, the military song "Over There." She paused to order us beers. We sipped and watched the "European showdown" between the '85 LeBaron GTS, Audi 5000S, Mercedes 190E, and BMW 525E.

"The LeBaron GTS will keep on beating them until *it's over, over there*," Donna sang along with the voiceover. "See, we think we win," she said.

Donna said, just watch, Chrysler had already downsized 10,000 jobs, and she predicted within a year they'd declare bankruptcy.

What else did Donna know?

"In a way, the change will be sexy," she said, which made her doubly sad.

I had no idea what was going on, but the car was in good shape, and she was into deals. We came to a long-term rental agreement with the option to buy. She offered me dinner and I stayed for a night.

Donna's house was full of textiles and statues. She was a traveler. She spent the last twenty years exploring Europe, including Turkey, as well as Asia, and Africa. She said she never really knew what she was good at doing, eventually settling on being a speech patholo-gist after years of outlining possibilities—entrepreneur, medical researcher, CEO, venture capitalist, marketing brand manager, busi-ness consultant, private investigator, military strategist. We sat down to eat, and she gave me a fan. "They say these summer temperatures are the highest on record." I also heard it was the third lowest year for rainfall but opted to keep things light. I asked about Hawaii, where she was born. She said, "growing up on an island is unique." And that's all she'd say about it. Over a dinner of jalapeño boats and chicken skewers, Donna asked me if I liked men. I remember thinking it was a peculiar question, and then wondering why I found it peculiar.

"I find myself envious of their bodies and education," I said. "It sounds ludicrous, I'm sure, but that's that."

"No," Donna said. "I get it. Seems we've desperation in common."

I liked Donna, but something about her made me uncomfortable.

She asked me what I liked to do. I said poetry. She said *poetry* like she was sounding out the word for the first time.

"What do you like about it?"

"It's something to do."

That night, she told me she thought about writing, about being a writer.

"Though," she admitted, "saying I want to write is different than saying I want to be a writer. Writing demands intimacy."

This was difficult for her, she said. I should have said closeness, the delicate kind, was difficult for me, too, almost impossible.

There was a lot I could have shared with Donna and that Donna could have told me about. Donna had lived, like really lived. She knew about car engines and more about harsh weather than I ever would. And now that my mind spent more time going backward on the timeline, I could have told her about what I was doing before coming to Alaska, how not long after my sister was sent to Alaska, Sylvia suffered a massive stroke that affected the left side of her brain, destroying her parietal and temporal lobes, the areas of the brain responsible for emotions, memory, the senses, and speech.

After our mother's stroke, her grasp of the world was light. Her state of being was a sort of state of being. She would scan my person as if I was someone she should recognize. Henry had withdrawn and was of no help. He spent his days not answering my calls. Therefore, I had hired a woman named Gladys from an online ad agency to assist me in caring for our mother, as our mother had done for her mother. Then not long after Sylvia had her stroke, I returned home to find her limp in her bed. Henry was not home. I called 911. I screamed out to Gladys, but she was nowhere to be found. Not even in front of the television where she often planted herself.

I could have told Donna that I had returned home to find that our mother, what I had not known then was the brightest light of my tiny life, had died alone. I was almost certain it wasn't her preference and the pain of that had me lost.

I can remember that day our mother died walking into our apartment in Chicago to find the space palpably empty in an incalculable way, as if all the light there ever was in the universe had been retracted. The walls ached. The ground moved. I went in their bedroom and found our mother unresponsive on the bed. I spent so long with her body there, since that was all that had remained, tirelessly scanning her face. A stunningly ugly face. The most delightfully unformulaic face I'd ever seen, save for Joanne's. The kind songwriters wrote ballads about because they didn't know what else to do.

For hours, I kept my mouth pressed up to Sylvia's mouth, which was cold, sweet, and charred, tasting of old tobacco. Her eyes were softly closed. Her hands were on her stomach, relaxed, and much smaller than I had remembered, even from just hours before. I crawled into bed with her until the paramedics arrived. In bed with our mother, I wished for time to bend in another direction, and heard Virginia Woolf: "Whatever else may perish and disappear, what lies here is steadfast. Here one might say to those sliding lights, those fumbling airs that breathe and bend over the bed itself, here you can neither touch nor destroy. Upon which, wearily, ghostly, as if they had feather-light fingers and the light persistency of feathers, they would look, once, on the shut eyes, and the loosely clasping fingers, and fold their garments wearily and disappear."

At least our mother died in bed surrounded by her landscape paintings, which had become more Cubist in their style. I was fortunate to be able to rub lotion onto her arms until I saw it absorb. For thirty-some years, our mother made her own shampoo, a mix of lavender oil, Original VO5, and tap water. She often said we looked to artifacts—stains, indentations like bruises and bite marks, the emptying and filling of drawers, checked and unchecked items on shopping lists, complete meals, and the leftovers—as evidence to point to something. A place in time where the act of being occurred. Each time she unraveled those dusty, worn items from our family's past, she liked to say to us that all that material might one day come in handy.

"These things that at first glance appear to be trash, might one day be the map we find ourselves needing."

The next day, as I drove along, I realized I could not describe Donna. I had to pull over. I poured the gallon of water I kept in the backseat on my face. Drenched, sitting there on the side of the road, just as tired as I was minutes before. I was supposed to be an archivist preserving the details like our mother. Recalling what Jo wore the day she returned home to declare that she had made a new friend in Seraphina; or how Henry made swoony eyes at Sylvia after she reported Jupiter had entered Aquarius. A sprinkle of salt that realized an apple's flavor. And I could not knit together Donna. I could not picture her face, and that alarmed me. I would not drive on until I saw her. I shut my eyes and tried to *see* Donna. I worked to conjure her in my mind but I couldn't. I thought about turning back around, driving like a fool, knocking on her door, and hugging her. And in that moment, I could smell her.

"Just remember we're in the middle of nowhere," were her last words to me as I filled the car's tank to capacity.

FORWARD MOTION

Ignoring all the advice, I speedily drove along the Haul in my long-term rental from Donna Acker and felt amused and stupendous and flat-out awesome. I was warned that if I wanted to make a call from the road, there was only time between Fairbanks and Coldfoot to do it.

On speaker phone, Jo said it was a bad decision to rent a Chrysler LeBaron GTS.

"No, it was an adventurous decision," I countered.

"Bernie," my sister continued. "Any purchasing decision based on '80s nostalgia is a bad one. It was the decade sex education went retail. Words generally associated with pornography were being applied to things like hair. Pump. Volume. Curl. Squirt. Spray. Fluff. Tease. Hold."

"PAY ATTENTION!" Jo screamed at me while I was driving. When it was me—and my eyes—on the road, *paying attention*.

"I can't drive and listen to you."

"Please go back to being an invalid," I finally said.

It was a two-day journey from Fairbanks to Deadhorse. From Fairbanks, I passed the Yukon River, No Name Creek—which sits in a low valley of boreal forest—and Finger Mountain, before stopping off in Coldfoot, a truck stop with a post office. For the rest of the drive, from there to Jo, there would be little sense of regular living. I would have to do without many amenities during that final seven-hour stretch. There were no auto body shops, gas stations, flush toilets, places to eat, medical facilities, hotels or motels, police, cellphone service, Internet connection, radio reception—nothing. I was going to make the most out of Coldfoot, not really a town but a "census-designated place," supposedly named after travelers who turned around because they got cold feet. Imagine cold feet in Alaska.

At the only rest stop in Coldfoot, a rustic, warm inn serving breakfast all day, I overheard the man next to me tell another man, "There's a pretty woman behind every tree on the North Slope." Obviously, there were no trees. I ate a thick and delicious burger and read a list on the back of the menu. "10 Reasons Out of a Possible 1,000 That Make Living in Coldfoot Unique." Number ten was the wonderful lack of television, politics, news, crime, pollution, freeways, congestion, lines, rudeness, hurriedness, traffic, and all that blather about O. J. Simpson. Still, life had its hardships. It could be colder for longer than one's imagination could handle. Such that the windows in Coldfoot were constructed with three panes of glass.

While I could, I tried calling Paul. We had kept in touch, as they say. Though he rarely had time. Last I learned, Paul had been made full professor at our alma mater. He and his wife had a toddler, with twins on the way. His wife ridiculed his weight gain. He had found he was too exhausted to have friends. He consistently liked to point out that was the one flaw with marrying a younger woman—that he was older. We used to laugh about it, making light of what was not light, just like I had grown up doing.

As it happened, Paul had lied. For a long time, he had fabricated his reality. He did have a wife. But he had one son, a bunny, and an elderly dog. He was still an adjunct. In his last phone message, in defense of his actions, he said he had only been exaggerating.

The phone rang. Paul answered.

"Why lie?" I asked.

"I want you," he said.

"What does lying to me have to do with wanting me?"

"I am competitive, I guess," Paul said.

He admitted that it had been going on for a long time. He confirmed his wife—younger wife—was real.

"When she wants to be," he said about her.

"That's not nice" I said.

"What does nice have to do with us?" he asked.

"Stop," I said.

"I won't."

And we left it there, like that, like just after a foghorn sounds. I prolonged this abstraction between us. I would draw out this immediate sensation like a yogic breathes to have more time to think. I was not sure I could be mine and his at the same time. Until he called back.

"I need to know if you're eating reindeer sausage with your omelet," Paul said.

"Your attention span needs work."

"Tell me what you know about Alaska."

"I'm toying with getting a job in oil."

"I need a shower. Maybe an enema. I've been talking to myself too much. I have so much to tell you," I told Paul, assuming he was still on the line.

"I gotta run," he said, like it was the premature end of a novel.

In all the time I had known Paul, I was never the one to say goodbye. Never once, in person, or on the telephone had I ever said: "bye," "later," "peace," "see you soon," "see ya," "see you never," "take care," "have a good night," "goodbye."

He always had the final parting words.

Before leaving Chicago, I did what I could to educate myself about life in Prudhoe Bay. I was looking forward to experiencing the month of August. I thought about putting together a trip to the Kobuk Valley National Park in Alaska, but it was useless due to the government shutdown. A click on "Deadhorse sample trips" on Alaska's official vacation and travel information website, *Travel Alaska*, came up empty. Deadhorse was an unincorporated community of seasonal workers situated on a precipice of water, like the dead end of a trail. The town was near the Arctic Ocean, adjacent to Prudhoe Bay, a ragged remote chunk of the Arctic Coastal Tundra, the heart of Alaska's oil patch, and home to the 800-mile Trans-Alaska oil pipeline.

Chief executive of BP, John Browne, also known as the "Sun King," was worth millions, like 13.6 million dollars. I thought maybe we might rob him. With that kind of purchasing power, Joanne and I could procure 1.645 billion Cool Ranch Doritos, which run approximately $1 a bag, with 121 Cool Ranch Doritos in each bag. (Tests indicate you only get 80 whole Doritos and 41 broken ones.)

I'd read someplace that the Alaska Airlines' CEO Brad Tilden explained his company had a soul. "It has a spirit," he liked to say. The use of the Eskimo on their planes was the ultimate personification of "who we are," Brad offered up. If I had a direct line to Brad, I would have given him a quick call to point out the Eskimo is a term sullied by colonialism, and unless you are a native to the circumpolar region, you probably shouldn't use the word. Brad took home a salary of $5,238,064 and loved a good soul, while natives remained on the economic fringes, experiencing some of the highest rates of accidental deaths, suicides, alcoholism, homicides, fetal alcohol syndrome, and domestic violence in America. I figured if I got a job in oil, I could sabotage operations from the inside. But I would have to wait for the right moment to make a play. Since much of my existence revolved around (bad) food, I had to investigate how food would fit in with my plans.

I learned food services made time in the oil camps bearable. In most camps, restaurant-quality meals were served four times a day to accommodate 24-hour operations. "All you can eat" meals were a dream come true for any American person—it's in our DNA. Steak and shrimp Fridays, and for Christmas a special of lobster tails. The oil companies provided "spike rooms," in what amounted to large convenience store-styled snack bars. Yes. Hot dogs, chili cheese nachos, personal-sized frozen pepperoni pizzas, glazed donuts, cookies, ice cream, candy, and soda available 24 hours a day. Apparently, workers could take whatever they liked, if they weren't obnoxious about it—in other words, if they didn't abuse the privilege.

In the Arctic, skeins of fog paused on the tops of spruce trees and summer was for the birds. At the beginning of their breeding season, the Arctic teemed with terrestrial and aquatic insects for birds to devour. Paul wanted to know how I felt. I told him I wasn't sure. He said he didn't believe me. I changed the subject to Donna Acker and asked if he'd ever forgotten the face of a person after spending hours with them, like I had with Donna. I told him about Fairbanks, Alaska's second-largest city, how it was surrounded by forest. Every summer, lightning sparks forest fires, filling the air with smoke. Donna said the fires had started early. The fires burned for two and a half months due to the hot and dry weather. An area roughly the size of New Hampshire had already incinerated. I was lucky, by the time I arrived, that things had much improved.

Did you know that parts of Alaska were at one time called Russian America? From mid-May through mid-July, the sun doesn't set. The sun doesn't rise from mid-November through mid-January. Vehicles are left running 24-hours a day from September through May, otherwise they wouldn't start again. Alaska was a stranger despite my learning about it, but the property in Deadhorse wasn't as much. I'd had a sense about the property and about what I was getting myself into with my sister before arriving. I had been the one tasked with going over the real estate materials with our parents. In the time since her relocation, Jo had mailed letters describing the place as well as photographs of the land, her greenhouse, and the trailer.

It was 6pm. Soon it would be time to check into my room inside of the trailer, not quite a hotel. The sun was as bright as ever outside. I was still in the café at the rest stop in Coldfoot. Breakfast may have been served all day, but my omelet had grown a bitter mustache. I ordered a glass of white wine that came in a pint glass, which I drank like a beer. Thanks to my friends in Fairbanks, I was warned that this was one of the only places along the eternal road to buy alcohol legally. After checking into my room, which I figured was practice for what was soon to be my new life with Jo, I got in bed and drew an imaginary outline of the North American continent on the ceiling.

The next morning, I woke up to a dead mouse in a trap outside my door, and an elderly shirtless man in the common room talking to the television. I thought of what the bartender said back in Fairbanks, that bonds of any kind form quickly in this kind of solitude. If I could have called someone I would have, but I needed to get on the road, where I would quickly run out of reception. I turned on the car and found the only radio station I could find, which would last no more than two minutes. I could get into summers in Alaska—the sun barely set, and the 65-degree days were a welcome break from the hot, humid ones in Chicago. As I drove along in my irresponsibly chic Chrysler LeBaron, commercial trucks passed by with decapitated caribou heads strapped to their grills. I saw a breathtaking sky and the constant steel pipeline, my only companion, which followed me along the highway. I noted refrigerated trucks hauling food, tankers moving heating oil and water, and tractor-trailers with huge modular housing units, each hurling stones at my windows. The last threatened to run me off the road. Eventually, at 20 miles per hour, I crossed the Atigun Pass, the winding mountain road's highest point of altitude, and, at that juncture, was only midway on my journey to her.

I arrived to the Deadhorse property with some light left to spare and made a point of parking far enough away to surprise my sister. I left my belongings in the LeBaron and went looking for Joanne. There were several old lawn chairs, most of them stripped of their dully-colored woven fabric, set up to face her greenhouse and rows of crops. There was a stack of empty cans of beer on top of a flattened bag of potato chips. I wondered if she'd had company out here. I found Jo alone, standing on the steps in front of the trailer, amusing herself.

"I'm thinking we should water your plants," I called out.

She looked disheveled. She looked exhausted. Her dark hair locked into place; a style held together by an excess of grease, arrived at by weeks of not bathing.

I asked: "Have you been eating?"

"What's this?" Jo asked me, her face lifting, breaking into a half-smile, and pointing to a bump on her middle finger.

"A plantar's wart, I suppose," I answered, foolishly.

It wasn't a real question. In the sense that it wasn't a question which had an answer.

Jo then lifted her middle finger and shoved it in my face.

I seriously considered turning around and driving back to Coldfoot. As far as I was concerned, the land of white wine in pint glasses and all-day breakfast options was far more appealing than taking shit from my sister.

She then grabbed my hand and took me inside what would become our new home.

Turned out Jo, over the course of three years in Deadhorse, had made two friends—both male. Mike and Cicero, two eager clerks who were about the only figures close enough to be considered in relative proximity. Both had cute butts and worked full time as clerks at the all-service general store, which also served as the local post office. Deadhorse itself was not an ideal place for variety; the place did not present many options to get laid, but it was near a host of national parks: Arctic National Wildlife Refuge, Gates of the Arctic National Park and Preserve, Kobuk National Preserve, Kobuk Valley National Park, which contained the Great Kobuk Sand Dunes—the largest active sand dunes found in the Arctic. One review of the town (if one could call it a town), called it the ugliest place alive and the pinnacle of odoriferous living. Essentially a graveyard of oil tanks, acetylene fires, heavy-machine repair shops, and spill-abatement companies, and where everyone my sister encountered wondered what in god's name she was doing there.

"Healing," was what she said.

Because the area provided much of the state's revenue from oil, there were certain amenities that were accessible, like telecommunications, medicine, food, a supply store, and a post office. We would have what we needed until there was a shortage. Groceries arrived mostly by ship or plane, and the area was exposed to a litany of both man-made and natural disasters. Summer fog and winter storms could ground planes for weeks. Emptying the general store of milk and bread. At any moment, the resources could cease coming, so it was essential to store what one could. Jo did. She stored lowbush blueberries—also known as alpine, bog, and bilberry—that caribou loved.

Jo told me the reason there weren't billboards along the highway was because people will shoot them. Her trailer was filled with books. She had painted the ceiling a bright yellow and had amassed a modest collection of secondhand chairs, bookshelves, lamps, plates, and cutlery from Ikea. The other rooms, a bathroom and kitchenette, were sparsely decorated as she'd imagined the Japanese lived in Japan: brown paper on the walls, tan matts covered parts of the floor, and little furniture. She was still in a weak physical condition, but she had begun cultivating the half-acre with what energy she did have. She used fish carcasses and seaweed to enrich the soil and set up bins to collect water. She went about building her own irrigation systems. She planted rows of crops: tomatoes, kale, cabbage, onions, beets, potatoes, radishes, and carrots. She designed a greenhouse for her crops. Her approximated greenhouse structure, assembled from thick clear polycarbonate sheeting and held up with metal poles, housed and protected the plants from the fluctuating light and climate. She monitored the land from the small porch she consistently varnished to help preserve. She waited for wildlife: blackfish, lamprey, goshawk, curlew, dall sheep, marmot, muskox, caribou, and wolves.

Jo said when the exchange between individuals and the environment reached a point of little food or water, massive heat, and flooding—catastrophe was for nature a necessary tool for regeneration.

Before leaving for Alaska, Preston and I had decided he would be my internet boyfriend and we would be simple about it. Which was to say, we would see where the arrangement took us without putting any pressure on it. We'd matured from simply feeling each other and having sex online to building something together, which we agreed was the best use of his art-making practice and my philosophy degree yet. When I shared my life with my sister, she said the arrangement between Preston and I sounded like a diet challenge—a fad destined to fail.

I first learned about Preston in high school when I met Paul. Back then, Paul showed me pictures of his close friend and rival, the conceptual artist Preston, who lived in Hoboken, who could grow facial hair, and had a mullet. Preston was gross. He was rough, in that he seemed capable of throwing himself into any situation. He had these peaked-lips, no doubt his best feature, and a broken front tooth, the result of a bet. (He never said whether it was a bet he'd won or lost, and when it came to Preston nothing was obvious.) I remember Paul's soon-to-be wife and mother of his "children" (a human boy, a bunny, and an elderly dog), saying that Preston could not come to their wedding unless he fixed his tooth, which Preston would not do. He attended the wedding anyway, and that was where we met, at the hotel's glassy pool, and where I spent the rest of the evening dripping. Preston introduced himself as a modest dreamer, but even then, I knew he wanted the world.

Paul's wedding was held at the Palmer House in Chicago, its own kind of relic. The hotel claimed Charles Dickens had once visited, which might have made sense given that his youngest brother was buried in Chicago and had left children behind, but in fact Charles skipped the city entirely. He blamed the shitty winter. I remember watching Paul's wedding guests splash around in the hotel swimming pool like sex symbols of a bygone era, and saying to Preston—handsome and unnamed at the time—that "swimming pools were infestations," before jumping in fully clothed.

We ended up talking all night about the differences between legends and conspiracies. I remember he looked like one of those healthy, plump-yet-scrappy city birds. A look that said to me, evolutionarily speaking, that he was doing well.

That was the last and only time I encountered Preston in the flesh, at Paul's wedding after college, which at that moment, living in a trailer with my sister at the edge of the world, seemed like a memory taken from the Paleolithic age.

2000'S

It was 2007, yet the cigarette tax in New York City, which had gone up $1.50 per pack in 2002 was still plaguing New Yorkers. Preston had taken to ordering cigarettes from Switzerland through yessmoke.com. When that website quickly shuttered, he asked his friend the poet Paul Violi to buy them from the Indian reservation. For us, the Alaskan weather could be prohibitive and that was on our mind.

Jo and I worked to entertain ourselves in the 400-square-foot trailer. Our morning conversations, that began in one part of the space and ended in another, could start like this—I might say, "Hamlet tried to find languages that spoke to people, and it was a raging nightmare." Jo might say, "Hamlet, along with the audience, saw the ghost. Gertrude, also present, saw nothing." And by the time we both said, "As in anything," we had moved to the finish line (our bathroom).

During this period of mutuality, Jo and I joined the Alaska Pioneers Fruit Growing Association and tried to contact our father. We would call Henry, and again get the answering machine. Paul left a message for me asking, "how many times must I declare it?" I called Paul, left a message saying "hi," and heard nothing back. In the interim, I wrote Preston emails to say I wanted to see him naked later. Jo and I tweaked recipes, filled online shopping carts with items we never intended to purchase, and took walks around the property, weather and light permitting. By evening, we were looking to Poppy for guidance.

Our great-grandmother, Poppy, was from a time when language mattered. Her interests lay in Alchemy and the body. Venus and Chaos. With Poppy and our mother in mind, my sister and I would get back to fermenting pears. We would take the cores and stems, a by-product of poached pears, and transform them into a spirit we called *Try Us*. Which we did on repeat. (Remember, we had to work to entertain ourselves. We rarely left the property.)

Jo and I pickled beets, carrots, cucumbers, rose petals, and corn. For a few weeks, we opened and closed them every other day to release the gasses. We made bread and turned poison into booze. Elderflower vodka was tricky since elderberry roots, stems, and seeds were poisonous. Eating them builds up cyanide levels in the body. If sprigs were used without the stems, nobody died.

Preston would call every night, naked, just as I had asked. I wanted to see every part of that man who lived in Brooklyn, and who I watched squirm inside of the computer's frame like a sea monkey.

Our days were filled with routines. These were long any time of year, regardless of the dramatic fluctuations of light in Alaska. In the early mornings, my sleep-deprived sister preferred to run around the compound, and the 400-square-foot trailer, screaming: "Nietzsche defended idleness!" while I made us coffee. After she exhausted herself, she returned to her projects exploring the great themes of America. At the time, she used Tater Tots to make still life portraits to accomplish this. (A fair amount of Mary and the Baby.) She inserted all sorts of dried fruits and hardware into the Tots to give them their individual character and arranged them in all sorts of ways.

"Did you know the inventor of the Tot farmed during the Great Depression and was prone to hyperbolic business proverbs?" I remember Jo asked.

My favorite was: "You can never go broke by taking a profit."

Joanne put Mary and baby on a heavily sanitized bible with a pack of matches.

"How do you think Mary Magdalene would be depicted today?" Jo asked.

"Perhaps she would represent the ideal portrait of a sinner?" I wondered.

"Or perhaps the ideal portrait of humility."

Around about 8am I would set up to teach my three online college writing courses. I was teaching ecological writing classes disguised as core philosophy classes and demanding to know what drove Patricia Highsmith's Tom Ripley to do the things that he did. "Why did Tom make problems while vacationing at a cliffside resort on an island in Italy?" The students wanted to understand and explaining to them that Tom was an American sociopath, an American prodigy, a kind of national ideal, did nothing to appease them. The students who rarely came to class had read the Highsmith novel in its entirety, whereas *Hyperobjects: Philosophy and Ecology after the End of the World* was a bust. They were convinced, perturbed even, that the white guy (Tom), average and bland by any measure, wasn't enjoying himself, basking in the sun and sea or lounging by the pool gently liquefying.

"I mean, he's on an Italian island," they protested.

"Well, that's just it—Tom Ripley *was* enjoying himself," I said. "And in no small way it was because he was unassuming."

But the once delinquent students ignored me and continued to demand answers. They were after a purpose.

"There must be a purpose," my students said, "otherwise what was all of this for?"

In our trailer, Jo and I clashed, as Newton's rule of balance and motion required things to do. We cooked too, mostly the vegetables we tried to grow, and otherwise the ones that were easy to come by, like potatoes, since most things had to be flown in from elsewhere. We ate and distilled, made clothes, prepared for the worst, and read about internet culture advancing the promise of liberation across the world, this same world that the internet was determined

285

to make small, when my sister and I were absolutely ok with the world being gigantic. Why not learn to be unafraid of largess? Why not go someplace?

Projects included things like keeping our Etsy account active and updated. We were selling some of our own fashions: home dyed and sewn pieces, mostly t-shirts and sweatshirts with idiosyncratic pseudo-French puns, as well as vintage European military underwear with the word "Balzac" emblazoned on the crotch. And (unsystematically) training ourselves to re-enter society. (This exercise was in no way rigorous.) Our stated purpose was to become more machine-like, though not permanently, lest America turn itself into a complete loony bin. But we would prepare for deep dark holes and webs of all kinds, because our countrymen were worshippers of the machine. Virginia Woolf wrote that, "one cannot live outside the machine for perhaps more than half an hour." Otherwise, my sister and I came to believe, drunk on elderflower vodka wearing only homemade undergarments—you would disintegrate.

Around the 5 o'clock hour we would initiate this "training," such as it were, by embodying, roughly, the idea of "progress," which for us meant: Be the plug *and* be the electrical system. That was what power responded to. Therefore, it was the thing most of all we wished to destroy. My sister and I took turns shocking each other with the static current we collected from the carpet. And for once in our relationship, we had no preference—we found that we enjoyed, equally, being both the plug and being the electrical system, in whichever (fair) order the routine presented itself that evening. If the two of us had doubts about the success of this exercise, we simply consulted the women in our family who knew when all else failed how to return to water. Our faces and bodies looked like plain donuts—they were dense, swollen, and regular. As plain donuts, we would *be* machines in order to kill The Machine, i.e. Capitalism.

Under a luminous 1am Arctic sun, the two of us worked on configuring our approach to society and sold underwear. The evenings were spent drawing, painting, and working on our life-size depictions of walruses on the walls. Where we lived, big game hunting was big money. In Alaska, "the hunt" was called "The Chase" and was cataloged: The Arctic "Grand Slam" (caribou, musk ox, polar bear, and walrus) comparable to the "African Big Five" (leopard, lion, elephant, rhino, and cape buffalo). There were global directories prompting camp talk of "Collecting the Cats," "Finishing the Plains," or "Doing Africa."

The walrus ranked as one of the most bizarre, therefore sought-after hunts, ever.

Painting them would not save them, but it became a way for us to save ourselves.

All of these ideas, what in the fresh dewy morning we came to think of as exercises in futility, sounded like solid ones all day long, most days, until we woke up.

In the trailer, months passed uninterrupted.

MIKE AND CICERO

At night, after cleaning up, Mike and Cicero, the clerks from the general store who were smitten with my sister, would dutifully come over and lay their hearts out. I would grade essays in a corner. Joanne would have Mike and Cicero compete for her attention. Reverting to times past with Seraphina on the farm, she asked them to draw caribou or rhino or cape buffalo, which they did neurotically, and she would decide on a winner. They could draw those animals by heart, and extraordinarily, which complicated her decision-making. She would snuggle up to that night's winner, each vying to be her person however she deemed fit—daddy to her unborn children, ex-lover, floozy, nymph.

Like a family, the four of us sat on poorly assembled Ikea furniture and watched television via satellite and ate pie that we had warmed up in the microwave. We did not know yet then, but by 2009, everyone in America would have a microwave. It was still only 2007. In the meantime, waiting for the near future, Joanne would sit cozily with her winner and wait for the information to overwhelm us. I remember eating pie waiting for Barack Obama to announce on a frigid day in Springfield, 90 miles due east of where the Fareown women lay in their cemetery plot in rural Illinois, that he was running for president of America. I remember being relieved that we were in Alaska with Mike and Cicero who were content being from Alaska, which was America like Puerto Rico and Hawaii—where Obama was born—were also America, though some denied it.

I remember Joanne biting at my sleeve, and like a flea in the dark, saying: "The party is just beginning."

There was no single exercise that would prepare me for life in America perhaps better than a life spent being with my sister.

Pie dropping from her mouth, Joanne said future president Obama would inherit a broken political system, a financial crisis, and a recession. Bit of pie across her lap, and growing deeply agitated toward the television—just as Henry had been many times before— Jo pinned the discord on my arriving in Alaska.

When the time came, there would be many who knew everything there was to know about numbers and statistics who would call it the worst financial crisis since the Great Depression. (We had heard those words before.) Even the wealthy would cut back, in such a notable way it would be covered by reputable writers and published in reputable magazines and newspapers.

I can remember reading one such piece and being informed about their approach to the market's fall, and the takeaway was this: the wealthy still spoke with their buildings' concierge, but their requests had changed. Instead of reservations at high-end restaurants like Daniel or Per Se, concierges were being asked to make them for more reasonably priced restaurants. One concierge was asked to find a reliable shoe repair shop that could handle 10 to 15 pairs of designer shoes at a time, as opposed to another number, presumably more expansive, which the article omitted. Instead of center orchestra seats at the Met, any seats were deemed OK if they were on opening night.

On social media, users would bemoan First Lady Michelle Obama's planting of fruits and vegetables in the White House Garden and the financial markets would collapse. For years, bankers had been slicing and dicing millions of garbage housing loans and selling them on to investors as mortgage-backed securities, which would fail, and by 2006, this was the case for seven out of every ten new mortgages.

Then there was news, new news. Paul's wife had taken the kid and pets and left him. His call with the news came when I was asleep.

The next morning, I listened to the voicemail message in secret, hiding underneath a blanket as if he could see me. I did not like how Paul made me feel—tingly and unbearable in the parts of my body I deemed off-limits. I deleted Paul's message and emailed Preston to meet naked. Preston immediately responded to say he was free in an hour, but after that he had an art opening in Soho to attend.

I texted him: "My body is a masterpiece that you should bow down to."

"My aphorism Bernie." He wrote.

And when I didn't say anything, since that was part of the momentum of pleasure, he responded: "Yes, I am well aware and I'm on my knees on the F Train bowing down now."

"Are you getting looks?"

"Bernadette, what do you think?"

"Blow the New York art scene," I texted Preston.

"Why don't you come to New York City and say that," he wrote.

I called him a shapeshifter, a coward, a moving target.

He said it was me that didn't know when to stop and come into focus.

All this back and forth over email, me love-hating all over the keyboard like a loser, which at the age I was I really should have grown out of. Preston said he would start fasting and not stop until I bought a plane ticket and emailed the receipt. I did want his art dick in my mouth for real, but I would never give that gift to myself like a little pillow of dried lavender tucked away in a dresser drawer. There was no point in freshening up the situation. It would ruin everything.

"The sadist must not kill the masochist because the torture must continue," Joanne said, uninvited, standing behind me.

The thing about "wanting," like hunger, was that it was defined by what you wanted, or what you needed, or some combination of the two. The wanting experience could take you down if you let it.

I salvaged Paul's message from my deleted messages folder. I listened to his words again. What would Paul be like without a wife to tend to? If they divorced, who would take sole custody of the child and the bunny, which I imagined were identical. There were so many animals to care for, and I was not mother material. Jo and I would certainly kill a child, which for my sister may have been precisely the point of motherhood.

Surely this complicated matters. Was he even a good dad, even to his elderly dog? No, I knew Paul was the best dad. He was made for fatherhood, but the women in our family were not made for mothering, which had me questioning our compatibility.

I called him back. He answered after the first ring.

"We can talk about whatever," I said. "Your call."

This made him laugh because it was just the right amount of self-effacing idiocy that might make any listener lightly pee their pants.

Paul wanted to go back in time to high school, at the end of 1995. I was all about going back in time, but I wasn't sure I wanted to go back that far.

"I thought you were past sticking to strict timelines," Paul said, about the tail end of '95 and having sex in Hello's shed.

"I have become harder to recognize after almost two years quarantined in an Alaskan trailer with my sister, where females in the past had been sent to get healthy," I said to him.

"Yes," I added. "I may have a BA in philosophy, which might one day seem significant, but for now I am just in Deadhorse."

Paul turned his attention to Preston, how Preston was suited to his role as artist, but made no mention of my seeing him, even though it was only ever online. At least I figured Paul knew this, but I had no way of knowing what Paul did or didn't know. Paul was recalling a Mexican bar they—the PPs—used to hit up in Jersey City. A place I should visit if I hadn't been, which Paul knew I had not (which is just something inclusive people add when they're about to go on and on without stopping). I took the opportunity to uncrinkle my underwear that wormed its way into my asshole, and prepared myself to be still. Paul continued. He explained it was less like an old man dive bar than a brightly lit Latin club with multiple television screens airing soccer games, and there were no white people except for him and

291

Preston. Coronas were seventy-five cents, and they came out frozen from an ice box. The beers were literally frozen.

"I remember," Paul said, "really appreciating the people working there. They were nice to us even though we were weird and white and in their space."

Paul wanted to return to the bar, as well as a rundown hat factory next door that he and Preston used to go into, to try on hats but never buy because the hats were too expensive.

"I've always regretted that," Paul said.

Across from the Mexican dive bar there were two competing pizza joints that continually cut their prices to compete with the other. So, the PPs would get cheap beer and a whole pie for like five bucks.

"We lived off that feeling—like the future is right there just waiting for you to look at it. Though I know how you feel about that concept, *the future*," he said to me.

"No," I wanted to say. "No, Paul, that's not me."

Or was it?

I came away from this conversation thinking that I was Joanne as much as Jo was Joanne. It was dizzying and yet it was so clear.

NEWS AND WINTER

Jo's night terrors had returned. Perhaps more worrisome was rec-ognizing that they'd never left in the first place. At that time, they involved images of biblical angels and emptied bank vaults. Some evenings my sister would wander the Deadhorse property with her hand over her heart reciting our national anthem, while I stood by keeping watch. I recall one such evening she found a dead caribou, several yards away from the trailer. We gathered our supplies from inside and went back out to skin the animal and then we went out to bury her. Later that same evening, Mike and Cicero came over and told us about their fathers, who were also best friends, and what they'd had them do as boys.

When they were boys, they would dig a hole to bury frozen chunks of caribou blood. Inside the dark mass, they were taught to hide a semicircular blade, edge facing up. They were told they would need to wait. They were told they would need to be patient. Mike explained that eventually, a wolf would come and find and lick the frozen caribou blood. The wolf's tongue would go numb as he licked and licked, until the wolf's tongue sliced open, and his own blood spilled out. Their fathers would take them as boys to follow the blood trail to the wolf, where they watched and learned.

"We didn't understand," Cicero said.

"Therefore, we stopped watching the wolves like this, got jobs and got a place together."

During this period, if Jo slept, she only did so if Mike or Cicero or both agreed to stay in the trailer until she fell asleep. Regardless, she would not sleep for very long. Often, she would wake up in a rage, knocking books off the shelves, smashing plates, and a few times she broke the rocking chair into pieces. She fractured several bones in her left foot and broke some in her hands. She gave herself two black eyes, and grew increasingly elusive, regularly walking around the property alone. She did not appreciate being worried over. Her face went blank. It was the same ghostly expression she would get in the hospital when they stuffed her full of colored pills. I needed space. I took Preston's penis in my mouth over the screen. His hands, remotely, in the bends of my legs. He would pull his computer toward him, while I moved toward the screen. Leaning in for a wet kiss tasted of skin and filth. When I wasn't with Preston over the internet, I made (re)directorial signs in arrow-shapes and placed these around the Deadhorse property to limit Jo's movements. There were signs indicating the Sag River, Dalton Highway, the trailer, and so on.

"An arrow can be moved," Jo said. "It can be shifted."

And with a slide of her hand, my sister twisted the *Danger* arrow so that it pointed to the Sharpie located at the bottom of the shallow river. I had been searching all over for that Sharpie.

From then on, Joanne made her way around the property blind-folded. As if to prove a point. According to my sister, who was sleep-deprived, living where we lived—America—was to live in a state of contradictions. For Jo, living in America constituted the expression, "a means to an end." She liked to say "a means to an end" was how a lot of Americans viewed existence on Earth. Though they didn't see *the end* the way she saw the end. Or the way I did, when I eventually saw it, too.

And when I asked Jo how she managed to walk around blind-folded without landing herself in a ditch, running into a tree, tripping over a rock, she answered: "You do it because you want to." Then she winked.

In this, I understood what I was supposed to: once an amateur, always an amateur.

Labor Day arrived, and I remember being thankful that this holiday caused my sister to rest. It was a day which I can break down because it was a revelatory day that happened slowly enough to be properly remembered. Joanne napped and I took the opportunity to call Henry; again, I got his answering machine. The outgoing message was mine, which I had made before leaving Chicago, and had remained unchanged: "Henry's here, but unavailable at this time. (Most of the time.) I'm Bernadette, or Bernie, or Joanne's younger sister, and I'm with Jo in Alaska for a stint. Only call Alaska if there's a serious emergency, 907-685-1800."

I left our father another phone message. I did not ask the whereabouts of the portrait, or how he was faring in the studio apartment in Chicago, nor did I provide any updates about Jo's condition, which had stabilized. In this message to Henry about Jo's health, I simply said, "You need to call." I saw the details our family had overlooked or simply ignored. All those years our family had used Joanne to distract ourselves from looking at ourselves. We pointed at her when the world unraveled. It was *she* who provoked those on the outside, we had decided. It was Jo who caused Henry's violent temperament, Sylvia's exhaustion, and my needy jealousy. It was she who made us say the things we should not have said. She represented our hope, which was to say our collective despair that the things we wanted to desperately change would not change. And she knew the entire time. Jo had made some deal at infancy with God or the devil (the same, she would say), to run into it, the proverbial "it," and not away from it. She trusted she would end up someplace.

"I suppose you could say Jo had faith," I said to our father's voicemail machine. When the recording popped on to ask me if I was satisfied with my message, I was not, so I hit delete.

For Simone Weil, in her day, the great (male) thinkers veered away from God, but Weil declared that it was the very uncompromising nature of her intellectual probity that had led her to a *sense* of God. *A sense* had been enough for Jo to believe in me and in our family. In other words, to believe in America. I remember this revelation astonished me to the core. I remember being ecstatic that I could still be astonished by America. This belief in possibility laid bare the tension that had for all those years fueled my sister's decisions.

I remember my stomach ached: Had I created a nastier, smaller, more insulated world inside of an already larger, nasty world, so we could forgive each other and ignore ourselves?

He was our father and I would call Henry again to tell him again on tape that I loved him. On the machine a second time, I included something about constellations, how these web-shapes linked principles of exclusion and inclusion. I rambled on; I said something about Holism, the theory that parts of a whole were intimately connected and thus cannot exist alone.

"Dad, you should really call us back," I said on his voicemail.

Then the answering machine cut me off to ask again if I was satisfied with my message. I called back a third time to finish my train of thought.

"The word *love* is a placeholder," I said in my last voice message to Henry.

"And like a baby's bib, I'm starting to think the baby needs to learn to just put the food in its mouth." I couldn't say I even believed in babies.

And before the machine could cut me off for a third time, I cut myself off.

8 p.m. There were still two hours of light left. Earth was golden. I turned to face the windows looking out onto the beaver slough between the trailer and Sag River. Yellow-rumped warblers and other birds darted around.

Then came months of darkness. The period when you were reminded the place was brutal and not meant for human habitation.

An Arctic storm was scheduled to arrive and was guaranteed to receive disaster declaration status. The plans for the weekend involved letting the time pass, which was easier to do in the dark. No expectations, also significantly easier to do living remotely in Alaska. My evenings would be spent subjugating myself, sitting castrated while Jo read to me from texts I already knew. After weeks of darkness, on a night when my sister and I were feeling rather anxious, more so than average, we made a Godly banquet of food: potatoes in a lot of different ways. Preston's recent trip to see a Medieval exhibition at the Met in New York City had been our inspiration for this Godly feast. He had written to tell me about a carved wooden coffin the size of a key chain, popped open to reveal the infernal roasting awaiting those who did not practice charity. I shared Preston's letter with my sister, who decided, right then and there, that we would live up to—and complete as fully as we were able to—the mind-warp challenge. We would produce an illuminated scene of abundance, which was triply absurd in Deadhorse since neither food nor other basic items were abundant.

The deal was Jo would photograph the illusion, and I would carefully paint a portrait of the illusion like one would a celebrity or king. These images would become the new background for our Etsy account selling homemade goods. The two of us did as we had agreed. We made a Godly banquet of food (really an assortment of potato products), and laid the dishes out on top of our most colorful articles of clothing, which we had put down on the dining table in lieu of majestic tapestries. Like the fancy tapestries we had seen in books and online belonging to wealthy barons from the 14th century who feasted while towns and cities and villages of people starved to death.

We added to this banquet nightly for the sake of doing something other than watching the television. Another dark night, Jo and I made miniature homemade ice sculptures of the Virgin and Child. We created many versions of the popular duo to accompany this banquet table of nonsense that we had assembled and left to rot.

The everlasting, sometimes controversial duo joined this collection of absurd, perverse pleasures, which sat spoiling on the array of colorful clothing we had laid out on the table. We would eat the rotten matter and get sick just like true worshippers of religion. And it must be said that we were also pretty cold without those items to wear. But as Jo was quick to point out: "Not as cold as that slut Mary and the Baby."

"Cruel," I said.

"Fine," she said.

We were hellbent on assembling things—little windup toys bopping here and there about the 400-square-foot trailer. But we wouldn't need to worry about waste. We would eat what we could and then Mike and Cicero would finish the rest. Those two were suckers for leftovers, suckers for anything having to do with Joanne, and they were so smitten they wouldn't notice the rancid smells.

Sometimes the trailer, especially during those darker days, seemed like one long extended funeral with no end. I wondered whether it was the best place to start a new phase of life. I had spent so much time with death (thank you, mother), I had wanted some time off. Yet, there I was, in Deadhorse, where the smell of cock shit intensified. I finally figured out that it was coming from the closet next to the bathroom.

"Is there a dead man in there?" I asked Jo, worried perhaps she succumbed to the castration curse that had afflicted so many women before us, and butchered Mike and Cicero.

"Why?" my sister seemed puzzled. "No," she said, dismissively.

"Watch this," Jo said, taking her pie and rubbing it all over her face.

We didn't have face soap. Jo knew we couldn't simply drive to the general store, also the post office, to buy some. And we had leaned on Jerry (the plumber), and Mike and Cicero (the two were madly in love with her), one too many times to do us favors. Without those three we would be in bad shape, which was putting the situation mildly.

They brought us our mail, our *The New Yorker* subscription, and the occasional letter from Henry or Paul. They brought over blankets, towels, soap, and pantry staples. Those three looked out for us when mental capacities were at a minimum, and general supplies were short. Jerry fixed leaks or whatever else needed fixing at near to no cost. Mike and Cicero went so far as to bring over tapes, a tape deck, and record player to get us through the fifty-five days of complete darkness. Jo liked having those two as "friends," though I was sure that was not how they saw my sister. My car, the LeBaron, had proven useless for year-round driving in Alaska. So much so, that out of pity, Donna said at some point she would come pick up the damn thing herself. Until then, the LeBaron GTS would sit as it had been sitting, like a corpse in the yard, now a giant planter for herbs we were growing.

I said: "But it really smells." Like it would make a difference.

"Say it, Bernie. Get it off your flat chest. You think I killed our father and stuffed his body in the closet."

"No," I said, "we don't have that kind of room."

Besides, it was Mike or Cicero who I had imagined she had taken out.

Honestly, my chest wasn't all that flat. Preston loved my tits. He had a close-up of my breasts; every freckle popped in the high contrast picture he used as his screensaver.

"Small titties," Jo was adamant, pie all over her face.

We were out of face soap, and the television reported on the major floods, fires, and severe weather systems sweeping Earth. We didn't bother searching the internet to learn more. I didn't even grade my online essays, and went on ignoring the smell coming from the closet next to the bathroom.

The phone rang. It was Henry. He was calling from a payphone; the connection was crackly, and we pressed him to tell us where he was. How had he even come across a payphone in those days? Were there any payphones left in America?

"Put me on speaker," our father said flatly.

Henry was calling for a reason and that wasn't the reason why he was calling. He said he only found jokes useful when thinking about death, and cited Walter Cronkite's rules for old men, which Cronkite never delivered on air: Never trust a fart. Never pass up a drink. Never ignore an erection.

Jo looked at me sympathetically.

"Get to it," she said, firmly.

Henry was calling from the last payphone on Earth to say he was moving to Tampa with Gladys, the caretaker I had hired part-time when the work of caring for Sylvia had become too much and I was desperate to get to Alaska. There was much that I didn't know, but I know that four billion years ago, Earth was a lifeless place. And then in a series of chain reactions, life began. I remember struggling to picture our mother's soul in my head—what did a soul look like? A thermometer. A dog's perspective. An hourglass. An egg and ham everything bagel sandwich. I tried but I couldn't picture her soul. But I could picture her hands.

With Sylvia gone, he desired companionship. He wondered if we might be willing to consider selling the farm. A new life with Gladys would require funds.

"You know how Gladys can be," he said.

Gladys looked like the state she came from, Florida. And much like the origin of her name, she was a princess carrying a small sword. She had a sunny disposition, bright, prickly blue eyes that she used to get her way—which was to say, to make you feel loved. She refused to bathe our mother but found a way for Sylvia to continue to paint while in bed by surrounding her with mirrors. Often, Gladys sat on the couch beneath the portrait to watch soap operas like *Days of Our Lives* and *As the World Turns*, which she loved since it took place in a fictional town in Illinois, and she felt like she lived in a novel.

Gladys said things like: "Be sure you see the body!" Characters came back from the dead in Gladys' world. Her favorite was the hottest couple from the late '80s, Steve "patch" (he wore an eye patch) and Kayla "the mute" (whose brother it was that had gouged out Steve's eye). It was so touching when Kayla finally—after being married to Steve's brother, and being raped by Steve's brother—regains her voice after she and Steve sign their vows.

Almost like Philomela in the myth of "Tereus" in reverse. But I did not share that with Gladys, because if I did, she would have turned into an avalanche of advice. It was enough that she liked saying that if I wanted a baby—which I should want, as perky and springy as I was—I should be honest about it: "Don't go around poking holes in condoms. That simply wasn't right."

I remember thinking that what I thought I had understood about television was only the half of it. I learned a lot about wild sex and resurrection when Gladys was around.

"Would you girls consider selling?"

I don't know what made us angry more, that our father called us girls, or that he wanted us to sell so he could start a new life in Tampa, not far from those agricultural pools, a deceptively happy pink hue, resulting from anaerobic bacteria that digest the fetid slurry, a combination of animal excrement and chemicals. Sylvia's will had stipulated her inheritance be passed down to her daughters, just as her mother and her mother had done. And we could decide what we wanted to do with this arrangement when it came time for children. If we had them. There was a long pause before Henry finally asked us for our forgiveness and hung up. He sent a sad face and raincloud emoji a few hours later. A few hours after that, three hearts: one purple, one green, and one brown. It didn't matter where he was getting this shit. I was depleted. We both were. So was the Chrysler LeBaron GTS that Donna would never retrieve, though I would have liked to see her again.

JOANNE WANTS A CHILD

In Alaska, there was an altered sense of what constitutes a day. It was like living on the moon. I remember the light going away, the air mildly algid. Our mother had said the key to love was grace, not forgiveness. More than ever, I wished I had snatched our mother's heart from her chest to preserve it. I remember thinking about preservation, which had me thinking back to 1987 when Jo called me outside to witness her fall.

"What was it you wanted me to see?" I asked.

Jo said that the morning of the roof incident, all those years ago on the farm in Illinois, that she had woken up in our attic space to an overwhelming, suffocating sensation that her belief in the human project had been hijacked by deception, terror, and bewilderment. The crisis wasn't a one-time event. It was constant. It was ecological as well as emotional.

"I had to try something," Jo explained of the incident.

I said I understood. I said I too had to try something myself.

"I wanted to see you," I told my sister. "I was close to dying myself."

This sentence unlocked the trailer, fresh oxygen filled the space. Joanne talked about her miscarriages, and how DNA transfers from babies to their mothers, even babies that have not been brought to term. Jo showed me what she had been working on—her "dream creature," like Mary Shelley's Frankenstein. I asked who in the end she preferred, Mike or Cicero, and Jo said, like Shelley, it didn't matter which body it came from.

"What about our mother?"

Joanne had all but ignored Sylvia's death, even in her newfound quest for progeny. Sylvia died and Jo had remained silent, leaving me alone in our apartment in Chicago to handle the details and to care for our father and Jesus was nowhere to be found, except occasionally stenciled beneath the freeway.

Many things about the period right after our mother's death escaped me. An alternative world did form, much as they had formed at various points in my life. But that one was entirely unique. Sylvia's death was a downpouring of darkness. Following her death, I prepared to be stationary. I set myself up in front of the living room windows like a storefront display. I kept with me some writing materials, a bag of chips, and an itchy wool blanket our mother kept around to remind us of our skin.

Weeks went by in that apartment in Chicago. Seasons changed. Television shows went off the air. People voted. People were outraged. My cellphone rang. Robocalls. The bank. Forty missed calls from Paul. Harriet. My jobs. The bank, again. I let the voicemail fill up. I let my phone die. I relied on fresh air and salty chips to satiate. My gums were receding and there was nothing to be done about it.

I sat. Sometimes you want to see something so badly you need to stay still and as alive as possible in the very same place and wait like it was not waiting but something else altogether. I waited. I wrote my sister postcards. I lost track of our father. I remembered our first summer in Chicago. Joanne and I went outside and scattered wildflower seeds all over the neighborhood. Since that time, they had grown tall, colorful, and wily. Harriet brought over more chips, bottles of water, and a fat joint to share. I remember I took the fat joint from her hands and smoked the whole thing down to the nub, down to the tips of my fingers where the heat burned. The best thing about Harriet was that she let me be.

I wrote my sister letters and postcards in rapid succession. I wrote to her about our mother because once seated on an orange bucket from Home Depot indeterminately, what else was there to do but communicate in fragments? I tried to save the light. Using our mother's compact mirror, I tried to capture the sun's last light by bouncing it into my water bottle. Then one day I received a postcard from Joanne, which said to visit her in Alaska. Jo wrote that in Deadhorse there were few STDs, snacks could be had, and babies could be made.

Steps were taken. I remember getting off my orange bucket from Home Depot. I reread Jo's postcard and there existed in me a new transformative energy. Jo revealed her interest in childrearing in a hand drawn postcard, which depicted a fountain labeled "urinal," and I showered. I did something I never do. I went out, ducked into the first clothing store I saw, and compulsively bought an expensive outfit: slim, navy-blue slacks, and a red and white nautical button up. Dressed like a power symbol (and one of leisure), I went to the lawyer's office downtown, and signed the deeds to the farm property. In that moment, Jo and I had become the owners.

Wearing that same compulsive outfit showcasing my power, I gave my notice to each of my employers. The wealthy poet gifted me a deck of tarot cards and said to use them anyway I wanted. I asked him why he gave me things, and he asked me if I really wanted an answer. I imagined stacking up a bunch of his muted silk pillows, positioning myself somehow, and demanding he take me from behind, haiku-style. "There, Paul," I thought—"that's what I'm capable of." I remember planning my trip to Jo by shutting myself up in the public library for weeks, a place nobody went.

I remember I stopped by Professor Tim O.'s office to return the books I had borrowed, which I'd held onto long since graduating. He was the best thing that ever happened to me, in terms of freeing my mind. I told my students to read to save your life, which they already knew. Alfred Jarry said the absurd exercises of the mind would further prepare them for life in America. With Gladys' help, I moved Henry into a studio apartment in our same building. I sold our father's Chevy. I held a successful two-day yard sale for the belongings that wouldn't fit. (Most of them.) The oak table sold first. Even Henry's hydro equipment and used textbooks sold. I put our thriving pots of herbs on his windowsills. I hung the portrait of our parents at the fair above his Murphy bed. I borrowed Harriet's Costco card and stocked Henry's cupboards with Lubriderm, TP, rotini pasta, and red sauce.

I changed the outgoing answering machine message to include the landline number for the trailer in Alaska, for emergencies only. I changed my cell number, gave it to the important people, and noted I'd be in Alaska for "an unspecified amount of time," but that I would stay in contact. I brushed dead flies off boxes of Sylvia's worn place settings. I found a flea. One flea indicated many fleas. I put Henry's prized Moisture Cube, our mother's collection of worn place settings, and other familial "valuables" into a storage unit. I gave our aging dog, Tall, to Harriet, who loved to love, and I loved her for it. I took the electric pressure cooker nobody wanted, stuffed it with some granny underwear, and boarded my flight to Fairbanks, Alaska.

And that was in part how I got to Deadhorse.

2007 CONTINUED, ALASKA EXISTED
AS A SEQUENCE OF EVENTS

The trailer was like a bento box. Without distinct walls to delineate separate interior spaces, like kitchen, bedroom, dining, and living room, we had to do so with different intentions. We played house like children. The best thing about the trailer was, regardless of light (whether we had it or not), the Alaskan outdoors opened up in front of us like a stage curtain does before a show. There was a period (and by this time I had trouble keeping time straight), when Jo rarely left the confines of the trailer to wander outside. She had shrunken in her clothes. Her body limped beneath the fabric, like she was wearing a canopy instead of a dress. "That's the style, Bernie," she had explained to me, looking like a ghost in a trash bag. I remember working to appear untroubled. When I did mention that she was chillier than her usual frigid state, the skin around my sister's eyes recoiled. Jo said Woolf had wondered why the sickbed hadn't been among, "The prime themes of literature."

Marcel Proust thought of his bed as his ship, a place to craft and set sail. He preferred to write in bed and ended up spending much of his life in bed. German poet Heinrich Heine's *Matratzengruft* translated to "mattress-grave."

"Bernie, you make things more difficult than they are," Joanne told me, one night while holding a dull kitchen knife in her hand. She asked if I wanted to play Scrabble. I was a lot of things—and *not* a lot of things—but I knew a clue when I saw one.

We had been cooking, therefore I had ignored her and continued rinsing vegetables. I should have been thinking about what would come next in my life, but I remember I found myself bemoaning the terrible water pressure, which dribbled out like baby spittle. Jo chopped garlic with the dull knife. Of course, it had made me anxious watching her cut something as small as a clove of garlic with a dull knife. That was the point. We prepped and cooked in a scene in which anything could happen. Ignoring incidents, potential and otherwise. There was the loss of our mother, and then of our father to Gladys, and Jo's recent downturn, after months and months of progress. She had been feeling more grounded. We dressed the lasagna with gobs of cheese and loads of garlicky tomato sauce, before putting it in the oven. We cut up apples and oranges for dessert, stirring the mulled spices in the pot like characters in medieval lands might have done.

For that period, to the best of our abilities, we lived separate lives in the 10' x 40' trailer. On our own handheld devices we played music, or favorite radio programs—hers the classical station, and mine news radio. The situation was not ideal. The situation was intolerable. I remember trying to get my sister's attention. I fumbled around, constructed vertical mountain-like colonies out of chopsticks and rubber bands. I drew and cut out paper figures that represented family members. I placed these figures on oil pipelines like rodeo cowboys on horses, doused them in kerosene and lit them on fire. None of what I did compelled her to like me. I set the paper family on her bed in a cuddly formation and my sister dumped a pitcher of water over them. "Then came the flood," Joanne had said.

The women on our mother's side—those women who were installed in our minds like a security system—were many things, but they could also be cruel. I remember our mother saying, when I'd asked her about it, that those women weren't into manners and general niceties. "Keep in mind," our had mother said, "women have long been scrutinized."

Then one day Jo said the storm was approaching. Thrilled, she pointed to the birds arranging themselves side by side on a perch; drawing their heads and necks down into their feathers, where they sat motionless and made a plan. Jo called to me to come outside to observe the thick white clouds as they closed in on us.

"We have storm issues," a man on television said about the upcoming weather.

We lost electricity. And Mike and Cicero dutifully came over with more snacks, flashlights, and batteries. That night a storm came and Joanne did not stay inside. I wrapped wool blankets courtesy of Cicero and Mike around my neck, and tried not to think about what Jo was up to.

Outside, lightning struck; it came barreling down. Trees were snapped in half, threading the debris into visible knots all throughout the sky. Scarring thunder followed. After, sulfurous and violent rainfall. The ground rattled and shook. In bed, my teeth rattled. My head ached. I listened as the upsweeping winds took hold of small animals and carried them elsewhere. The sounds were immense and encompassing. Massive flooding came, which tore through the property. I remember an overwhelming smell of darkness.

The morning after the Federal Disaster, shivering, black and blue with a newly chipped front tooth, Joanne came home. Mike and Cicero had made waffles.

"The air is decisive," Joanne said, taking a seat at the table.

"You must be starving," they offered her waffles, one after the other, pat-a-cake.

My sister ignored their competing gestures.

"I am always starving," she said.

Jo went back to talking about the air. She said the air was so sharp and so fresh, it tore her face. She showed us the lacerations on her cheeks. They were torn, red and blue, and throbbing. Her skin was palpitating like a heart. Then she left the room. I heard the shower turn on. When Joanne emerged, she said she was ready.

"For what?" I asked.

"Waffles, fuckwad," she said.

Jo took a seat beside me, her younger sister who had many questions regarding her whereabouts the night of the storm.

"Look," she said, pointing to blisters forming on her hands and knees. "In real time," she said before laughing. "The snow burns with new life on my skin in real time."

Then came Joanne's birthday. As was Alaskan custom, my sister took the forecast into account when picking out her clothing. She emerged from the bathroom in multiple layers, over which she wore her latest personalized sweater vest: "tout le monde." Mike and Cicero came over with freshly baked brownies, more groceries, and soap. There was a bounce in her step. Jo seemed to be feeling better. She pulled out her dictionary, a standard dictionary she had been amending since we were kids. She turned to the word, "pleasure." Jo said Cicero's dick was a loaded pistol. Cicero dropped the grocery bag that was in his hand. Jo said Mike's tongue was a sneaky lizard. I worked to contain the contents of my stomach. Jo went on in her usual fashion, doubling down. She pulled out illustrations promising eight explosive techniques on how to finger your way to an orgasm. I was not a child. I said so: "I am not a child."

Nevertheless, my sister insisted on reading the definition of "penis," though not before stating she preferred the word "cock."

Jo explained cock was not only a male genital organ of higher vertebrates, the ship transferring sperm during intercourse, a seizure of power, the vessel that loved stroking—it also served for the elimination of urine.

I was not amused. *Pleasure. Cock.* I thought about what those words meant while secluded in Deadhorse, where we had been living like porcupines. Holed up like porcupines inside hollow trees.

"Did you know a gang of porcupines was called a prickle?"

Mike and Cicero were awkwardly attempting to look busy by peering obsessively into their phones.

"Like us, they hardly ever venture out."

I said: "For me, intimacy with someone else is better experienced with something, like a wall or a screen."

"With a barrier, you mean," Jo amended.

I remember Jo dropping the topic on the floor like a dirty towel. She said she was glad I was articulating my discomfort.

"It's a start," she had said.

The storm had revitalized Joanne, which meant we could get back to updating our Etsy account. To celebrate her turn toward a positive attitude, and relative openness to my presence, I mail-ordered a high-quality geodesic dome designed in Denmark but mailed from Minnesota. It arrived in many irresponsible pieces, which was fortunate because assembling it kept us busy. We caulked and then re-caulked the windows, since the first round we'd done poorly. We phoned Mike and Cicero, each pretending to be Joanne. They would come over straight away. (I never understood how they could leave their shifts at the general store like that. Jo said they just closed the doors, which didn't help me understand the situation any better.) Our Alaskan world was more at ease with Mike and Cicero around.

My sister and I busied ourselves with our new friends, the putting together of the geodesic dome, and building up our online fashion collection. Over the course of the next week of positivity, we grew our business model to include vats, instead of using mixing bowls and dying in batches. We were now dying fabrics in vats of coffee, hibiscus, turmeric, saffron, and mushrooms. We made tees with slogans like, "Free Gluten" and "Tit for Tat." We expanded our collection to include loose articles of clothing, which we hand-sewed for both men and women to wear. We called the latest garments "Poofs," and said they were there to hide your burritos, which we ate tons of. The traffic on our philistine website was out of control. Our online presence was taking off. A few boutique retailers in L.A., Houston, and Upstate New York had emailed us to place orders.

Ever since Sarah Palin had made Alaska freaky—which was to say, authentic—urban dwellers had taken an interest in what went on in the Arctic.

It just so happened we were there selling clothing. While Palin's freaky may have been a big draw, it may not have been the only reason. Someone important in the web sphere, someone influential who remained anonymous, had linked our clothing to "wellness," and that was what really set us apart. Jo and I agreed that we needed to get our shit together. Of course, to accomplish this we did nothing but close our computers and go outside. Wellness—the concept—was a full-scale hijack, but by all accounts, the money and attention were not something we could poo poo.

By the end of that post-storm week, we had successfully completed the dome and Jo had seen Henry in a vision in Alaska. He had been there with us, in her mind. Unaffected by arthritis, he was fishing in Sag River's bend, wading through the river's currents, stripping hooks from the jaws of trout, releasing the fish back to the water. He wanted both to cook the fish and to free the fish. Our father spent his life conflicted by his responsibility—to family, himself, to nature—and now he was a one-note man, an ultra-conservative living with wide-eyed, fancy-free Gladys in Florida.

"Our father has always been drawn to extremes," Jo said.

"He always said if we wanted to see a redwood forest, we should get ourselves a room in a hospital," I added.

It was Henry that had sent Jo to the remote wilderness so that she could learn how to use solitude well, like she had learned to use a mandolin well. Send Jo to a place where the differences between outdoors and indoors were made even more extreme, where the elements could not be manipulated, where they did not acquiesce to our needs, and where the human-animal spectacle would be confronted with another kind of humility. Sylvia agreed. It was Henry who had pointed out that the greatest earthquake ever experienced in North America happened in Alaska on Good Friday in 1964, even the J.C. Penney had not survived the destruction. It was a place that strained to make itself real, to others. It was Henry who felt Deadhorse would equip Jo to handle a world where germs (including ourselves) were spreading fast and wide, and these fears only worked to solidify America's quest for cleanliness. To further our preference of chemical disinfectants and antibiotics over air and sunlight; to rid the natural world of microorganisms. Sylvia and Henry agreed Jo needed solitude—in what may have been their last collaboration as a couple.

Separation was key to forming the twentieth century American dream. And when our parents looked around, they saw the expansion of this separation increasing, between ourselves and each other, between the rich and the poor. The future, which had been here festering for some time, they said, demanded people get used to separation, with an emphasis on managing the personal, from spiritual to indoor health. Now a person could mold their office space to suit their needs: earbuds, light visors, HEPA filters, light-diffusing curtains, to control the temperature and air flow.

GOD

Joanne had said we should go back to the beginning. For her, that meant starting with language, which took effect after being born. From birth, "woman" was defined as "tool," and a tool was an object man used for violence, in other words: women were the initial enemy of men. And since *man* was *God*, it could be said that women were the initial enemy of God. A tough break, if you asked me, which nobody did.

I remember wanting something less challenging to explore for the afternoon, and asking if we could talk about the glories of soft serve ice cream, which had Jo evaluating her want of Mike or Cicero. Both. Neither. That summer, temperatures were hitting triple-digits. Heat was scorching sugar maple trees at Chicago's Botanic Garden. Eastern Colorado's farmland was drying up, forcing farmers to cut their crops early to sell as feed and recoup some of their losses. In Kansas, farmers' profits were wiped out by the record drought. Farmers were working hard to hang on to their small farms, some operating for over five generations. Residents of a very dry and dusty Midwest hoped that remnants of Hurricane Isaac might bring a little relief. Cows dropped dead. Wells went dry. Corn dried up. Then came the active fire behavior. Fires burned across ten parched western states.

"What makes wars start?"

Even though it was a question I was born to answer, I felt sick. I was thirsty. I wanted water but not too much, which made me sicker still.

"What a mess."

"Storms were the primal mess from which worlds were made," my sister said. "Everything longs for something."

I wanted Paul. To talk with him, but he was traveling Europe. I never knew what time zone he was in anymore. Him doing his thing had somehow managed to seem cruel, which had managed to make me aware of my selfishness, which had me questioning my intentions. It was a period of feeling stuck and bad moods. Preston wanted to use our bodies to communicate and to explore what it felt like to be intimate on the computer screen, while I was feeling past that sort of exchange. This was a period spent listening to Laurie Anderson's "The Dream Before." The truth was, I was experiencing a sort of vertigo. Faces of those I knew, and those I didn't know, were rapidly flashing before me; those I envied, loathed, loved, and protected. I wanted to write about the people I loved, to describe their intricacies, but I didn't know how. Maybe I was scared that if I tried, I might erase them. All these years later and I still was not sure exactly what I wanted.

I prepared to touch myself because that was what an aspiring young citizen did when they were at a loss for words. I understood how that worked best. I was as temporary as anyone else. Jane Austen sent her older sister, Cassandra—considered the drab one—many letters, which Cassandra would go on to burn after Jane's death. Many fans would decry her actions. But why can't some things be left, quietly—why must we have our hands in everything? I looked for my underwear. I put my jeans back on. I didn't know where my underwear had gone. It has been said that we're living "in an age of Cassandra," a reference to the Greek goddess who was punished for turning down Apollo's affections and therefore was cursed—her life-saving prophecies would go ignored. We create these outcomes and then immediately go back to wondering how it happens.

There were rattling sounds outside. This brought Jo around to revolution.

"Now is the time," she said, packing up supplies from the closet—nuts and chips, gum, slingshot, water bottles, long-sleeved shirts and pants, compasses, an atlas, flashlights, solar batteries—and placing them into a large duffel bag. Her mind was clear; it was frightening.

Jo said we must resist the social brandings that wish to eviscerate us.

Jo said she was ready to face America.

Jo said she would not be found dead with bullet holes in her back, even a crooked one.

Jo said her relationship with Seraphina was about lust and desire and being female. She said she wanted to love Seraphina mightily, because she was the sort of magical creature accustomed to receiving love. It was all she knew. Jo tried as hard as she could to give her more of all she knew—this love—and Seraphina felt more love if she saw you suffer, so Jo did that too, assuming love belonged to Seraphina and to Seraphina only. Eventually you despised yourself more than you ever had before, and it would take Joanne years to find forgiveness.

Jo said she was better, but it was impossible to tell.

She wanted to talk about Paul Klee, his *Angelus Novus*, an image of a seraph going who knows where that later became Walter Benjamin's *Angel of History*.

In this image, onlookers witness what appears to be a chain of events, but the Angel sees the past as one single catastrophe: rubble on top of rubble on top of rubble piled high, reaching both demons and saints. Just as the Angel wished to linger in the moment, awaken the dead, and piece together the broken pieces, a violent storm from Paradise has caught itself in the Angel's wings—they no longer closed—saying, as all angels must: unite, wake-up, or perish before being blown backward into the future by the storm of progress.

Eventually Joanne would wear herself out and fall asleep. I would unpack the duffel bag and put the supplies away. I had come to believe that the trailer had an infection. A virus. I would wipe my eyes, fill a glass full of vodka, and salute Satan. American persons and things were making everyone sick.

At night, after Jo collapsed from exhaustion, I sipped vodka until I downed it. *Think, loser, think.* I would try to think. The climate warmed, allergies worsened, and the pharmaceutical companies were ready to sell solutions. *Create problems to create solutions.* Everything was clear with vodka. Wellness was an industry like sickness was an industry. Like adulthood, equally childhood was a Capitalist scheme. The goal was to keep up the charade.

I drank more and broke out in hives. Miasm. We both had a genetic predisposition to disease-truth. We were inheritors of defect. I downed the vodka. I Googled: "giving away an animal?" I got back news of earthquakes and the "biggest wildfires in history." Drunk, I sloppily emailed Preston to tell him that we should activate our souls if we wanted to continue. I wrote Paul a postcard in cursive that he would not be able to decipher and addressed it to Père Lachaise Cemetery. The front of which was a photograph of Duchamp's urinal, otherwise known as *Fountain*.

The gift the storm had brought would not last. Again, Jo was refusing to leave the bed, which had to do with her two preoccupations: what it meant to reach the point of no return, and *Macbeth*. *Macbeth* had suggested another model of yielding was sleep. And for a time, my sister had an interest in yielding. She gave herself to sleeping in her bed wedged up against the wall, in a trailer on a property that at one time cared for young females. Jo said it was time that I accept the state she was in. Jo's skin was that sickly mixture of damp and flaky. I went to touch her, dab her brow, and remove the dead skin. She said "no." She said the end was where we started from. I agreed and we slept with the windows unfastened, listening to the wind as it came through the property like an operatic swell.

My sister was ill. She was shutting down. A decision had to be made about whether to take her in to seek medical attention, an option she was adamantly opposed to. I called Mike and Cicero for advice. They arrived at the trailer in minutes. They immediately, and uncompetitively, drove Jo to receive medical treatment. She had a severe case of pneumonia and was administered an infusion of antibiotics. She would need to remain in the treatment center for a couple of nights. The nurses shoved tubes into her arms without blinking. My older sister, wild-eyed, demanded I run back to the trailer and grab her neon green "Mon Cocteau" shirt. I was sure nobody present would find that amusing, but I did what she wanted. She was an invalid, incapacitated, yet again, but what choice did I have?

I dropped Mike back at the store, borrowed his truck, and drove all the way back to the trailer to grab Jo's neon shirt. She hadn't even asked me nicely. I promised myself I would never have children. I was never the one who wanted to live in England, foul weather, all that. I saw myself with an older woman who knew a ton about vaginas and living full-time in the sun.

Mike and Cicero longed for my sister. They weren't the brightest, but I was grateful they were kind to her and were committed. Over the course of our time together in Alaska, Joanne went back and forth between the two of them. Out with Mike, and then out with Cicero, each date raising the stakes for the other, which was why Cicero had gifted me his custom-rigged 2000 RAV4 with triple-tread tires and a CB radio. The RAV4 wasn't his only car, he had the big truck of course, but it was his favorite one. The car that held meaning, therefore it was a bold move on his part to give it to me. It was a gesture Jo noticed. Cicero depended on that RAV4 to transfer his band's instruments from gig to gig, really one person's garage or another's. He relied on its being there when he experienced writer's block and couldn't come up with lyrics. That car was an inspiration. It also stored his stash of Ritalin. The bottom line was that Cicero, in an act of love, had sacrificed his beloved RAV4, and now the next move, as moves pertained to winning Jo's affection, was up to Mike; the ball was in his court.

I wanted to see how it would all play out; it had been a great source of entertainment since being in Alaska. I had decided it would be my last weekend in Deadhorse before hitting the road, and Jo, having been released from the hospital and prescribed a regiment of antibiotics, would have no choice but to stay with me. My past self would have been nervous about her decision. She would have done something to torture herself—which was to say, me—but my present self knew she had grown more stable, though in true form she remained unpredictable.

The plan was to just enjoy the time together, to not set our expectations high, and to try our best to ground them in reality, or at least aim for something reasonable, and not set them as we had as junk kids in the attic—in our imaginations. The check list: make a cassoulet, bundle up, open the doors to the outside, and enjoy the frigid glacial air. Watch Netflix. Listen to the radio. Drink vodka, which I had allowed back into my life. Joanne said I was miserable past the point of recognition without it. "Whatever you say, Joanne," was what I said to her.

We would sift through our materials. Laugh at the discombobulated passages, the disjunctive narratives, and overall ridiculousness.

"What is it?" Jo asked me.

"God, we were children. Junk kids then, janky now," I said, though I wasn't sure it was what I had wanted to say. To be honest, the thought of leaving this solitary, epically manipulated yet beautiful place, weighed on me.

Jo said of us that we were fools. We were continual inheritors of defect. We should not be underestimated.

I did not want to talk about insanity, i.e. children. Or about kin. I did not want to think about my DNA. I did not want to be reminded the two of us belonged by descent to America's most coveted psychopaths of bodies of water and God-related paraphernalia. Sisters Fannie and Vida Fareown, who, according to our mother, were healthy and polyamorous, as were their nine younger sisters and their twenty-five female cousins; Poppy Fareown, intellectual nutcase who may have been the only one in the family to have made good decisions; Vie Fareown, medicinal savior arsonist; Sylvia Fareown, radiant bi-polar wonder; Joanne Fareown, a psycho's psycho. All capable of immense cruelty.

What did I want from myself?

I put in earplugs and wrapped a sheet over my face; let me just say, this took a lot of hand passes to work and made me look like an origami warrior.

Paul called from wherever he was to see if we were OK. He had heard Joanne was pregnant. He called it a Federal Disaster. After all this time way out here, I should have yearned for a connection, but I was annoyed. I felt like I was being held accountable.

"Don't you have your own issues," I said to Paul.

"You do know that studies show a correlation between loneliness and aggression, right?" Paul asked and hung up.

I punted whether to confront this. Instead, I asked Jo if she had posted something about her pregnancy and my leaving Deadhorse on social media, to which she said nothing with such a straight void face it became blurry. Her void became my migraine. Paul called back incessantly until he eventually left a voicemail. I kept his phone message new for days before listening to it.

SWEEPING FRONTIERS

In Alaska, the sound of your own body was an orchestra compared to the quiet outside. I was leaving, which meant I felt like I was abandoning something carelessly. What is our responsibility to others? Those that walk in the eyes of God believe God created Eve because Adam—in other words, man—should not be alone. I honestly did not know what I was responsible for: whose heart, which chores and routines, in terms of proper acceptable hygiene and modes of socializing in both private and public, which aspirations were within reach. What was I responsible for?

I was a mess that wanted to be an origin. Antigonus landed on Bohemia, a desert country near the sea, where a beast of a bear bit into his body, chomped through his bones, because beasts also get hungry. I thought about what my sister had said—that we all long for something. I agreed to hang around a few extra days to help clean up the debris and put the geodesic dome back together.

That week, when it was light out, we worked to clean and rebuild what the storm had wrecked. Jo and Cicero were gross with affection. I asked Jo if this was it—had she decided on Cicero because he was named after an eloquent Roman politician from 43 BC (an orator who knew how to use his mouth), or the town in Illinois.

"I'm dying to know," I said.

"Of course, that's where you'd take it," Jo answered. "You do realize this entire time you've been talking to yourself."

"Where would I take it? This entire time?"

Something hugely disruptive had happened here. This was not the order of events. Joanne was the reliable degenerate.

Jo said: "You spend an inordinate amount of time seducing yourself."

I said: "And here I thought you had turned a mental health corner."

The misleading inversion of characters had me thinking about women taking revenge. The Roman statesman Marcus Tullius Cicero tried escaping by sea, unimaginative even by the standards of his day. His assassins caught him en route, slit his throat, and sent his head and hands to the political leader, Mark Antony, and Fulvia, his beloved wife. Fulvia put Cicero's decapitated head on her lap, opened his mouth so wide his jaw cracked, pulled out his tongue like the path to the end of the earth, and proceeded to stab his tongue multiple times with a pin taken from her hair. The very tool political men use as weapons.

In the days that remained, I remember I slept well. Mike, who was cool with Jo and Cicero being an item, and who took the blow well for someone who also loved her madly, often brought over Gatorade and stayed for dinner. We were a good family unit. The day I was set to leave I got my period. At 5am the two of us, Jo and I, sat in the bathroom and had final words. I was reluctantly putting in a tampon because I still believed they should be free and "should anyone get squeamish if my blood leaks all over your airplane then pitch in," I said, inserting the blasphemous object into my vagina anyhow. Jo was pointing out that even super absorbent "radiant" tampons, which promised up to eight hours of leak and odor free protection, had trouble stopping a heavy flow.

I said, "There is nothing radiant, in any way shape or form, about a string hanging from my vagina."

There was also absolutely nothing appealing about shoving a silicone cup up inside my vagina to catch "the flow" either. Anyone who claimed they felt like a badass with their Diva Cup, Lily ultra-soft cup, or anything else made of questionable materials shoved up their vagina catching their flow, was lying. Not to mention it took a shit ton of toilet paper to hide used tampons in the trash bin from the eyes of people who could not handle natural disturbances, like seeing a cotton cylinder bloodied.

Jo told me to continue my rant and to open up my Gatorade for additional support. The drive would be long, she said.

If Jules Michelet was right, that it was the sorceress that conceived *nature*, what would that then mean in terms of our DNA? And we know now that DNA transferred both ways, from mother to child, and child to mother.

I put a cup's worth of vodka in my Gatorade and made a new flavor.

I said: "Therefore, we rebel. Rebellion comes from the pain of mental torment. The sorceress, also the neurotic, also the double, outsider, ecstatic, drifter, carnie, hawker, juggler, tumbler, acrobat—those anomalies, those persons of pervasive perversions—mirrored the agony of the people whom *she* had provided for over thousands of years."

Jo then told me to shut up, she'd had quite enough of me. She put peppermint toothpaste first on her toothbrush and then put a fraction of what she gave herself onto my toothbrush, handing me the inferior one.

"Have you read Dostoevsky's 'The Double'?" Jo, brushing her teeth, wanted to know, which of course I had not, which of course she had known.

She explained it told the story of how an impersonator destroyed the original. How did the copy do this? Well, the copy was more charming, more lovely, and much smarter than the person being impersonated. The copy—the replica if you will—goes on to make better friends with the original's friends. The latest version of the person had even supplanted the original version of the person at work. Everyone seemed grateful for the replica. The replica version was better in every way at everything than the original was. Everyone was pleased with the copy, except for the original that is.

It was time to get on the road. I was in a hurry to depart, hoping it might alleviate Jo's drabble that had been lodged in my head. I had risen at 5 AM, and for what? Not to experience an enjoyable morning, but instead be plagued by notions of replicas and copies replacing what was certifiably real in my head. I would not waste any more time. Besides, rain was expected in the forecast. With the help of Mike and Cicero, we readied the few boxes to be shipped to the storage unit in Chicago and put the last of my things in the RAV4. Jo did not come outside. In fact, I would not see her before leaving. She would not show her face.

I have read that many find Deadhorse barren and dismal. They incorrectly call it a town, which I think may be the source of the problem. Deadhorse is a worksite. I once stumbled across an article where it was called the most horrific place on Earth. It went further, saying if Stalin had built a gulag in the cargo section of JFK airport, it would look like Deadhorse.

"This place will always suit me," I thought, driving off, as the sun tossed a brilliant wash of orange daylight over the misty arctic oil fields.

REARVIEW

As I drove along in my comfortable RAV4, courtesy of Cicero, I ate dry oatmeal. I swallowed it down with instant black coffee and couldn't help but think we had spent an inordinate portion of our lives pretending, trying as we might, to fit in. Those last few months, Jo had said I was trying to establish something I was under-evaluating. Wearing nothing but tights, her inert breasts and stomach exposed, my sister told me this. I wanted to touch her skin.

I sped along the road. I was starting to see why Cicero loved the car so dearly. Jo liked to say about potential, especially in places and people we deem to have none, that Jeanne d'Arc was from farmers. "Joan was decapitated, and perhaps not an icon to replicate," I remember pointing out. I was averse to eternal life, even narratively.

"She was also made into a Saint, fucking idiot," Jo had said.

As teenagers back in Chicago, outside of our Aldi store—which was to say, the one we frequented—my sister would saddle up her frayed bicycle basket with plastic shopping bags, bike locks, and chains, and we would ride together through the city. Her long, loose, dark hair flapping around like an uncivilized creature. Her back arched, spine crooked, and neck bent backward, sucking in the sky like through a straw. Jo rode dangerously fast, opening her throat: "Even if you part my soul from my body, I will confess nothing!" she would scream.

I would spend my first night camped two miles off the road, on a willow-covered knoll with another expansive view. The rains had stopped for the day. The temperature was comfortable. By the time I had finished cooking macaroni for dinner it was nearly midnight, but the skies were scarcely darker than at noon. Both a bright sun and a full moon were overhead.

Fifty-five hours later, the car and I were far enough away from my sister to enjoy her as a memory. I could not say I was making exceptional time, but I was not in a hurry. Between Christian songs, the announcers on the radio were discussing the weeklong wildfires blazing in the Los Angeles hillsides. One caller blamed the city; another caller blamed the governor. One caller even brought up his mother-in-law. He said his mother-in-law hated the state of California so much she said that it deserved to burn. It was an un-Christian state too late for redemption, and exactly why those in the Donner-Reed Party making the journey suffered for it.

I had never been to California. That famously fraught place was foreign to me, but Paul, who was then separated from his wife and living and working in Japan for part of the year, had sent me every one of Joan Didion's books. Her images of highways, and her family's legendary potato masher, an object which had made the long journey west, had penetrated my mind. Now when I pictured freeways, I pictured them as strips of blinking green and red jewels with migrating Midwestern potato mashers like drones hovering above them.

That night, I camped again. And in the morning, I was woken up by bird calls. Outside my tent I spotted four ravens, big as balloons, circling in the milky sky. The air tasted like pine. I got back in my car and drove on.

I passed fields of cottongrass rippling in the wind and blush fireweed lighting up the landscape. I rolled down the windows and switched the radio channel. Turned out the wild horses I heard about a day earlier had escaped from a western movie set in Hollywood. Imagine that. I had about seven hours left to get from Minot, North Dakota, to Minneapolis. Minneapolis was the goal, anyway, before bad weather would eventually decide my fate. I listened to *Fear and*

Loathing in Las Vegas on tape as I passed through American towns, versions of their former selves. Much of the country felt ghostly. Whatever these towns once were, these days they were roadside stops with all the familiar trimmings: signs, gas stations, fast-food chains, and shoddy construction.

MORE ABOUT SUPER 8

After my evening with Isa at the karaoke punk bar, my hands up her dress in the bathroom stall (easy to do given its short length), our bodies rubbing on popular, time-less sentiments and slogans etched into the walls, we never went out together again. Isa would return to the motel and work her shifts. She would acknowledge me if I was around. But mostly by then, week number whatever (by that point I had lost track), I kept to myself organizing materials and formalizing plans.

Then one afternoon there was a knock on my door. Isa was standing in the doorway fiddling with her necklace, a long colorful beaded thing that hit her navel. I made it, she said, pulling on the beads and inspecting them. That wasn't why she was there. She had stopped by to say she would be leaving town for Taos, New Mexico, for a few weeks. I asked her to come inside, and when I moved my hand in that familiar sweeping gesture to introduce my room, I noticed it was in a pitiful state.

Isa declined. Her grandmother, her father's mother, was dying alone in New Mexico. And she had asked for her granddaughter's presence while she did this—die. Even though it probably wouldn't take long before her grandmother would die, a sentiment Isa contended was honest, but, in a way, felt embarrassed about. Isa admitted she would miss the Super 8.

"The way the motel bent time and made the smallest, most mundane things like a battery-run calculator or the annual wall calendar

Reeba was sure to replace at the start of every year, stand out like a viral tweet," Isa said.

"I don't even like her," Isa said about her grandmother. "My father was an animal and she reminded me of him. Her son's nickname was Rage, if that's any clue," she said with a smile.

Isa said she was glad we met. She also said it would probably be good for me—it would be in my best interest—if I left Minnesota, since I had been in Bloomington much longer than I had intended. She hoped I had gotten what I came for. In terms of finding myself, like all Americans seemed set on doing. She wouldn't want to read about it, or about herself, in print. Should it come to that. And while that in and of itself wasn't a problem, she said it seemed clear to her that I was ready to depart by the look of my room. That was it.

After that, Isa was gone. I watched her walk down the hallway. The things I thought but did not say: I would miss knowing Isa was near, and I would spend a portion of the rest of my life imagining I knew more about her. It was probably too early to make such robust proclamations, but what then were proclamations for.

Henry was unsettled too. He was alive and living in Florida, but I wasn't sure I would ever see him again, and I wasn't sure it was entirely up to me now that he'd mostly vanished from our lives.

I did need to be kinder.

I, too, thought about weather systems.

JUNK KIDS FOREVER

Like so many on farms, we had lived among a vast Illinois landscape replete with geometric agricultural patterns, shapes defined by their muted browns and golds. I have always wondered what Henry David Thoreau would have written.

In my motel room I kept the lighting to a minimum. I tried to get a good night's sleep. Instead, I called Paul who was back in Chicago for the U.S. portion of his year. The part of the year he spent time with his son, reminding himself of all the reasons he had left America. (I did not ask about the bunny. The dog was dead.) In Paul's new, updated life, he had a Japanese girlfriend named Mariko. They had met while he was working there. Though I didn't ask, Paul was sure to tell me Mariko was smarter than anyone he had ever met, including his wife, who he was still separated from. And I wasn't seen as relevant in this comparative category. Turned out Paul's wife agreed with him, Mariko was a gem. Plus, she liked his living part-time time in Japan. Not to mention the money was fantastic. His wife approved of the situation between he and Mariko on the condition they remain a supportive family unit whether he was in Japan or in America.

Paul's voice made me want to envision him low and welcoming, like a painting done in watercolor. Watercolors were not disarming. Nothing about watercolor paint was intimidating in the way that oil paints were.

I told Paul, who I could hear breathing, that Southern air smelled of olive oil. Air from the north had a turpentine scent. He was jealous I had a custom-cool compact sports utility vehicle, and wondered what I had done to be gifted such a find. I told him to focus on what I was saying.

"Where are the eyes?" he asked.

"I do not like that," I said.

He knew why. That sentiment did not belong to him. It belonged to Joanne. He had no business borrowing it to get to me.

The real question was did Paul know there were different smells at the magnetic poles, which the magnetic compass of a bird registers?

"I've seen what's in my head," I said. "But in a bird's head there are bundles of magnetic crystals that respond to Earth's magnetic field."

"Bernie, you're as close to a bird as they come."

Please just don't say what you think I want to hear, Paul.

But I said: "I'm not a bird, though I am considering the permanence of a lightless time, a time without investigation, a time washed with the deceit of certainty. I am thinking of Old Abe."

"Do you need me to get on a plane and meet you?"

"If you came to this motel, your wife and your smart girlfriend in Japan would not be pleased."

"What do you want?" Paul asked. "I am capable of this," he said.

There was a silence that lasted an eternity. I knew he was still there on the line because I could hear his tongue hitting the roof of his mouth, making that suction sound he made when he was nervous. Decades of our relationship coming down to this moment, and I wanted nothing more in the world than to be predictable—to ask Paul if he loved his brilliant new girlfriend. To ask Paul if he had ever loved the mother of his child and other animals. Yes, in part this was because I was jealous. And about his son: Would he welcome me if he met me? Would his son think of me as a traitor? By then he might have been too old to care. Or maybe he would need a new bunny—was that what kids his age played with? By then his son was probably busy with his own worries and failures. He would think nothing of me.

I wondered how old they were now, and this thinking about the years that had passed, and actually doing the math to figure out how much time we were looking at exactly had caught me out of depth, like a schoolgirl. I became a prune in order to aid my previous constipated self. And by *previous*, I meant several minutes ago. I was sitting on the toilet entertaining the meaning of life, which I blamed for my irregular bowel movements.

In terms of Paul and having sex in this motel and whether he should get on a plane or not, I wanted to do the predictable thing, as I was intended to do, but which was it? Was it giving in and seeing Paul romantically? Was it further restraining ourselves? I no longer knew the answer. I did know I was tired of letting reason get in my way. I also knew Paul had made a point of reading every book there was on Lyndon B. Johnson.

If I asked Paul to come to this Super 8, people would get hurt. If Paul were to come of his own accord, people would get hurt. The truth of it was, I did want him to come, but I wasn't sure I wanted him to stay.

I told Paul who I was in that moment, fan shaking, rattling above my head uncontrollably. I told him about my ravenous appetite for a young woman who wore tight articles of clothing and who very well might hate me, for the absurd layered nachos, consisting of chili cheese fries—altogether—and then the two of us having sex together—not over a screen—full of nacho chili cheese fries, bloated and miserable, when getting naked or having sex is least optimal.

I shared with him how self-denial had become a form of desire. I denied-desired him.

"Don't you see? It's complicated, like the color sea-green was complicated."

That which was reduced to a limited color through language.

"I'll get back to you," I said to Paul, and hung up the phone before he could say anything more, including responding or hanging up first.

I remembered the feeling of Isa on my neck and of Paul on my face. I remember thinking hot, warm air coming from the mouth was disgusting, and I distinctly remember liking it more than I had ever thought possible. I felt unhinged and in need of an anchor. For a moment, I considered contacting Preston, but he was now this bigshot artist who had decided to go all in; really narrow his focus down to an institutional critique, in the vein of German artist, Hans Haacke. Worse, he was in love with me. Flat out, he said he wanted to make *this work*. I told him I prized his lack of effort, and that grunge was over. He called me cruel. He ignored me and what I said. Instead, he declared his deep feelings over text, email, on his Facebook account and website, repeatedly, which I hadn't known I had accounts for until Jo informed me; I had a slew of nasty messages and many of my followers had un-followed me. If Jo was amused, I was fine. I asked for my social media passwords.

"My profile picture is of a porcupine?" I asked my sister.

"You should have seen last week's."

I had received furious messages from people I had never met telling me to marry the guy. "Shit or get off the pot, Bitch," was liked over seven thousand times. It seemed to me in that moment that the world I had felt secluded from in many ways while living in Alaska had become even more dated.

Preston's remedy to whatever sort of relationship we had, was to bluntly message me over and over: "we're in love," and it was time for "next steps." He went all over New York City painting giant, lopsided pink hearts on the sidewalks. *The New York Times* wrote an article about a heartbroken artist showcasing love on the streets of the Big (heartless) Apple. The artist was putting himself out there and why wasn't this love reciprocated? Who was this chick? Preston told the reporter from *The New York Times* that he wanted to acknowledge me and to thank me for being myself, and for being his inspiration.

In the end, Preston left me no choice but to give him space to recover from his feelings.

I wondered what Jo was up to in Alaska, but before I had time to picture my sister inside the tent inside the trailer, I heard a sound that wouldn't stop. I got up, turned on every light in the room that worked. There was a wasp that was trapped inside, buzzing, and smacking its small body against the ceiling. I was no longer living in a remote trailer in Deadhorse, though I was still surrounded by contradictions. There were stores around, well-lit, fully-stocked, name-brand ones, tons of them. Target stayed open late. I considered going to Target to buy a can of sky-blue paint and repainting the room's ceiling. Target would have options for blue—Esmeralda, Drip, Sunken Pool, and Ethereal Mood—I figured I couldn't go wrong. I would paint the ceiling a Sunken Pool blue and hope the trapped wasp might die more appropriately.

My phone then rang. It was my sister with news.

Jo was six-and-a-half months pregnant. She had thought her body had finally reached that mature state and figured out to hold onto fat, to build that desirable, luscious frame she never had and always wanted. And her body had, of course, but for the baby growing inside of her. She and Cicero were having a baby. Of course, she would not call it a miracle. Up until that moment she had been, presumably, under the impression that she wouldn't be able to bring a baby to term. Her baby was healthy as can be.

"Babies are *babies* and they happen," Jo said of her pregnancy.

"You kept it from me," I said.

I heard loud chomping sounds and wondered what she was devouring.

"Tortilla chips," she said.

Joanne said she was going to name her baby Chaos. Of course she was kidding. I knew she was winking. But what I was really desperate to know was how she had kept this from me.

"Bernie, this isn't a replacement for you," Jo said, knowing it was a lie.

Jo said: "And there's something else."

But it turned out that my sister couldn't remember. She said I might have to call back about that detail, an assortment of details, call back to get the information regarding whatever it was, later. "Pregnancy brain," she said, of her regularly blanking mind and getting off the phone early, before we had a chance to say anything worthwhile, anything of significance, before we had a chance to talk about how our relationship would be changed forever. "Just remember," Jo had said, before ending the call, "you and I, the two of us, we were always both the players and the backdrops."

From an internet café I wrote an email to Jo and Henry about a dream. The microwave had its 50-year birthday. Gwyneth Paltrow's 250-million-dollar face would be everywhere. Really, everywhere. The trusty American department store Sears would be relegated to the dustbin of history; thousands of Americans would lose their jobs. It was too much to cover on voicemail. And a letter would take too long to reach them.

In my email, I wrote that in my dream I was attempting to outrun an unwelcome feeling that had been following me. Racing through terrain devoid of all living matter, through cleared and desolate fields, running so far and so out of breath I collapsed to the ground. I wanted to scream to be heard, but the surroundings were still. I found myself on top of a cliff, where the air had thinned. There, it occurred to me that I could build a human slingshot, or a slingshot fit for humans. A contraption to propel us upward; first by making a large rubber band into the shape of a triangle, then by securing the oversized band to two giant tree trunks. I would do my best to make sure the seats were sturdy and comfortable. The turbulence would be heavy. I knew it was possible. There was a slingshot in Dubai that had launched a person at 125mph. He went as far as three hundred meters. If there were a glider involved, the person could go much further, but the wings would have to extend after the launch because the launch force would rip them off a conventional glider. I imagined the human slingshot contraption's wings would be something like the German aviator Otto Lilienthal's, but retractable.

Anyway, I wrote in what over the course of minutes had become a three-part email.

Jo G-chatted back immediately, "Bernie, is that your plan?"

It was sunrise when I opened my eyes to the agitated ceiling fan. I wondered if my personal credit card information was secure. Wyndham Hotels and Resorts, the company that owned Super 8, formally known as Super 8 Motels, and other hotel chains across America, had promised data security, but in a few years' time would allow hackers to steal data from over 600,000 customers. Nothing close to Yahoo's data breach affecting 3 billion users.

I was getting ahead of myself. I had to pee. I was feeling fancy in that strung out, spectacular, expired rockstar way in my Super 8 room which smelled of urine. The wasp was dead. It was time to see the country, but I would remain in this room a little longer just to be sure my head was screwed on tight. There was a mini-fridge and cable, and between commercials for sleeping pills and fiber supplements, they were re-airing a 2003 *National Geographic* documentary searching for *The Afghan Girl*. (Based on Steve McCurry's 1985 cover photo.) "Steve," because in my motel room I was on a first name basis with everyone, traveled to refugee camps in Pakistan to find the girl with no name in his portrait that had captivated America. Eventually, he found her. (She wasn't missing.) And when he did, she was wearing a veil, and the metaphor became: she was one of millions lost to the veil.

This might seem random, but one day we could have a female president. If we can manage not to chant hatred around her as they chanted around Marie Antoinette before decapitating her.

My plan was to start again, eventually zigzag through the middle of the country and later drive to the eastern most tip, Quoddy Head Point in Maine. I had some time before needing to settle, some savings, and the laptop Henry had shipped to the Super 8. His way of apologizing for being an asshole. Being alone, and for a moment in control of your own time, was a big deal in anyone's life: artist, philosopher, woman. For the moment, I would keep an eye on the expansive parking lot I could see from my room, and where my trusty RAV4 was surely dying, the nondescript acres of industrial parks and power plants. Plus, thousands of acres of razed farmland I could not see. I planned to finish all seven seasons of *The Good Wife* back-to-back.

Did you know historically that hotels were places where women could be solitary?

Recent thinking suggested that hotels were for couples, but I still believed hotels were places to be alone. Though the key was that in a hotel, one was never alone. Furthermore, I was in a motel, which was to say my room could be accessed through the parking lot. If Jo were here in room 508 smelling of fries and lubricant, and not fresh on a fishing boat freezing her pregnant ass off, she would find this line of questioning antiquated and stab me with something.

"Bernie, you have not changed," Jo would tell me.

I would counter by highlighting my victorious sexual rendezvous online; my scholarship to, and subsequent degree from, a prestigious educational institution; not to mention the few friends I had made and kept over the years.

Jo would laugh like it was her last day on Earth and keep the next few sentences in her head, reserving the thoughts for herself. My sister knew that whatever I would use to fill in the blanks would be merciless. That was the point.

ACTUAL AIR

From Quoddy Head Point, Maine, my plan was to then drive the perimeter of America down to its southernmost tip, a place above water at low tide, Western Dry Rocks, Florida, where I would sit Henry down and ask him what it meant to be a good man and end up staying a week or two to complete a short documentary about air conditioners, since nobody in Florida could sanely spend time outside. But even that being the case, air conditioning has not saved anyone there from going insane.

From there, I would get back into my car, put on the Silver Jews, and head to Cape Alava, Washington, making sure to see the Spiral Jetty in Utah along the way. An earthwork located in the north arm of Great Salt Lake, which had been visible since 2002. It would remain that way due to Climate Change and drought. Windows down, I would continue driving until I reached Cape Alava, and then on to Point Barrow, Alaska, where Jo would give birth in Samuel Simmonds Medical Hospital in Utqiagvik, America's northernmost town. A place where people lived for two months in darkness, ate bowls of cereal in perpetual night, until February arrived, where minutes of sunlight were gained each day, until 24 hours of daylight was reached and would remain until mid-August, giving way to the best days of sunshine across the tundra.

Together, the two of us had seen the Arctic Ocean surrounded by the fistic force of light.

Jo wrote to me of the coming sunshine: "It's going to get wonderful. Life is going to spring back to us."

My pregnant sister—almost seven months—was about to embark on a five-month Alaskan fishing trip with Cicero.

Of course she was.

It was my last night staying in the Super 8 in Bloomington. I had paid my bill in advance. Reeba, knowing I would be taking off at sunrise—before the stampede of children in need—made me a goody bag for my trip. She packed a box of chocolate chip granola bars and a few old European postcards she'd collected from an antique shop. Reeba had touched me. What else was there to do but think about places and people?

The RAV4 was packed. I had my packing skills down; each little belonging had a spot which fit nicely with the others. I parked the thing in a well-lit spot near a noticeable security camera. I brushed my teeth and went to bed early. I was nervous. In bed I tried not to think about theft. I tried to ignore myself. The more I tried to not think, the more I lay there awake. Did you know koalas sleep twenty hours a day and still manage to contract chlamydia? That's a lot of beauty rest.

I fell asleep briefly, one of those spells that felt like hours but was really a few minutes, before being woken by a reoccurring dream. It was really something to wake up daily in a stained motel room after successively dreaming of railroads and time. Trains can go anywhere. Time dreams are peculiar. I dreamt again that I saw our mother as a very old woman on a Viennese train, embroidering an image of a basket on a pillow. Lying on the bed, in that middle state—not quite awake, not quite asleep—I let myself back inside the train because the very old woman on the train, who was our mother, had asked me to. I expanded my throat and stomach like a bellow, spread my limbs to every corner of the room like a crucifix, and then fell off the bed, hitting my funny bone on the wooden desk.

I rose from the floor slowly. In bed, I tucked the sheets and covers around my neck like a collar.

Did you know if the queen looks down with the crown on her head her neck will snap?

Of course, I could hear Jo, I was her fool. And it was just the sort of unhelpful metaphor she was known for. Naturally, my sister had to add her two cents when I was having trouble relaxing, her prickly eyes bright, poking me in the dark room, her face the face she wore when she had a point to make, which was always.

And then an overwhelming sense of urgent dread took over. My sister was having a baby at sea. Was she continuing this lineage? No, that seemed much too easy. Much too obvious. Or was it her plan to smother them both, and the idea of us all, at sea? Just as the classics had taught us to do.

It was 7pm. Perhaps too early for dreams. I left the bed and tried to pry open the windows to let in the fine Midwestern air, which got me nowhere. Motels lock the windows for security reasons. I imagined the distant sounds of combines and running tractor motors. I knew those sounds were there. I put on a pair of cut-off shorts and one of Jo's "Tit for Tat" sweatshirts and took a seat at the shoddy desk. At least it was made of wood. Sylvia would have appreciated that. There I was, a person with a quality degree, yet, I still had nothing cohesive to offer. I etched into the desk a picture frame, also a see-through box, or a level square. Maybe a cube, or an energy bar, and when I looked again it became a portal. Jo used to say there was a reason that entire civilizations collapsed. My sister would not be defined by someone other than herself. She refused to end up dead and naked on a gurney. Never a hamster. Her life would include a series of incidents and confrontations, some of her own making, some of which belonged to others that she would scrutinize like her own flesh. My sister would live a life of confrontation. She would bite, disrupt, stink, abhor, and never die. Joanne, you were a thorn in my skull. It no longer mattered which of us was demented first.

In my room I started to question whether motels were the best places to recover from a lifetime spent in America. I grabbed the nearest trash can to vomit. Inside were receipts, an apple core, condom wrappers. All this time and the trash had not been emptied. Those items did not belong to me.

I took a beer from the sloshy ice bucket.

Last we spoke, Jo was boarding an Alaskan fishing boat, pregnant with her daughter. She was headed to sea, entering a new level of hardship, carrying the hope of a new generation. She was a rebel who never shied away from accusations of sentimentality. And from our stubborn and hardy lineage, she defiantly carried a child that embodied her survival and defined us both, the us that could be. Joanne wanted this—motherhood—she told me as much over the phone. She had said she had more love to give. And I asked her why, why she was doing what she was doing? To put it another way: Why was she hellbent on making bad decisions, like getting on an Alaskan fishing boat pregnant? She shot me her middle finger straight into the camera's lens.

I said: "Sometimes, I love you."

"You mean indefinitely," Jo said.

Love in our family was like a rubber band. It was just as Joanne said: "I will love you, indefinitely."

2009

Old Abe was a bald eagle. He was born in Wisconsin at the start of the Civil War. Abe was too young to fledge when an Ojibwa chief chopped down the tree where he was roosting. The chief murdered his sole sibling, beat off his parents, and then traded the bird for a bushel of corn. Some Union soldiers adopted Abe as a mascot. The soldiers toted him around, dressed the bird in dangly red, white, and blue ribbons. Abe fought alongside American soldiers for America. He was lauded by the likes of Ulysses S. Grant and General Sherman. Abe could fiddle. He could shake hands with a talon. The war ended, and Old Abe was incarcerated in the basement of Wisconsin's capitol. His wings were routinely clipped. He was neglected and almost starved to death, before eventually dying from smoke inhalation in a fire. His corpse was mounted, displayed in a glass box, and incinerated in another fire.

It seemed to me humiliation was the worst of all violence. From birth, stories of the women in our family had me inches from death by humiliation. I had often tried to disassociate from that sensation—the proximity to the fragility of life, because the feeling overwhelmed me. Now I let it penetrate my insides. And I would do my best to collect, care for, and record, much like our mother had, everything that has endured around us. I remember Sylvia speaking of the women in our family as a sense—which was to say, she described them less as figures, beings in human form, and more vaguely as senses. Sylvia could *sense* these water women everywhere:

supermarkets, television commercials, and the library. In many cases (perhaps in most cases), they weren't even related. In each instance, these women in their updated, modern context—because of course they were all dead—represented a different version of Sylvia at different stages in her life. They were her as an infant, toddler, teenager, middle-aged woman, and so forth. They were Jo, I was them, but they were also not any of us.

Up until her stroke, Sylvia said that the very act of living in America had excluded grace. Grace was a thing for our mother. I tried grace out like a rental car, but I was often scarred by what I saw in the world, what I saw in myself.

Did you know the astronomer Percival Lowell thought he was observing Venus, but really, he was observing his own eye? The spokes he saw in 1914, the ones that he used to make his maps of Venus' atmosphere, were really the pulmonary vasculature of his retina, a sign of dangerously high blood pressure. Lowell died of a brain hemorrhage.

Just then, Jo sent an email with a picture attached. The picture was of her, her hands wrapped around her growing belly, beneath the large portrait of our parents at the county fair holding luminescent oranges. Henry had it wrapped and sent to Alaska, a good luck charm for the boat voyage, Jo told me our father had said. I thought to myself: "There it is—the generations."

I was about to write my sister back something about how I found feasting on our own lives to be extraordinarily gratifying. That Van Gogh's last painting before killing himself was of a landscape of cornfields with birds flying out of it. I was not going to kill myself, the windows didn't even open, but certain details are hard to extract from the mind.

I studied the email attachment like it would evaporate. There Jo was in the picture, flushed, pregnant, standing in front of Henry and Sylvia standing in front of a painted backdrop depicting California's luscious San Fernando Valley. If I were writing an autobiography, it would begin the moment that portrait was taken at the county fair.

I would wander into the image on a fine summer day, with citrus heavy in my pockets, smelling of fried donuts, and feel the stirrings of identification. It was said of sisters Jane and Cassandra Austen that they were of one mind. Scratching my breasts, I had come to see that much like Jane and Cassandra, in many ways, we—Jo and I—had become, or always were, indistinguishable.

America Project. Poof. I would complete this novelistic existence exercise solo. I have stocked up on books from my online library that can take weeks, sometimes even months, to get. I was glad Americans were reading. Joanne was on an Alaskan fishing boat. She looked more and more like our mother, who had over time resembled her mother more and more. I called a slew of help hotlines just to hear the sound of someone who cared. I spent an ungodly amount of time trying to fix the curtain's cord, which in the end I could not fix. To see anything, I had to manually pull the long and heavy blackout curtains to either side of the windows. I opened them. I found myself longing for soil and longing to sit beside the Fareown graveyard on the farm. I found myself fingering the initials our relatives had carved into the barn's wooden beams. Maybe that was it, directly in front of my face was the point: The land has no need for people, and people have a need for land, and that cataclysmic error was my legacy.

It was still light out. I got undressed and briefly thought about contacting Paul. Undressed, I briefly thought about texting Preston. I did neither. Instead, I stood there loving myself and touching myself, my bones and the flesh between them, picturing both of their faces melting like a Lucian Freud painting—blotchy and dismantling on stretched canvas. After I came, I changed my old underwear out for a fresh pair. In the drawer I found a brown velvet ribbon. Who would buy a brown velvet ribbon? Whoever had, had decided to leave it here in this motel. I sliced it in half. I then tied each curtain with some ribbon to make it nicer. It was my last night, and I was celebrating.

The television was on. The weather report indicated clear bright skies. Yet, it was pouring rain. So much about the context I found myself in was laughable. I had a vehicle that could pass for a van. If it even started anymore. I hadn't left this motel in months, save for taking a trip to the Mall of America, stopping by the coffeehouse where Bobby Zimmerman alchemized into Bob Dylan, and taking a cab to meet Isa at the punk bar for karaoke and bathroom sex.

Looking at my RAV4 aging in the parking lot, I could say I had the rhetorical skills to convince someone my RAV4 was a van if I wanted to. More, if I wanted to, I might again decide to have sex with a stranger. Perhaps next time I will penetrate a stranger in my persuadable van and not in a bathroom stall next to eternal declarations, after downing multiple shots of an unknown substance, after singing ABBA like it was the last thing on Earth we would ever do. The audience that night with Isa was enlivened. The crowd went mad when we sang ABBA together. I sang, she sang. Honestly, I never thought we would ever get the chance to be alone, though it was all I had wanted from the start. Which I see even more clearly now.

Standing nude in front of the open window I saw in my reflection our mother's breasts as my own. Her shoulders, which were my sister's too, in an image where I belonged in that very moment. I dared myself to cut my hair, unevenly. Of course, I could do it. I was Sylvia's daughter. I was from a line of women who did as they pleased, even if they suffered for it.

"Why are you doing this?" I heard Jo.

Or was it myself that I heard.

"Sometimes you just do things."

I went to the bathroom to wash my face. All that remained was the complimentary little square bar of soap that nearly disintegrated in one's hands. People assume those free little squares of soap aren't worth opening. But those little squares smell good.

I took the scissors out from my backpack, turned off the news, and chopped off my hair in my motel room with the blackout curtains drawn open and kept in place with a brown ribbon. The rain hit the window's glass at an angle. When I focused and looked closely, I saw a portrait of myself reflected in the window's glass, which framed the parking lot outside, a few deciduous trees, the big rainy blue and gray sky above, and below that my bare feet standing on the motel's psychedelic carpet. There Bernadette was—my whole naked figure standing there looking, surrounded by industrialized parks and motorized vehicles and signs of nature in the distance. America could be beautiful.

THE END

ACKNOWLEDGEMENTS

Nick, my love for you is the size and shape of the universe, ever expanding.

Thank you, Martha Wydysh and Trident for seeing a spark in Bernie and Jo and in me. In us fools, really.

Two Dollar Radio, you're rad and that is anarchy. Thank you, Eric Obenauf and Eliza Wood-Obenauf—nobody else knew what to do with this book. You have made writing an unlonely process and I love you for it. Thank you, Brett Gregory for helping me to navigate social media like a champ and for championing this book on our behalf. I feel your support as far away as I am and it means so much to me.

Thank you, Renee Gladman. You've always pushed me to dive in—to simply be a writer as I've so wished only to be. I love you for so many things, like the truth. Thank you, Paul La Farge. Our correspondence has taken us to the earliest caves, to the burrito stand, to illness, to childbirth, and back to limitless horizons. Thank you, John Edgar Wideman. The stories I wrote in graduate school made sense to you. I have never forgotten. Thank you, Leslie Scalapino. You are here. Tucked inside my sunhat. See? Thank you, Aunt Sherry for opening up your strawberry-filled ancestral home in Geneseo to me as a kid. Thank you Mom for taking me there. Thank you to all those in Illinois who for years have shared their time to indulge my interests, including providing the jars with which I could take some soil home.

Thank you readers, T.C. Boyle, Karen K., Porochista Khakpour, Kimberly King Parsons, Justin Taylor, Elif Batuman, Amelia Gray, Daniel Alarcón, Samantha Hunt, J. Ryan Stradal, Edan Lepucki, Robin McLean, BTS, David Wallace-Wells, Caroline Bergvall, Ann Lauterbach, Carole Maso, Brian Evenson, Joanna Howard, Brian Conn, Forrest Gander, Mom.

Thank you to my friends. KKB, you are my sister.

Thank you to my family for your love and support. Jesse, I'm grateful that we're in this world together. I'm not sure I'd be able to be in it without you.

Thank you to those female stars, Skylar Jean, Claire, Mafalda, Zadie, Nico.

And Nick Bredie, thank you again because I do not want to stop.